Most Highly Favored Daughter

Janice Lane Palko

JANICE LANE PALKO

To Sadie

You've enriched all our lives with joy and love,

and I can't wait to see how the story of your life unfolds.

.

A sister is both your mirror—and your opposite.

-Elizabeth Fishel

Chapter 1 – Sunday, January 25

The mallet paused above Cara's head and then swiftly crashed onto the wedge, driving the pointed vee into her skull. *Why am I not dead? Death would be relief.* The mallet arced again, readying for another strike as Cara thrashed against the restraints. It delivered another cranium-crushing blow, and Cara's eyes flew open. *Where am I?* The phone rang again inducing another skull-splitting shock of pain. Her heart racing and head throbbing, she disentangled herself from the twisted bed linens and reached for the phone to silence its painful trill. As she brought the receiver to her ear, she glanced down at herself and froze. *Why am I naked?*

"Hello," she said, trying to recover her wits, but her mind was spinning in an endless loop of questions and yielding no answers.

"Where the hell have you been, Cara?"

It took a moment, but she finally placed the voice. It was Wesley.

Where the hell have I been? Every light in the hotel suite was blazing, and her clothes were strewn all over. *What happened? Why do I feel so strange? What did I do?*

"Right here," she said, buying time to clear her mind of the fog obscuring her memory.

"I've been calling you all morning, and you never answered. I left messages on your cell phone. It's nearly noon. I was about to call the front desk to have them check on you. Why weren't you answering?"

I don't know. I don't know anything. She tried to think back, but her mind felt as if someone had poured thick oatmeal into it. Her hair had worked itself loose and hung in disheveled strands about her face. Bobby pins littered the white cotton sheets like black ants. A roiling tide of panic rose in her as she looked over her body. She appeared to be unharmed, yet why did she feel as if she'd been beaten?

Cara spied her blue silk gown lying in a heap on the gray plush carpeting. *I wore it to the awards banquet. I was honored last night. With the Mother Teresa medallion. The medal? Where was it?* Her eyes searched the room for it until she caught a glimpse of herself in the mirror above the dresser and realized that the ribbon was still around her neck. The gold medal, however, was dangling between her shoulder blades. She righted the medal and then pulled a blanket around herself. Goose flesh rose on her skin but not because she was cold, but because thinking about the possibilities of what had happened in this room froze her blood.

Why would I be so careless with such an expensive dress? What did I do last night after the banquet?

"Cara! Are you listening to me? What the hell is with you?"

I got sick. Yes, I remember that. At least, that was something, a bread crumb she hoped that would lead her down the road to fully remembering how she had gotten in this state.

"I'm sorry, Wesley," Cara said, feeling a bit calmer now that she had, at least, some excuse to offer her husband. "I must have gotten food poisoning or some super virus. I remember feeling sick last night after I talked to you, and I must have passed out."

"Passed out? Who blacks out from the flu?"

"I don't know. All I remember is feeling terribly ill and coming back to the room. Maybe I was dehydrated."

"How much did you have to drink?"

She pulled the blankets more tightly around her and checked her hand to make sure that her engagement and wedding rings were still there. Thankfully, they were. She touched her earlobes and found that her grandmother's aquamarine and diamond earrings were still dangling from her lobes. *At least, I wasn't robbed.*

"Cara, are you still there? How much did you drink last night?"

"I don't know. I'm not your child, Wesley. I didn't think I had to keep a tally and report in."

"I've been going out of my mind. I thought something terrible happened to you."

"Nothing's happened to me. I'm fine." *Am I? Why can't I remember anything past feeling sick? Did I strip off my clothes? Did I have a fever?* She touched her cheek with the back of her hand. It felt cool. Had she done something bad like that other time? She closed her eyes, near tears. *Why can't I remember?*

"Are you sure you don't have someone with you?"

Her eyes flew open. "What? Are you accusing me of hooking up with someone?"

"Come on, Cara. I'm not stupid. You're there all by yourself in a hotel room, and when I called you last night, you were in a bar."

That's right. I was in a bar. Another crumb.

"Then I tried calling all morning and no one answers. It doesn't take a genius to connect the dots."

She stood, pulling the blankets off the bed. "How can you say such a thing? I booked this room for us. So we could be together. *You were the one who stood me up.* Maybe you're feeling guilty." Her head began to spin, and she sank back onto the bed, clutching her temple.

"Guilty? For what?" his voice boomed out of the phone making her head pound like a jack hammer. "Working? Trying to make a nice life together? You forget, I don't have the connections and name recognition you do. Some of us have to work hard."

She stifled a scream. She worked hard too and being so well known was no picnic, but she felt too feeble to argue. Cara sighed. "Look, Wesley, I'm sorry. I love you. I'd never cheat on you. You know that. I got sick last night—the sickest I think I've ever been. I came back to the room and fell asleep. That's all. Seriously, you don't think I'd ever want someone else, do you?"

He didn't answer.

"Do you?"

"I'm sorry, Cara. It's just that sometimes I get so crazy when I think of all the other guys you could have married."

Exasperated, she closed her eyes. "Wesley, don't."

"It's true. You could have married any number of other men. How did your grandmother phrase it? 'Someone more suitable.'"

"But I didn't want them," Cara said softly. "I wanted you."

The silence hung there. They'd been over this so many times, it was maddening.

"I'm just glad you're OK. I was calling to tell you that my plane will be boarding soon," he said. "I'll be home before dinner."

"Good."

"Love you," he said and then hung up.

She put the receiver in its cradle, and her stomach rumbled with hunger. *I don't think I threw up last night. My stomach doesn't have that kicked-in-the-gut feeling. Perhaps I was drunk.* She tallied the drinks she'd had during the evening but concluded that too much alcohol wasn't it. She'd certainly had more to drink on other occasions without feeling this hung over.

Maybe I'm pregnant. She held her head in her hands. You'd have to have had sex for that, she thought. With Wesley so involved in the Nelson fraud case, she couldn't remember the last time they'd made love. That was why she had booked the suite for them in the first place.

Sighing, Cara picked up the phone again and dialed room service. She ordered dry toast and tea, and after pulling on her nightgown and straightening the bed linens, she crawled back under the covers, rolling onto her side, clutching a pillow. As she closed her eyes, she heard her grandmother's voice in her lilting Irish brogue coming through clearly in her cloudy head, "A wee bit of tea and toast is just the thing to cure what ails you."

Cara smiled wryly, thinking she'd need more than a cup of tea and slice of toast to fix this mess. As she tried, once again, to reconstruct the previous evening, a thought reached out and clutched her, sending a ripple of panic through her. *What if this is like the last time?*

One other time while she was still a child, she'd had a memory lapse, and many times over the years, she had trod down that well-worn path in her mind hoping to discover what her subconscious kept from her, but each time her foray into the past had led her into forests of confusion and dead ends of frustration. No matter how she tried, she couldn't remember. Her pulse quickened and her heart beat into her ears as fear seized her. *I couldn't remember then, and if I can't remember now, will the same thing happen?* The metallic taste of terror was on her tongue as she pondered the next question, the one that provoked the most turmoil in her heart: *Will I be abandoned again?*

JANICE LANE PALKO

Chapter 2 – The Previous Evening

Rarely did Cara Cavanaugh Hawthorne Wells wish she were Sophia, but this night was one of them.

What do I do with my hands? Her mind was divided between listening to the speaker standing at the lectern next to her and trying to calm her nerves. Her palms were perspiring, and she knew that if she dared to touch her blue silk gown, they would leave ghastly marks on the delicate fabric.

As her heart fluttered in her chest, she purposefully folded her hands like a dutiful school girl, resting them on the edge of the table as she had been taught by Sister Mary Bernard in first grade. Sitting stiffly on the dais, she pasted on a smile. *Can they tell how nervous I am? Do I look as self-conscious as I feel? What must they think of me?*

The master of ceremonies for this year's Mother Teresa Humanitarian Awards banquet, Herbert Stumpfel, a bespectacled, doughy man with a receding hairline, was expounding on the past honorees, which included such luminaries as Paul Newman and the Dalai Lama. Cara felt decidedly out of place in the pantheon of recipients.

The moisture in her body must have migrated to her palms, as her mouth was suddenly as dry as the shimmery powder the stylist had dusted over her face and décolleté when she'd had her hair and makeup done that afternoon.

Cara lifted the crystal water goblet, the slivers of ice softly rattling against the glass from her trembling hands. The chilled lemon water sent a cascade of shivers down her spine. Her strapless gown combined with the frigid air pumping out of the vent above her left her so cold her teeth were nearly chattering.

Young lady, pull yourself together. Cara heard Grandmother Cavanaugh's voice in her mind. *Sit up straight, raise your head, and smile. Ninety percent of life is appearances, my dear. And may I remind you that you are a Cavanaugh, and no matter what you may be thinking or feeling, you are to act with dignity and grace.*

Cara envisioned her maternal grandmother lying on her deathbed, ashen and wasting from pancreatic cancer. Even in her last days, she insisted on having her sparse white hair styled and makeup applied.

How she would have loved this evening. Cara set the goblet back on the crisp white linen tablecloth as the memory of her grandmother warmed her heart if not her chilled body. The daughter of poor Irish immigrants, Nora Maloney Cavanaugh had worked hard, married well, and fought her entire life to keep a grip on all that she'd achieved. Her grandmother valued titles, awards, and honors, and although Cara often felt intimidated by the woman who had raised her after her mother's death, she loved and missed her deeply.

Cara gazed out over the dimly lit Grand Ballroom of the William Pitt Hotel. The opulent room was filled with politicians, clergy, media, the upper crust of Pittsburgh society as well as elites from all over the country and even some dignitaries from around the globe.

Dear Lord, please help me get through this night.

She made out the silhouette of Lia Minor, her devoted assistant and friend, at a table near the front. Lia was seated with the other members of Comfort Connection's Advisory Board and staff.

It seemed that everyone she knew was there to join in honoring her from former classmates and teachers to her dentist and manicurist. *Everyone except for my family. What would all these people think of me if they realized that their honoree had no family in attendance to share her big night?*

Wesley Wells, her husband, had phoned just as the limousine had arrived at their Sewickley home to transport her to the banquet. He'd called to say that his deposition had taken longer than expected, and although he had been able to make his return flight, the plane had been delayed on the tarmac at LaGuardia for another round of deicing. Much to Cara's disappointment, he informed her that he would miss the dinner portion of the evening but hoped to be there in time to see her receive her medal.

Her father, Laurence Hawthorne, the patriarch of the Allegheny Food & Beverage Group, one of the world's largest commodities corporations, was currently in Slovakia on emergency business and would not return to the states for another few days. And Sophia? Who knew where her younger sister was. The only way to keep track of her would be to implant her with a GPS device.

Cara noticed that she'd let shoulders droop from disappointment then quickly straightened her posture. *Perhaps it's best they're not here. They may have made me more nervous, especially Sophia.* Her sister was worse than a loose cannon; Sophia was an electromagnetic pulse of recklessness capable of rendering everyone speechless with her outrageous behavior. As images of Sophia sloshing her drink and her breasts nearly spilling out of her dress at the last event they had attended together ran through Cara's mind, she was abruptly brought back to the present by a round of applause. Herbert Stumpfel was ceding the microphone to Bishop Niccolo Fiorito, who was barreling toward the lectern.

Cara stifled a chuckle when she saw her dear friend and mentor decked out in his clerical finery. He looked more like an aging bantam-weight boxer than a shepherd of the church, a Rocky Balboa in ecclesiastical regalia. He had thick salt and pepper hair and a perpetual five o'clock shadow. His large nose was balanced by sparkling blue eyes, framed by lush black lashes. He was a short, square block of flesh, and although Cara knew he held the utmost respect for his office and all its trappings, she also knew he was a simple man.

She'd first met him when she was in college after the All Souls' Day Mass. He'd found her weeping in the cathedral while she'd been lighting a candle. He'd asked her what was wrong, and she'd introduced herself and told him that she was worried about her mother's soul because she had committed suicide. He told her that he was familiar with the family and the circumstances of her mother's death. Coming from such a prominent family, Cara knew that most people over a certain age in Pittsburgh were well aware of her mother's scandalous death. He assured her that God was merciful and loved her mother even though she'd taken her own life. He'd been so kind and understanding, they had become fast friends. She loved his humility and warmth.

Cara had learned that he'd been a missionary priest, spending most of his vocation serving the poor in Chimbote, Peru. He once confided in her that he felt foolish wearing his clerical robes. In fact, after last Easter's Mass at St. Paul Cathedral, as he stood outside the great stone church greeting the congregation, he whispered into Cara's ear, "Don't I look like an overgrown Infant of Prague statue?"

Most people referred to him as Your Grace; however, he preferred that Cara call him Father Nicco. It took her a while to get used to such familiarity, but it didn't take any time to develop a deep affection for this kind-hearted, unpretentious man, who many felt would shortly be elevated to Cardinal, a prince of the Roman

Catholic Church.

On his way to the podium, he reached out and briefly clasped Cara's hand, giving it a firm, warm, reassuring squeeze. She smiled and was amused to see him give her a little wink as he pulled out his notes.

After Father Nicco greeted the dignitaries and audience, he turned and nodded toward her and then said with the faintest hint of an Italian accent, "Ladies and Gentlemen, it is my great privilege tonight to present this year's Mother Teresa Award. But first I'd like to tell you a bit about our recipient." He laughed, his whole upper torso shaking. "You thought I'd make this quick, eh? Wrong, my friends. You can't give a priest a microphone and expect him to make it snappy!" Laughter rippled throughout the ballroom.

Cara watched his blue eyes twinkling under the intense spotlight as he looked about the hall relishing the laughter. He was so comfortable speaking before a crowd. Some people are born for the spotlight. Sophia lived for it. When the bright light shone on her, she blossomed like a hot house flower under its rays, while I wither, Cara thought.

"Our recipient is most appropriately named," Father Nicco said. "For those of you who may be unfamiliar with Italian, 'Cara' means 'dear.' And Cara Cavanaugh Hawthorne, our honoree, is truly a dear. Although born into a life of privilege, with the face of an angel and the intellect of a scholar, Cara, our dear, has turned away from more worldly pursuits and has devoted herself to ministering to grieving children. In a few short years, she and her nonprofit organization, Comfort Connection, have made an extraordinary difference in the lives of children dealing with grief."

An accomplished orator, he paused briefly to allow his words to register. He then grasped the sides of the lectern and lowered his voice. "When that bridge over the Monongahela River collapsed last year taking the lives of sixteen, it was Cara and her organization that came to the aid of the traumatized and bereft children whose parents perished. And it was she who immediately sprang into action forming a Comfort Connection program to help children in an Erie elementary school after a school bus tragically overturned last winter, killing twenty-eight of their classmates. And it is Cara who has now made it her goal to develop satellite Comfort Connection programs for every school district in the nation."

She felt herself blushing from the praise.

"Her effect on the spiritual and emotional well-being of thousands of children is incalculable," Father Nicco said. "As one sweet child, Maura Vilsac, so aptly phrased it when I recently visited Comfort Connection, 'Cara kissed the boo-boo on my heart.'"

A murmur of appreciation rose in the room, and Cara lowered her head, tears welling in her eyes as she recalled little Maura and the pain that child had suffered from witnessing her step-father beat her mother to death.

"The Lord," boomed Father Nicco, "in his Sermon on the Mount proclaimed: 'Blessed are they who mourn for they shall be comforted.' To that, I say blessed are our children for they shall be comforted not only by the Lord, but also by the good souls at Comfort Connection and by their dearest soul, founder Cara Cavanaugh Hawthorne Wells."

Thunderous applause filled the enormous ballroom.

"Ladies and Gentlemen," Father Nicco said as he turned to face Cara, "I am proud to present this year's Mother Teresa Award for Charity to Humanity to Cara Cavanaugh Hawthorne Wells!"

The crowd applauded and rose. The ovation was so loud Cara could barely hear her mind as it intoned a silent prayer. *Lord, be with me. Help me get through this speech.* With her legs shaking, she stood. Father Nicco came, took her hand, and escorted her to the center of the dais where an aide met them and handed him a blue velvet box. The spotlight engulfed them and blinded Cara.

Father Nicco opened the box and took out a large gold medallion that was attached to a ribbon of yellow and white, the colors of the Vatican. Cara, her heart pounding so loudly that it seemed to drown out the applause, bent her head, and Father Nicco placed the medallion around her neck.

Covering it with her hand and clasping it to her heart, she looked up at him and whispered, "Thank you."

Father Nicco grasped her upper arms and gently kissed one of her cheeks and then the other. "No, thank you, Cara *mia.*" A photographer moved in and snapped several photos while flashes from cameras and cell phones all over the ballroom lit up the place like fireworks.

This must be what it is like to be Sophia.

Father Nicco then stepped aside, leaving Cara alone in the spotlight.

She tentatively approached the microphone, the residue of the flashes in her eyes making it difficult to see. *Breathe, Cara. Breathe.* She leaned forward and said, "Thank you." She was too close to the microphone, and her words thumped out into the crowd. She smiled nervously and adjusted the microphone a bit. "Let's try that again. Thank you." She then acknowledged the dignitaries in attendance and began her speech. "I am truly honored to receive such a distinguished award, especially one named after Mother Teresa, someone I greatly admire." As she began to thank her staff, advisory board, and benefactors, Cara felt a wave of calm descend upon her.

"Yes, Bishop Fiorito is correct," she said. "As you may know, I was born with many advantages. But there was one advantage that I did not have while growing up." She paused. "A mother." She had rehearsed her acceptance speech at home and speaking about her mother had not been a part of it. *Why did I go off on this tangent? Now what do I do? I can't just change the subject. I'm committed. I have to continue talking about what happened with my mother.*

When she began to speak again, she found it difficult because of the lump rising in her throat. Cara was surprised by the wave of emotion now washing over her after all these years. *Please, Lord, help me get through this without falling apart.* After stopping for a moment to collect herself, she began again. "I'm sorry," she said with a wavering voice. "I find it difficult to speak publicly about my past, but as some of you may know, sadly, my mother took her own life when I was only four."

The crowd gasped.

"As the presence of a mother shapes her child, the lack of her presence shapes her child as well. Unfortunately, my mother's absence shaped me into a sad, lonely little girl. Even though I had a supportive family, for many years I grieved and no one knew what to do about it. Why?" Cara gave a slight shrug. "Perhaps because they were grieving too and didn't know how to deal with their own sorrow, let alone a child's."

As the audience listened with rapt attention, Cara realized that she had a grand opportunity before her. She had a captive, receptive, well-heeled audience to whom she could pitch her dream of making Comfort Connection a national program.

She detailed how she had met the bishop while attending college at Mercy University in Pittsburgh. How he had come upon her sitting alone, crying after the All Souls' Day Mass. And after talking to her, how he had urged her to seek grief counseling.

"It was then," Cara said, "while I was going through counseling that I realized that grief programs for children are too few. I didn't want other children to suffer for years with unresolved grief as I had, so I began an outreach program, Comfort Connection. And it just grew and grew."

Cara looked out over the crowd. "Some of you, right now, may be feeling sad or lonely or depressed or may be wrestling with feelings of loss too. If so, I have found that the greatest balm for my troubles has been to help someone in need. There are grieving children all across this country. I'd like to help them because they can't become the people God destined them to be if they are burdened with sorrow. I appeal to you. I can't do it alone. Please help me help these children. Help me lift their burden of grief. And in doing so, you'll also be helping yourself. On behalf of all grieving children, I thank you for this award, for your support, and for allowing me to share my story."

Cara stepped away from the microphone, and the crowd rose, clapping loudly. She smiled, heartened that she'd won their approval. As Father Nicco and those on the dais moved to congratulate her and more cameras flashed, she had never felt more confident. With a little luck, Cara knew that there'd be no stopping her or her dream of expanding Comfort Connection now.

As she took her seat, she placed her hand over the cold medal to prevent it from bouncing off her chest as she scooted her chair in. While Herbert Stumpfel made some concluding remarks, she sighed deeply and relaxed. *Thank you, Lord, for getting me through that.* Then

Cara felt a warm glow of satisfaction radiating in her heart. She took a sip of her wine, silently toasting herself, and sensed that no matter what happened in the future, this night would come to be one she'd never forget.

Chapter 3

Lia wrapped Cara in a hug. "Oh, congratulations!" When she released her, she asked. "May I see it?"

Cara held out the gold medallion emblazoned with a bas-relief of Mother Teresa on one side and the diocesan coat of arms on the other. "I look like Count Dracula with this thing around my neck," Cara said.

Lia gently brushed a finger over the likeness of the Albania saint and then flipped over the gold disk. "Count Dracula? No way." Lia's green eyes were animated with excitement as she spoke. "But you do look regal. Like Queen Elizabeth when she poses for those state photos in all her finery."

As she readjusted the ribbon, Cara wondered how long she would have to wear the medal. She was truly thrilled to be honored, but she felt so conspicuous. She wanted to stow it in her purse, but she didn't want to appear ungrateful.

"Talk about looking regal," Cara said, as she surveyed her assistant. At thirty-eight, twelve years Cara's senior, Cornelia—Lia Minor—had a lovely face, with a delicate porcelain complexion, capped by a striking shade of copper hair. Lia was soft and round with an ample bosom, which, in another age, would have made her the model for many a Renaissance master. Unfortunately, in this age where jutting bones and ripped abs were the pinnacles of beauty, she was summarily dismissed as "A girl with such a beautiful face." Meaning she'd be gorgeous if she'd lose some weight.

Cara had helped Lia shop for the burnt orange, iridescent off-the-shoulder gown, the color of which seemed made especially for Lia. It accented the creaminess of her assistant's pale shoulders and Titian hair. "You look positively gorgeous," Cara said.

"It's amazing what a little makeup and the proper undergarments can do." They both laughed, recalling the sales clerk at the boutique who had sold Lia the dress. She'd lectured them both about how it didn't matter if the dress cost $6,000 or $60, "without a proper foundation, the dress would be a disaster."

"Thank you for insisting I try this on and lending me your jewelry," Lia said as she fingered the topaz necklace that had been left to Cara by her grandmother. "But I'm terrified I'm going to lose it."

"Don't worry about it. It's insured, and I never wear it. At least, if grandmother can't be here, her jewelry can. I've got her aquamarines on," Cara said as she touched an earlobe.

"Oh, Cara, she'd be so proud of you. Tonight has been the most incredible evening. The food, the dignitaries, your acceptance speech—it was wonderful. You had everyone in tears. Why, I even saw Mike Rivers over at the next table dabbing his eyes. A hard-boiled journalist like that and you had him blubbering."

"I don't know what came over me," Cara said. "I didn't intend to talk about my mother's death, and I certainly didn't intend to make them cry. I just wanted to stress how important Comfort Connection is to grieving children, and it all came spilling out."

Lia smiled. "Maybe it was the Holy Spirit leading you." Then Cara watched as her friend's expression froze on her face and her eyes became as bright and big as the Mother Teresa medallion. Lia reached out and clutched Cara's arm. "Don't turn around," she whispered, "but the bishop is walking over, and he's bringing Francesco D'Amore."

"Who?"

"Francesco D'Amore! The opera star. The young, handsome opera star and owner of the Francesco's Gelato franchise." Lia's voice was on the edge of hysteria. "The one I told you about from *People* magazine. Who's forty, single, and likes 'fleshy' women." A squeak escaped her lips like steam from a pressure relief valve as Father Nicco touched Cara's arm.

"Cara *mia*, excuse me for interrupting, but I'd like to introduce you to my *amico*. "This is Francesco D'Amore. He's very interested in

Comfort Connection. I have to speak with Senator Marshall for a moment, but I'm sure you can answer Francesco's questions."

"Certainly," Cara said.

Father Nicco smiled and strolled away.

Cara offered her hand to the tall, imposing man with the shoulder-length, wavy black hair and fashionable stubble. Francesco took it, but instead of shaking it, he kissed it and clasped it to his heart. His espresso-colored eyes searched Cara's face as he struggled to speak. "Ms. Hawthorne er Mrs. Wells . . ."

"Wells is my married name. I use my maiden name, Hawthorne, professionally, but I prefer you call me Cara."

"Cara, you have touched me," he said beating her hand against his chest."

Cara thought him overly dramatic, a caricature, like Adam Sandler when he played "Opera Man."

"I've been looking for a charitable organization to . . . How should I say? Patronize? I am sure you are aware that I lost my twin sister when I was small."

Cara stifled a snicker. No, she was not aware of that, and she didn't want to tell him that until a few minutes ago, she'd not even been aware of him.

"I read about the tragedy," Lia said, insinuating herself into the conversation. "You were so traumatized that you stopped speaking. And it was only through—"

Francesco dropped Cara's hand and turned to gaze at Lia. "Singing opera that I regained my voice," he said, as his eyes devoured Lia's ample breasts as if they were two mounds of his vanilla gelato. "And who may I ask is this *bella signora?*"

Cara watched a wave of crimson flood Lia's cheeks. "This is Cornelia Minor," she said. My executive assistant."

Lia offered her hand. "Pleased to meet you."

Francesco took Lia's manicured hand into both of his. "Miss Minor, a woman of major beauty, I am pleased to meet you too." He kissed her hand.

As Cara watched Lia lower her eyes coquettishly, she felt a tap on her shoulder. She turned to see a tall, lean, elderly gentleman standing there. "Ms. Hawthorne, pardon me for interrupting, but I'm wondering if I may have a word with you."

"Of course," Cara said. She was beginning to feel like a third wheel anyway. "Francesco, please excuse me," she said. "I'm grateful that you're interested in Comfort Connection, and I'd be happy to talk to you in more depth at a later time." Her eyes locked on her assistant. "Or I'm sure Lia would be happy to assist you."

"I look forward to seeing you again," Francesco said and then turned to Lia. "Perhaps we could discuss this over a bottle of Prosecco."

Cara, amused, watched the pair head toward the bar. Lia looked over her shoulder and flashed her eyes at Cara.

"Miss Hawthorne," the man said, "I'm Sanford Coskins."

Cara couldn't believe her ears, and she berated herself for not recognizing him. His distinctive shock of white hair and black bolo tie should have given him away. So this was the legendary Sanford Coskins. The man held more patents than Edison and had more money than Bill Gates. A very private man, he was rarely seen in public, keeping mostly to his sprawling Idaho ranch.

"It's an honor to meet you, Mr. Coskins," Cara said.

"Sandy, please call me Sandy. I was very impressed with you and what you've told us about your organization, and I'd like to offer my support."

"I'm very flattered." Cara felt as if she were going to split out of her skin with excitement.

"Don't be. You're a hard worker, and I value that. I've worked hard for my money too, so before I throw my backing behind a charity, I investigate it. Thoroughly. And I was impressed, but I wanted to meet you first. I get a sense about people. I've done my homework, Miss Hawthorne, and I must say that you and your organization are quite remarkable." He nervously fingered his tie. "I lost my father when I was a boy—farming accident. It was a tough time. Anyway," he said, appearing to shrug off the painful memory, as he reached into his breast pocket, extracted a card, and handed it to her, "this is my private line. I'll be out of the country for the next three days, but when I return, I'd like you to call me so we can discuss how I can best help Comfort Connection."

Cara could barely contain her joy, but she heard her grandmother's voice admonishing her like she had when she was a child and she'd gotten, in her grandmother's mind, too emotional. *Goodness, don't go all giddy on me, Cara. Act like you've been here before.* Cara reigned in her enthusiasm and calmly said, "Thank you, Sandy. I'll certainly be in touch." She tucked his card into her beaded evening bag and smiled radiantly as he turned and walked away.

It went on like that for the remainder of the night with people introducing themselves, congratulating her, and offering their assistance. As the evening drew to a close, Cara, though grateful, was exhausted. The stress of speaking before such a large crowd and the toll of meeting and making small talk with strangers all night had sapped her of energy. Her face ached from smiling, and her feet, trapped in the blue satin spiked heels, were throbbing. She glanced at the platinum and diamond watch on her wrist. It was a quarter to eleven. She realized then that Wesley had not arrived in time to see her receive the award, and a mixture of anger and hurt clutched her heart. *When is he going to get here? It's been hours since he'd called. It would be nice if he phoned to congratulate me or, at least, keep me informed. It would be nice if he thought of something or someone else besides his career.*

Rather than returning home, she'd booked them a room at the hotel and had planned a romantic evening with him. It was so late now and she was so tired, the best she could hope for was to try to rekindle their love tomorrow morning after room service delivered her a huge breakfast. Too nervous to eat her dinner, she'd only picked at her food and now she was hungry. And truth be told, a bit tipsy. All night it seemed that someone had been handing her a drink. Cara wanted to find Father Nicco, bid him goodnight, go to her room, perhaps break into the mini-bar peanuts, and take a long hot bubble bath and then order room service while she waited for Wesley.

The crowd in the ballroom was slowly thinning. She hadn't seen Lia since she'd entrusted her to "Opera Man." Cara smiled. At least, someone was enjoying a little romance.

She spied Father Nicco seated at a table with several other men. He was rearranging the salt and pepper shakers animatedly and going on in Italian.

"Sorry to interrupt," she said, as she touched his arm, "but I wanted to say goodnight."

"You're not interrupting." He rose. "I was explaining the wisdom of allowing a striker to roam freely."

Cara laughed. She should have known. Father Nicco's devotion to his beloved football, commonly known as soccer in the U.S., was only surpassed by his love for the church.

They stepped a few feet away from the table. "Father Nicco, thank you. Thank you for everything. Your support, your lovely introduction, and most of all for your friendship." She gave him a peck on the cheek.

He took her face in his hands, and his blue eyes became serious. "You're welcome, Cara *mia*, but it was my pleasure. I'm proud of you. I'm proud to know you. I'm proud of God for creating you."

She laughed at his extravagant praise. "You're going to make me cry."

"You know who else who would be proud of you? Your grandmother and your mother."

She felt a lump rise in her throat as he hugged her.

"How are you getting home?" he asked when he released her.

"I'm staying here tonight. Wesley is supposed to join me."

"Yes, where is Wesley? I didn't see him."

"His flight was delayed because of bad weather in New York. He should be arriving soon."

"He missed all of this? Ah, what a shame," he said as he escorted her to the lobby. "Well, dear, give him my love."

As she walked toward the elevator, she wished that she could infuse Wesley with some of Father Nicco's warmth and love. Wesley definitely needed it.

Chapter 4

"Miss Hawthorne! Excuse me, Miss Hawthorne!"

Cara groaned. She didn't think she could raise another smile or shake another hand. She only wanted to get to her room and relax.

"Please wait, Miss Hawthorne!"

Please, Lord, give me patience. Cara turned to see an attractive, young woman with a blonde pageboy hairstyle scurrying toward her, the jacket of her navy pinstripe suit flapping as her stiletto heels clicked on the shiny lobby floor.

"Oh, thank you for stopping, Miss Hawthorne," the woman said breathlessly. "I hate to bother you, but I'm Anne Neville, a correspondent with *Sonic Wayve.*" She held out her hand. "I was wondering if you had a moment?"

Cara shook the young woman's hand. "*Sonic Wayve?* I'm afraid I'm not familiar."

"We're an industry magazine, out of L.A. catering to musicians, producers, promoters, industry types, and I was hoping to speak to you about an article I'm doing."

"Are you sure you've got the right person? I'm not . . . I don't have anything to do with music."

"Yes, I'm sure you're the right person," the young woman said as she smoothed her hair, which Cara thought pointless since there wasn't a strand out of place. "I'm doing a feature on the effect of grief on musicians, and I wanted to get some quotes from you."

"But I'm not a grief expert. I leave that to the therapists and counselors."

"I'm aware of that, but I thought that your receiving the Mother Teresa award for the work you do would be pertinent."

Cara scrunched her nose. "I don't see how I'd be of much help."

The reporter touched Cara's arm, and her face became very serious. "But I could be of help to you. Many famous—and I might add—wealthy musicians, singers, and producers read our magazine. You may not be aware of this but Paul McCartney, Bono, and Madonna, to name a few, all lost their mothers when they were very young. When they read about your story and your work, I'm betting that many of them may want to help your foundation."

"Do you really think so?"

"Most definitely. This could help you and Comfort Connection immeasurably. Think Bob Geldof and Live Aid, or John Mellencamp and Farm Aid."

Cara knew the value of celebrity backing. She shrugged. "I guess it couldn't hurt."

"Great! Why don't we go into the lounge, I'll buy you a drink, and we can chat there."

Cara's feet were screaming with pain, and she couldn't wait to take her hair out of this updo. The hair pins were digging into her scalp. *Maybe I should get my hair cut like her pageboy. It seems so sleek and simple.* "Could we do it tomorrow, please? I'm really quite exhausted."

"I've got to catch a plane early tomorrow. It'll only take a few minutes. I promise."

Before Cara could refuse, the reporter put a hand on her elbow and began to guide her toward the lounge.

They found a small table in the far corner of the dimly lit bar. A cocktail waitress soon appeared. Cara tried to order a club soda, but Anne Neville insisted that they have champagne to celebrate Cara's award.

When the drinks arrived, Cara took a sip, but not before accepting a congratulatory toast from Ms. Neville.

"Now, Ms. Hawthorne," Anne Neville said, opening a notepad, "as I said before, many artists have suffered great losses. Do you think grief begets sensitivity and, therefore, artistic creativity?"

"Wow," Cara said, and then chuckled. "That's a tough question. You said this would be easy. I'll have to think about that for a minute." She mentally inventoried the children who had come to Comfort Connection. Certainly, some of them seemed gifted artistically, but was that due to grief? She couldn't say for certain. "I don't know," Cara said. "But what I do know is that grief definitely changes a person. Perhaps it makes—"

Cara's iPhone rang inside her evening bag. "Excuse me." She pulled out her phone. "I'm sorry," she said while looking at the screen. "It's my husband. He's traveling. I have to take his call. It'll only be a moment."

Cara tapped the phone's screen. "Wesley, where are you? What? You're still there?" She heard her voice becoming louder. "But you were on the plane," she said lowering her volume. "And I reserved us a suite. You missed the entire banquet and my receiving the award. And now you're not going to come at all? That's just wonderful."

The reporter tried to look interested in her notes, but Cara could tell by the way she cocked her ear toward her that she was eavesdropping. She didn't want a marital spat ending up in the article. She wasn't Sophia; she cared about her privacy. And her reputation.

Cara pulled the phone away from her ear and looked at Ms. Neville. "The reception is poor in here. I'm going to step into the lobby."

"Who are you talking to?" Wesley's voice squawked as she made her way to the entrance of the lounge.

"A reporter was interviewing me. I didn't want her to hear us arguing," she whispered.

"I'm not arguing. You're the one who's getting upset."

"Don't you think I have a right to be? The biggest night of my life and my husband is nowhere to be seen."

"I was working. It wasn't like I was out in Las Vegas clubbing like your sister."

So that's where Sophia is, Cara thought, doubling her anger. Partying in Vegas. That was certainly more important than supporting your sister.

"You've known since October that this night was coming," she said. "You could have rearranged your schedule. How does your absence make me look?"

"Cut me a break. It's not my fault the witness chose this time to take a turn for the worse. I had to get his deposition before he croaked. You know that."

"Couldn't one of your associates have done it?"

"I've told you this case is so high profile, it has the potential to make or break my career. I can't let some newbie handle so much responsibility."

Exasperated, she sighed. "When will you be home?"

"I'm going to try to catch the first plane out tomorrow. I should be there in the early afternoon. I'll call you in the morning."

"Fine." She ended the call and stuffed the phone back into her purse.

Before she reentered the bar, she checked her reflection in the pane of glass outside and saw that her frustration with Wesley was evident on her face.

Once again, she pasted a smile on and rejoined the reporter at the table. "I'm sorry for the interruption. Now, what was your question?" Cara took a large gulp of champagne. *May as well drink up. I've no reason to remain awake.* She felt it splash as it hit her empty stomach. While the reporter leafed through her notebook, Cara thought of herself sleeping alone in the enormous king-sized bed in the suite. She took another long sip and felt the buzz dulling her anger, dulling her senses.

"Let me read this back to you," the reporter said, "so that perhaps you'll be able to pick up on your train of thought."

As the reporter spoke, Cara felt odd, as if she were receding from consciousness, as if she were being enveloped in cotton. *Must be all the drinks I had on an empty stomach.* She began to feel queasy. This was not a normal alcohol buzz; this was something more paralyzing. She had to get to her room before she threw up or worse blacked out. *Wouldn't that look lovely in tomorrow's* Tribune-Review? *A picture of me passed out in a bar wearing the Mother Teresa medallion.*

"I'm sorry. I have to cut this short," Cara slurred as she rubbed her forehead. "I'm not feeling very well." *Dear Lord, just let me get back to my room.*

"Are you OK?" the reporter asked as she rose and came to Cara's side.

Cara stood on unsteady legs and staggered toward the lobby.

"Miss Hawthorne, we can do this another time," Anne Neville said following her. "You look awful. Do you want me to call a doctor? Your husband? Someone?"

"No, I'll be fine," Cara said, reeling and feeling as though she were talking to Anne Neville from another galaxy. "I just need to lie down."

"Let me help you to your room."

The reporter pushed the button for the elevator and escorted her inside. Cara was grateful that it was empty in case she got sick to her stomach.

"Is your room key in your bag?"

Cara nodded, leaning against the elevator's rear wall, the movement of which intensified her queasiness. The reporter searched the bag, and Cara was relieved when she heard the woman say, "Found it. Do you know the room number?"

From somewhere deep in her cloudy brain, the number came: "1915," Cara said. As she watched the elevator's floor indicator light rising in numeric order, she felt herself descending into her consciousness, folding into herself.

The doors opened and sagging onto the arm of Anne Neville, Cara aimed herself toward her room, staggering toward its door. If only I can lie down, she thought, her vision becoming blurry.

"Here we are," Cara heard the reporter say, her voice far away as if she were calling to Cara from deep inside a well.

The door opened, Cara stumbled toward the bed, and collapsed on top of it, her contact with consciousness severing.

Chapter 5

After eating the breakfast that room service had delivered, Cara decided she'd better check her iPhone to make sure no one else had been trying to get in touch with her. When she picked up her phone, she recalled that she had spoken with Wesley just before taking ill. That key unlocked the memory of the evening for her—the banquet, meeting the reporter, and suddenly getting sick came flooding back. However, as she caught a cab home, she was still mulling over in her mind, one question: How she had wound up naked in the bed? She concluded that she was so sick she had stripped off her clothing and fell into bed. By the time she had arrived home, Cara had dismissed the whole episode from her mind because she had more important things to consider.

Uncharacteristically, she skipped Mass because she still felt as if a parasite had invaded her body and was sapping her energy. She had taken a long, hot bath and dressed in her pink velour Victoria Secret sweat suit and spent the next few hours relaxing on the sofa in the den while compiling a list of prospective donors to contact from the people she'd met at the banquet. With each passing hour, she'd begun to feel a bit better.

When she heard Wesley's Lexus turn into the driveway, she peered out the palladium window of their Sewickley home and saw him exit the car. His blond hair caught the late afternoon January sunshine and glowed like a halo. Cara watched as he folded his athletic frame and reached into the backseat. He took out his garment bag and standing, flung it over his shoulder. Her heart skipped a beat. He looked like one of those ruggedly handsome sailors in those Old Spice commercials that ran on television when she was a girl. And watching him, she felt as excited as a woman who had been waiting months for her man to come home from the sea. It had been more than a month since he'd made love to her, and she longed for him.

Cara was pleased that he had this effect on her. She recalled how angry she had been with him when he had called her last night to say that he wouldn't be coming at all that she thought perhaps he'd killed any feeling she had for him.

He grabbed his leather briefcase and strode up the walk, his black wool overcoat flapping, revealing his royal blue crew neck sweater and khaki slacks. Cara told herself to put last night behind her. Perhaps by loading so many expectations on having a romantic evening, she had set herself up for disappointment. Hadn't Wesley often accused her of placing the bar so high that no one could ever live up to her measures?

When she heard the doorknob turn, she left the den and came into the foyer as Wesley crossed the threshold. "Finally, you're home." She went to give him a kiss.

He pulled back before she could place her lips on his cheek. "You still have that bug? You don't look very good."

Cara was taken aback. She caught a glimpse of herself in the mirror over the small wrought iron and marble table in the foyer. She did look a bit pale. "You're all compliments," she said.

"Sorry, but I have to be in court tomorrow. I can't get sick." He dropped the briefcase, went to the foyer table, and began to riffle through the pile of mail.

"How was your flight?" she asked, placing a hand on his arm.

He tossed the mail aside. "Miserable. They bumped me out of first class, and I was forced to sit among a pack of obnoxious kids coming back from a ski weekend in the Adirondacks."

Wesley took off his coat and draped it over the newel post.

"Are you hungry? I can fix us omelets," she said, taking his coat from the post and walking to the closet. Her appetite was finally returning.

He grabbed the coat from her. "I don't want it in the closet," he said tossing it back onto the post. The coat hit the post and slid onto the floor. "I have more things in my trunk, and then I have to put the car in the garage. A limb came down in the driveway, and I have to move it. And no, I'm not hungry. I grabbed something at the airport."

She wrapped her arms around his neck and peered up into his face. "I'm so glad you're home. I missed you. I'm sorry I was snippy with you last night. It's just that I had reserved us a room, and I really wanted to be with you. But you're home now. We could have our romantic evening here at home."

He reached up and clasped her wrists, his hands cold on her skin as he broke the hold she had on him. "Sorry, honey, but I'm really tired, and I have work to do. And besides you're sick."

She stepped back, stunned by his callousness. Tears came to her eyes.

He sighed. "Oh, Cara, don't overreact. I hate it when you act like a wounded puppy. I've got work to do." He grabbed the briefcase and headed toward the den.

She hung the coat back on the post and followed after him, watching as he set his briefcase on the massive cherry desk and pressed the buttons, releasing the case's latches with a snap.

Cara held it closed. "Don't shut me out, Wesley. I'm not overreacting. The most important night of my life— And you weren't there for me."

"I'm not going to discuss this again. I had to go out of town."

"I understand that, but I had plans for us afterward. Couldn't you have gotten an earlier flight before it started to snow?"

He collapsed into the leather desk chair and massaged his temple. Then he reached for her hand, but she kept it to her side. "Cara, I admire you, and I'm proud of you for trying to make the world a better place, but the world doesn't always work the way you want it to. Things don't always work out according to plan—according to your plan."

His words stung. If she had one fault it was that she was controlling, but if she had tried to micromanage anything, it was because all she wanted was to be with him. And she wanted him to want to be with her.

She took his cold hand, and he pulled her on to his lap. "I'm sorry, sweetheart," he said. "It was a long, tiring trip. I wish I could have been there. I saw your photo in the *New York Times* and *USA Today*. You looked amazing."

She rested her head on his shoulder. He smelled like coffee and bacon no doubt from his breakfast at the airport. It felt so good to be this near to him again. "I haven't seen the paper," she said. "I was still feeling a bit woozy when I came home. I turned down the ringer on the phone and took a bath."

"How do you feel now?"

"Much better. I think I must have gotten a case of food poisoning. I'm going to call Lia later to see if she may have gotten sick too. Did any of the articles mention anything about my wanting to expand Comfort Connection?"

"No, they pretty much focused on— No, they didn't."

"What were you going to say?"

"Nothing. It can wait. Hey, you haven't shown me your medal."

She raised her head and stared into his eyes. "You started to say they focused on something. What was it? What did the article say?"

He closed his eyes and sighed. "I wasn't going to tell you now, let you enjoy your moment in the spotlight, but I guess you're bound to find out anyway." He stroked her hair as if she were a child, adding to her apprehension. "There's something else in the paper," he said, "that overshadowed your receiving the award."

What with getting ready for the banquet, the evening itself, and then taking sick, she'd been in a virtual media blackout for the past thirty-six hours. Had there been a catastrophe or a terrorist attack? Surely, someone would have mentioned it last night. "What is it?"

"More like who is it?"

Alarmed, she immediately thought of her father. As the CEO of a well-known corporation, he was a target for terrorists or anarchists. "Did something happen to Daddy?"

"Not your father. Sophia."

She stood. Images of violent car or plane crashes flashed in her mind. Or maybe she has been kidnapped. As a co-heiress to the Cavanaugh and Hawthorne fortunes, she was a prime target too. "Is she OK? What's happened to her?" Cara heard the fear in her voice.

Wesley stood and placed his hands firmly on her shoulders. "Don't get upset, sweetheart. She's fine. For Sophia that is."

He lifted the lid on his briefcase, took out *The New York Times* and handed it to Cara. She examined the front page where the headline screamed, "A Tale of Two Sisters." Below the headline was a picture of Cara accepting her medal juxtaposed to one of Sophia barely wearing a skimpy dress, holding a Margarita, her head thrown back, laughing. The caption read: The Hawthorne Sisters - While one garners honors the other courts disgrace.

"Oh, no," Cara cried. "What has she done?" She quickly scanned the article, passing over the few short paragraphs that touched on her award to get to the heart of the story. After reading a few sentences, she dropped the paper onto the desk and groaned. She looked at Wesley. "What would possess her?" She sunk into the desk chair and covered her face with her hands. "Oh, Sophia. Why? Why would you marry a 'Buns of Fun' male stripper?"

Chapter 6

"What time is it in Vegas?" Cara glanced at the clock on the mantle. "I'm calling her. She should be sober by now."

"But she may be busy recording her honeymoon sex tape to release on the Internet," Wesley said.

"You don't think she'd . . ." Cara's voice trailed off as she contemplated whether her sister would stoop to such depravity. She and Wesley both knew she would. Cara suddenly felt queasy again. "What was she thinking?"

Wesley laughed. "Sophia think? She acts on whatever impulse strikes her fancy."

"You find this funny?"

"No, but you have to admit it's rather comical to think that the two of you came from the same family."

Cara shook her head and reached for the phone. Instead of a dial tone, she heard the beep-beep-beep indicating that there were messages in her voicemail. "I forgot to check the phone after shutting off the ringer. We have messages. Maybe she's called to explain that it's a joke," Cara said as she punched in her pass code. The computer-generated voice said she had twenty-eight messages. She sat on the edge of the desk and covered her face with her hand as she listened to them. There were messages from *People* and *US* magazines, *TMZ, The Enquirer, The Washington Post*—each voice sounding more rapacious as they implored Cara to call and satisfy their lust for gossip with a comment on her sister's surprise marriage.

Cara couldn't stand to listen to any longer. She slammed down the receiver and clenched her teeth. "I'm going to kill her."

Wesley stared at Cara. "What is it?"

"All the messages are from the press. She has reduced us to the Kardashians. It's good that Grandmother is dead or this would have killed her."

Wesley touched her shoulder as if to reassure her that everything would be fine. Cara picked up the phone and dialed Sophia, a tide of anger rising and washing away the shock. The phone rang and rang and then went to her sister's voicemail. Cara hung up. "She's not answering."

Wesley snickered. "If you were Sophia, would you answer?"

Cara couldn't even begin to contemplate Sophia's thought processes.

Wesley sat in the wingchair near the fireplace, reading the newspaper. "I wonder if she'll take our new brother-in-law's surname? It says here that he is known as Peter N. Vee."

Cara closed her eyes and groaned.

Wesley folded the paper and shrugged. "At least he's an educated man. He's familiar with Freud."

Cara moved to the desk chair. "I'm calling my father. He'll put a stop to this. They can annul this. Britney Spears had her Vegas wedding annulled."

"Where is he today?"

"I believe Tokyo."

"What time is it there? He may be asleep," Wesley said as he glanced at the Rolex on his wrist. "They're thirteen hours ahead."

"I don't care what time it is. He has to know about this."

Wesley stood and slapped the paper on the desk. "I'm going to unpack." He left the den.

As Cara listened to the phone ringing and ringing, she anticipated her father's reaction. She knew he'd be outraged. Perhaps now he'd realize how indulgent he had been with Sophia. Shoplifting, pot smoking, and DUIs were one thing, but marrying a male stripper was a new low—even for Sophia. Her father had always dismissed Sophia's antics as youthful dalliances, but Sophia was no longer a child. She was twenty-two, and it was time he put a stop to her reckless behavior.

"Hello," her father said gruffly. Cara envisioned him dressed in his silk pajamas reaching for his half-moon pewter frame glasses to read the time on the bedside clock, his thick blond hair threaded with gray, not a hair out of place, as if he'd never gone to bed. Her father even while sleeping was impeccable. Nothing seemed to disturb his appearance or rattle his composure, perhaps that's why his name was being bandied about as a nominee for Ambassador to United Nations. His years of experience living abroad and traveling the globe as the CEO of Allegheny Food & Beverage Group had made him well known on the world stage. In addition to having friends all over the world, her father had the temperament of diplomat. He was tactful and self-possessed, always looked smart and behaved properly.

"I hated to wake you, but I had to call."

"Cara, what is the matter?" he asked, his voice sounding thick from sleeping.

"Sophia is what's the matter. Have you seen what she's done now?"

Cara heard him sigh heavily.

"No, but I'm sure you will tell me. What has you so concerned now?"

She would not let him trivialize this. "She has married a Vegas stripper."

"Your sister has married a showgirl?"

"No, no. She married a male stripper. A member of the 'Buns of Fun' male dance troupe."

"That's reassuring. At least she's carrying on with a man."

"You're not upset? She's brought disgrace to our family. Again. I'm trying to acquire funding for Comfort Connection, and she goes and pulls this stunt! And what about you? This can't help your career. How is this going to look?"

"Are you sure this is true and not some sensational rumor launched by the tabloids to sell papers?"

"It's in *The New York Times* and *U.S.A Today*. I've got a ton of messages from the paparazzi—all wanting to know what we think of her marriage. What are we going to do?"

"Cara, calm down. This is not the end of the world. People make mistakes all the time."

Mistake? Bouncing a check is a mistake. Getting a speeding ticket is a mistake, but marrying a Vegas Romeo is more than a mistake!

"It's late. I'll be home tomorrow. I'll take care of it then."

Cara turned the newspaper over. She couldn't bear to look at Sophia's photo any longer. "What do I do in the meantime? What do

I tell the media? They're hounding me. They want my comments."

"Tell them Sophia is a grown woman and that you admire her sense of adventure and *joie de vivre*."

"You can't expect me to say that. This is a disgrace!"

"You sound just like your grandmother. Lighten up, Cara darling. If you don't take it so seriously, neither will the press. In fact, you could use a bit of Sophia's zest for life. I don't mean to find fault, but do yourself a favor. Stop taking everything so seriously. You're becoming rather dull."

Sophia marries a stripper, and I'm one the one he criticizes? I should have known. Why can't I get it through my thick skull that Sophia is his favorite, and there's nothing I can do or she can do to change the way he feels about me?

"Fine then. Have a safe trip home." She hung up the phone and dumped the newspapers into the trash.

Chapter 7

When Cara walked into their master bathroom, Wesley was putting away his toiletries. She sat on the edge of the marble jetted tub and watched him.

"How did your father take the news?" Wesley asked as he stowed his razor in the cabinet.

He seemed more relaxed now. Cara was glad that his mood had softened. The stress of traveling and taking the deposition must have put him on edge. That's why he'd been so short when he'd arrived home. "Oh, he was his usual unruffled self." She pushed off with both of her hands and stood. "I promised myself I wouldn't let it get to me, but I am so furious, Wesley. I don't know how he does it, but he, once again, has managed to portray me as the one with the problem. Sophia marries a stripper, and he has the audacity to call me," she touched her chest for emphasis, "dull! Dull? Do you believe it?"

In the bathroom mirror, Cara caught Wesley's lips as they briefly curled into a smirk.

She put a hand on her hip. "So you think I'm dull too?"

"What?" He turned and wrapped his arms around her. "No, no. Why would you think that?"

She looked up at him. "I saw you smirking in the mirror. You think I'm annoying too, don't you?"

He kissed the top of her head. "Cara, I don't know why you let him get to you like that. Sophia's his baby. That's why he cuts her slack all the time. What's he going to say? If he condemns her, it's an indictment of his parenting skills."

"So you don't think he favors her? That this is all in my mind? That his turning it around on me is merely his way of covering for the poor job he did of raising her?"

"Yes, I do."

Cara shook her head. "So you think minimizing and excusing her behavior makes him feel better, but that doesn't explain why he chose to ship me off to live with grandmother after mother died and keep Sophia with him in Thailand."

Wesley sighed heavily and released her. "How many times have we been over this, Cara?" He looked her squarely in the eye, commanding her attention. "Your father couldn't manage two small children on his own and decided that you were the most stable psychologically and would adjust more rapidly to living with your grandmother in the states. Sophia was younger, and he wanted to provide some continuity for her life. And don't forget, your grandmother was elderly and wasn't up to caring for an infant."

No wonder he was on the fast track in the firm. When he pleaded his case, you couldn't help but believe him.

"Maybe that was the wrong choice," he said, "but I don't know what I'd have done if I were a single father with two little girls. I can understand that. Why can't you? Why do you have to keep torturing yourself by going over this?" He touched her shoulder and went into the bedroom.

She followed and sat next to him on the bed as he removed his shoes. "You never answered my question," she said.

"What question was that?"

"Am I dull?"

Wesley's shoulders rose and fell in a great sigh.

Cara stood and peered down at him. "I guess I have my answer."

"Cara—" Wesley reached for her, but she stood stiffly, a mixture of anger and hurt swirling inside her.

"I know I can be controlling and a bit of a perfectionist," she said, as the hurt overwhelmed the anger, and she began to blink back tears.

"My father said I take things too seriously, and that I should adopt some of Sophia's," she rolled her eyes, "*joie de vivre.*"

"Cara, listen to yourself. You're a grown woman; you don't need your father's approval anymore. Good Lord, half the world came to town last night to honor you. You have their approval. Isn't that enough? Wallowing in self-pity and vying for your father's affection with Sophia is sick. This whole thing with your father? Yeah, that's what's dull."

She had to admit that she was wallowing in self-pity. *Why do I always allow my father to upset me like this? So what if he loves Sophia more than me. What do I care what he says?* "You're right." She sat next to Wesley on the bed and touched his hand. It was warmer now. "I'm sorry."

"No need to be."

"I'll stop talking about my father. I promise, but I have to ask you something. He said I could use a little of her zest for life." She paused, afraid to ask the question for fear of Wesley's answer. "Do you think I'm a wet blanket, that I lack *joie de vivre?*"

"Honestly?"

She squeezed his hand. "Please tell me. I won't get angry."

He covered her hand with his. "Don't take this the wrong way, honey, but no one I know is as kind or good as you. It's not easy being around a saint."

"I'm no saint," she said, her voice rising as she pulled her hand away.

"Not now anyway. Father Nicco hasn't put in for your canonization yet." He was smiling, but she didn't think it at all funny. Wesley touched her cheek. "Can I be honest with you?"

She nodded because she was afraid if she spoke, she would start to cry.

"You are too hard on yourself, which sometimes makes you a bit staid—so perfect and predictable. Sometimes I wish that you would loosen up a bit, cut yourself some slack, let your hair down—get a little edgy."

"OK," Cara said, a weak smile covering how wounded she felt by Wesley's words. "I'll try to change. I'll try to loosen up. If it's edgy you want, it's edgy you will get."

Wesley went back into the bathroom to finish stowing away his toiletries.

Cara remained on the bed. *Now I know why they call it edgy.* Because even contemplating changing her behavior made her feel as if she were skirting the rim of a deep, black pit.

Chapter 8

Cara couldn't believe how much better she felt when she awoke on Monday morning. The haziness had left her mind, and she'd slept so soundly that Wesley's kiss on her cheek when he left for the office barely registered in her subconscious. They'd spent the rest of their Sunday hunkered down in the house as the temperature had started to plunge after dinner, dropping into the teens. She tried to concentrate on planning her strategy for appealing to those potential benefactors she'd met at the awards banquet, but she found her mind wandering to her father's and Wesley's criticism, accusing her of being too stuffy. She tried to let it go, but like a sore tooth that your tongue keeps prodding, she couldn't help but repeatedly going back to it.

Neither of them was very hungry so she made them grilled cheese sandwiches for dinner. Wesley turned on the local news on the massive television in the family room. He insisted on purchasing a sixty-five-inch screen, but Cara found it so large that it felt as if she were absorbed into the picture, making her motion sick when he watched movies with a lot of action like *The Dark Night Rises*.

However, she found watching the news a bit of a relief as it turned her attention from her character flaws to monitoring the broadcast for news on her sister's scandalous marriage. This year, the Super Bowl was going to be held in Pittsburgh. The big game was set for February 8—thirteen days from now—and already the city's enthusiasm for hosting it and the plunging temperatures had overshadowed the news of her sister's marriage, which mercifully merited only a five-second mention on the broadcast.

After the news, Wesley had retreated into the den to work on his case, and he had risen before her this morning because he wanted to get an early start on the day.

Cara had spent the remainder of the evening in the solarium, off the kitchen, attempting to watch *Masterpiece Theatre*, but questions arced in her brain like sparks from a live wire. *What would receiving the medal mean for Comfort Connection in the long run? Where was Sophia now, and what would happen with her hasty marriage? Why did her father's approval mean so much to her?* And the most puzzling question of all—one that had been shuttled to the back of her mind: *What had happened in that hotel room after she had taken sick?* She tried to convince herself that she had just gotten sick, but something was not right. Only she couldn't put her finger on what was out of order.

When she went to bed, as was her habit, she read her devotional book, and the scripture passage had seemed hand-selected for her. It was Proverbs 3:5-6: *Trust in the Lord with all your heart, and do not lean on your own understanding. In all your ways acknowledge him, and he will make straight your paths.*

Cara repeated the verse several times to herself, and each time that she did, she felt her cares settling in her mind, like wrinkles smoothing under a hot iron. Whatever happened with Comfort Connection, Sophia, and her father was out of her hands. And whatever had happened to her in the hotel room after the banquet didn't matter anymore. It was in the past and tomorrow was a new day. She was feeling better and ready to improve her life—even to be willing to try to be less controlling to please Wesley. She vowed that she'd do her best and let God do the rest.

Before turning off the light, she leaned over and kissed Wesley's cheek and whispered, "I love you." He was nearly asleep, and he mumbled something back to her. As she slid beneath the toasty flannel sheets last night, she felt confident that tomorrow she'd be led on a straighter, brighter path.

As soon as her alarm sounded on Monday morning, she rose. She could not wait to get to the office and begin to call the contacts she'd made at the award ceremony. Perhaps she would acquire enough support to run a Public Service Announcement during the Super Bowl. *I wonder how much that costs?* Cara especially couldn't wait to speak with Sanford Coskins when he returned to the country.

Earning his stamp of approval would signal to other philanthropists and foundations that Comfort Connection was a worthy endeavor, and if they followed his lead, funds would soon be pouring into Comfort Connection's coffers. There would be no stopping the good that Comfort Connection could do. She was so jazzed that even when she remembered Sophia's disastrous marriage while brushing her teeth, it didn't dampen her enthusiasm.

Cara showered and dressed in her red knitted dress and matching bolero jacket. Wesley called it her super woman suit, and today she felt very powerful as if she could leap tall buildings in a single bound or at least harness the good will coming Comfort Connection's way.

After dressing and straightening her wavy hair and applying her makeup, she entered the kitchen. Weak winter sunshine crept in through the multi-paned windows, offering the faintest hint of warmth and the slimmest promise that the temperature may rise out of the teens. She poured herself a cup of coffee from the pot that Wesley had brewed earlier and toasted an English muffin. She knew she should eat something more substantial. Wesley was always urging her to retain a housekeeper who could make them a proper breakfast, but Cara had grown up with domestic help and Wesley hadn't. No matter how much their housekeeper tried to remain invisible, Cara always felt her presence and found it intrusive. *What if we'd had a housekeeper here last night?* Cara didn't want some stranger listening to the conversation that she and Wesley had had last night. She valued her privacy. She felt uncomfortable enough being in the spotlight when she was awarded the medal, she didn't want some housekeeper tattling to the tabloids on everything that went on in her home. No, she was happy with a low profile; Sophia could keep the limelight to herself.

The medal. I should take it with me into the office. Lia had been the only one to see it up close, and Cara was sure that the rest of her staff would want to admire it. Sadness washed over her. In all the commotion with Sophia's marriage, Cara had forgotten to show it to Wesley. She knew she should be proud of the medal, but she noticed that nothing had gone right since it had been placed around her neck. It was silly, but Cara wondered if it could be cursed. "Get a grip, Cara," she mused to herself. "It was blessed by Father Nicco. It can't be cursed."

As she raised her cup, the slanting rays of the sun caught her engagement ring and refracted in a shower of rainbows on the granite countertop. Her ring had been another area where she and Wesley had differed. She adjusted it on her finger. She would have been perfectly content to have used Grandma Cavanaugh's modest engagement ring, but Wesley insisted on this ostentatious three-carat, pear-shaped diamond. Wesley was desperate to climb out of the depths of his humble beginnings and get to the top. Cara knew that once you arrived at the top, the view wasn't always that great. But she couldn't get Wesley to understand that. She'd have traded in the housekeepers, private schools, piano lessons, debutante balls—all of it—for a home with a mother and father and a normal upbringing.

She remembered the vow she made before she fell asleep, and she released Wesley's insecurity to Divine Providence as well.

Before heading out the back door into the cold of the breezeway that linked the house to the double garage, she retrieved the velvet box holding the medal.

As she drove across the Fort Duquesne Bridge into downtown Pittsburgh, Cara noticed chunks of ice floating on the Ohio River like miniature icebergs and was grateful that she had indoor parking and didn't have to brave the weather walking the streets to her office. After parking her Escalade in the garage of the former Westinghouse Tower at 11 Stanwix Street, she took the elevator to the lobby and then boarded another elevator that took her the eighteenth floor and their offices.

Comfort Connection occupied a small suite of offices suitable to the nonprofit's minimal staff. Cara limited the personnel because she didn't want staffing costs drawing on their limited funds. And if she were honest with herself, the smaller the operation, the greater control she could exert over it.

When she walked into the reception area, Nina Anzeloni, their receptionist, was not at her desk, but Cara could hear laughter and excited voices coming from down the hall in Lia's office. When Cara poked her head around the door frame, she saw Nina; Marjorie Walsh, their accountant; Stacy Ostrowski, their wunderkind, fresh out Robert Morris University's marketing program who knew all about the Internet; and Tess Adams, their Development Director; crowded around Lia, who was holding up her iPhone.

"Morning," Cara said.

"There's the star now," Lia said. "Come on in. I was showing everyone the photos I took at the awards ceremony."

Cara deposited her purse and tote on Lia's desk. "Let's see." Cara scrunched up her nose. "Oh, I look awful."

"You do not," said Nina. "I wish I could have been there. It would have been more exciting than my great-grandmother's ninetieth birthday."

"It was a fantastic night," Marjorie said.

Cara looked at Lia. "So how did it go with the *Phantom of the Opera?*"

Lia shuffled through the photos on her phone. "Here's a selfie of us." In the photo, Lia and Francesco were toasting.

"Lia thinks he's gay," Stacy said.

Cara was shocked. After the way he'd practically drooled over Lia's breasts, she'd have never suspected. "Why's that?"

Lia shrugged. "Oh, I don't know. For all his bluster complimenting me when he first met us, when I was alone with him in the bar, he never once flirted with me again."

"And she looked *really* hot," Stacy said.

"He may be the Liberace of this time," said Tess, who, in her early sixties, had to explain to Stacy exactly who Liberace was.

"Whether he is gay or not," Lia said with a wink, "I couldn't run off with him to Italy anyhow. I'm needed here."

"It's his loss," Tess said, "because you looked beautiful on Saturday night." She looked at Cara. "As did you. I had such a wonderful time, Cara. Thank you for inviting us."

"It was my pleasure," said Cara, who was grateful that at least the office staff had accompanied her to the event.

"Please send those photos to me, Lia," Stacy said. "I'll load them onto our website." She turned to Cara. "The media took a ton of pictures of you. We should get some and post them."

"Yes, I can use them in our next appeal for funds too," Allison said. "And I'd like a photo of the medal too."

"Good thing I brought it with me then," said Cara as she rooted in her purse for the velvet box.

Everyone examined and admired the Mother Teresa medal until the ringing of the phone interrupted them. Lia answered it and then pushed the hold button. "Cara, it's *The New York Daily News*."

"Ask them what they are calling about. I suppose you saw what my sister did over the weekend?"

Lia shook her head. "Yes. It's like she couldn't stand for you to be the center of attention."

"I don't want to talk to anyone about that. You'll have to be on guard and really the screen the calls today," Cara said.

"Got it. Award, yes; Sophia, no." Lia took the phone off hold and interrogated the reporter. She put the call on hold again and looked at Cara. "They want to speak to you about your award. Do you want to talk to them now or shall I have them call back?"

"I'll talk to them now. Tell them to hold until I can get into the office." Cara collected the medal, picked up her purse and tote, and went to her office, pleased for the opportunity to promote the organization again. As she opened her office door, she called back to Lia, "No one called from *Sonic Wayve*, did they?"

"*Sonic Wayve*? What's that?" asked Lia.

"It's a music magazine," Stacy said.

"I've never heard of it," Tess said.

Allison chuckled. "It sounds more like an electric toothbrush."

"One of their journalists wanted to interview me on Saturday night, but I had to beg off," Cara said. "I believe her name was Anne Neville. If she calls, put her through please."

Cara hoped the journalist would call. Perhaps she would be able to fill in some of the gaps in Cara's memory of Saturday night. She had tried to stop worrying about what had happened and release it to

God as well, but she still had an uneasy feeling. She'd had the flu several times before and never had memory loss been a symptom. Oh, well, it doesn't matter now anyway what happened, Cara reasoned. I'm not Sophia. *It's not like I did anything wrong or anything scandalous.*

Chapter 9

By the time Cara arrived home after work that evening, she was exhausted. She'd spent most of the day on the phone either giving interviews to the media or calling potential benefactors. To her delight, Lia had arranged with Sanford Coskins' secretary for Cara to speak with him on Thursday. What would she do without Lia? To her assistant's credit, only one duplicitous reporter had gotten past Lia to Cara. He had claimed to want to speak with her about her award but had started into a line of questioning regarding Sophia.

Wesley had called while she was driving and said that he would be home near seven o'clock, and if she could wait for dinner, he would pick up a pizza for them on his way. Grateful for some quiet time at home, she thought she'd unwind with a glass of pinot noir and a soak in their tub.

She hit the remote, which opened the wrought iron gate to their short driveway and pulled into the detached garage. Hustling through the drafty breezeway, she let herself into the warmth of the house via the backdoor, disarming the alarm system.

Their house was a stately, old Victorian, which had belonged to her grandmother before she and her grandfather had built their estate, Kerry Glen, in Sewickley Heights. Cara and Sophia had inherited both the estate and this home when their grandmother died. Sophia showed no interest in either place, deeming them both "ancient and boring." The estate was virtually in mothballs; only a skeleton crew of maintenance people kept it in good repair. Her father also had an estate in Sewickley Heights, Hawthorne Hall, which he'd inherited, but he chose to live in a penthouse on Mt. Washington. Recently, Wesley had been urging Cara to move into Kerry Glen. Perhaps when they had children, but, for now, Cara loved being in the heart of Sewickley. The village had all the appeal of a small town but was only a short drive from downtown Pittsburgh. But more than that, she loved this house. Her mother had grown up in it, and in some way, Cara felt the house connected her with the mother she could barely remember.

Before she and Wesley had gotten married, they'd had it restored and where appropriate, updated. Cara thought the house the perfect marriage of old-world charm and modern convenience.

She traveled through the kitchen, down the long center hall to the foyer, where she deposited her briefcase beside the foyer table. Then as she hung her black wool coat in the closet, she remembered that Lia had returned her grandmother's topaz jewelry. Cara promptly took the jewelry box from her purse into the den and locked it in the safe. As she headed toward the kitchen, she saw the mail lying beneath the brass slot. She bent to pick up the pile, and she noticed that among the standard-sized white envelopes was a large, unmarked manila one. Puzzled, she rose and flipped it over. Without postage or an address, it obviously hadn't been delivered by their mail carrier.

She shook the envelope. Nothing rattled inside it, just the soft swishing of papers shifting. Cara walked into the den and held it up to the desk lamp, but she could discern nothing inside the envelope. *Could it be anthrax?* Her family was famous and wealthy, but they'd never been a target before.

"Oh, you are being ridiculous," Cara said to herself as she grabbed the letter opener and slit the seal. Releasing the breath that she had been subconsciously holding when no powder spilled out, Cara pulled out a folder. When she opened it, that same breath caught in her throat in a sharp gasp.

The folder contained a series of eight-by-ten photos. Cara riffled through them, and at first, the images didn't register in her brain. It was as if she had been concussed, as if a nuclear bomb had been set off in her hand, sending a shock wave to her mind and stunning her. They were a collection of pornographic photos, each one more graphic and depraved than the previous. With faltering fingers, she closed the folder and vomited into the wastebasket beneath the desk.

When she had finished retching, she slumped in the chair, her head spinning, bile sour on her tongue. Suddenly, she stood because she felt like running or calling for help, but there was nowhere to go and no one who could explain what she had just seen. She wiped her mouth with the back of her hand and found her way to the powder room to empty the waste basket and rinse it out. She swished some water in her mouth to clear the sourness on her tongue. But as she headed back to the den, Cara could not see her surroundings. All she could see were those photos, lingering before her eyes, blinding her like the flash of a bright light. Numb, she sank back into the desk chair, staring at the folder. "I don't understand," she whispered as she re-examined the envelope. Her hands shook as she opened the folder again, and as she looked at the photos once more, she covered her mouth as tears came to her eyes. "Oh, dear God," she moaned.

At first glance, she had thought that the naked woman in the photos was Sophia, but when she realized that she was looking at herself, that was when she had gotten sick. *But who was the naked little boy in the photos with her doing those unspeakable acts?*

As the shock of being assaulted by such repulsive, graphic images wore off, she collected herself and scrutinized the photos more carefully. Perhaps she had been Photoshopped into the scenes, but as she examined them, it became clear that it was she in the photos. Her distinctive engagement ring was there as was the medallion hanging between her naked breasts. *The medallion!* Now she recognized the room. It was her suite at the William Pitt. Cara studied the child in the photos as well. *Who was this poor little boy? Who would allow their child to do such perverted acts? Who had brought him to her room?* It was difficult to tell, but he looked to be no more than eight years old and Asian. She wiped away a tear and pushed away from the desk. "Now I know what happened after I blacked out."

Then her shock transformed into anger. The reporter must have drugged her. That would explain the sudden wooziness, the blacking out, and memory loss, but it didn't explain who she was and why she would do this. Nor did it explain what kind of sick, twisted bastard would exploit a child this way. As Cara cradled her head in her hands, she noticed a slip of paper lying on the rug. *It must have fallen out of the envelope when I extracted the folder.*

She picked it up. The plain white paper was the kind anyone with a printer may have. Unfolding the note, she noticed that there were few lines of type on the page, but they were all in caps and bolded. It read:

WOULDN'T EVERONE BE SHOCKED AND REPULSED TO KNOW THE REAL CARA CAVANAUGH HAWTHORNE? THERE ARE MANY MORE PHOTOS & UNLESS YOU LEAVE $250,000 IN UNMARKED BILLS IN A BACKPACK UNDER THE FAR LEFT BENCH OUTSIDE GATEWAY PLAZA AT 9:15 P.M. THURSDAY NIGHT, I WILL RELEASE THESE PHOTOS TO THE PRESS AND EXPOSE AND RUIN YOU.

"Blackmail!" said Cara. *Who hates me so badly that they would go to the trouble of drugging me, staging these deplorable acts with a child, and photographing them?* She rapidly turned over faces and incidents in her mind, trying to find someone who would have a motive to do this, but unless she were extremely naïve or unaware, she could come up with no one who was that vile.

The phone trilled, startling her and she and began to shake. Could it be the blackmailer? She looked at the caller ID and sighed with relief. It was Wesley calling from his cell phone.

"Hey, Cara, I forgot to ask. What would you like on the pizza?"

She looked at her wristwatch. Was it seven already? Wesley would be home soon. Suddenly, she felt ashamed, and although she knew she had done nothing wrong, she felt guilty, as if Wesley could see her through the phone and knew her to be a child molester.

"Mushrooms," she managed to answer. *Is this how rape victims feel?*

"OK. Mushrooms it is. Be home in a bit." Wesley hung up.

Rape? She hadn't thought of that. Then a cold chill coursed through her body. Had she been raped as well? Had she, as well as the boy, been violated? How could she tell if she had been assaulted? She thought back to Sunday morning when she had showered. She hadn't noticed any bruises, and she didn't feel sore anywhere. *Please, God, don't let me have been raped.*

But whether or not she had actually been raped, she had been victimized. Who had removed her clothing against her will and positioned her in such demeaning poses? Someone had put this child up to these atrocious acts too. There was no child with the reporter; she had to have had an accomplice.

Her mind flashed back to the reporter. She didn't seem capable of such a despicable plot. *Appearances are deceiving,* she heard her grandmother's voice echoing in her mind. If someone could be evil enough to devise this sick scheme, what would stop them from raping her as well while she was unconscious?

At that thought, she vomited in the wastebasket again.

Chapter 10

When Cara heard Wesley at the door, she quickly stuffed the note and photos into the envelope and stashed them in the desk drawer. She needed time to think about what she should do. She'd need Wesley's support and expertise, but she didn't want to hit him with this as soon as he walked in the door.

Cara met him in the foyer. "Hi, honey," he said as he kissed her cheek.

"Let me get that," she said as she took the pizza box from him, "while you hang up your coat." The box was warm and felt comforting on her chilled, trembling hands.

While Wesley headed for the closet, Cara walked into the kitchen where she set the box on the granite counter of the center island. Had it only been this morning when she'd been thinking of how great a day it was going to be for Comfort Connection? Now, with the arrival of that envelope, everything had changed.

"Want some wine?" Wesley asked as he sauntered into the kitchen, loosening his tie.

Cara startled at his question.

"Wow, you're jumpy tonight. You feeling OK? You look a little pale."

She sighed. "Oh, it's just been a long day."

He poured wine for them and handed a glass to Cara. "No doubt filled with adulation."

"Oh, yes. My adoring public." She heard the sarcasm in her voice. Cara kicked off her heels and took a seat in one of the stools at the island. Wesley joined her. She had lost her appetite but managed to feign enthusiasm for the pizza. As they caught each other up on their respective days, Cara had to force herself to pay attention as her mind kept gravitating to those photos lying in the desk drawer.

"You haven't eaten much, Cara," Wesley said. "You sure you're still not under the weather?"

Cara crumpled her napkin. "No, I'm feeling fine, but there's something about Saturday night that I need to discuss with you."

Wesley set his glass down and rose. "We're not going to rehash that again. I said I'm sorry. What more do you want me to say or do?"

Cara closed her eyes and rubbed her temples. She wished this would all go away. When she opened her eyes, she saw Wesley looking down at her puzzled. "There's something else," she said. "Remember, when you called yesterday morning, and I said I didn't know what had happened? Now, I think I know."

"I don't understand."

She rose. "Stay here. I have to get something." Cara went into the den, retrieved the envelope, and then came into the kitchen, standing next to him, the tile floor cold on her feet. She held the envelope behind her back. "When you called me on Saturday night, I was in the bar with a reporter who snagged me on the way to my room." Cara told him everything that had happened and how the last thing she remembered was feeling ill and being escorted to her room. "When your call awakened me on Sunday morning, I was shocked to find that I was in bed, naked, and with the linens in a twist. My dress was in a heap on the floor, my hair was undone, and I was wearing my award with the medallion down my back. You know me. I'm not like that."

He looked at her sternly. "What are you trying to tell me? What I thought? That you drank too much and had a one-night stand?"

"No! No!" Cara said. She held the envelope in front of her. "I found this when I got home today. It had been shoved through the mail slot."

"What is it?"

He reached for the envelope, but Cara pulled it to her chest. Even though Wesley was her husband, she was still embarrassed for him to see her in these photos. She wanted to prepare him for their shocking nature. "I think I was drugged and set up for some reason."

"What? How?"

She pulled out the note and handed it to Wesley.

"You're being blackmailed?" Alarm flashed in his eyes. "What photos are they talking about?"

Cara slid the folder out, placed it on the counter, and opened it. She watched as the color drained from Wesley's face. "Good, God," he murmured as he shuffled through them, his eyes darting all over the images. "Who is this boy?"

"I don't know," Cara said, the tears coming now. "I don't know anything." She covered her face and began to sob. "You do believe me?"

Wesley put the photos down and rose to wrap her in his arms. "Oh, sweetheart."

She was cold and the warmth of his arms felt reassuring. "Why would someone do this to me?" she wailed. What would she do without him? This was too horrible to bear alone. "What am I going to do, Wesley?" she said between sobs. "Every time I look at these photos, I get sick to my stomach," she said. "I feel like a little piece of my soul dies each time I see them."

He released her, then put his hands on either side of her face, forcing her to look at him. "Cara, Cara, listen to me. This is outrageous, but we'll get through this. Do you hear me? We'll get through this."

His certitude calmed her some.

"Now," Wesley said, "let's think this over rationally." As they sat at the kitchen island, they both were at a loss as to anyone who had a vendetta against Cara. "I'm betting it's just some lowlife who wants to make a quick buck," he said.

"What do I do? I hate to cave in to criminals, but I fear what would happen if these photos got out. It could ruin Comfort Connection."

"Not to mention you." He frowned. "I can't tell you what to do, Cara. It's your money and your reputation, but this could also have a devastating effect on your father's career—his nomination for the ambassadorship—if the rumors are to be believed." Almost as an afterthought, he added, "Not to mention mine. Combine this with Sophia's wedding, and we'd be tabloid fodder for months."

Cara closed her eyes and shook her head. "We'll all be ruined."

They sat silently for a while then Cara spoke, "Do you think if I give them the money, this will be the end of it? Or will they come back for more?"

"I can't say, but if they did, then you could go to the authorities."

It didn't feel right, to give into whomever these repulsive reprobates were, but Cara was confused. If the photos were released to the press, it would ruin everything. Comfort Connection would never be allowed to remain standing and all that she had strived for would be lost. Who would help all the grieving children? Wesley was right. Her father was angling for the ambassadorship, and if word of these photos got out, it would destroy his opportunity not to mention the blow it would strike to Wesley's law career.

And then there was Sophia. Any reckless thing that she had ever done would pale in comparison to this. Whether Cara was guilty or not, Sophia would delight in this. No one was more reviled than child molesters, and Cara couldn't bear the thought of being regarded as one. "So you think I should pay them off? Make it all go away?"

"As an officer of the court, I'm obligated to uphold the law. But I'm also your husband, and I'm worried about what this could do to you and everything you've worked for if these photos ever became public. You and I both know how the least little whiff of sexual impropriety with children ruins lives. People would be calling for your head. I hate to give in to these creeps, Cara, but unfortunately, giving them what they want may be your best recourse." He took her hand, and the concern in his eyes made Cara's heartache. She hated the people for doing this to her, but she was even more enraged that it also hurt the people she loved.

He squeezed her hand. "It makes me furious," Wesley said, "but we really have no choice."

Chapter 11

"Come in, dear," said Cara's father, as he ushered her into his palatial office at the USX Tower. The floor-to-ceiling windows exposed a sweeping view of Pittsburgh's Golden Triangle. Gray, heavy clouds shrouded the city, giving everything a funereal quality to match the weightiness of the problem hanging over Cara.

"How was your trip?" Cara asked, as she shrugged off her black wool coat.

Her father kissed her cheek. "Tiring. I have to keep reminding myself that it's Tuesday morning. It's so easy to lose track of time. And one gets so weary of glad-handing."

Cara did notice a pinched look about his eyes, and the light gray suit he was wearing seemed to drain the color from his complexion. She hated to drag her father into this, but she needed his opinion. As soon as Wesley had gone into the shower last night, she had called her father. It's not that she wanted to keep her desire to consult her father from Wesley; it's that Wesley often reacted emotionally and her father had a way of divorcing his emotions from a problem. His "sound judgment" was one of his most valuable qualities—that is according to the recent profile *Forbes* magazine had done on him.

"I'm sorry to bother you as soon as you've arrived home, but I need to talk to you." Cara unwrapped the Burberry scarf encircling her neck.

"The message you left sounded so desperate, my dear. If it's about Sophia again, I do wish you'd stop worrying yourself so much about your sister. Not everyone can be as level-headed and focused as you. Sophia will find her way . . . eventually. Sometimes we have to be patient."

Since the photos had arrived, Cara hadn't given much thought to Sophia. "No, I want to talk to you about something else . . . something much worse."

"Worse?" He raised his eyebrows. "Have a seat, dear," he said, indicating one of the burgundy leather chairs clustered around the walnut conference table. "Would you like some coffee? Have you eaten? I can have Sheila get us something."

Cara took a seat, keeping her leather bag containing the photos on her lap. It was irrational; no one was going to steal the bag. One had to pass through security to get into her father's office, but she didn't want to let the photos out of her reach, not even so much as to set the bag on the floor near her feet. "No, thank you. I'm fine." She felt as if she were carrying her reputation in that bag.

He took the chair next to Cara and smiled expectantly. "I hope you and Wesley are well. I've been so busy with work—and I'm sure you've heard the rumors that I'm being considered for appointment as U.N. Ambassador—that I fear I've neglected you."

"No, don't worry, Father, we're fine. Are the rumors true?"

"Yes, they are—but that is between you and me. You must not tell Wesley yet. Sadly, it seems that Ambassador Chambers has terminal cancer and will soon be stepping down. While I was traveling, I was contacted by the White House and informed that I was being considered and was asked whether I would be interested in the position."

"That's terribly sad for Ambassador Chambers."

"Yes, it's a pity. He's a good man."

"So how do you feel about the position? Do you want it?"

"I would love it, Cara. As you know, my degrees are in International Affairs and that has always been my passion. I only agreed to come on board with the company out of family loyalty, devotion to my parents. This morning, I received a list of documents I need to turn over to the White House so that they can vet my credentials, business, personal life—everything. The list is quite extensive."

"You should have no problem there. You've certainly done a fine job. You're the one who made Allegheny Food & Beverage a global success. You would be hard to replace as CEO, but if this is truly your passion, I hope they nominate you."

"Everyone is replaceable, sweetheart." He patted her hand. "But thank you. Now, what's troubling you? When you walked in, you looked terribly distressed."

"That's because I am." She paused, not knowing how to broach the subject.

"Tell me."

"I'm being blackmailed."

Her father grabbed the edge of the table as if to regain his equilibrium. "Blackmailed? I don't understand."

"Neither do I." Cara then reiterated the entire sequence of events leading up to the arrival of the despicable photos. She pulled out the manila envelope from her leather bag. "These photos of me and a little boy were slipped through my mail slot. They want money or they threaten to send the photos to the media." Her lower lip began to tremble as she fought to hold back tears. "I don't know what to do, Father."

Laurence Hawthorne leaned back in his chair, running his hands over his face. "'The depravity of man is at once the most empirically verifiable reality but at the same time the most intellectually resisted fact.' Malcolm Muggeridge never said truer words." He looked pointedly at her. "I can't comprehend how someone could do something so evil. And why? Who would want to do this to you, Cara?"

"I don't know. Do you want to see the photos?" She said softly. "I have one that I can show that's not as graphic."

He raised a hand. "No, Cara. I don't. If there is an offensive photo of a child, it could be construed that you are in possession of child pornography, and I do not want to be accused of trafficking in it by looking at the photos—no matter the motive. No, I definitely don't want to be associated, especially with the ambassadorship on the line." His blue eyes fixed on her. "Can you think of anyone . . . someone you offended or alienated? I know you don't mean to be, but sometimes you can appear to be a bit aloof or condescending."

I'm not only dull, but he also thinks I'm aloof or condescending, thought Cara, trying to keep her hurt from registering on her face. "Pardon me?"

"I'm not saying it's a justification, but sometimes you can be a bit high and mighty. And don't forget you are also beautiful and wealthy—that alone is enough to provoke some people. Someone may have taken offense to that. A friend who is jealous of you? Was there anyone you rebuffed or fired? Any old boyfriends?"

Cara shook her head. "No, I can think of no one. So what do I do? I need your guidance. Wesley thinks I should give them the money to avert a scandal. He thinks any word of this to the public will harm

Comfort Connection. Not to mention his chance for becoming partner."

Laurence Hawthorne closed his eyes as if contemplating Cara's options. When he opened them, he stared intently at her. "It's detestable, but I believe Wesley is right. I know $250,000 seems like a vast sum of money, but when you think about the cost to Comfort Connection, your reputation, Wesley's reputation, and his opportunity for advancement, that may be a pittance in comparison."

Not to mention your political advancement, Cara thought.

"If I were you, Cara, I'd take the money from your inheritance and pay it. I know it's odious, but once you've lost your reputation, you've lost everything."

She slid the photos back into her bag. No, you're wrong, Cara thought, still annoyed by his characterization of her. Once you've lost the truth? That, Father, is when you've lost everything

Chapter 12

After leaving her father's office, Cara went to hers, but she couldn't concentrate on the work at hand. She hadn't mentioned the photos to anyone on her staff because this was her problem and the less people knew about it the better, especially if she were going to pay off her blackmailers. *Pay off her blackmailers.* The phrase had the taint of guilt.

At noon, the National Weather Service issued a severe weather warning for Western Pennsylvania. The warning had come as an alert on several of their cell phones. While the staff clustered in front of the windows looking out at the January sky, Lia clicked on the weather bulletin. They groaned when the she read the segment of the warning that said the area would be hit with a sleet and ice storm around rush hour. Everyone groaned but Cara; she was glad for the inclement weather. At two o'clock, she dismissed the office staff, grateful that she could retreat to her home, give up the pretense of trying to be productive, and hash out once and for all what she was going to do about the photos.

Near dinner time, it was as if Old Man Winter had opened his bag of tricks. The wind came howling, dropping temperatures and showcasing an impressive repertoire of snow, freezing rain, and sleet. It had even thundered, making Cara startle as she sat in the family room, pen and paper in hand making a "pros and cons" list of her alternatives for dealing with the photos. She rose and stood at the back windows, peering out into their small fenced yard and saw the evergreens bowing in submission to the blast of cold air buffeting them. Wind sang in shrill tones through the cracks in the window frames. She hit the remote and turned on the local news where she learned a new meteorological term, "thunder snow." She also learned that traffic was choking the city with a cord of red taillights that wrapped around the parkways, cutting off the chance that anyone was going to get home from work on time.

Cara called Wesley. "Have you left yet?" she asked when he picked up his iPhone.

"No, I was going to wrap things up here in a minute and then head out."

"You may want to wait a while. I had the news on, and they're reporting that drive times are taking four times longer than normal."

She heard Wesley sigh. "Great. I was going to work from home, and now I'll have to waste time sitting in traffic."

"It might be wiser to go and get something to eat, and maybe by then, traffic will have subsided and you can drive home."

"Where are you, Cara?"

"Home. I let everyone in the office go before the storm hit."

"At least, you're safe and snug."

Safe, Cara thought, but how could she be snug with a blackmailer haunting her?

"How are you holding up, honey?"

"I'm plugging along."

"Have you done anything about getting the money together?"

"I'm working on it."

"Good. I guess I'll head to dinner and see how things look after that. I'll keep you posted."

But things hadn't improved by eight-thirty when Wesley called again. "Hi honey," he said. "Man, it's a mess out there. The sidewalks are as slick as the ice at the CONSOL Center, and I just checked my traffic app, and there's a tractor-trailer jackknifed on the Veteran's Bridge. Fender-benders are everywhere from Butler to Bridgeville. If you don't mind, I'm going to get a hotel room at the Doubletree."

"No, I'd much rather know you are safe in a hotel than stuck in this storm," Cara said. She didn't want to tell him that she was also relieved to be alone. She needed the time to sort things out.

After ending the phone call, she opened a can of vegetable soup and heated it in the microwave. While she ate, she sat at the island going over all the angles of her dilemma until she found her thoughts repeatedly taking the same course until ruts were worn into her thought processes.

Near ten o'clock, Cara texted Wesley that she was going to take a bath and then head to bed. She went into the master bath and ran the water in their jetted tub, adding the lavender scented bath salts that Lia had given her for Christmas.

As she slowly slipped into the water, she exhaled with relief. The heat penetrated her tired muscles and warmed her bones, and she wished that the answer to her problem could seep into her mind like the heat of the bath water into her body.

Clearly, she knew where Wesley and her father stood. Then her mind began to wander. *What would grandmother do?* Cara smiled and inhaled the calming, clarifying scent of the lavender. Without a doubt, Nora Maloney Cavanaugh would have fought. Then she thought of her mother. What would she do?

Cara tried to remember what her mother looked like. She knew that she was dark-haired and petite, and that she resembled her, but no matter how hard she tried, she could not remember her face. It was as if her mind had pixilated her mother's features as if she were an undercover informant on the evening news.

She did remember a few things about her, though. How cool her hand felt on her feverish head when she'd had strep throat and how soft her breasts were when Cara lay on them listening to thump of her mother's heart.

Again, Cara tried to recall that last day, the day her mother took her life, but trying to remember was like trying to hold on to the water in her bath, eventually her recollections slipped through her fingers.

Was my mother a fighter? If she had been, she must have lost her fire because throwing yourself out a window was not the action of a battler, but of someone who had surrendered. *Are we all battlers until we come to something larger than our will to fight? Do we all have a Waterloo? Are these photos mine?*

The water quickly cooled, and Cara found herself shivering as she stood and dried off and then wrapped herself in her robe. Before dressing in her warmest pajamas, she turned on her heated blanket to take the chill off the sheets. Without Wesley beside her, she knew the bed would be cold.

Although the bed was cozy and she was warm when she slipped beneath the covers, Cara could not sleep. She lay there in the blackness listening to the sleet pinging off the window panes. Whenever she closed her eyes, those images of her naked doing unspeakable acts with that poor little boy were before her as if they had been tattooed on the insides of her eyelids.

Rage burned within her. She didn't anger easily, but as she tossed and turned, she entertained elaborate fantasies of what she would do to the culprits if she ever got hold of them. *How dare they drug me! How dare they strip me naked and manipulate my body into such vile poses! How dare they threaten Comfort Connection's existence and jeopardize all the children it helps! How dare they take an innocent little boy and use him for such depravity!*

She didn't know which was racing faster—her mind or her heart. She rolled over onto her side and tried to calm herself. *Why have I been singled out? What have I done to deserve this?*

In the stillness of her heart, Cara heard Grandmother Cavanaugh's voice echo. *There's nothing more putrid, Cara, than self-pity.* Once, when Cara had been in high school, she had tried out for the lead in the school play. They were performing *Thoroughly Modern Millie*, and everyone, including Cara, thought she was a shoe-in for Millie. She had been stunned when Jennifer Blackwell got the part. Devastated, Cara had spent days moping about.

A smile crept across Cara's lips as she recalled her grandmother and how she brooked no whining. She pictured her fair cheeks flushing crimson when she had determined that Cara had indulged her misfortune long enough.

"You think anyone took pity on me when I came to this country with nothing in me pocketbook and just the clothes on my back?" she'd asked, her hands on her hips, her Irish brogue becoming thicker as she worked herself into a lather. "Did I sit around bemoaning my fate? No, my dear girl, I certainly did not. I had to fight and scrape for every penny. Now, what kind of girl are you? What are you made of?" She gently slapped Cara's arm. "Mind now, you either pull yourself together and get out there and show the world that your cut from the same cloth as Nora Maloney Cavanaugh or curl up and die quickly so I can have Hilda sweep you up and put you out with the trash. I'll not have some malcontent lying around littering my parlor."

Cara sat up in bed, hugging her knees to her chest.

The question is not what others would do, but what do I want to do? What am I made of? What would grandmother think of my giving away her hard-earned money that she had left me to blackmailers?

Cara could almost hear her grandmother shouting across eternity. *Pay a fortune to some cur to buy his silence about something I've not done? Oh, I think not, my dear girl. No, this blaggard will be sorry he ever crossed paths with Nora Maloney Cavanaugh!*

As Cara sat there recalling her grandmother's strength when faced with seemingly insurmountable obstacles—the prejudice she'd endured as an uneducated immigrant who dared to rise above her station—Cara felt the anger receding and a contented peacefulness flow in. The peacefulness settled into something more substantial—resolve. And as Cara slid back under the covers and drifted off to sleep, she knew exactly what she was made of. Cara also knew exactly what she was going to do about those terrible pictures when morning came.

Chapter 13

"Thank you for seeing me on such short notice," Cara said. Father Nicco took her hands, and she kissed him on his cheek. It was early on Wednesday morning, and she was glad that the temperature had surged above freezing during the night, melting the ice so that she could come to see her mentor. Now a cold, hard rain was falling, as if to threaten that with a mere drop in a degree or two of temperature, the city could once again be at the mercy of ice.

"Come in, my dear, and have a seat," he said as he led her into his stately office. "Would you like some espresso?" The bishop waved his hand toward a mahogany credenza. "My staff bought me a machine for Christmas. The espresso is not quite as good as that in *Italia*." He looked rather sheepish. "Don't tell them that, but it's still enjoyable."

"No, thank you." Cara was wired as it was; she didn't need caffeine to add to her anxiety. She took a seat and watched as her mentor settled into the leather club chair next to her.

"Then would you care for a pizzelle? I made them last night," he said, proffering a silver platter laden with the waffle-like Italian cookies." All the diocesan activities were canceled because of the weather so I got out my iron and enjoyed my evening at home. They're lemon almond." Father Nicco loved to make pizzelles and often said that they were like humans, "a mish-mash of ingredients until God gets hold of them and imprints them with his likeness. He was always experimenting with new flavor combinations, and his recipes had even been featured in *The Post-Gazette's* food section.

Cara took one. "These are delicious."

"I'm thinking I should add poppy seeds."

"I don't know. They seem perfect as is."

He took one himself, set the tray on his desk, and then smiled at her. "So Cara *mia*, what is on your mind?"

When she'd finally fallen asleep last night, she had been convinced that this was what she had wanted to do. But now, she was no longer sure. It had been hard enough showing the photos to Wesley, but the thought of bringing Father Nicco into this mess now seemed to be too much. She wished Wesley had been there to tell him of her plan, but even though she had texted him to call her when he was awake, he hadn't yet replied.

She sighed. *Where to begin?* "I need your help."

He smiled, his bright blue eyes twinkling. "I am here to serve."

"I'm being blackmailed." She saw the smile fade from his lips.

"Blackmailed? Ah, Cara *mia*, you can't be serious."

"I am."

He set his pizzelle on his napkin. "Whatever for?"

Cara told Father Nicco what had happened after the banquet and how she had suddenly taken ill and then could not remember anything. She pulled the envelope from the leather portfolio resting in her lap. "Then when I returned home from work on Monday, this was waiting for me." She heard the anger invading her voice as she held up the envelope. "It had been put through the mail slot."

Father Nicco touched her arm. "What is it, dear?"

She pulled out the note and handed it to him.

He read it and looked at her quizzically. "Photos? What kind of photos are they talking about?"

Cara felt the rage transform into tears. "Only the vilest, most disgusting pictures that can be imagined of me and a small boy in sexually explicit poses."

"*Mama mia.*" The color drained from Father Nicco's face, making him look like a black and white depiction of himself, his heavy beard contrasting with the paleness of his skin.

She extracted the folder from the envelope. "I was drugged and someone staged these."

"Do you care to show them to me?"

It had been humiliating enough to have to show them to Wesley, and he was her husband, but she felt she needed to at least show Father Nicco one of the photos so he could understand just how diabolical a plot had been perpetrated against her. This morning she had taken the least explicit of the photos that she could find, one where only a side view of her breast was exposed, and she had covered that area with a small sticky note.

She slid that photo out of the sleeve. "I can show you this one. It's the tamest; the others make me want to vomit every time I look at them."

Father Nicco tentatively took the photo from her and gazed at it. Then he covered his face with his hands. After a long pause, he ran them through his thick gray hair. "*Mama mia*," he said again this time softly. Then sighing, he looked at Cara and took her hand. She hadn't realized that she had been trembling until his strong, thick hand held hers. It felt steady as a rock. "You know, Cara *mia*, I've been hearing confessions for decades, and I'd thought I'd heard and seen it all. But I'm amazed that there is no bottom to the depth of man's sinfulness."

"So you do believe me then?"

"Believe what?"

"That I would never do something like this?"

He squeezed her hand. "Of course, Cara *mia*. I know you. I know your heart."

"Thank you. That's why I came to you. I need your help."

"What can I do?"

"I want to fight this. Fight them. Fight whoever did this. It's not a question of money. Wesley thought that perhaps it would be best to give in to their demands, to avoid scandal for me and Comfort Connection. I spoke with my father, and he thinks I should give them what they want too. And in light of Sophia's latest escapade—you've heard, I assume, of her—" Cara rolled her eyes, "marriage?"

He pursed his lips. "Yes, I've heard."

"At first, I was inclined to agree with them," Cara said, "but the more I thought of that little boy . . . and of my grandmother . . . I knew she would never let this be. I have to fight this. It has brought the fighting Irish out in me."

Father Nicco chuckled. "I only met your grandmother once. My, she was *altezzoso*, feisty. No, this would not sit well with her at all."

"I have to fight, but I don't know how. That's why I came to you. Do you have any ideas?"

He closed his eyes and massaged his beard. Then he opened his blue eyes and they blazed with determination. "Ephesians says: 'Stand firm, girding your waist with the truth, and clothing yourself with the breastplate of justice.'" He pointed at her. "We fight this with the truth, Cara *mia*. When I was elevated to bishop, the diocese was in the throes of the child sexual abuse scandals. No matter if you are a priest, layperson, or child, when something bad happens, whether you are responsible or not, the first inclination is to cover up the unpleasantness or sinfulness—you remember Adam and Eve. But that is the wrong option. That's where some in the church faltered. The greatest weapon is the truth. We must expose the truth. Evil has no power over it."

Already Cara was feeling more resolute. "So what do I do?"

He rose and strode to his desk, grabbing a yellow legal pad and pen, and then he sat next to her. "In football, you need to have a strategy. The same with battling evil. We make a plan." He bowed his head. "But first, we pray for guidance from the Lord for the best way to beat this *bastardo male*."

Chapter 14

Jake Gold turned on the television in his office on the second floor of the Buhl Building precisely at three fifteen as he had been instructed by Father Nicco. A red "Breaking News" banner scrolled across the bottom of the screen of KDKA's noon broadcast.

"Mike, we are here live at the Pittsburgh Roman Catholic Diocesan offices for a press conference called by Bishop Niccolo Fiorito and noted Pittsburgh philanthropist and socialite Cara Cavanaugh Hawthorne," said Tiffaknee Reynolds, the young reporter whose parents apparently thought it clever to spell her name so unusually. She was speaking in hushed tones into the microphone as if it were a golf match. "Hawthorne, who is a descendent of two of Pittsburgh's most prominent families—the Cavanaughs, who made their fortune in railroads, and the Hawthornes, the owners of mega-corporation Allegheny Food & Beverage—as you may remember, was last Saturday night honored with the Mother Teresa Medal for her work with her nonprofit organization Comfort Connection, which helps grieving children. When the press conference was called, it said it was

103

to make an important announcement. Speculation is that Cara Hawthorne is going to announce that she will be using some of her family's vast wealth to fund a Pittsburgh Catholic Heritage Museum. A museum of this sort has been talked about for years. Here they are now," said Tiffaknee. "Let's listen."

Jake sat on the edge of his desk and watched as the bishop, wearing a black suit and white clerical collar, strode to the table, followed by a beautiful dark-haired young woman. Of course, he'd heard of Cara Cavanaugh Hawthorne. How could you not if you lived in Pittsburgh? The Cavanaugh and Hawthorne names were as common as Mellon, Carnegie, and Rooney, but he'd never paid much attention to the faces attached to those names. Until now. With her stunning blue eyes, luxuriously thick dark hair, and trim figure snug in a white knit dress, she could give Kate Middleton a run for her money, Jake thought, as he watched the pair take their seats at the table in front of a backdrop sporting the diocesan coat of arms.

Although she moved gracefully when taking her seat, Jake could tell by the way Cara Cavanaugh Hawthorne fiddled with the enormous diamond ring on her left hand that she was nervous. After what Father Nicco had told him about what was going on, Jake thought that she should be. Father was utterly convinced that she was innocent, but Jake wasn't so sure. He'd been around too many like her before, and he knew women in her position would say or do anything to preserve their precious reputation and status. *And money. Never forget the money.*

Jake saw Father Nicco reach over and cover Cara's hand before looking straight ahead with fierceness in his eyes, the same look he'd given Jake when he'd had provided the bishop with incontrovertible evidence that the accuser who had claimed retired Bishop Quinn had molested him as a child, was using a fictitious name and had never grown up in Pittsburgh.

Then Father Nicco smiled broadly and looked straight into the cameras. "Thank you all for coming on this pleasant January afternoon." The mention of the weather brought snickers because it was still raining. "However, I'm afraid that the nature of this press conference is gruesomely unpleasant. And I ask that you hold your questions until the end, and then we will try to answer them the best that we can."

The reporters fell silent.

"Cara Cavanaugh Hawthorne," he nodded at his table mate, "whom the diocese and Vatican honored only days ago with the Mother Teresa Medal, came to me this morning with a terrible problem, and I offered to schedule this press conference to support her in this most repugnant battle."

Even through the television, Jake could hear the reporters murmuring. Apparently, they'd had no clue about what Father Nicco was speaking.

"I will now cede the microphone to Cara." Father Nicco looked at her and nodded.

Jake watched as Cara Cavanaugh Hawthorne took a deep breath, her breasts rising and falling, and then picked up a paper. "Thank you for coming," she said, her voice sounding reedy as she read from a written statement. "As you know, I was most graciously honored with the Mother Teresa medal last Saturday night. After the gala, I was approached by a woman who identified herself as a reporter for *Sonic Wayve* magazine." The camera focused in on her lovely face, and Jake had to remind himself that he was not to be fooled by her beauty. She quickly read a detailed account of what she said happened with the reporter and how she had taken ill and had blacked out—the same information Father Nicco had provided Jake when he had called earlier. She paused for a moment as if to gather strength, which Jake found a bit theatrical.

"On Monday evening when I came home from working at Comfort Connection," continued Cara, "I found an envelope in my foyer that had been slipped through my mail slot." Her chin began to quiver as she lost her composure.

Jake shook his head. *What an actress.*

Covering her face with her hands, she began to cry. Then Father Nicco gripped her shoulder. "Cara *mia*, you can do this," whispered Father Nicco, but the microphones caught it. "If not for yourself, for that little boy."

Cara raised her head, and Father Nicco handed her his handkerchief. She dried her eyes and took a sip of water. "I'm sorry," she said, "but inside that envelope was a note and pictures of me, naked in compromising positions with a young boy."

A collective gasp escaped from the mouths of the press corps.

Cara read the text of the blackmail note. Then she looked up and stared into the cameras. "I believe I was drugged and blacked out, and then exploited as was this poor child." She leaned forward, her jaw set. "I have a message for whomever did this. I will not give you $250,000. I will not let you intimidate me. I will not let you do this to an innocent child. And I will not rest until I find you, and you are sent to prison."

"Before the bishop and I came here, we spoke to the FBI, which now has the envelope and its contents. While they investigate, I want to assure whomever did this that I will not rest until you are punished for violating me and most importantly for abusing this beautiful child." Her cheeks flushed. She looked at Father Nicco. "What is it Jesus said? 'It is better for him if a millstone is hanged about his neck, and he is thrown into the sea than he should harm a child.'" She gripped the edge of the table. "Let me tell you, you sicko. I'm coming for you, and I'm bringing a millstone with your name engraved on it."

Jake snickered.

Appearing spent, she slouched back into the chair. Father Nicco patted her hand and whispered. "Bravo, Cara *mia*. Next time, I need to call down fire and brimstone, may I contact you?"

She seemed so reserved and controlled that Jake was surprised by her outburst. *Maybe there's much more beneath that lovely façade*, thought Jake. *But what was it? The passionate heart of a philanthropist or the warped soul of a child abuser?*

"I am offering a $25,000 reward for anyone who can provide a tip that leads to the conviction of whoever is behind this," Cara said.

"Why should we believe you?" called a reporter.

Startled, Cara looked up. "Pardon me?"

"How are we to be sure that you haven't been caught up in a scandal and are concocting this story as a cover?" The reporter had expressed exactly what Jake was thinking.

Before Cara could respond, another reporter shouted, "Your sister is not exactly a paragon of virtue. Why are we to believe that you are above reproach?"

"Did you know your sister was going to marry a male stripper?" shouted one reporter.

"When can we see the photos?" shouted another.

"What kind of sexual abuse are we talking about?" someone else called.

The press conference was deteriorating into chaos, and Jake could tell from how pale Cara looked that she had been blindsided by the reception her remarks had received.

"Bishop Fiorito, should you be associating with someone accused of child sexual abuse after all that the church has been through?"

Father Nicco turned from looking at Cara to gaze out at the sea of reporters, his blue eyes turning as biting as the cold rain hitting Jake's office window. "Silence, please!" he commanded, extending his hands. Jake knew Father Nicco to be a charming, affable man, but he also knew that this reporter was going to be sorry he had ever posed that question.

Slowly, the reporters settled into stillness. After a moment, father smiled genially. "I was hoping I was not going to have to call you a brood of vipers. As to whom I should associate myself with? First of all, I trust Cara implicitly and vouch for her character. She would never do something so heinous. Also, may I remind you that even if she weren't above reproach, that as a disciple of Jesus, it is my calling to associate with sinners, to bring the good news of salvation to all. Jesus dined with tax collectors, cured lepers, spoke to prostitutes . . ." Father Nicco paused then laid a finger beside his cheek as if he were trying to recall something. "Hmm, no, I guess Jesus never had to deal with the press. Maybe that's where I've gotten myself into trouble, hanging out with the likes of you."

Jake chuckled as he watched Father Nicco gaze around the room wearing a mischievous smile. "OK, even you, I would hang out with in obedience and devotion to Christ."

The reporters laughed although a bit nervously, thought Jake.

"Use the brains God gave you, people," continued Father Nicco. "For what purposes would Cara stage something like this? To gain fame or fortune? She already has both. We have answered all the questions that we are going to for now. I look forward to seeing you soon when we can announce an arrest in this case. In the meantime, instead of trying Cara in the court of public opinion, I encourage you to be real journalists and seek to uncover the truth. Good afternoon."

Father Nicco touched Cara's arm. "Come along, my dear."

The broadcast cut away again to Tiffaknee Reynolds. "As you have heard, Mike, a remarkable story here unfolding in Pittsburgh involving prominent Pittsburgher Cara Cavanaugh Hawthorne, who alleges that she was drugged and framed with child sexual abuse and is now being extorted."

"Incredible," said Mike the anchorman, shaking his head. "I guess the big question is: Can we believe Cara Cavanaugh Hawthorne?"

Jake shut off the television and stared out the window of his office, watching the rain run in silver rivulets down the glass. *Yes, you got that right, Mike. That is the question. Can we believe Cara Cavanaugh Hawthorne?*

Chapter 15

Cara leaned against the wall and exhaled loudly. "What just happened in there?" She looked at Father Nicco as he shut the door to the conference room behind them. How could the media turn on them so quickly? "I should have never dragged you into this."

"Nonsense," Father Nicco said. "You didn't drag me into anything. I am your friend and the truth is the truth—whether they," he waved his hand toward the door, "want to believe it or not."

"Maybe I should have paid the blackmailers off privately like Wesley and my father advised."

"And how would that make you feel?" He took her elbow and began to lead her back toward his office. "Cara *mia*, I know you are frightened, angry, and if the truth be told, a bit shocked to find yourself so suddenly fallen from grace in the eyes of the media."

Cara blushed. He was so perceptive at times, it shocked her. Perhaps she was a bit naïve or arrogant to assume that somehow she would be exempt from rough treatment by the press. "What a fool I was to expect them to believe me."

"Ah, Cara *mia*, one is always blindsided by evil. But either way, it is right to fight for the truth just as it is right to fight for justice. And just as it is right to fight for yourself." He squeezed her elbow and then released it.

"But what about you? And the church? The media was more than happy to lump you and the church in with me, who they now seem hell-bent on portraying as a sexual predator. The church has finally begun to heal from the sexual abuse scandals. I don't want to reopen the wounds."

As they passed people in the hallways, many nodded politely and kept on going. Cara could feel the change in the way people regarded her now. If Father Nicco had noticed it, he didn't say, but knowing him, Cara thought, he'd long ago gotten past caring what others thought of him.

"As a priest, it is part of my ministry to find the glory of God working in all circumstances. The scandals in the church where a terrible blight, but I've learned some truths while dealing with them that may help you. One, not everyone is as they seem to be and may not be looking for the truth. Some will act out of ambition to make a name for themselves or to line their pocket or to protect something they hold dear. Your life will most certainly come under intense scrutiny now. I know the FBI promised to get to the bottom of this, but with the Super Bowl being played here in the city in a few days and the heightened security, I fear your case may not get the proper attention until after the game."

Cara had not thought of that. She'd heard on the news how all available law enforcement resources were being utilized to make sure that the city and Heinz Field were safe from terrorists or anyone else who wanted to seize the opportunity of the Super Bowl to wreak havoc.

"So what do I do? Sit and wait?"

They were back at his office now. He closed the door and offered her a seat. "No," said Father Nicco as he sat behind his desk. "There are some things I think you should do that would benefit you. The first is that I'm going to give you the name of a private investigator I retained during the scandals. I can't urge you strongly enough to let him conduct his own parallel investigation to find out who is behind this blackmail scheme, make sure that your interests are being represented, and the truth be revealed."

Father Nicco's words were so ominous, Cara shivered.

"I called him before the press conference while you were in the conference room drafting your statement and told him the circumstances. As a favor to me, he has agreed to work with you. My second piece of advice is to retain a good lawyer. I'm sure Wesley can recommend someone. And my last piece of advice is the most important." He reached across the desk. "Give me your hand." The firmness of his grip and warmth of his palm and fingers steadied her nerves a bit. "Rely on the Lord, Cara. I implore you. I fear you are in for a trying time, a time when you may feel that you have been abandoned." He squeezed her hand tightly. "But I want you to remember that I am here for you, and most importantly, to remember that the Lord is here for you too. Rely on His Holy Spirit living within you for guidance."

Father Nicco opened his desk drawer and took out a business card. He came to her and handed it to Cara. She felt like a knight being presented with a sword for use in battle.

"Jacob Gold?" Cara said reading the card.

"Yes. He goes by Jake, and I warn you he's a bit *scontroso*.

"*Scontroso?*"

"Grumpy, gruff. But underneath his rough exterior, he has the heart of a lion."

"Gruff? How do you mean?"

"Hard-boiled. Tough. He was in the IDF."

"As in Israel Defense Forces?"

Father Nicco nodded.

"Seriously? What's he doing as a private investigator?"

"He's retired. He was wounded while serving, and lost an arm."

"How in the world did you ever connect with a member of the IDF?"

"As you know, I often make pastoral visits to the hospital to anoint the sick, and on one occasion when I happened to be there, I met Jake. He had returned to the area—he grew up in Pittsburgh—and was recuperating from a recent surgery to his arm. This was 2006, a World Cup year. The year *Italia* was crowned the world champions." Father Nicco smiled with pride for his beloved team. "Jake was watching the semifinal match between Portugal and France. I struck up a conversation, and we became friends. For a time, he was at loose ends, not knowing which direction he should go with his life since his military career had ended, but eventually, he figured out that he could channel his great intellect and training into becoming a private investigator."

Cara had to laugh. "You amaze me. I would never have dreamed that you would have a friend who was in the IDF."

The sparkle returned to Father Nicco's eyes as he laughed. "Sometimes I amaze myself!" He shrugged. "Anyway, I retained Jake when a number of our priests were accused of sexual abuse. There were a few accusers I felt certain were jumping on the bandwagon and trying to extort money from the church. I wanted him to investigate, to protect the church if it needed it, and if some of the accused were, indeed, guilty, I wanted to know that too. Jake may be a bit jaded after all that he's been through, but if there's anything he has a passion for, it's the truth. From his investigation, I learned that one of the accusers was a convicted felon scamming for money. When confronted with what Jake had discovered about him, he dropped the charges. Unfortunately, Jake also discovered that one of our priests was using a family home as a place to bring teens and abuse them." Father Nicco shook his head in disgust. "He does excellent, thorough work. He's like a surgeon with the truth, separating flesh from bone."

"I certainly hope he can get to the bottom of this and exonerate me so that I can get back to my work at Comfort Connection."

"And I as well. I told him you would be calling him."

"I'll get in touch with him as soon as I get home." Cara began to gather her things. "Now, I should be going. I've taken up too much of your day as it is. I'm sure you have other pressing matters."

"Wait, please," Father Nicco said, placing a hand on Cara's shoulder, stopping her from rising. "Before you leave, take some pizzelles with you." He placed some on a plate and covered them with a napkin. She smiled and wondered if Jesus had been born an Italian, would the Eucharist have been pizzelles and wine?

"Now I want to call down God's blessing on you."

Cara bowed her head. As Father Nicco raised his hands above her, he called for God to fortify and protect her in battle. Cara felt comforted, but as she thought about how the media had turned on her and the black heart of the person who had conceived of this plot, Cara felt woefully weak and vastly overpowered.

Chapter 16

Street lights cast a pinkish glow, illuminating the fat rain drops in the descending twilight as Cara drove down Broad Street in Sewickley toward home, past the bistros, bookstores, and boutiques. Sewickley was an Indian word for "sweet water," but the water flowing in town was anything but sweet. Near the curb, small rivers ran with the cold rain that had been steadily falling all day and collected in large puddles near catch basins that had been inundated.

When Cara turned off Broad Street and drove toward her house, her shoulder muscles tensed. Through the staccato swipe of her windshield wipers, she spied several mobile satellite news trucks parked on her normally quiet, tree-lined street, and a huddle of media personnel collected on the sidewalk under huge umbrellas, each sporting the logo of their respective news channel. "Oh, good lord," she mumbled to herself as she looked in her rearview mirror to see if she could back out of her street. *Maybe I should head to a coffee shop on Beaver Street to wait them out.* But a car came behind her, hemming her in. Besides, she thought, where can I go in town that I'm not known, especially after such a sensational press conference? Sadly, it seemed these days that the more salacious a story, the faster it became viral. Viral was a good word, thought Cara, as she slowed her car and aimed to turn into her driveway because the way the media reacted when they spotted her made her sick.

The cluster of reporters moved en masse toward her Escalade, crowding the driveway. Cara feared she'd hit one of them. Her heart thumping, she fixed her eyes on the black wrought iron gate as she nervously pushed the remote button for it to open. As she crept down the short driveway alongside her house to the rear of her property, she kept checking her mirrors to see if anyone had followed. As she was about to hit the other remote button to open the garage door, a reporter popped from, it seemed, out of nowhere and stood defiantly in front of her car. He must have been inspired by the Tiananmen Square protester because he stood in front of her car, his arms outstretched. Cara knew that if she allowed him to prevent her from proceeding, she would be devoured by the media, so she slowly inched her way ahead in a game of vehicular chicken until the reporter caved and moved aside.

Safely in the garage, she hit the button that lowered the door. Although she was shaking, she had to laugh as the reporter, still shouting questions, peeked under the lowering door like he was in a game of Limbo with it until he was nearly lying on the ground. Exhaling loudly, she tilted her head back and tried to make sense of what was happening to her. Was it only last week that she was preparing to accept the Mother Teresa award? It seemed like a lifetime ago.

Gathering her things, she exited the car and made her way through the breezeway, which on a rainy January night like this Cara thought would be more aptly called the wind tunnel as the cold rain pelted her from the side. Reporters called to her, but she hunkered down in the collar of her coat and was relieved when she entered the sanctuary of her home through the kitchen door.

"Oh, dear God!" She startled when she saw Wesley sitting at the granite-topped island. "You surprised me!"

"Then I'm not the only one," he said.

"I didn't expect you to be home," said Cara, setting her purse on the counter and beginning to remove her wet coat.

"And I didn't expect you to blindside me."

Cara paused, her arm half way out of her sleeve. "Pardon me?"

"When I left here yesterday, I was under the impression that you were going to keep this mess with *your pictures* quiet. Then today, I'm sitting in my office and the phones start to ring off the hook, and then a reporter tries to barge into my office to get my reaction to my wife's press conference. What the hell, Cara?" Wesley said, the blood vessels in his neck squirming like worms. "A press conference? What's going on here? First, I can't get hold of you, then *your photos* show up, and then you go behind my back and hold a media spectacle without even so much as alerting me."

"They aren't *my pictures*, Wesley," Cara said tartly. "They are the work of some deeply demented individual." She heard her tone and took a minute to compose herself before she lost control and took out the stress of the day on Wesley. She walked toward him and touched his arm. "I'm sorry. I should have called you, but when I changed my mind, you weren't here. I texted you early this morning, but you didn't answer. Then things happened so fast. It was crazy. I decided I wanted to fight this, fight whoever is doing this. I can't let some psycho ruin me, my reputation, Comfort Connection."

"That's all well and good for you, isn't it," Wesley said, loosening his tie with a quick jerk. "But what about me? Have you ever considered how this would affect my life, my reputation, my career? They were none too pleased at the office. You've opened Pandora's box here, Cara. Hell, to get into my own home, I had to park two streets over and sneak in through the back yard. Now we've got those vultures," he waved his hand toward the front of the house, "camped out on our doorstep. No doubt our private lives are being sifted through as we speak. I can hardly wait for Geraldo to arrive."

Cara touched his shoulder. "I'm sorry this has happened, but I can't throw money away to pay off some scum. And what if I had given them the money? What was to prevent them from coming back for more? I can't live with this hanging over my head, wondering if those pictures are going to show up in the *Enquirer*. I can't leave control of my life in someone else's hands."

He rose, her hand sliding from him. "It's always about control with you, Cara, isn't it? You always have to be behind the wheel and the rest of us are just along for the ride, aren't we?"

"It's not about control, Wesley, and you know it. It's about principle. And the truth."

Wesley was silent for a moment, then he cocked his head and looked down at Cara. "You know, I had a professor in law school who once give a lecture on the truth, and you know what he said, Cara?"

She felt like she was being cross-examined, and resentment was building in her, making her eyes throb. "No, what?"

"Well, he quoted Camus, who said, 'A taste for truth at any cost is a passion which spares nothing."

Cara sighed and took his hand. "I didn't mean for this to hurt you, Wesley, but you've got to understand. I need to do this."

He slid his hand from her grasp then touched a piece of paper lying on the granite counter top.

Cara looked at him. "What's this?"

"Your father. He called. He wants to know what the hell is going on too." Wesley walked out of the kitchen.

"Where are you going?" she called.

"To mix some Margaritas. I hear Geraldo likes tequila."

*****

Cara poured herself a glass of Cabernet and headed for the den. She took a sip of the wine, which warmed her physically, but could not touch the chill that she felt descending upon her marriage. *Why didn't I just call Wesley? He had every right to know.* But Cara knew why she hadn't included him in her plan. Because she knew he would have objected to it, once again, placing his needs before hers. *But haven't I placed my needs before his?* She rubbed her temples. The truth is the truth, and I'm sorry, Wesley, if you don't share that, she thought, as she dialed her father. And the truth trumps all.

"What were you thinking, Cara?" said her father when he picked up the phone.

Not even a "hello," Cara thought. She sighed, steeling herself for another round of "beat up on Cara." "I suppose you're referring to the press conference?"

"Yes, of course, that's what I'm referring to."

Sometimes when her father was angry instead of blowing up and unleashing his wrath, he became more calm and controlled, but you could sense the anger just below the veneer like a skim of hardened lava over a volcano cauldron.

"I had a change of heart, and I talked it over with Father Nicco, and he advised—"

"I should have known he was behind this. I'm sorry, Cara, I know you put stock in his wisdom, but he's a cleric. What does he know of the real world and how it works?"

"That's unfair. He's one of the wisest men I've ever met, and if you may recall, he's had experience dealing with situations like this. He was able to clear Cardinal Quinn when he was falsely accused. He advised me to get it all out in the open. Shine the light of truth on the situation."

"Then he, above all people, should have known how things like this spiral out of control. Now, I've got the press hounding me, Cara. Several reporters called already. They'll be going over all of our lives with a fine-tooth comb." He paused. "Are you prepared to have them drag your mother's suicide through the press again?"

What was there to dredge up? My mother was suffering from post-partum depression after Sophia's birth and threw herself off our Penthouse balcony.

"I've had enough trouble coming to terms with that, trying to raise you and your sister, and now to have it rehashed . . . I did not need this, especially with the ambassadorship on the line. It's too painful."

"I'm sorry you've been ensnared in this, but I'm the one here with the most to lose—my money, my reputation, and my life's work."

"I hope you know what you are doing," said her father, whose exasperation with her was spilling over into his voice.

"I do," Cara said, cringing as she said that because that was a lie. She had no idea what she was doing or where this was headed. She only knew that now that she had chosen this path, there was no going back. As if to reassure herself as well as her father, Cara said, "Father Nicco advised me to retain a private investigator to help get to the bottom of this."

"What?" Her father laughed derisively. "I think he's been watching too many reruns of *Father Dowling Mysteries.*"

Cara rolled her eyes. Sometimes her father's arrogance, especially when it came to Father Nicco, was so annoying.

"The private investigator was able to help him flush out the bogus claimants during the church's sexual abuse scandal."

"Oh, fantastic. Now we'll be associated with that mess. If I didn't know better, between you and your sister, I'd think you were out to get me."

"No, father," Cara said dryly. "I can assure you the only thing I'm out to get is the truth." She then did something she'd never done before—she hung up on her father.

Chapter 17

Cara quickly finished her wine, went upstairs to their room, and changed into jeans and a Comfort Connection sweatshirt. She was feeling a bit tipsy, but when she caught her reflection in the mirror and saw the sweatshirt, it dawned on her that she had also forgotten to alert her staff about the blackmail scandal. She'd called earlier in the day to say that she wouldn't be coming in, but she'd never called again to alert them to what was happening. *Great. More people angry with me.* No one would be in the office now, but she decided she'd better call Lia at home. Her "to-call list" was growing longer by the minute. She needed to call Lia, Jake, and a lawyer. She would need Wesley's help with the selection of a lawyer, but at the moment, he was downstairs engrossed in an ESPN program about the history of NFL football in Pittsburgh and the city's first Super Bowl. He was still angry with her, and she didn't want to broach the subject of finding one just yet. That left Lia and Jake. Whom should she call first?

She decided Lia, who when she picked up the phone, seemed a bit cool with her. But true to her ever-direct nature, Lia plunged right into the situation, asking a million questions and scolding Cara for not clueing the office as to what was going on earlier.

"You made us all look foolish," Lia said, "especially when the phones started blowing up with reporters asking for a reaction from Comfort Connection."

"I'm sorry," Cara said. "I'm not thinking straight. When something this awful happens, your first instinct is to bury it, and then when I decided to go public with it, I didn't tell anyone. Maybe because I was afraid that my resolve was so shaky, I would chicken out."

"Next time, Cara, I hope your first instinct is to call your friends. I agree, you need to fight this, but don't make the mistake again of thinking you have to fight this on your own. We're all here for you."

"Thank you. You don't know how much that means to me," Cara said. "For the next day or so, I'm going to work from home to avoid the press converging on the offices and because I have things I need to take care of with regard to this mess. Is there anything pressing?"

Lia paused. "I hate to tell you this, but Sanford Coskins' office called right before I left for the day and said they'd like to beg off meeting with you until this 'unfortunate episode' is resolved."

Cara sighed. "Did we get any other calls like that?"

"A few."

Now the scandal was crippling Comfort Connection and the grieving children she cared so much about. She needed to get to the bottom of who was behind the photos and she needed to do it fast. She hung up with Lia and retrieved Jake Gold's card from her purse.

*****

Cara waited until Wesley went into the den to catch up on some paperwork, then she went into the guest bedroom and called Jake Gold from her cell phone. She'd eventually tell Wesley that she was hiring a private investigator; she just didn't want to deal with his reaction to this piece of news now. She was sure he would point out the fact that if she had just decided to pay the blackmailers, she wouldn't need the services of an investigator. Her call went to Jake Gold's voice mail, and she left him a brief message.

As she was ending the call, she heard the doorbell chime. Should she answer it? What if it was the press? No, she couldn't face them again. Not tonight, not on an empty stomach, not with her head buzzing from the wine. She went to the top of the stairs and called down. "Can you see who it is please, Wesley? I'm afraid it's the press."

He came out of the den and looked up the stairs at her. "Can't we just ignore it?" The doorbell chimed again. Then there was heavy knocking.

"Please, Wesley, do me a favor and tell them I'm not available and to please leave."

Wesley shook his head as if to say, "See I warned you, Cara, this would happen if you made this public," and went to the door."

Cara stepped out of sight upstairs where she could still hear and get a glimpse of who was calling yet not be seen. Wesley opened the door, and Cara was taken aback when she heard the voice of the person there say, "Good evening. My name is Agent Delia Crosley and this Agent Samson Pappas. We're with the Federal Bureau of Investigations. Is Cara Cavanaugh Hawthorne at home? We'd like to ask her a few questions."

She was further dismayed when Wesley introduced himself and told the agents that she was upstairs, but then she remembered Wesley commenting many times while watching news reports on television, "never lie to the FBI."

Cara heard him tell the agents to step into the foyer and close the door behind them. He guided them into the den and instructed them to be seated. "Wait here, while I get Cara."

Wesley came up the stairs where he found her skulking behind the door frame. "The FBI is here, Cara. They want to talk to you."

Cara trembled. "Father Nicco and I just talked to the FBI this afternoon. He took me to meet the Special Agent in Charge in Pittsburgh, who is a friend of his. We explained everything to him. What do they want now? I guess it's routine follow-up questioning?"

"Maybe. Maybe not," said Wesley.

"What do you mean?"

"You're assuming that everyone sees you as innocent. You may not realize it, but if they don't believe your story, you are in a lot of trouble. The first, being in possession of graphic sexual content involving a child."

Cara felt herself go pale. Common sense would dictate that no one would take photos like these and then tell the world about them if they were involved in kiddie porn or abusing children.

"Look," Wesley said earnestly, "go down there and greet them, but don't let them question you without an attorney being present."

"But won't that look suspicious, like I have something to hide?"

"Cara, you've got to get over caring what things look like. You're in a mess right now, and you don't want to make it worse by being charged with a crime."

Charged with a crime? Could they possibly do that? Cara's knees went weak. *Time to face the music, kiddo,* she heard her grandmother's voice in her mind. Cara got hold of herself and straightened her spine. She glanced in the mirror in the hallway and smoothed her hair before descending the stairs after Wesley. As she walked into the den, the agents rose.

"Hello," Cara said, trying to sound calm, but she knew her voice sounded pathetically shaky.

"Hello, Ms. Hawthorne," said the tall, thin young woman whose straight, auburn hair accented the smattering of freckles escaping detection under her foundation. "I'm Agent Delia Crosley and this is Agent Samson Pappas," she said, nodding to a man who was in his early forties and whose broad shoulders seemed to make him appear to be as wide as he was tall. "We're with the Federal Bureau of Investigations, and we've been assigned to your case. We'd like to ask you a few questions."

Cara looked to Wesley for help.

"Although I'm an attorney," Wesley said, "for obvious reasons, I'm not representing my wife, and I advised Cara not to answer any questions until her legal counsel is present."

"I understand," said Agent Crosley, but we only have a few questions, and we're trying to help." She opened a portfolio and turned to face Cara. "From the press conference you held today, you stated that you received the photographs by having them slipped through your mail slot. When was that?"

"You don't have to answer that, Cara," Wesley interjected.

The question seemed harmless, and she wanted to appear cooperative because she had nothing to hide. "It was Monday." Out of the corner of her eye, she saw Wesley shaking his head at her.

"And you claim that they were taken after the Mother Teresa awards last Saturday night, January 24?" asked Agent Pappas, who leaned in closer, resting his elbows on his knees. "Are you aware that by now, there would most likely be no way to test to see if any drugs were in your system to support your claim that you were drugged and framed?"

Cara looked puzzled. "No, I'm not aware of that."

Wesley stood. "OK, I'm sorry, Agents Crosley and Pappas. I'm going to have to ask you to leave. Cara's attorney will be in touch with you as soon as possible. And then, you can question her."

"Very well then," said Agent Crosley, who stood and reached into a pocket of her portfolio. She handed Cara, who remained seated, a card. "Here's where you can reach us."

Agent Pappas rose and shook Wesley's hand. "A pleasure to meet you." He held his hand out to Cara; she didn't like him but shook his hand anyway. His grip was firm, and she felt like an animal with a limb caught in a trap when he held it. "Looking forward to talking with you soon, Mrs. Hawthorne, and getting to the bottom of this."

Agent Crosley shook Cara's hand as well. "Thank you, Mrs. Hawthorne."

"Actually, it's Mrs. Wells," said Cara.

"Mrs. Wells it is then," Agent Pappas said with a false smile as he left the room.

Cara remained seated while Wesley showed them out.

"They're gone," said Wesley as he returned to the den.

She covered her face with her hands and doubled over in tears.

"Cara, what's wrong?" he asked as he knelt next to her, his hand on her back.

She looked up, her face streaked with tears. "What do you think they meant by that question? That I faked being drugged and hired someone to take pictures of me and that little boy?"

Wesley patted her back. "Look, sweetheart. That's their job. You have to see it from their point of view. They don't know you like we do. As FBI agents, they've seen crazier things. They're just doing what they've been trained to do."

"Is it true that the drug is now out of my system? Don't chemicals deposit in your hair or something? I've seen that on *CSI*. I could have my hair tested. Call in Cyril Wecht. He was friends with my grandmother. I'm sure my father must know him too."

"Cara, calm down. You're rambling. Not everything on *CSI* happens in real life. I'm no toxicologist either. We'll call you an attorney. He can devise a defense strategy."

"Defense strategy? You make it sound like I'm guilty of something." Panic gripped her. She wanted to flee, but where could she escape this?

"I know you aren't guilty. But they don't. An attorney will help clear you."

She clutched her throbbing head. "But why would anyone think I would do something like that? Create these photos and then go to the press and the FBI?"

Wesley rose, took her hand, and pulled her from the chair, wrapping her in his arms. "You are too good sometimes, Cara," he said, smoothing her hair. "Too naïve. People do a lot of insane, nasty, underhanded things in this world for a variety of reasons. Who can say why?"

Why? I can say why, Cara thought as Wesley consoled her. I'm going to learn why, and when I do the person who did this to me is going to be sorry.

Chapter 18

Wesley calmed Cara, and she then listened while he called his friend from law school, Clifford Martel, a noted criminal defense attorney and arranged for him to be Cara's attorney. Attorney Martel agreed to call Agents Crosley and Pappas to allot a time where he could be present for Cara's questioning. He also said he would be in touch when he had set something up with the FBI. Then he would meet with Cara to prepare her for their questioning.

It was near nine o'clock now and with the intrusion of the press into their lives, their argument, and the arrival of the FBI, neither of them had eaten dinner yet. Although she was relieved that Wesley had found her an attorney, Cara didn't have much of an appetite, so she and Wesley had omelets. After picking at hers for a while, she tried to call her father to apologize for hanging up on him, but her call went to voice mail. She tried to remember his itinerary. He traveled so much, it seemed that he clocked more hours in the air than on the ground. Cara consulted her phone where she confirmed that he was en route to Paris and would not return to the U.S. for two more days.

Wesley was more sympathetic to her plight after seeing how distraught she'd become from the FBI's visit, and after dinner, they discussed what, if anything, she should say to Comfort Connection's supporters. They decided that it would be best if she drafted a statement for release to the public. While he went into the den to do some work, Cara sat at the kitchen island, pen in hand, trying to draft a statement that would reflect confidence that this matter would soon be resolved and that she would soon be back at the helm of Comfort Connection. It was a greater task than she had imagined. With the FBI involved now and no clue as to who would want to frame her with such a despicable deed, it was hard to find the words.

As she was about to dodge the task entirely by making a cup of tea, her cell phone vibrated. I hope someone from the press hasn't gotten hold of my phone number, she thought as she looked at the screen. The name Jacob Gold appeared. She had completely forgotten about him.

"Hello," Cara said.

"Jake Gold here," he said, "returning your call."

"Thanks for calling me back. I suppose Father Nicco—or I mean Bishop Fiorito—spoke to you about my situation."

"Yes, he did."

"And do you think you'd be able to help me?"

"As a favor to Father Nicco, yes."

Is it my imagination or does he sound condescending? "What do you mean, as a favor?"

"I'll cut to the chase. What you're asking me to do is not my usual thing, but Father Nicco helped me out a lot a few years ago when I was getting things started, so I owe him."

"I would be paying you so it wouldn't be just a favor."

"Yeah, so when do you want to meet?"

"As soon as possible. I want to get this resolved."

"Why don't you come to my office at ten tomorrow morning? I'm in the Buhl Building downtown."

"Would it be too much trouble if you were to come here?" she asked. She sounded so timid, she was annoyed with herself. Cara walked into the living room and carefully pulled back the curtain. There were still a few reporters milling about on the street. "I'm a bit of a prisoner in my own home right now because of the press. They've camped out in front of my house."

He sighed. "I'll be there. What's the address?"

As she gave him her address, Cara felt even more morose. She could tell Jake Gold's heart was not in helping her. As she ended the call, she wondered if she had done the right thing by not giving into the blackmailer. How was she going to clear her name and regain her reputation when her husband, the FBI, and even her private investigator was unsupportive?

*****

The doorbell chimed at precisely ten o'clock the next morning, and Cara checked herself in the mirror. She wasn't exactly sure what to wear when meeting with a private investigator because she'd never met one before. She didn't know why she was so nervous about meeting Jake Gold. He was not the FBI or the press. He could do her no harm. Yet, thinking about meeting with him in the morning had kept her tossing and turning all night. She'd assured herself when she was getting dressed that if Father Nicco thought highly of Jake Gold, he must be fine. But there was something in his tone when she'd spoken to him last night that unnerved her. She could tell that he didn't like her already, and she felt as if she had to prove herself worthy of his assistance. She was glad Wesley had already gone to work. She would explain to him about Jake when he came home later if Jake was still working on her behalf.

As she stood in her walk-in closet staring at her wardrobe, she berated herself for feeling so vulnerable, for seeking Jake Gold's approval, a man she had never met. Cara eventually decided that her gray gabardine slacks, blue blouse, and black leather ballet flats were appropriate. She wanted to appear serious, not flashy like Sophia always did. She had left her dark hair hanging loosely.

As she glanced in the mirror, Cara couldn't deny that this situation was taking a toll on her. She looked as gray as her slacks. *After this episode is over, she and Wesley should take some time off and head to Florida or the Caribbean,* she thought. As she descended the stairs, she saw the distorted frame of a dark figure through the leaded glass panel flanking the front door.

Near midnight, the rain had stopped and the temperature overnight had dipped below zero chasing away the press. The day had dawned with brilliant sunshine, but it was still so cold, the rays seemed like brittle shards of light. Cara inhaled deeply and opened the door. "Hello, you must be Mr. Gold. Come in."

Jake Gold stepped across the threshold without saying a word. He was younger than she expected, probably early thirties and everything about him was dark and brooding from his wavy black hair to his brows and onyx eyes to his fashionably stubbled beard. He wore a black wool military-styled jacket that was zipped up to his chin, black jeans, and black Dr. Martens. He was not much taller than Cara but his presence loomed larger. Sunbeams glinted off the titanium briefcase that he was carrying.

As he came in and wiped his feet, Cara could feel the cold radiating from him, and she wasn't sure if it was from the arctic temperature outside or from his presence. She closed the door behind him and smiled warmly.

He didn't return the smile.

"Thank you for coming here on such a frigid morning," Cara said. "I really appreciate it." She thrust out her hand. "I'm Cara." Then she remembered that he'd lost an arm, but before she could retract her hand, he thrust his prosthetic hand into hers. She felt herself recoil for a moment at the unnatural feel of it and how cold it was, then she caught herself. Cara wondered if he had done this to unnerve her.

"Jake Gold." He glanced around the foyer. "That a Simon Willard clock?" he said as he eyed the antique grandfather clock on the far wall.

"Why, yes, it is," said Cara, astonished that he would know such a thing.

"My parents had one similar to it."

"Really? Let me take your coat, Mr. Gold," she said.

He slid his prosthetic arm from one sleeve, then shrugged off the other. He had broad shoulders and was wearing a black pattern-on-pattern fitted shirt that conformed to his well-muscled body. "It's Jake. I prefer Jake."

"Sure. Jake it is then. Would you like something to drink? I made a fresh pot of coffee."

"No, thank you."

"So Father Nicco told me that you did some work for him," Cara said. "He certainly sings your praises."

Jake Gold's black eyes locked on her, and she felt as if she were staring into a double-barreled gun. "He does the same for you."

"He definitely is one of a kind," Cara said, trying to jumpstart a conversation.

"Yes."

When they amputated his arm, they must have removed his personality too, Cara thought. "Well, then," she said, "you are probably busy. Let's go into the den where we can talk."

Cara took a seat in the chair behind the desk and offered the upholstered one in front of it to Jake.

She noticed him glancing around the room. From his muscle-bound physique to his piercing gaze, everything about him seemed taut.

"I don't know what Father Nicco has told you about my case—"

"I watched the press conference, but I'd like to hear what happened from you, the unsanitized version, in greater detail." He set the briefcase on his lap, opened the latches, and extracted a tablet and pen. Cara was a bit amazed to see how well his prosthesis clasped the pen.

"Why don't you start with the awards banquet? It was at the William Pitt?"

She nodded.

"Did anything unusual happen during it?"

"No, nothing unusual happened until I was headed back to my room." Cara filled him in on everything that had happened, and he took notes. When she mentioned being detained by a reporter, his head rose.

"Didn't you find that a bit odd?"

"I did at first, but then she convinced me that it would benefit the kids at Comfort Connection if I granted her an interview." She told him about getting sick and the reporter helping her and not remembering anything after that until the next morning when Wesley had awoken her. Cara told Jake that she'd assumed that she'd gotten the flu or something until the photos arrived.

"Where are the photos and note now?"

"I turned the originals over to the FBI, but I have copies locked in this desk drawer."

"I'd like to see them."

"I'd rather not show the photos. They're graphic . . . and . . . embarrassing." Cara could feel herself starting to blush.

He leaned forward. "I'm not interested in how you feel. If you want me to find out who's trying to tap into your fortune, I've got to see them."

"I'm not holding them back because I've had my feeling hurts," Cara said. "I've been violated. I may not remember it, but that doesn't matter. I was stripped, abused, and humiliated, and it's all preserved in photographs."

"I understand that," Jake said, tapping the pen off the sole of his boot. "But if you want me to get to the bottom of this, I have to see the photos."

Cara pushed away from the desk. "I can't. I won't."

"Look, I'm a professional. I've been to war. I can assure you, I've seen worse."

"Father Nicco told me you were injured. Let me ask you. Would you like to have had that moment captured for others to gawk at? Every time I look at those pictures, I feel shame even though I did nothing wrong. It was difficult enough to show them to my own husband, let alone strangers."

Jake sighed heavily.

They were at a standoff. Cara could sense that he was about to get up and leave. She had to do something. "I can show you the note, and I have one photo that is less explicit. Maybe that will help." She reached for the key, unlocked the desk drawer, and removed the manila envelope, sliding out a copy of the extortion note and handing it to Jake.

He read it and handed it back to her. "Nothing remarkable about this."

"Here's the least humiliating photo." It was a side shot of her naked body; her arm was partially obscuring her breast as it was reaching out to fondle the small genitals of the little Asian boy.

She was surprised that he seemed unfazed by what he was viewing. Had his heart been removed as well?

"Have you ever seen this kid before? He's not one of your clients?"

"No, I don't know him." Cara felt tears coming to her eyes. She brushed one away that began to roll down her cheek. "That's what really gets me about all of this," she said. "I know extortion is awful, and I know this has been a violation of me, but when I think of this little boy . . ." her voice trailed off. "How scared he must have been. Was he afraid of me? More than anything I want to find him and tell him that I don't do things to hurt children. I love children and try to help them." She felt stupid for crying in front of him. He probably never cried. He was so hard-boiled his tear ducts had probably closed over. She wiped her cheeks and fumbled for a tissue. "Sorry. I just hate whoever did this to him and me."

"OK," she heard Jake say as she dabbed at her eyes, trying to save her makeup, "let's get to work then and nail the bastards."

She stopped and looked at him. "Then you'll help me?"

"Look, Ms. Hawthorne—"

"Cara, please call me Cara."

He shifted in his chair. "Cara, I admit I only agreed to meet with you as a favor to Father Nicco. When I watched you during the press conference, you struck me as another spoiled socialite who'd gotten herself into some deep shit and was looking for a way to weasel out of it. I intended to come here, let you try to explain and worm your way out of this, and then I'd agree to do a half-assed investigation, which would result in allowing the avalanche of shit to rain down on you and send you to jail."

"But now?" Cara asked, afraid to hear what else he had to say.

"I've changed my mind."

"Why?" Cara asked.

"That kid," he said, stabbing the photo with his prosthetic finger. "When you talked about that boy. OK, I believe that you didn't do this, but I've worked with a lot of innocent people who've had bad things happen to them." He shook his head as if he quite didn't understand himself. "But this little boy. Man, his face looks so . . . detached. A kid his age and in this kind of situation should be terrified or bawling his eyes out," Jake held the photo out to Cara. "But look at his expression. It's like he's not even there. What else has he seen? Or been made to do?"

Cara smiled. "So you do have a soft spot."

Jake smiled back at her. "Yeah, it's my brain. Because something tells me I'd have to be soft in the head to take on a case like this."

Chapter 19

For the first time since the photos had arrived, Cara felt that she had regained some control over her life, that she was no longer sitting helplessly like fate's punching bag. After Jake left, she spent the rest of the day trying to work from home to keep Comfort Connection operating. The temperature had hovered all day around zero. Even for January in Pittsburgh, it was uncharacteristically cold. Cara liked summer much better, but today she was grateful for the polar air that had gripped the city as it had driven the media indoors and away from her doorstep. She stood at the family room window, watching the weak winter sun set over her small back yard, the silhouetted homes against the red-streaked sky. As she went to her phone intending to call Wesley to see when he had planned on coming home for dinner, the doorbell chimed.

She was not expecting anyone, and as she made her way into the foyer, she hoped it wasn't that eager reporter who had followed her to the garage, thinking he was going to make a name for himself by staging an ambush interview. At the door, she turned on the porch light and pulled back the curtain on the leaded side panel. The person was so bundled up in a hat, scarf, and bulky coat, it was difficult to distinguish features, but Cara could tell that it was a woman.

Cautiously, Cara opened the door slightly. "Can I help you?"

The woman raised her face out of the collar of the coat.

"Oh my God, Sophia! What are you doing here?"

As her sister turned, the light from the porch lamp fully illuminated her face.

"Good, God what happened to you?" Cara exclaimed, her hands flying to cover her mouth. Then Cara looked about to see if anyone else had seen Sophia come to her door. Thankfully, no one was out. She grabbed her sister's arm and pulled her inside the house, locking the door behind her.

Sophia stood there haplessly as Cara pulled the knitted hat from her sister's head. She had a massive bruise on her forehead and her lip was puffy as was her nose. Dried blood had caked inside one nostril. "What happened? Were you in an accident?"

No response. Cara grabbed Sophia's arms; her sister winced and tried to pull away. "Sophia, look at me. Tell me what happened to you."

She fell into Cara's arms, sobbing uncontrollably. Alarmed, Cara cradled her sister, stroking her silky blonde hair that waved like fine tentacles from static electricity. It wasn't like Sophia to be so fragile. "It's OK. You'll be OK. What happened? Are you hurt terribly?"

"He . . . beat . . . me," she said between quivers of her lip.

"Who beat you?" Cara asked, her anger rising as she held her sister away, trying to assess how injured she may be.

"Pavel."

"Who's Pavel?"

"Pavel Nestorov—Peter N. Vee."

"The guy you married?"

"The guy I supposedly married." She shook her head. "I don't know. I was drunk."

"And he beat you?"

"Yes, he's a mad man. He's all hopped up on steroids."

Cara began to peel the coat away from her sister. She was shocked at how thin Sophia appeared in her black yoga pants and pink sweater. "Do you need to see a doctor? Did he hurt you anywhere else?"

"No, I think I'll be fine."

"You're frozen," Cara said as she picked up Sophia's delicate hand. It still felt as small as it had when she was a little girl, Cara thought as she led her sister into the kitchen. "Let me make you some tea. Are you hungry?"

"No, I ate on the road."

"Father has been trying to call you, but you never answered."

"I left my phone in Vegas."

"How did you get here?"

"I couldn't fly looking like this. I rented a car and drove."

"You drove all the way from Vegas in this condition?"

"I holed up in a motel in St. George, Utah, until I felt well enough to drive. It's amazing how those Mormons don't know anything about me. When I rented the car, my picture was on the front page of the paper next to the counter, and no one made the connection."

Cara didn't want to comment that the reason no one recognized Sophia was because she looked more like a vagrant than the beautiful girl in the photos the papers had published. Cara changed the subject instead. "What if you had internal injuries?"

"Then I would have blacked out at the wheel and been put out of my misery."

"Don't say such an awful thing."

Cara made her a cup of tea and set it before Sophia, who gingerly took a seat at the kitchen island.

"Now tell me what happened," Cara said, standing across the island from Sophia and studying her younger sister. Cara had to admit, that Sophia truly was beautiful, even looking emaciated, rumpled, and bruised, her platinum hair and deep blue eyes, gave her an ethereal beauty, a waifish quality. She was like a sprite or a fairy, someone you couldn't actually believe could be human and be this beautiful. No wonder the paparazzi followed her everywhere.

"I don't know. I was in Vegas with some friends, and we were gambling and partying—what everybody does in Vegas, and I guess I drank too much. Then the next thing I know I'm in a hotel room in Caesars with this guy I don't even remember meeting the night before."

Cara closed her eyes, shaking her head. "What were you thinking, Sophia?"

"Listen, do you want to hear the rest or are you going to sit there and pass judgment on me like you always do?"

Cara held her tongue. *Perhaps I pass judgment because you so lack judgment of your own,* thought Cara. "No, no. Go on."

"At first, he was nice to me, but let's just say the 'roids were wreaking their havoc as he couldn't," she flashed her blue eyes, "perform so to speak. I didn't care, but I began to tease him that he'd have to change his stage name to Peter Nogo, and that if he didn't watch out, he'd soon have to give up stripping all together as the 'roids would make his breasts larger than mine." Sophia cringed before speaking again. "That's when he went ballistic on me, and he began to knock me around. Luckily, a bellhop in the hall heard the commotion, and he called security. While they restrained him, I threw on some clothes, grabbed what I could of my things, and took off."

"Oh, Sophia," Cara said, slumping over the granite counter top. "When are you going to learn?"

"Learn what? How to molest children?"

Cara's head shot up.

"I heard about your escapades on the radio while I was driving here," said Sophia. "You're the hottest subject on talk radio. All these years on my back about my 'lifestyle' while you've got some really sick shit going on."

"You don't actually believe that I did that? You know me. You know I would never do something like that."

"Cara," Sophia said, looking dubiously at her. "Do we ever really know a person, what's going on inside?"

"I swear, Sophia—"

"Relax, Cara. I know you'd never do that. You'd never want to risk tarnishing your golden reputation." The sarcasm oozed like a toxin from Sophia's lips.

Perhaps because she had been laid bare in the photos and in the media, she felt as if everything may as well be out in the open, but Cara was still surprised when she heard herself saying, "Why do you hate me so, Sophia?"

Sophia laughed, opening the cut on her lip. As she reached for a napkin to blot the trickle of blood, she said, "I don't hate you. See, I graced you with my resplendent presence." She struck a pose while seated in the stool. "I just hate your superior attitude. Lording your loftiness over everyone."

"I don't do that. You read too much into everything. Maybe it's your way of deflecting guilt."

Sophia put her hands on her hips. "Guilt about what?"

Cara looked at Sophia incredulously. "You're serious?"

"Yes, I'm serious. What do I have to feel guilty about?"

"For starters, you just wound up in bed with a psycho after a drunken orgy and Vegas wedding. Not to mention the shame you've brought to the family and the money and talent you've wasted."

"OK, I was drunk, but it wasn't an orgy. God, Cara, I'm only twenty-two, I'm not ready to sit home in a cold, old mansion like you playing Mother Teresa." Sophia massaged her temple. "Do you have a Tylenol? I have a splitting headache."

Cara went to the kitchen cupboard and got Sophia a pill and a glass of water. "Here."

Sophia threw the capsule back and washed it down.

"I'm not saying you have to sit home, but can't you use some discretion. It's embarrassing reading about you in the papers. I keep wondering what Grandma Cavanaugh would think about your antics?"

"I wouldn't know. Grandma didn't want me."

"Oh, come on. You know that's not true. She wanted you. But father thought it would be less disruptive for you to stay with him, a parent you knew rather than to send you back to the U.S. to a grandparent you didn't know."

"Oh, yeah, I'm the lucky one."

"How do you think I felt? Being forced to leave you and father behind?" Cara started to cry. "You were too young to remember, but I missed you so much." She touched Sophia's arm and looked at her. "I still do."

"Don't get all weepy on me. I haven't gone anywhere," Sophia said.

"But I miss the sweet Sophia, the little girl who used to draw me pictures and send them to me in the mail. The one who used to visit me during summer vacation."

"Things happen. People change."

"Not at their core," Cara said. "As much as we'd like to believe that people do change. At their heart, they don't." She dried her eyes. "Just as you know, I could never hurt a child, like in those photos, I know that inside of you remains that sweet, innocent Sophia."

"Perhaps that's your greatest flaw, Cara. You believe there's too much in people when there's really nothing there."

Chapter 20

Sophia asked Cara if she could stay there for a few days until her bruises healed, and Cara said that she could stay as long as she liked. Sophia had parked her rental car in front of the house, and Cara insisted that it be moved to the alley that ran behind their house so as not to attract further attention from the media. That's all I need, Cara thought as she bundled herself up and headed to the car, is to have the media discover that Sophia is living in the house with me. Not only would the local press be stationed outside the house, but also every tabloid and media outlet in the country would descend upon them.

As Cara went to her sister's candy apple red Lincoln, she laughed. Only Sophia would think that a red luxury car was traveling incognito. Cara brought the few items that Sophia had managed to escape with into the house, and she had to admit that no matter how disruptive a presence her sister was, Cara was relieved to have her in the house because that way she could keep tabs on her better. She moved Sophia's things into the guest room while she sent her sister to take a hot bath.

Cara surmised that whatever was in her sister's suitcase was not suitable for a sub-freezing evening in Pittsburgh. Although Sophia was four inches taller than Cara, they were both slender. Cara found a pair of yoga pants and sweatshirt and laid them on the guest bed. "I'm going to go downstairs and start dinner," Cara called through the bathroom door.

Sophia called back. "OK, and if father calls, DO NOT tell him that I'm here. I'm not up to seeing him just yet."

"But he's been worried about you."

"I'll call him when I get out, and I'll tell him I'm staying with friends in Los Angeles."

As Cara was staring into the refrigerator, trying to figure out what to make for dinner, Wesley came in. He kissed her on the cheek, but by his stiff body language, she could sense that he was still annoyed with her. Before she could warn him that Sophia was here and would be staying with them for a while, Sophia sauntered in wearing Cara's white terry bathrobe, her freshly washed hair hanging in loose waves. Even battered, she looked like an angel as she padded into the kitchen in her bare feet.

"Wesley," she said exuding charm, as she kissed her brother-in-law on the cheek. "You're just the guy I need. Know any good lawyers because I need an annulment?"

Wesley looked shocked. "When and how did you get here?" He gazed at the bruises on her face. "And what the hell happened to you?"

She plopped onto a stool at the kitchen island, a long tan leg exposed, which Cara saw that Wesley had not missed. Cara was grateful that Sophia and Wesley were fond of each other, but sometimes it seemed that when they were together, they often conspired against her, making her feel like the odd man out.

"Long story," said Sophia.

"Long stories always call for a drink." Wesley walked over to the wine rack and selected a bottle. "How about something to toast your nuptials?"

"I don't think you need another drink, Sophia," Cara said. "I still think you should be seen by a physician."

Sophia looked at Cara, with a there-you-go-again face.

"What do you want for dinner?" Cara asked to change the subject. "I have some steaks we could grill."

"I'm in the mood for Thai food. Why don't you call and place an order," said Wesley. "Then we can unwind a bit and hear how the TMZ set lives," Wesley said, eyeing Sophia.

Sophia laughed. Cara didn't like Wesley encouraging her.

After arriving at a consensus of what to order for dinner, Wesley poured them all glasses of wine.

"She's had Tylenol. Don't give her a glass, Wesley," said Cara. "It will damage her liver."

"My liver is beyond repair. Give me that," said Sophia, grabbing the glass of wine.

Wesley went to the fridge. "How about some cheese too? I'm kind of into cheese now."

"Instead of kinky sex?" said Sophia, gulping the wine.

Wesley laughed.

"Oh, right," said Sophia. "I forgot you're married to Cara. But hey, I heard she gets it on with little boys."

"Sophia!" Cara exclaimed, astonished that her sister could find humor in her situation and a child being exploited.

Wesley took out several wedges of cheese and placed them on the bamboo cutting board. "Where's my cheese knife?" he asked Cara.

"In with the silverware in the dining room."

"If you saw those vile pictures, you wouldn't be laughing," said Cara. "Some poor child was forced to do repulsive acts. My heart aches for him."

Sophia held up her hands. "OK, OK. I was merely trying to ease the tension."

"What tension?"

"Come on. Between you and Wesley. Man, the body language between you two is—"

"We are fine," Cara said cutting her off before Wesley came back. "This situation . . . it's been a shock for all of us."

Wesley returned with a small ornate curved knife, which was forked on the end, and began carving the blocks of cheese and setting the chunks on a silver platter. "I took a cheese appreciation course recently," Wesley said to Sophia. "It was very enlightening and amazing how certain ones bring out the best in a wine."

"I always said you were a cheesy lawyer," Sophia said laughing and popping a cube of cheese into her mouth.

"Ha ha. Try this. It's imported, a Danish blue called Mycella, like a Danish gorgonzola." He stabbed a piece and fed it to Sophia.

"Umm, that's good," said Sophia.

Wesley took a seat next to his sister-in-law at the island. "So what china pattern have you and Mr. Envy registered for?"

"Wesley, it's no joking matter," Cara said. "The idiot beat her."

"Ah, so that explains the bruises," Wesley said. "I thought maybe you were just a little too enthusiastic on the honeymoon. So what happened?"

Sophia told Wesley about how she wound up married to Peter N. Vee.

Wesley shook his head. "Wow, that guy was a lunatic. Had I woke up and found you in my bed, I think I'd have found something better to do with you than beat the crap out of you."

"Ah, that was the problem," said Sophia. "The 'roids may have strengthened his muscles but they weakened something else. And he didn't like being teased about it."

"Even so," said Wesley. "I wouldn't have beaten you."

"Yeah, well everyone's not a peach like you, Wes. But now I need an annulment. That attorney you set me up with when I was charged with the DUI, do you know if he also handles annulments?"

"If not, I can recommend someone who—" The doorbell interrupted Wesley.

"Are you expecting anyone?" Cara asked. Wesley shook his head no. She turned to her sister. "Does anyone know you're here, Sophia?"

"I didn't tell anyone," she said. "I hope the press hasn't tracked me down somehow. I don't want my battered face on the cover of all the newspapers and magazines."

"Will you please see who it is, Wesley?" asked Cara.

He sighed and rose. "OK, make the poor sap without a scandal do all the work."

Cara and Sophia remained quiet while listening to hear who was at the door.

"Well, Laurence," Wesley said loudly enough for Cara and Sophia to hear him in the kitchen. "What brings you out into the cold?"

Sophia looked at Cara alarmed. "Oh no, father! I'm not up to facing him."

"Hide in the solarium," Cara whispered as she hustled her sister into the small windowed room off the kitchen. "Here, take your drink," Cara said. "And if you get cold, there's a fleece throw on the hassock."

"Good thinking, Cara," said Sophia as she sat on the hassock in the dark, chilly solarium. Cara went to shut the door, but Sophia whispered, "Leave it open a crack. I want to hear what he says about me if my name comes up in conversation."

Cara rolled her eyes. Sophia's first concern was always Sophia.

Laurence Hawthorne strode into the kitchen a split second after Cara returned from the solarium. He looked distinguished in his gray pinstripe suit, white shirt, and dove gray paisley tie. He was so handsome and polished, Cara, thought he could have been a movie star. She went over and kissed him on the cheek. "Hello, Father. I'm surprised to see you. I thought you were in Paris."

"No, I canceled that. I was summoned to Washington."

"Washington?" Cara asked.

"Anything to do with the ambassadorship?" Wesley asked.

Laurence looked at Cara, who put her hands up defensively. "I haven't said anything."

Wesley turned to Cara. "You haven't said anything about what? Now, what haven't you told me?"

Laurence turned to Wesley. "Don't fault Cara. When I met with her, I mentioned that I am being considered for the ambassadorship because Ambassador Chambers has terminal cancer. I swore her to secrecy." Laurence frowned. "Ambassador Chamber's illness won't be made public just yet; however, he is declining rapidly. I met with him yesterday. So sad." Laurence closed his eyes for a moment as if to blot out the vision of how ill Ambassador Chambers was. "I was asked to come to Washington to begin the vetting process. I was on my way home from the airport, and I had my driver stop here for a moment." He took Cara's hands. "I wanted to check on you, to see how you are doing. And to apologize. I'm afraid I was a bit terse with you. Forgive me." He shook his silver-haired head. "This has been so unpleasant for you—for all of us."

"Thank you, Father," Cara said, grateful that he wasn't upset with her for hanging up on him. "Would you like a drink? Or some cheese? We were trying some of this delicious cheese Wesley selected."

"No, I can't stay, but I wanted to let you know that I contacted some friends in the FBI."

"Oh, Father, I wish you hadn't. I don't want preferential treatment," Cara said.

"I didn't ask for preferential treatment. I offered to work with them to provide as much help as I possibly can."

"I don't understand," Cara said. "How can you help them?"

"Some of my staff have brought it to my attention that the boy in the photos may be a victim of child sex trafficking. I wanted the FBI to know that I have lots of contacts—connections I've made over my career. International ones as well. I don't know how much I can be of assistance, but I'm eager to help to solve this, to clear your name." Laurence Hawthorne looked at both of them. "Clear all of our names actually."

Cara thought this was the best time to tell Wesley about her hiring Jake. He couldn't blow up at her if her father was there. "In that vein," Cara said, as she turned to Wesley, "I wanted to tell you that today I talked to a private investigator, and I've retained him."

Wesley looked stunned and angry, but he appeared to be trying to tamp down his anger. "I don't like that idea, Cara. It makes you look guilty—like O.J. conducting his own search for the killers."

"I still think it's a mistake," said her father.

Wesley looked at Laurence. "You knew about this?"

"Cara mentioned that she was considering it, and I voiced my concerns."

"Are you sure he's not just someone out to drain you of your money?" Wesley asked.

Cara felt as if she were being double-teamed. "His name is Jake Gold, and he comes highly recommended."

"By whom?" Wesley asked.

"Father Nicco," said her father, his disapproval evident in his tone.

"Yes," Cara said. "Father Nicco recommended him. He retained him when Cardinal Quinn was falsely accused of child sexual abuse."

Laurence scoffed. "If I knew you were so set on this, I'm sure I could have come up with someone more suitable."

"Jake is very reputable. He flushed out the background of the Cardinal's accuser, tracing him to several other false claims of sexual abuse of teachers and ministers around the country."

"What exactly are you paying him to do?" Wesley asked.

"Get to the bottom of this. Find out who is behind the photos, and most importantly, find out who is responsible for exploiting that little boy," Cara said, feeling her face flushing with annoyance.

Laurence sighed. "If it makes you feel more in control of the situation, then go ahead."

"It's not a question of wanting to feel in control," Cara said indignantly. "It's a question of clearing my name, getting justice for this child, and putting these sickos in jail."

The doorbell chimed again. "That's probably dinner," Wesley said, turning to Cara.

"Let me get my purse."

"Wait, I've got it," Wesley said as he headed for the door. "It might be the press."

"Are you sure you can't stay for dinner, Father?" asked Cara. "We've ordered Thai."

"No, I'm sure.

"Cara," Wesley called from the foyer, "can you give me a hand?"

Cara left the kitchen and then returned with two brown bags. She moved the cheese platter to the counter near the sink, and then unloaded the containers of takeout.

"Are you sure you won't stay?" she asked her father again.

Laurence removed his hand from his suit pants pocket and looked at his Rolex watch. "No, I've got to run. You and Wesley enjoy your dinner, my dear."

They walked him to the door. He kissed Cara on the cheek. "Take care, darling, and know that we are all here for you. Let's hope that this unfortunate episode will soon be over and that we can all get back to our lives."

Chapter 21

"A private investigator?" Sophia strolled in from the solarium, wrapped in the green fleece throw.

"You heard that?" Cara asked, hoping that Sophia's comments would not provoke Wesley.

"I don't miss anything," said Sophia. "How else do you learn a person's secrets?"

"Why didn't you tell me you were thinking of hiring a PI?" Wesley asked, facing Cara.

"Is he handsome?" Sophia asked, taking off the throw and draping it over the back of the stool. "Silly question. Aren't they all? I mean why would you hire one if he's not handsome?"

"That wasn't one of my requirements," Cara said.

Sophia took a seat at the island and finished her glass of wine. "I didn't ask what your requirements were. I asked if he was handsome."

"I guess in a dark, rugged way." Cara waved her hands. "But what's that have to do with anything?" *Does Sophia take anything seriously?*

"So this has gone beyond phone calls. You've met with him already?" Wesley asked. "When were you doing to tell me about this?"

"I met with him today. I didn't have a chance to tell you, Wesley," Cara said as she removed the containers of food from the brown bag. "Sophia arrived as soon as I got home, and then you came and my father."

"Do you know if this guy is licensed and bonded? Is he insured? Did you sign a contract? What's he charging you?"

"I'm not a moron, Wesley." She opened one container and pulled a serving spoon from the silverware drawer. "Of course, I signed a contract. And I did a little homework. It's a standard contract, and he charges the going rate."

"Let's see the contract."

Cara slammed a spoon into the bowl of Pad Thai. "You know, Wesley, you are always accusing me of being a control freak. Listen to you. I can handle this."

"Oh yeah, right. You're in control. You walk off with a stranger who drugs you."

"Who drugged you?" Sophia exclaimed, looking too interested by

Cara's estimation.

"I haven't had time to explain to her what happened yet," Cara said to Wesley. Then she turned to Sophia and briefly told her about what happened after the awards banquet and how she had received the blackmail photos in the mail.

Sophia shook her head. "That is pretty bad, Cara. At least, I knew Peter a few hours before I went off with him."

"I didn't go off with her. I was drugged." She looked back at Wesley. "How can you say I went off with a stranger? You know I was slipped something."

"Cara, after the past few days, with the arrival of these photos, your staging a press conference against my wishes, and then keeping it from me that you've already hired a PI—I'm beginning to realize that I don't know a lot about you."

"What's that supposed to mean?"

Wesley walked out of the kitchen. Cara followed. "You don't believe me, do you?"

She grabbed his arm. Wesley said nothing. "Admit it. You don't believe me." She looked back at Sophia, who was standing in the kitchen's archway looking startled and smug at the same time.

He stopped and looked down on Cara. "Does it make a difference whether I believe you or not because either way you do whatever you want, whatever makes you look good." Wesley walked toward the den.

"That's fine," Cara called after him. "I don't need your help." She looked at Sophia. "And I don't need yours either. The control freak will take care of this all by herself."

"I'm glad you don't need my help," Sophia said, "because I'm going to need yours."

Puzzled, Cara stared at Sophia, who grabbed the doorframe. "Either this wine is really potent or you've been cloned."

"What are you talking about?"

Sophia blinked her eyes. "I'm seeing two of everything."

Cara rushed to her side. "That's it. You're going to the hospital." Cara guided Sophia back into the kitchen, sitting her on the stool.

"Wesley! Wesley!" Cara shouted. "Help me!"

Wesley came into the kitchen, annoyance still clouding his face, but his countenance changed to one of alarm as he saw Sophia slumped in the stool, her head resting on the granite counter. "What's wrong?"

"She has double vision. And she's had a headache since she arrived. She needs to be seen by a physician."

He pulled his cell phone out. "I'll call 9-1-1."

"No," Cara and Sophia shouted in unison. "I don't want anyone to see me looking like this," Sophia said.

"The Hawthorne sisters don't need any more drama," Cara added.

"But her brain could be hemorrhaging. You remember what happened to that actress—Natasha Richardson," Wesley said.

"I'll go to the hospital, but I'm not going by ambulance," said Sophia who raised her head to look at Wesley. The movement must have been too sudden because she suddenly vomited down the front of Cara's robe.

Wesley winced. "If she's going by car, she's going in yours, Cara. I don't want her messing up my Lexus."

*****

"Thank goodness, it's only a concussion," Cara said as the doctor left them. When they arrived at Sewickley Hospital, they were relieved to find that the Emergency Room was not crowded. The two other patients—a boy of about four, who had a gash on his head and whose young parents were so distraught, they couldn't have cared less that the Hawthorne sisters were there, and an elderly woman and her daughter. The white-haired old woman kept complaining that she had to pee again, which Cara surmised was probably the symptoms of a bladder infection.

After Wesley had wheeled Sophia in and Cara had explained her sister's symptoms to the nurse on duty, Sophia was bumped to the top of the patient-to-be-seen list. Immediately, Sophia was taken into a curtained room. In rapid succession, she was examined by a physician and sent for a CT scan. Although Cara was grateful that her sister had been seen right away, it also alarmed her. Apparently, her symptoms were indicative of severe head trauma.

She was relieved when the attending physician, a handsome, tall man told Sophia that there was no sign of bleeding in her brain, but that she had a concussion and wouldn't feel herself for a bit.

Cara knew that something was not right with Sophia's brain even before the doctor gave his diagnosis because her sister normally would have been flirting with the handsome doctor instead of lying on the exam table with her eyes closed.

Sophia was discharged with the instructions to rest and avoid mental activities that tax the brain.

As Wesley drove them home, Cara thought that perhaps the concussion was a blessing in disguise. Sophia had always been difficult to control. Now Cara would no longer have to worry about what her sister was going to do. She looked over at Sophia who had her eyes closed once again and was dozing. The concussion had accomplished what no one else had ever been able to do—rein in Sophia.

At least for the moment, thought Cara.

Chapter 22

On Monday morning, Jake called Cara from his apartment in Bellevue as soon as he woke up and asked her to come by his office around one o'clock. Since their meeting the previous week, he had been working his leads and contacts, and he was excited to share what he'd learned. As he was combing his hair, he looked at his prosthetic hand. He'd gone to Israel to escape what he'd thought were superficial people, but as he looked at his mechanical hand, he wondered what Cara thought of it? *Does that make me superficial?* It didn't matter anyway, he told himself, Cara is a client and a married one at that, but for the first time since he'd come back to the states—since he'd recovered from his injury—he could feel the old juices returning to his parched and hard-baked life.

He missed his hand, but what he missed even more was the chase. It was Ground Hog Day. He'd seen the reports from nearby Punxsutawney on the news this morning while he was eating his breakfast, the drunken college kids cheering Phil, the befuddled groundhog, as he was held aloft and presented to the crowd. For the last few years, Jake had to admit that he felt a bit like Bill Murray in the movie *Ground Hog Day*. Every day was the same—work and home, work and home. *But at least Bill Murray eventually made some progress and got the girl. I am stuck.* He loved pursuing a target and capturing or eliminating it. His thoughts drifted again to Cara. He should not like her if he were to true to himself—she was the epitome of everything he disdained—money, status, and privilege— everything he'd gone to Israel and joined the IDF to escape, yet there was something about her, something that made him want to be more than what he was, which if he were honest with himself was husk of the person he'd been. Certainly, she was beautiful, but he'd know beautiful women before. *Maybe it's part of that need for the chase. Because she's so out of reach, she's a challenge. That's why I can't stop thinking about her.*

When he arrived at the office, he spent the rest of the morning organizing his findings and tidying. Other tenants in the building had turned their offices into trendy, retro workspaces. As he looked around at his metal desk and aluminum folding chairs, he cringed. He needed to clear the binders from the chairs before Cara arrived. His office would not inspire much respect from clients. When his eyes lighted on the coffee pot on the cheap folding table in the corner, he groaned. He'd never noticed before how stained the small coffee pot was. *How can I offer her coffee from this thing? She'll be afraid of contracting a disease.* Quickly, he found a sponge and spent too much time trying to make it presentable.

As he was rummaging through an overhead cabinet for another coffee cup that was not chipped or stained brown, he heard the door behind him. Cara stood in the doorway holding onto the doorknob looking startled.

"Oh, I'm sorry," she said. Cara was dressed in black slacks, black turtleneck, and a herringbone checked jacket, set off with a red scarf.

I've been hired by Audrey Hepburn, thought Jake.

"I should have knocked. I thought you'd have a secretary or receptionist or something."

Jake pulled his black buttoned-down striped shirt over the waist of his black jeans. "No, it's just me. I work better alone."

Cara smiled. "Ah, the proverbial lone wolf. I understand. The sisters always gave me low marks in 'Works Well with Others' when I was in grade school."

"I can't imagine you ever got less than stellar marks anywhere. I bet you have a whole room of trophies in your home and the Mother Teresa award was just the latest addition."

"You'd lose that bet," she said as she entered the office and closed the door. "I guess I'm not a team player. I've been told I can be a bit controlling. That's probably why I contacted you. I'm not content to leave this investigation to someone over whom I have no control."

Jake looked at her askance.

"I don't mean I have control over you. What I mean is that I don't want to be out of the loop. If I left this solely in the hands of the FBI, I'd never know what's going on."

"That's why I asked you to come here today," Jake said, "to get you up-to-date on what I've been doing." He moved a stack of binders from the chair to the top of the bookcase "Why don't you have a seat."

Cara settled into the aluminum folding chair, and if she thought his office a disaster, she didn't let it show on her face.

Jake went behind his desk and sat. "Anything new on your end?" he asked. "Any more photos or letters arrive?"

"No, thank goodness. I would have called you if I'd gotten anything more. Although—" Cara stopped talking.

"Although what?"

"I guess it won't hurt to tell you. She hasn't sworn me to secrecy."

"Who hasn't sworn you to secrecy?"

"Sophia. My sister. She showed up on my doorstep Thursday night."

"So is that a secret?"

"Well, yes. I suppose you heard about her hasty Vegas marriage. Evidently, it was a match made in hell because her groom," Cara rolled her eyes at the word, "beat her up. She drove cross country to my house. Wesley, my husband, and I took her to the Emergency Room when she started to have double vision. Thankfully, she had nothing more serious than a mild concussion. She's been staying with me, resting, and trying to get rid of her persistent headache."

Jake remembered well the incessant pain of the concussion he'd suffered after one of his captors had beaten him.

"She doesn't want anyone to know she's here. I've spent the past three days taking care of her, which in some ways has been a blessing. It kept me from obsessing about this blackmail scheme."

"That's my job anyway, Cara. I wanted to let you know that I've been nosing around a bit, getting in touch with some contacts, and I've come to the conclusion that we're not dealing with professionals here."

Cara looked intrigued. "Why do you say that?"

He turned his laptop screen toward her. "I was able to obtain video from the hotel's security camera." He touched a button and a grainy black and white video appeared. He looked at her, his dark eyes studying her face.

"How did you do that?" she asked.

"You don't need to know."

"Oh, my God. That's her," Cara exclaimed, pointing at the screen. "That's the reporter." She looked up at him. "You found her. You are amazing!"

He felt the heat rising in his chest. It had been a long time since any woman had told him he was amazing. *Get a grip, Jake.* He came around the desk and moved some folders from the other lawn chair and sat. "Watch closely." He adjusted the screen so that there was no glare. "See, she's just outside the ballroom waiting for you, and right there—look, she adjusts a wig."

"She *was* in disguise. Now that I think of it, I remember having a brief flash of insight where I thought her hair was cute and a subconscious inkling that it looked too perfect. But then Wesley called, and then I began to feel so strange, I forgot about that."

"Since she was in disguise, I wasn't sure if we'd find anything on the recordings of the parking garage, but I was able to isolate an image of her emerging from a car, a Honda Civic. I went to the surveillance video from the camera located at the entrance of the hotel parking lot and found the car again." He pointed to the ghostly images on the screen. "You can see her clearly here. Same face but different hair style." He froze the screen on a three-quarters profile of a woman who looked to be the same person as the woman who had posed as a reporter her but with short dark hair. "Do you know her?"

Cara studied the image and shook her head. "No, I wish I did."

"I've been trying to ID her through the rental car. I'm still working to match that. It's going to take a while."

"Wow, you've made a lot of headway," Cara said. "You *are* good."

Jake felt a rush of blood surge through him. *Focus Jake. She's a client.* But she'd awoken something in him that longed for her to tell him that he was good but not in a professional way. "Yeah, well I have a lot more work to do before we can nail her," he said, shrugging off the compliment and the urge to kiss her. "I find it a bit unusual that one woman's behind this. She must have had help. How could she have gotten a small boy up to your room without some? I'm still working to see if I can get video with the boy on it."

"I agree she must have had an accomplice," Cara said. "But the craziest thing is I still can't figure out what her motive is."

"Could be money. Who knows? Maybe her coffee was cold, and she got pissed and is taking it out on you. Maybe she saw a picture of you and hates you because you're beautiful. It could be something random."

Cara looked at him.

Why did I say she was beautiful? I've become a cliché. The private eye hitting on a client.

He abruptly closed the laptop and went behind his desk. "While I try to run down the lead with the rental car companies, I thought that tonight, I'd head uptown. My contact in the police department says they've been having a huge problem with teen prostitutes there." He picked up a still photo that he'd made from the video. "I'm going to show the glamour shot of our friend here around to see if I get a nibble."

"May I come with you?"

He stared at her, surprised at her question. "No."

"Why not?"

"Because I'm the investigator."

"But I'm the one who has been accused."

"This isn't a debutante ball, Cara. This is a side of Pittsburgh you've never seen before—prostitutes, pimps, drugs. At night. In the cold."

"Then I'll be sure to wear my mink and bring my lady's maid," she said sarcastically. Cara scrutinized him, making him feel as if she were stalking him. "I'm going and you can't stop me."

He backed away. "I call the shots here. You do what I say."

"I'm paying you so I get to do whatever I deem fitting."

Any attraction he felt for her withered with her lording her money over him.

"Isn't that always the way it is with you people?"

"*You people?* What does that mean?"

He shrugged.

She reached across the desk and grabbed his arm, his prosthetic arm, startling him. Most people were repelled by it, but here she was grasping it. He wished he could feel her touch, but all he had was a sense of pressure radiating up through his false limb to the stub that remained of his arm. It was a metaphor for his life. He couldn't really feel anything anymore—only pressure to contain himself before he imploded.

"Ever since we've met, I've sensed hostility toward me," Cara said, withdrawing her hand. "You know, Jake, I was born into this life, the money, the notoriety. I didn't get a choice. So I don't know what your problem is. Did you get snubbed by a prep school or get tossed off the tennis courts at the country club for not wearing whites?"

"No. I snubbed them."

"Pardon me?"

"I had all that, but it bored me, and I walked away."

"And joined the IDF? Wasn't the French Foreign Legion taking recruits?"

He smirked at her wit. "I was born into the same scene as you, but I opted out."

"And you think I should have too? Is that it? That's why you've got it out for me. Maybe I'm tougher than you think, Jake. Tougher than you. I chose not to drop out of life."

He grabbed her arm with his prosthetic hand. "Hey, Your Highness,

I wouldn't call having an arm blown off by a grenade exactly dropping out."

Cara looked at him with fierce determination, then something changed, something he couldn't read, and she softened her gaze. "I'm sorry. That was unkind of me. Obviously, I don't know all that you've been through, and it was presumptuous of me to think that I know what your life has been like. You don't have to like me. I've hired you to do a job and obviously you're great at it. I apologize."

"For a humanitarian you sure have a wicked tongue."

She smiled sheepishly, which about melted the soles of his Doc Martens. "Especially when facing an injustice. Like there being no good reason why I can't come with you tonight."

"How about I'm a lone wolf? You said it first."

"Yes, you are and a pretty damn intimidating one. You'll probably scare away anyone that could help us with that scowl and snarl."

He smiled. "I don't scowl and snarl."

She looked at him dubiously.

"If I do, it doesn't seem to scare you."

"You got that right, Jake." She rose and put her hands on her hips. "So what time and where are we meeting?"

Chapter 23

Cara spent the rest of Monday working from home. Support for Comfort Connection was dwindling, and when Lia phoned that afternoon to tell her that several of the children had been pulled from their grief counseling program by their parents or guardians, Cara knew that she had to find her blackmailer fast and prove her innocence or Comfort Connection was doomed.

Dear God, help us. Help me, she pleaded.

When she wasn't obsessing over how to keep Comfort Connection afloat, she was fussing over Sophia. Wesley was not home from the office when Cara left to meet Jake that evening. She left him a voice mail saying that she had prepared lasagna for him and Sophia, who was still suffering from a headache although her double vision had subsided and her swelling and bruising were nearly gone. She checked on her sister before leaving, but she was napping and Cara didn't want to wake her.

Dressed in jeans, a fleece L.L. Bean shirt layered over Under Armour, UGG boots, and her Columbia jacket, she drove to Jake's, an older home in Bellevue, which was only a fifteen-minute drive south on Route 65 from Sewickley. The behemoth of a red brick building had once been a single-family home and had been subdivided and converted into three apartments. Jake lived on the first floor. Cara walked up the cement front steps and crystals of salt crunched under her boots. She took care as she crossed the glossy floorboards of the porch in case they were slippery, entered the vestibule, a converted foyer, and pressed his doorbell.

Jake opened the door and invited Cara inside. He looked more like a cat burglar than a private investigator. Once again, he was dressed all in black from his boots and cargo pants to his thermal T-shirt, which Cara couldn't help but notice how it hugged his muscular shoulders and biceps.

"You dressed warm enough?" he asked. His black wool military style jacket was hanging from a peg on a wooden accordion rack on the wall next to the door. He checked the pockets of the coat, pulling out a pair of, what else? black gloves. "You have a pair? It's going to be cold out there."

The apartment was as sad and spare as his office. There were no curtains or drapes on the windows, but sun-faded blinds that looked as brittle and ancient as parchment. A green plaid, broken-down couch sat on a burnt orange oval braided rug directly in front of a huge, state-of-the-art flat screen TV. Typical man, thought Cara. He only needed what he wanted and wanted what he needed.

"I should be fine," she said. "Want me to drive?"

"No, I'm driving," he said.

I guess that's settled, thought Cara. No wonder he wears black all the time. There's no room for gradation.

He pulled on a shoulder holster and then tucked a gun into it.

"You're bringing a gun?"

He put on his jacket. "Yeah, you got a problem with that?"

Cara sighed. "I guess not. "

"Look, you asked to come along."

Cara held up her hands. "I know. I know."

"OK, then you have to do it my way. Do what I tell you to do. Got it?"

"Yes," she said grudgingly.

He opened the doors of—what else?—a black Honda CRV.

"You really like black," Cara said as she buckled herself in.

"Not especially, but with black you don't have to fuss or worry about matching." He cracked a devious smile. "It goes from the office to a night-on-the-town by just adding the right accessories."

"What?"

"I've seen *Glamour, Vogue, InStyle*—how they are always extolling the virtues of the little black dress."

Cara shook her head, laughing as they pulled away. "I can't picture you reading *Glamour.*"

"I didn't say I read any of them," said Jake as he glanced in the rearview mirror. "But I know them. I know a lot of things."

Cara chuckled. "I bet you do."

He reached into the back and retrieved a file folder, which he held out to her. "Hold on to this. I've got a photo of our extortionist with and without the wig and a photo of the little boy."

"Where are we going?"

"Uptown. It's not far from the William Pitt, and my contacts in the police department say that's where the action is these days. I figure we'll show the photos around see if anyone recognizes the woman or the boy."

They drove through downtown Pittsburgh. The city lights bled into distorted splashes of color in the sleet that had begun to fall. Super Bowl banners had been strung across all the bridges into the city, and the neon sign atop Mt. Washington flashed a message welcoming the Super Bowl and the fans to town. The game was this coming Sunday. *If this weather continues, the NFL is going to be sorry they awarded the game to the city*. It was so miserably wet and cold, Cara couldn't believe that anyone would be out soliciting prostitutes or peddling their flesh, but she'd heard reports on the news that, sadly, with the Super Bowl came an increase in prostitution. They drove past the CONSOL Energy Center, which was deserted. The Penguins must be on the road, thought Cara, as they looped around Center Avenue and turned onto Fifth Avenue. This area of town was in flux, dilapidated storefronts contrasted with new businesses that had sprung up around the arena.

Jake slowed the car, and a young black girl in high heels, denim mini skirt, and ratty fake fur jacket approached them.

Jake lowered his window.

"It's cold. You looking to keep warm with someone?" she asked.

She must be freezing, thought Cara, with her legs so exposed.

"Actually, sweetheart," said Jake. "I'm wondering if you've ever seen any of these people in the photos?" He shined a mini flashlight on the photos he took from Cara.

"You a cop?"

"Now, do I look like a cop?" Jake said with a wicked smile.

Cara was shocked at the charm he exuded.

"No, you look like some crazy-ass commando from the cover of one of those romance novels in CVS, called *Delicious and Dangerous*."

"I'll grant you the delicious part," he said with a wink, "but I'm just looking for a friend."

"I don't know nobody." She started to move away. Jake pulled a $20 out of his pocket.

She reached in and grabbed the $20. "Guess it don't hurt to look."

The girl poked her head in the car. "Who that? Your ho? No wonder you ain't interested. You already got a ho."

"No, she's not a ho." He looked a Cara wearing a smirk. "She's my sister. You ever seen this woman around here? Sometimes she wears a wig." Jake shuffled through the photos.

"Don't see ladies much around here. Mostly old, creepy guys. She don't look like anybody I know."

"How about this boy? You ever see him working the streets?"

"He's small and looks Chinese. My guys not into that freaky shit. Talk to Alex. He knows all the working boys. Alex is a pretty boy."

"Where can I find this pretty boy Alex?"

"He hangs out in the Loco Bean further up Fifth."

"What's he like?"

"Skinny. Thai. Everybody know Alex."

"Thanks, sweetheart. You be safe now."

"Yeah, yeah. Come back again, Mr. Delicious. Easiest $20 I make in a long time."

Jake put up the window and headed further along Fifth Avenue.

"That is so depressing," said Cara, pulling her jacket closer around her neck. "She looks barely fifteen."

"Yeah, it's a whole nother world, sister."

She chuckled. "Sister? How'd you come up with that?"

"I'm trained to think on my feet."

They drove several blocks and parked a few doors up from the Loco Bean, which was so shady looking Cara thought for sure more than coffee must be sold there.

"Come on," Jake said. "Let's get out and ask around a bit."

They entered through the glass double doors, and a chime rang. The only patron, if you could call him that, was a disheveled man sleeping in the last Formica booth. "I'm looking for Alex," Jake said to a small Asian woman behind the counter."

"You police?" she asked appearing rather frightened.

"No, I'm a friend."

"He was just here. He went around the corner to Thai Mei Down."

"Thanks," Jake called as he guided Cara out the door.

"Thai Mei Down?" asked Cara when they reached the street. "Why kind of place do you think that is?"

"S&M. Whips and leather," Jake said.

The apprehension must have registered on her face because Jake shook his head and laughed. "It's an Asian restaurant."

"Thank God," Cara said as she adjusted the collar of her coat.

A group of young men was smoking under the striped awning outside Thai Mei Down when Jake and Cara arrived there. A glowing neon light in the restaurant's window flashed "open" and intermittently turned them all a sickly shade of blue. "Any of you Alex?" asked Jake.

"I'm Alex. What do you want, handsome? You and your woman into kinky shit? Want to party with Alex?"

Alex looked to be about sixteen. He was lean and tall and had a smooth complexion and a huge smile, but his teeth had a yellow cast. He was wearing skinny jeans and a hoodie.

"No, we're looking for someone, and we were told you might be able to help." At Jake's disclosure, the other young men peeled away and headed inside Thai Mei Down.

"Who you looking for?" Alex said, grinding out his cigarette beneath the toe of his gold metallic Keds.

Cara handed Jake the photos. "Do you recognize this woman" Jake asked. "She's wearing a wig in this photo."

Alex lit another cigarette and took a prolonged drag. Cara noticed that the teen had stars tattooed on the four knuckles of his right hand. "No. Never seen her," he said exhaling a gray snake of smoke.

"How about him?" Jake pointed to the child.

The change in the young prostitute's expression told them that he did know the boy.

"You know him, don't you?" Jake said.

"Can't be sure. I know lots of people."

Jake pulled another $20 bill from his jacket pocket and held it between his thumb and index finger.

"Why you want to mess with him? He just a baby."

"We don't want to mess with him," Jake said. "We need to find him, help him."

"You can't help him."

Cara admired his protectiveness and moved closer to Alex. "But you do know him, and if we could help him, you'd help us to do it, wouldn't you?"

Alex stared at her.

Cara reached into her pocket and pulled out her Coach wristlet. She extracted a $50 bill.

Alex snatched the money from both of their hands. "Shit, his name is Tam."

"Can you take us to him?" Cara asked. "I only want to help him."

"How you going to help him? He don't know English. How else he going to live but do what he's told?"

"Where is he? Please. I can help both of you," she said.

Alex pulled a few more drags on the cigarette, then sighed. "OK, you wait here." He flicked the butt into the street. It landed in the water running along the curb and disappeared into the gurgling sewer catch basin.

Cara put her gloved hands on her red cheeks and began bouncing on her feet to keep warm. "Do you think he's going to bring him?"

Jake rubbed his gloved hands together. "You better hope so or you're out $50."

Cara found it strange that he wore a glove over his prosthetic hand. Maybe it was an attempt to avoid curiosity. Or maybe he only wanted to appear normal and whole.

After several minutes passed, Jake looked at his watch, and then Cara saw Alex further up the block as he came around a corner, dragging a child by the hand through the sleet. The boy was clad in an ill-fitting coat.

"Is it him? Does the boy look like the one in the photos?" she asked.

Jake squinted. "I can't tell."

"I tell Mama freaky dude want to party with little boy," Alex said, pushing the child forward. "This Tam."

The boy looked horribly frightened and confused, but when Cara crouched to see his face better, he blanched, seeming to recognize her and began to cry and cling to Alex's leg.

Distressed at her effect on him, Cara felt tears spring to her eyes. She appealed to Alex. "Tell him I'm not going to hurt him. I know someone made him do those awful things with me. I want to find the woman. I want to help him."

Alex translated for Cara while the child peeked from behind his legs.

"Tell him my name is Cara, but I need to know this woman." She held up the photo. The boy was obviously distressed by the photo of the woman. "What is her name?"

Alex looked at Cara. "Tam say the man called her Brin."

Cara looked up at Jake. "The man? Did you hear that? We were right; there was an accomplice."

"Ask him what the man's name was," said Jake.

Alex spoke to Tam in his native language again and then waited for the child to answer. "He say, 'honey.' She call him honey."

"Ask him if he remembers anything else," said Jake.

"The car had all colored dancing teddy bears on the window."

Puzzled, Cara looked at Jake.

"Dancing teddy bears? Hmm." Jake mused. "Ask him what he means by 'dancing teddy bears.'"

The small boy said something and then struck a pose, sticking out his leg.

Jake and Cara could not comprehend what he meant until Jake's black eyes became animated. "So our friend must be a Dead Head."

Jake's brilliant, thought Cara. How did he ever make that connection?

"If our blackmailer is driving a Cadillac with a Dead Head sticker, I'm going to die," Jake said to Cara, referencing the lyrics from the Don Henley song. He then turned to Alex. "Ask how they found Tam?"

The child replied and Alex said, "Mama make him go with woman." Tam began to cry and shake.

"Who's mama?" asked Jake.

"She his madam. She take care of all the sweet meat?"

Jake frowned. "Sweet meat?"

"That what they call the babies. Sweet meat make lots of money for mama. Men pay big dollar for fun with sweet meat."

Cara felt tears pooling in her eyes. "That's not right," she said.

"Please come home with me. I'll help you." She looked up at Alex. "Both of you. You don't have to live like this."

"That nice, lady," said Alex, "but The General will hunt us down and kill us."

"The General? Who's The General?" asked Jake.

"Mama work for The General. General nasty bastard. Once you belong to The General, you his for life." He pointed to his hand. "That's his mark. Now his forever."

"He branded you?" Cara asked, incredulous that Alex had been marked like he was cattle with four stars by this so-called General. She touched Alex's arm. "Please come with me. I promise you'll be safe."

Alex laughed. "Not safe anywhere from The General."

"I'm begging you."

Alex grabbed Tam's hand. "Come. Have to get back to Mama before she send someone after us. You got $100? I tell her freaky dude pay $100 to play with Tam's snake."

Sickened by the thought that someone would actually pay to do that to a child, Cara reached into her wristlet again. "Before I give you the money," she said to Alex, "I want to give you this too." She pulled out two business cards and a pen. "This is where I work, but I'm going to write my cell phone number and home address on the back," she said as she held the cards in her palm and wrote on them. "If either of you ever, I mean ever, need help or change your mind—call, and I'll come get you or come to my house." She handed Alex the card; he stuffed it in his pocket. "Tell him what I said," Cara commanded and watched as Alex took the other card, gave it to Tam, and told him of Cara's offer. Tam's eyes never left her face; he then tucked the card into his tennis shoe. Cara gave Alex the $100 bill.

Alex stuffed the money into his pocket and then grabbed Tam's hand.

Cara and Jake watched the pair walk into the night. Then they headed to Jake's car, the sleet stinging her cheeks.

"That was productive," Jake said as he turned to face Cara when they were back inside the shelter of the Honda. "We confirmed that there were two people in on this, got some leads on their names, and the Dead Head sticker clue is a godsend."

Cara barely heard a word he said. She was looking out the car's side window, preoccupied with wondering what would happen to Alex and Tam. She felt a tap on her arm.

"Hey, you OK?"

Cara nodded.

Jake reached over and grasped her by the chin, turning her head toward him. Tears were streaming down her face.

"Satisfied? I'm crying. I guess you're right. I'm not as tough as you," she said.

"No, but you're better than me. You still did good out there and still have your humanity."

"You don't have yours any longer?" she asked.

"Nah, it was amputated with my arm."

Liar, Cara thought. If you have no humanity, Jake, then why are you brushing the tears from my face?

Chapter 24

It was nearly ten o'clock when Cara pulled into her garage. Wesley's car was not in the next space. Working late again, she thought. He's going to give himself a heart attack if he didn't learn to relax and delegate some of his work.

Having Sophia in the house was like having her own personal Goldilocks. Crumbs on the granite counter told Cara that at least Sophia had been to the kitchen at some time and had regained her appetite. There was a message on her home voice mail from Father Nicco telling her that he was merely checking up on her. It was too late to return his call now so she headed up to bed. She peeked in on Sophia on her way to her room. Once again, Sophia was sleeping. Her blonde hair was fanned out on the pillow. She is Goldilocks, Cara mused. It was just as well that her sister was sleeping. After the evening she'd spent with Alex and Tam, she was in no mood for conversation.

Cara took a hot bath, the heat penetrating her chilled bones, and unwound with a glass of Merlot. She warmed the bed by turning on her heated blanket. The bath, wine, and cozy bed still did not induce sleep. As she lay there, Alex and Tam's faces haunted her. She knew how frightened she'd been when her mother had died and she'd been sent to live with her Grandmother. *And Grandma had loved me.* Even then it was difficult. She could not fathom the trauma that Tam had already experienced in his brief lifetime. How had he come to be in the United States as a human plaything? She hadn't noticed any star tattoo on Tam's small hands in the photos, which made Cara think that Tam must be a new arrival. Alex seemed to have abandoned any hope of ever escaping his fate, but perhaps there was still hope for Tam. *Please help me help them, Lord.*

Cara eventually drifted off to sleep, but she dreamed that she was looking for someone. She couldn't tell if it was a child or Wesley. When she awoke, she had expected to find Wesley in bed beside her, but his side of the bed was empty. She looked at the clock, and it was nearly two. Alarmed, she tried his cell phone, but it went to voice mail. She texted him and waited for his reply, placing the phone on the pillow next to her where her husband's head should rest. When the phone buzzed with a text several minutes later, she startled. "Roads were icy. Took a hotel room. TTYL"

As she lay there, she grew colder. Without Wesley beside her generating body heat, she could not get warm. She turned up the heated blanket to high and wished she could adjust life with the mere turn of a dial. She wished she could turn up Wesley's support of her and turn the world off so that children did not suffer.

The last time she remembered glancing at the clock, the luminous dial said three twenty-eight, but when her alarm went off at six, she'd felt as if she'd only slept for a few minutes. She padded down the stairs, looked out the living room window, and saw a slight dusting of snow like God had opened a container of baby powder and had shaken it over Sewickley. The roads didn't look slippery, but sometimes a dusting is all that it takes to turn them treacherous. Fortunately, there were no reporters camped outside.

She walked into the kitchen and clicked on the small television on the counter while she made herself a cup of tea. The morning news did not cheer her. In the corner of the TV screen was the temperature— twelve degrees. "Lots of reports of black ice this morning. Be careful out there on your way to work," advised the meteorologist before the broadcast cut back to the anchor. "Once again, a human trafficking task force has been formed for the upcoming Super Bowl," said the anchor. "According to authorities, the Super Bowl is one the largest sporting events in the world, and an event of that magnitude attracts human sex traffic. The mayor has pledged full support to the FBI, and on our website we have posted tips on how to spot those who may be victims of human trafficking and whom to call to report the crime."

He continued, "Next up, tailgating Pittsburgh style, and the who's who of celebrities who have already arrived in town for the big game."

"Wonderful," said Cara, shaking her head. "More creeps abusing children." No wonder there were no reporters outside her house. It was too cold and the city was in the grip of Super Bowl fever. Disheartened, she shut off the television and headed to the den to check her emails before she looked in on Sophia to see if she wanted any breakfast.

She missed going into the office, but she knew if she went there, she'd be nothing but a distraction. When she logged on to her email account, she was shocked to find a considerable number of messages calling her the foulest names she had ever heard.

Enraged, she shut down the computer. *Damn Wesley, damn the press, damn her detractors.* She was going to go into the office and try to put Comfort Connection into order.

She showered and dressed in her favorite suit, a plum tweed, with black patent leather buttons and trim on the lapels. She looked in on Sophia, who was half awake and asked if she wanted any breakfast before she left for the office. Sophia said her headache had dissipated somewhat and that she wasn't hungry at the moment, but if she got hungry while Cara was at the office, she could make herself something.

In that case, Cara thought she'd grab a bagel on the way to work. As she was about to head to her car, the doorbell chimed. She heard Sophia's bed squeak, apparently making a move to get out of bed. Cara left the kitchen and called up the stairs, "Don't get up, Sophia. I haven't left yet. I'll get it." Cara strode to the front door, moved the curtain aside, and saw a young man dressed in khakis and puffy down coat standing on her doorstep.

Cara cautiously opened the door.

"Are you Cara Cavanaugh Hawthorne?"

Puzzled, she said, "Yes."

"This is for you," he said, handing her an envelope.

"What's this?"

But the young man didn't reply; he merely turned and walked back down her front stairs.

Cara felt her mouth go dry. *Were these more photos and another demand for money?* Highly unlikely, she thought. Who hand-delivers blackmail letters? She closed the door and took the envelope into the den. Grabbing the letter opener, she slit it.

Cara unfolded the envelope's contents and felt as if she'd been blindsided by a powerful wave when she saw the title of the document. It was a Complaint for Divorce. Wesley was divorcing her.

Numb, she sank into the desk chair, and as she read through the document, a range of emotions assaulted her. Confusion and hurt gave way to rage when she read where the Complaint cited cruelty and alleged sexual misconduct with children. When she came to the section where Wesley was asking for half her property, she flew out of the chair. *After all I've done for him, paying for his law school education, and introducing him to powerful people to advance his career. Now he's leaving me and taking half of my money? How can he do this to me? He knows I had nothing to do with those pictures.* She began to cry. Her life was falling apart. She was being blackmailed and was under a suspicion of child abuse, her marriage was over and now Wesley wanted to loot her as well. *What has happened to that understanding, idealistic college student that I fell in love with? What has caused him to turn into a driven, status-seeking louse?*

Certainly, the last year had been rough on their marriage, but she as well as Wesley had blamed his workload. She never suspected that he was unhappy.

Cara was still sitting in shock in the den staring at the divorce papers debating whether to call Wesley when the doorbell rang again. She folded the documents, hid them in the desk drawer, and called up to Sophia again. "Change of plans. I'll be here for a while. I'll get the door again."

As she walked into the foyer, she caught a glimpse of herself in the mirror. Her eyes were red from crying. She brushed away tears and straightened her suit. It better not be a reporter, she thought.

She opened the door and was surprised to see Jake hunkered down in his parka wearing dark sunglasses making him look even more mysterious than ever. "Cara, sorry to bother you at home, but do you have a moment. "

It was a raw day. Cold and sunny, making the snow glare unbearable.

"Come in," she said as she held the door for Jake and then quickly closed it behind him. "I was going to head into the office and try to keep things afloat there, but I've already gotten waylaid. So no problem."

He took off his sunglasses and stuffed them into this jacket pocket. "I discovered something, and I really think I need to move on this quickly so I came right over in case you were here."

"Let me take your coat. I've just had some tea. Would you like some or coffee maybe?"

"Tea would be fine," he said as he followed her into the kitchen and took a seat at the island. He tilted his head and looked at her, and his gaze was so penetrating, she felt as if she were being put into an airline scanner that peered beneath your clothing. "You look a bit upset, Cara. Is something wrong?"

She didn't think she could talk about the divorce papers right now without crying, and this was personal. Jake didn't need to concern himself with her disaster of a marriage.

"No, I'm fine." she said, filling the hot water kettle.

"You've been working already this morning?" she asked to change the subject.

"That tip about the Dead Head sticker bothered me."

"Most people rent a car because they don't have use of one. We know because of the clue about the Dead Head sticker that she had a car. I figured our mystery girl probably left her car behind and either walked to a rental place or had someone drop her off. So I began asking questions at rental car companies near the hotel, showing our friend's picture around, and asking if they remembered her. I got a hit."

Cara was having difficulty concentrating on what Jake was saying because of the divorce filing, but she wanted to hear what he had discovered, so she redoubled her effort to shut out Wesley and her marital troubles and concentrate on what Jake was saying. She knew this was a big break because this was the most animated, she'd ever seen him.

"Someone recognized her?"

"Yes, the agent at Luxury for Less rentals near the Boulevard of the Allies recognized the woman in the photo. He said she was dropped off by a man driving a car sporting a Dead Head sticker. He said he noticed because he thinks it's funny all these young people with cars sporting Dead Head stickers when half of them have no idea who Jerry Garcia even was other than for the ice cream named after him."

"That's fantastic, Jake. Father Nicco was right. You are the best."

If he heard her compliment, he didn't acknowledge it. "I've got her name. It's Brianna Hoffman. Does that ring a bell?"

Cara let the name tumble through her mind. "No."

"No one you've ever met through work or school?"

"No."

"Damn. I thought maybe you would recognize her name. The only other thing I've been able to glean so far is that she's a law clerk at Gibson, Jones & Marshall."

Cara gasped. "That's where my husband works. He's an attorney there."

"Bingo!" Jake exclaimed. "Now, do you think she might have it in for your husband? Want to get back at him for some reason?"

Cara suddenly turned pale. "Not that I know of. I've never even heard him mention her name before."

Jake frowned. "Cara, is something wrong?"

"I'm not sure, Jake," Cara said as she stood. But as she began to tremble all over, Cara knew deep in her heart that something was indeed very wrong.

Chapter 25

Cara's eyes looked as if they had lost focus. Then Jake realized that she was about to faint and sprang from the stool, grasping her arm, and wrapping his prosthetic hand around her waist. As she crumpled, he picked her up and carried her into the nearby family room and laid her on the couch.

"Cara, are you OK?" he said, slapping her hand.

"Yes," she said weakly as she came around. "I just felt a bit lightheaded. I haven't eaten and . . . " She hesitated.

"And what?" asked Jake who was on one knee beside her.

"Nothing," she said, looking as if she would prefer to faint again to avoid revealing what was troubling her.

"Tell me, Cara. What is it?"

She covered her face with her hands. "I was served with divorce papers moments before you arrived."

"Oh," Jake said. *Now what the hell do I say or do?*

Cara scooted up, tears running down her cheeks. "I never saw this coming. I'm in total shock. And now this revelation that my blackmailer works in my husband's law firm? What does this all mean, Jake? Could she have something on Wesley too? Is the blackmail related to his filing for divorce?"

He rose and sat next to her on the couch. Jake had his suspicions, but he didn't want to add to Cara's misery by revealing them now. "I don't know. But there's only one way to find out. I'm going to check out our friend Brianna Hoffman. But don't breathe a word of this for now until I nail down the details."

Cara nodded and then began to cry harder. "My life is falling apart before my eyes," she said between sniffles.

Her despair was so intense it was tearing him apart. He'd heard men on the battlefield cry in pain, but he knew how to respond to their suffering—with action, unleashing hell on the enemy, but he didn't know how to assuage Cara's distress. He'd never been good with sympathetic words or platitudes. He was a man of action.

He looked at her. She was so beautiful, so perfect, so vulnerable, and he did the only thing that he knew how to do to comfort a woman. He slid his hand behind Cara's head and pulled her closer, kissing her. Her lips were soft and warm and salty from her tears, and to Jake's surprise, very responsive. She melted into his arms and returned the passion.

"Well . . . well . . . well . . . Look at what we have here!"

Jake froze and quickly released Cara. He looked up and saw a young blonde haired woman in a pair of pink plaid flannel pajama bottoms and tight white T-shirt that left little to the imagination standing over them with her hands on her hips. He immediately recognized her as Sophia Hawthorne, although looking less glamorous than the photos he'd seen of her. "I was listening to the radio in bed when the news came on, and they said that 'socialite Cara Hawthorne has been served with divorce papers.' I didn't believe what I was hearing, but maybe little sister was wrong. Because it seems sure seems that big sis has a little something going on besides liking little boys. Seems she likes big boys too."

Cara quickly brushed her hair back and sat up, straightening her skirt. "It's not what it looks like."

"Wait. Let me guess then. He's your dentist and he's giving you an oral exam with his tongue?" Sophia said.

Jake rose. "Cara's right. She had nothing to do with this."

Sophia smiled. "Certainly looked like she was involved to me."

"Jake, if you haven't already guessed. This is my sister, Sophia."

Sophia mocked a curtsy.

Jake nodded. "Nice to meet you, but you're wrong, Sophia. She was upset, and I took advantage of her and kissed her. It was all my fault." Sophia is stunningly beautiful, thought Jake, but in a Barbie doll, flashy sort of way, but he found Cara's classic, understated beauty more attractive. *Obviously, you do, Jake. You were just kissing Cara like her lips held the secret to life.*

"You don't have to explain," Sophia said. "Least of all to me. It's just nice to catch Cara every once in a while when her halo slips."

Cara rose too. "Jake is my private investigator."

Sophia breezed past Jake, looking him over, making it plain that she liked what she was seeing and plopped into the recliner. "You could investigate me anytime."

"Seriously, Sophia. I was upset. Wesley *has* served me with divorce papers."

"So it's true?" Sophia asked.

Jake touched Cara's arm. "I should be going. Let you fill your sister in on what's happening."

The phone began to ring. Neither Cara nor Sophia seemed eager to pick it up. Sophia looked at the caller ID. "It's father."

"Let it go to the answering machine," Cara said. "I can't deal with him now."

Jake made his way toward the foyer.

"I'll get your coat," Cara said.

"Nice to meet you, Jake," Sophia called. She had followed them and was stretching her arms overhead, making her breasts bounce under the T-shirt and baring her midriff as she stood in the doorway to the foyer. He could sense that Sophia was doing this for his benefit. He had no siblings, and he wondered if all sisters were this competitive?

Cara handed him his coat. After zipping it up, he stood there once again not knowing what to say or do.

Cara glared at Sophia. "Do you mind, Sophia? I'd like to talk to Jake privately."

Sophia sighed and rolled her eyes, retreating into the kitchen but not before mumbling, "I bet you'd like to get Jake in private."

"Cara," he motioned toward the family room. "What happened in there . . . I'm sorry. I-I'm not very good with words, and when I saw you so upset, I panicked and well, I did what comes naturally for me when I'm around a beautiful woman."

Cara smiled demurely. "It's OK."

"I'll be in touch." He put on the sunglasses and zipped his jacket tightly. "Take care," he said as he walked outside.

The cold morning air invigorated him. He stood for a moment on her front porch, then looked back at her door. *No, Cara, you're wrong. That kiss was not OK. It was awesome. And I sure as hell don't intend it to be our last.*

Chapter 26

After she closed the door, Cara leaned her forehead against the frame. A man who kisses like Jake doesn't need to be good with words, she thought. Then she quickly straightened up and got hold of herself. *Whether Wesley wants me or not, I'm still married, and I can't let my emotions get the better of me and leave me vulnerable. I won't be vulnerable again.*

Cara went back into the kitchen where Sophia was eating a banana and drinking a glass of orange juice.

"God, he's hot, Cara," Sophia said. "What's the scoop on him?"

"What do you mean?"

"His story. Is he married? Gay? Does he like blondes?" She said with a wicked smile.

"All I know about Jake is from what Father Nicco told me about him. He grew up in Pittsburgh, became disenchanted with his life here, and decided to drop out of Columbia and go to Israel to join the IDF. If you didn't notice, he has a prosthetic arm."

Sophia smirked. "I didn't notice. I was looking at his other parts, which, if I may say so, looked to be in fine working order."

Cara closed her eyes and shook her head. *Sophia must be feeling better.*

"How did he lose it?"

"I'm not really certain. He's very private. He doesn't say much."

"He doesn't need to." The way Sophia was staring at her made Cara uncomfortable.

"So are you having an affair? Is that why Wesley is suing for divorce?"

"No, I'm not having an affair, and I don't know why he kissed me. Half of the time I think he hates me." Cara felt a wave of sadness wash over her, and she took a seat at the island. "I'm totally blindsided by Wesley."

"Was there trouble in paradise?"

"Things were a bit strained, but we'd been trying to have a baby without much success, and he's been very busy at work. But I never suspected . . ."

"They said on the radio that he cited you for cruelty and sexual abuse. Do you think he seized on your being blackmailed as his chance to get out?"

"And to get money. He wants half of everything." She shrugged. "I never thought money was that important to him."

"No, I don't think it's the money, Cara. It's the status. No matter how much he tried to pretend it didn't bother him, you could tell that he was ashamed that he'd grown up poor."

"But that never mattered to me."

"I know, but I think deep down he resents you—us—for growing up privileged."

Where had Sophia come by all of this wisdom? "Oh, yeah, our lives were one big cotillion," Cara said bitterly. "Growing up continents apart."

"Always under the microscope," added Sophia. "Everyone waiting to pounce on the least little screw-up."

Cara was surprised by her statement. She had always thought Sophia had enjoyed being in the limelight, but perhaps she was like an ant under a magnifying glass in the sun. She moved and entertained in response to the heat.

"So what are you going to do, Cara? Do you still love him?"

"Yes, I do love him."

"Have you called him?"

"No, I was served the papers minutes before Jake came to the door."

"Is Jake making any headway?"

Cara narrowed her eyes at Sophia.

"I meant with the investigation, not you."

"A bit," Cara said softening her gaze. "But nothing concrete yet." She didn't want to reveal that Jake had identified the woman who had drugged her until he'd nailed everything else down.

"I guess I should call Wesley. And then a lawyer. Again."

"You can call the one I'm going to use for the annulment. Maybe he gives a family discount."

*****

Cara returned to the den and looked over the divorce papers again. She wasn't sure why. Perhaps she was hoping that it had all been a bad dream. She steeled herself and noticed she was shaking as she dialed Wesley's cell phone. She remembered how nervous she was the first time his name had come up on her caller ID. They'd met at an alternative spring break trip, building homes for the poor in Appalachia. He was so handsome and charming, and she admired how he knew his way around tools and construction. Wesley had explained to her that his father had been a handyman, but had died when Wesley was seventeen, plunging his mother and five siblings into a financial abyss. She admired how determined he was, how he had won a scholarship to Mercy University and was aiming to go to law school, secure a good position, and help his family. *When had he lost those noble qualities?* Cara was somewhat relieved when the call went to his voicemail.

Should she call his office? *The office.* Everything revolved around *the office.* Cara sighed. It had been nearly two years since she'd seen her in-laws. Although they had welcomed her into their family, it seemed that the more she embraced them, the more Wesley seemed to want to distance himself from his working-class roots. Two summers ago, Wesley had insulted his family by not inviting them to his law school graduation. At the time, he said they would just be bored by the whole affair, but Cara had the feeling that they embarrassed him.

Damn *the office*, thought Cara. Some things are more important than your career. She picked up the phone and dialed, not sure if he would take her call, but his secretary put her through.

"What's going on, Wesley?"

"Ah, Cara. Shouldn't I be asking you that?"

"What do you mean?"

"You know our marriage has been strained for a long time, and I kept asking myself what went wrong. Have I changed? But when those photos came, it all became clear to me. It was you who changed. Apparently, you are not the person I thought you were."

"Me?" Cara felt herself tense as red-hot rage flared in her. "You don't seriously think I would molest a child? And then send myself photos? It doesn't make sense."

"Unless you're the sicko who wanted those photos taken in the first place, and then your accomplice decided it would be more lucrative to extort some money from you."

"That is ridiculous."

"Is it? Our sex life has been non-existent. You surround yourself with kids. You set yourself up as some champion of children. Then these photos appear. It all fits, Cara. And it sickens me. I can't pretend. I can't live with a monster just to preserve your reputation."

Cara was reeling. She wanted to blurt out that Jake had found the woman who had drugged her and that she worked in his office, that he had also found the boy she hired, but she didn't want to blow the investigation.

"I don't give a damn about my reputation. I give a damn about my kids at Comfort Connection and that boy who was abused." She began to cry. "How could you possibly believe that about me?"

"Easy. It all fits. Who played Miss Virgin all the time? You always told me you were saving yourself for marriage because of your religious convictions, but now I'm beginning to believe it was because you had no real interest in men. You never cared about me."

"That's a lie, Wesley." She began to sob. "I still care about you. I do. Don't do this to me. Don't throw our marriage away until the truth is revealed."

"Face it, Cara," he said. "The truth has been revealed. You need help.

I shouldn't, but in some way I'll always have feelings for you. But sadly, what was once love has now degraded into pity." He sighed. "For all our sakes, admit what you did, plead for mercy, and get help."

She didn't like being pitied. "You're wrong about me, Wesley," she shouted into the phone. "I'm innocent. I'm going to prove it, and when I do, you're going to be sorry you ever doubted me."

She hung up the phone and flung the divorce papers across the room.

Chapter 27

When Cara emerged from the den, she was emotionally spent and her head was pounding. She took an Ibuprofen and went into the kitchen to make a small sandwich so as to avoid an upset stomach and was surprised that Sophia was still there. She was sitting at the island, with a tablet of paper and a pencil.

Sophia looked up when Cara came into the room. "Wow, that must have been rough. You look like hell."

At the moment, Cara didn't care what she looked like. It hurt that Wesley was divorcing her, but what hurt more was that he didn't believe her and thought she was a child molester. It galled her that the man she had been married to for four years, had shared her life with, shared her body with, could believe such a horrible thing about her.

She sat at the island with Sophia. "He believes that I molested that boy," Cara said flatly. Then she began to cry again.

"That's preposterous. Who blackmails themselves?" said Sophia, handing her a napkin.

Cara wiped her eyes. "That's what I said, but he believes I had those pictures taken and whoever took the photos turned on me and decided to blackmail me with them."

"Then why would you call in the FBI?"

"He thinks I turned them over to the FBI to cover myself."

Sophia shook her head. "He's a lawyer. They're always looking for angles."

Cara touched Sophia's hand. "Do you believe me?"

"Listen, Cara. You are a pretentious, pious, pain-in-the-ass, but you are not a pervert. Believe me. I've been around enough of them to know, and you're definitely not one. If anything, you're a prude."

"Thank you . . . I think. Well, I'm going to prove Wesley and all the doubters wrong. I don't care if it takes me until my dying breath."

"Cara, I know you think I'm all screwed up, and hell you are probably right. But I've learned some things along the way. You've got to stop worrying about what others think of you. What really matters is what you think about yourself."

*****

Cara needed some perspective on what was happening and someone to offer her hope that it would all turn out well and that meant she needed to call Father Nicco. After Sophia retired to the guest room for a nap, Cara called him. When he answered, his voice oozed with compassion. "Ah, Cara *mia*, I'm glad you called. Bridget heard the bad news on the radio and told me. I can't tell you how heartbroken I am over this."

The news of her divorce had already traveled to Bridget, his secretary? Cara was sure the media would once again descend upon her. "Me too," Cara said, her voice cracking. "Do you think there is any hope for Wesley and me?"

"Ah Cara *mia*, there is always hope. Especially for those who want to search for it. I'd be happy to talk to Wesley if you think it would help."

"I don't know. He seemed determined when I called him earlier to find out why he's doing this to me."

"Perhaps he would agree to see a marriage counselor instead. There are several great ones in the diocese. I could give you a referral. That might be best since you and I are so close, he might think me biased."

"I don't know how open he would be to that," Cara said. "He said some vile things to me."

"Things are said at the height of emotion. At least, suggest it to him.

It can't hurt."

"I don't want to make things worse."

"My dear, how can it make it worse? Your marriage is on the line. Give it a chance."

"But what if he perceives it as my being desperate and clingy?"

"Who cares how he perceives it. He made vows to you. It shouldn't be easy for him to walk away from them. He needs to be made aware of that."

"But what if he believes I'm guilty of child molestation?"

"Then he needs to be set straight. Speaking of which, how is Jake doing?"

Cara felt herself blush and a wave a guilt wash over her as she thought of Jake. Even with a missing limb, he somehow seemed more of a man than Wesley. "He was just here. He's making progress, but he wants to nail down some details."

"He's very good," said Father Nicco. "He'll get to the bottom of this. When you are cleared, Wesley will no longer have any reason to doubt you."

When he does exonerate me, Cara wondered, will there be anything left of her life to salvage?

She promised Father Nicco that she would, at least, ask Wesley to consider counseling, and, in turn, he promised to pray for them. After she hung up the phone, Cara sat for a moment trying to settle her mind. It seemed all too much to deal with. *Life is not served on a silver platter.* Cara heard her grandmother's voice in her mind. *You've got to work, my darling.*

Ah, but grandmother you've never had to face what I'm facing.

In her mind's eye, she could see her grandmother's bright blue eyes looking fiercely at her, compelling her to give up the self-pity.

Cara shook her head in amazement at how someone who'd been dead for six years could still exert so much influence over her. Resigned to her fate, she went to her desk and composed an email asking Wesley to consider counseling. She read it three times before hitting send.

When Cara returned to the kitchen, she was surprised to find that Sophia was back at the island and that she was sketching something. She'd always been the most artistic of the pair and had entered the Rhode Island School of Design as an Illustration major, but she had dabbled in various media from photography to oil painting. She had also ventured into the performing arts, winning the part of Ado Annie in *Oklahoma* in a community theater production. It was then that the lure of the klieg lights prompted her to drop out of college and try acting in Hollywood. Although she was beautiful and talented, there were hundreds of beautiful, talented young women in Hollywood. Her name and fortune had opened a few doors for her, but her reputation for being unreliable and a party girl, quickly shut those doors, reducing her to a bit of a joke.

"What are you drawing?" Cara asked, looking down at the roughed-in pencil drawing of a baby.

"Oh, I don't know. I've been thinking about a new venture."

"You're pregnant?"

Sophia looked at her perturbed. "No, I'm not pregnant. God forbid, but I'm thinking of starting a line of dolls. You know how I've always loved dolls. I need something that captures my passion."

"What about your movie career?"

"I never really wanted a Hollywood career; I just wanted my freedom. That's why I left school. And you and I both know I'm no Sandra Bullock."

"You got rave reviews for your part in *Power for Love.*"

"So I did, but I would like something that's all mine—my creation—from start to finish with my name on it. I could still do the occasional movie when I felt like it, but creating dolls would be a steady venture."

"That sounds wonderful," Cara said. "So you've been thinking about this for a while?"

"Yes. Staying in Utah, I thought of Marie Osmond and her line of dolls. Then while I was driving here, I came through Missouri, and I kept seeing ads for the Kewpie doll museum in Springfield. I can't seem to get dolls out of my mind."

"That's great. Maybe this is your calling. What kind of dolls do you envision?"

"I'm not quite sure yet, but dolls have always given me great pleasure, and when I was little and you left me, great comfort. I'd like to capture that in a doll. A doll that expresses emotions." She showed Cara her sketch pad.

"See this one. I've tentatively called it Fretful Francie."

The sketch was beautiful, depicting an innocent child, with a tentative, wide-eyed gaze.

"You know how sometimes you can't be strong for yourself, but you can be strong for others?"

Cara nodded, immediately thinking of Tam. While Cara had a hard time defending herself against the child molestation charges, she had no difficulty summoning the outrage and the courage to protect that little boy. Cara looked at Sophia, touching a section of the drawing and began to see her sister in a new light. Maybe she had sold Sophia short all these years. Maybe she was merely taking a lot longer to find her calling in life.

"I envision my dolls doing that for children. If a child is fretful, she can turn to this doll, see herself in it, and then find something within herself to be strong for her doll."

She showed another sketch to Cara. "This one is called Lonely Lola."

The doll's expression was one of melancholy. "I see a lonely little girl getting this doll and then playing with it, telling it that everyone gets lonely, that she'll be OK."

"That's pretty deep psychologically. If I remember correctly from psych class, that's called transference—when you transfer your emotions to something or someone else. Will you also make positive emotion dolls?"

"Sure, I don't see why not. I haven't thought about it. Maybe my first will be Conquering Cara, the doll that makes you believe you can overcome adversity."

Cara snickered. "I could certainly use something like that right about now."

Sophia began to make more sketches; the pencil making scratching sounds on the paper.

"I'm really proud of you, Sophia," Cara said, touching her sister's shoulder. "I think this is a fantastic idea."

Sophia looked up. "Then I guess you'd be open to giving me a loan for the start-up?"

Cara was taken aback. "Don't you have money?"

Sophia bit her lip. "Unfortunately, my funds have run a bit dry what with my DUI conviction and the legal fees and now with having to retain a lawyer for my divorce and annulment, I'm a bit short. Until I turn twenty-five and can get my hands on my trust fund, I'm stuck."

"Sophia, I'd love to help you, but I can't commit. With the blackmail scandal, donations have been drying up for Comfort Connection, and I'm afraid I will have to dip into my funds to keep it afloat until this is resolved. And with Wesley suing me for divorce and seeking a large settlement, I don't think it would be wise right now." Cara thought for a moment. "What about asking father?"

"I'd hate to do that." Sophia's face clouded over. "You know that would come with strings attached."

Cara knew how Sophia hated her father's lectures. She hated them too, but he seemed unable to refuse Sophia.

"I wish I could help. I think this is a great idea, and I'm really excited that you are getting serious about your life."

Sophia laughed. "Who said anything about getting serious?"

Chapter 28

Cara's head was still spinning from the shock of the divorce papers, Wesley's abandonment, and if she were truly honest with herself, Jake's kiss. She'd never been kissed like that, not even by Wesley. Had Wesley's heart never been in their marriage or was Jake just an exceptional kisser? That was the trouble with divorce, Cara thought. It casts a pall over everything in your marriage even the good times. It makes you go back and question everything, wondering if it all was a farce.

She went to her room to lie down and dozed off for a bit, and when she awoke, it was mid-afternoon. She figured she'd better do something constructive before her mind became preoccupied again with Jake's kiss. After heading to the den and checking her inbox several times to see if Wesley had responded to her overtures and finding nothing, she called Clifford Martel to inform him of Wesley's petition to divorce her and seek a referral from him for an attorney who practiced family law. She thought it would look unseemly if she and Sophia used the same attorney, and besides Sophia's lawyer had been recommended by Wesley, which would hardly make him her advocate.

Clifford recommended she get in touch with Lysandra Powell and told Cara that he would phone her to let her know that Cara would soon be calling. All that Cara knew of Lysandra was from seeing her on the news. She had represented Bonita Weatherford, the wife of Steelers wide receiver Drew Weatherford, when she'd sued him for divorce after learning that Drew had another wife in Seattle, where he had previously played. Cara wondered if she and Lysandra would be a good fit. Lysandra loved staging over-the-top press conferences and making headlines on the news. If Wesley refused to reconcile, Cara preferred to keep the divorce proceedings as low-key as possible.

Then Cara did something she had been putting off all day—she called her father. She was relieved when Sheila, his secretary, told her that he was out of the office.

After all the phone calls, she decided that she needed to get out of the house and actually do something rather than talk. Cara finally headed to the office around three.

When her staff realized she was in the reception area, they all came out of their cubicles and gathered around her voicing their support for her. Cara thanked them and said that they would have to work doubly hard to fund Comfort Connection until this blackmail thing blew over. Lia followed Cara into her office and brought her up to date on everything that was happening with Comfort Connection.

"You look so stressed. How are you holding up?" Lia asked.

Cara sighed. "I'm OK, considering."

"Considering what?"

"Don't play dumb, Lia. You must know."

Lia tilted her head. "Know what?"

"That Wesley has served me with divorce papers."

Lia slowly sank into the chair across from the desk. "What?" Her mouth moved but nothing was coming out. "I-I can't believe it."

"It's all over the news."

"We've been so busy I haven't paid attention to the news, mostly because I can't stand hearing how they are portraying you in the media." She shook her head. "Cara, I'm so sorry."

She filled Lia in on what was happening, but she didn't tell her that she'd retained Jake as he had instructed. She then asked her assistant to please tell the others not to comment on the blackmail case or Wesley's filing suit for divorce should anyone from the media call asking for a reaction.

"Certainly," she said.

"Anything I need to know about?" Cara asked.

"Actually, minutes before you walked in, the producer of *In the Spotlight* called. They want to do an in-depth interview with you tomorrow afternoon."

"Tell them no."

"Are you sure? It might help. If you granted an interview, it might give people get a greater sense of who you are and what you do here at Comfort Connection. It may help to dispel some suspicion."

"Like Jerry Sandusky did during the Penn State scandal? I don't think his interview helped him much."

"No, but you're not him."

"I don't know. When do you have to let them know?"

"ASAP."

"Let me think about it."

After Lia left the office, Cara sat contemplating whether to do the interview. Ordinarily, she would have called Wesley and asked his opinion, but sadly, that was no longer an option. She probably should call her father again and ask his advice, but he was so unsupportive after she had called the press conference to reveal that she was being blackmailed, she really didn't want to involve him. And if truth be told, Cara believed that his first concern was not her, but his prospects for being appointed ambassador. As was becoming a habit, she reached for the phone and dialed Father Nicco.

His cheery voice, for a moment however brief, gave Cara the hope that things would all be well. "It's the pest again."

"Ah, Cara *mia*. You are not a pest. I love hearing from you."

"I promise when this is over, that I won't call for six months."

"That would break my heart."

"I'm sorry to interrupt, but I need your advice. You're the only one who brings any clarity to this mess. *In the Spotlight* would like to interview me. Lia thinks it's a good idea, and part of me does too, but I'm afraid. Maybe it will do more harm than good. What do you think? I know you went on the show during the sex abuse scandals."

He paused a moment then blurted. "I think you should do it. I know Marsha Robbins, and I've always found her to be very fair when conducting an interview, unlike some of the other journalists. If she has an agenda, I'm not aware of it."

"But how do I prepare? What do I say?"

"Pray. Pray, Cara, and be yourself. Tell the truth. Ask the Holy Spirit to guide you and help you to rest in the peace of knowing that God, who has numbered every hair on your lovely head, is standing guard over you."

How I wish I had his unwavering faith. Cara thanked Father Nicco and hung up the phone. She buzzed Lia. "Call the producer at *In the Spotlight*. I'll do the interview." She sighed heavily, hoping that she would not regret this.

Chapter 29

Jake hated to call Cara so early on Wednesday morning, but it couldn't be avoided. He'd been in the office until very late the previous night watching and analyzing video he'd obtained from his sources yesterday afternoon until his eyes felt as if they were about to fall out of their sockets. He'd slept poorly, not wanting to face this day. Over the few years that he'd been in this business and his time in the IDF, he'd learned that people can be cruel and despicable, but he didn't know how to make others aware of that without devastating them.

"Hello," Cara said when she answered, her voice sounding husky from sleep.

"Cara, it's Jake. I'm sorry to wake you, but I've had a major break in the case."

"Fantastic," she said sounding more awake. "What is it?

"I think I've found Brianna Hoffman's accomplice."

"You are certainly a fast worker. Who is it?"

"I'd really not rather say over the phone."

"Can we meet somewhere for breakfast? I'm so excited that this might be over soon."

"I think it best that you come to my office," he said. "I picked up some pastries from the Lincoln Bakery if you're hungry."

"OK. I'll be there as soon as I can." She paused. "Oh, and Jake . . ."

"Yes?"

"Thank you."

As he hung up the phone, he wondered when he told her what he'd learned if she would still be thanking him.

*****

Cara knocked on Jake's office door in a little less than an hour after he had called her. She was dressed in jeans, a white ribbed sweater, black suede boots, and silver parka. Her hair was pulled back into a neat ponytail, and she was sporting red ear muffs. She wore very little makeup, and seeing her, he realized how young she really was. At thirty-seven, she was much too young for him he told himself as she walked into the office, an air of expectation illuminating her face.

"Morning. Have a seat," he said.

She plucked off the ear muffs, stuffed them into her pocket, and smoothed her hair. It was evident that she could barely contain her excitement. "So who is the creep who did this to Tam and me?" Cara asked as she perched on the edge of the lawn chair.

"Would you like a bear claw or cinnamon roll?" he said, holding the box in front of her. Cara selected a bear claw, and Jake handed her a napkin to set it on. "How about some coffee or tea?"

"I'm fine," Cara said. "The suspense is killing me, Jake. Tell me what you found out."

Jake sighed heavily and ran his good hand through his wavy black hair. "OK, but I want to caution you not to get too excited about what I found."

She took a bite of the bear claw and swallowed. "Why?"

Jake rose and brought his laptop with him. Taking a seat next to Cara in the other lawn chair, he set the laptop on his desk and clicked on a file, watching as a video loaded. "You remember I was able to ID this woman as the one in the hotel and the one who drove the car with the dancing bears bumper sticker," he said pointing to Brianna Hoffman on the screen.

"Yes, yes," Cara said. She was barely paying attention to him as her eyes were scanning the laptop screen for a clue.

"Well, I began to follow her, and as we guessed, she has an accomplice."

"So who is it?"

Jake hesitated. He rolled up his sleeves, stalling for time. What he was about to show Cara would rock her world even more than the photos that had been slipped through her mail slot.

He looked at her, and she had placed a hand on his prosthesis. God, he ached to actually feel her touch.

"Jake, tell me who it is?"

He clicked the play button of a grainy black and white video. Cara narrowed her eyes, watching intently as the same woman in the photos, Brianna Hoffman, walked out of an apartment building and got into the passenger side of a car. The video focused on the car's license plate then zoomed in on the driver. Jake studied Cara as her look of curiosity transformed into one of disbelief then dismay. He held his breath as he saw Cara view Brianna Hoffman get into the car and kiss a man—kiss Wesley Wells, kiss Cara's husband.

She looked at Jake, pale, as if she were a black and white face from the video. "Wesley? My husband is behind all of this?"

*****

Cara looked up at Jake, wiping her mouth with the back of her hand. "I'm sorry about that. As soon as my stomach settles, I'll empty your wastebasket."

"No, you sit," he said. "And steady yourself."

"But you shouldn't have to empty my vomit," she said closing her eyes.

He grabbed her shoulder. "Cara, I've been to war. Vomit is nothing." After emptying the wastebasket and rinsing it out in the bathroom down the hall, he returned with a glass of water and found Cara with her head lying on his desk.

"Here, have a drink."

She raised her head. The color was returning to her face, but she kept staring as she sipped the water as if the shock of what she'd seen had short-circuited her brain.

Cara set the paper cup on the desk and turned to him. "I'm so sorry. Until now, I've never been one to react this way before—vomiting."

"Well, you've never been betrayed before."

"Yes, that's true. I guess we never know how we are going to react to something until it actually happens."

They sat silently for a while. Jake didn't know what to say to Cara. He knew how to proceed legally, but how to comfort her—that was another thing. He felt like he was back in wilderness training, like he had been dropped in a hostile land without a map and provisions.

"Betrayed?" Cara said, looking beyond him to the window where thin rays of winter morning sun broke through the thick gray clouds. "I never realized before how close that word sounds like betrothed."

She looked at Jake pointedly, tears welling in her eyes. "I wonder if they share a common root? I'll have to look that up."

"Cara, I dreaded telling you this."

She stood and began to pace in his small office. "It's not your fault, Jake," she said, her voice becoming soft.

"There's more video just like that, but you don't need to see it," he said closing the lid of the laptop. "What gets me is for someone who was supposed to be smart, a law school grad and all of that, they were really careless."

She stopped pacing. "Probably because he never thought I'd fight the blackmail charges. I'm usually the kind that wants to keep the peace and avoid controversy. No wonder he was so emphatic that I give into the extortion demands. He probably had those divorce papers prepped and ready to go."

"He probably would have collected the money, revealed the plot, making you look guilty of child sexual abuse, and then divorced you."

She went to the window and gazed out at the gray day. "Thank God, I listened to my heart and Father Nicco's advice." She looked over her shoulder at Jake, "And thank God he sent me to you."

He came to her now and was standing behind her at the window, so close he could feel his attraction for her pulling him toward her. He wanted so much to take her in his arms and comfort her, but he willed himself not to. He was finding resisting her as difficult as repelling his torturers had been.

"Why do you think Wesley did this to me? I could understand maybe growing apart and seeking a divorce—but this, this is overkill." Her breath clouded the cold window, and she drew her finger across it. "First, it was my mother. I could understand her not caring about me, but she did she have to throw herself out of a thirty-three-story building to get away from me? Now Wesley. I could understand a divorce but did he have to grind my life into dust?" She turned and looked at Jake, tears streaming down her cheeks. "What is it about me, Jake, do you think, that makes people want to leave me so spectacularly?"

With his good hand, he brushed the tears from her cheeks and hugged her, resisting the urge to tell her that he didn't understand any of that when all that he wanted was to make love to her and keep her forever.

Chapter 30

Cara's mind wandered while the makeup artist fussed over her face for the *In the Spotlight* interview. *One good thing, if there could be anything good in all of this, is that, at least, I know I wasn't raped in that hotel room.* She folded her hands in her lap. They were freezing from nerves. *Was agreeing to do this interview a mistake?* Jake thought it was. She considered bolting, but she had already agreed to do the show. It would reflect badly on her if she reneged now. As much as she wanted to go on the interview and expose Wesley and Brianna, she pledged to Jake that she wouldn't. He wanted to make sure that they were in police custody before she even dropped a hint that she suspected who was behind the scandal. While she had been in the makeup chair, a tease for *In the Spotlight* had been broadcasted during the noon news on the monitor in the room. It was being billed as an exclusive interview that would "rock Pittsburgh" and would be aired later that evening at 10 p.m. on *In the Spotlight.* The news broadcast cut away to a story on the grounds keeping crew at Heinz Field and how they were preparing the playing field for this Sunday's Super Bowl. With all the turmoil in her life, Cara had forgotten that the city was caught up in the whirlwind of pregame hype.

Marsha Robbins, who appeared much thinner and more wrinkled in person, came into the makeup room and greeted Cara warmly. "As soon as you are done here, we can begin taping. We've set up in the studio. I want this to be casual," she said, touching Cara's hand and smiling, "like you're having a conversation with your best girlfriend."

Best girlfriend who is watched by millions of viewers. Even though she had nothing to hide, Cara knew that she had to be convincing because the court of public opinion was often harsher than the courts of the country's legal system, even when irrefutable evidence was provided.

Cara, her makeup done, was guided into the studio by a crew member. She thanked him and took her seat in a wing chair. She smoothed the skirt of her French blue wool suit and fluffed her silver, blue, and gray printed scarf. Lia told her to wear blue, saying, "It's the color of the Blessed Mother. You can't go wrong with that."

Crew members of the *In the Spotlight's* production team scurried around adjusting the lighting and cameras while one young woman attached a small microphone to her lapel. Then Marsha Robbins appeared, shook her hand, and offered her a drink of water before they began. Cara declined, and as soon as Marsha took her seat, it seemed that the camera's red light came on and Marsha began to introduce the piece and announce Cara as her guest.

Marsha led Cara step-by-step through the events of the awards night and how Cara received the pictures.

"So you don't deny that you are in those photos, naked, doing sexual acts with that young boy?" asked Marsha.

"No, unfortunately, it's me, but as I explained before," Cara said, feeling her cheeks flush with annoyance. She hoped the makeup was heavy enough to conceal the redness. "I was drugged."

Marsha leaned in. "You have proof of that? Why should we believe you? Many have speculated that you got caught and concocted this whole extortion plot as a stunt to exonerate yourself. How do you respond to that?"

She sounded just like Wesley. Angry, Cara curled her toes in her gray pumps, composing herself. "For now, people will have to trust me and those who know me and have vouched for me until the investigators can solve this and prove my innocence."

"So you believe that the investigators will resolve this?"

Cara wanted to blurt out that her husband was a lying cheat and had framed her, but she heard her grandmother in her mind saying, *Cara, darling, you know patience is a virtue.* She steadied herself and calmly replied, "Yes, I do."

"And yet, I have research here that indicates that your husband has just filed for divorce citing cruelty and sexual abuse. Obviously, your husband, the partner in your most intimate relationship, does not believe you."

Cara's eyes stung as she willed herself not to cry. "I prefer not to talk about that at the moment, but I'm confident that I'll be vindicated." She straightened her spine. "In fact, I'm offering a $25,000 reward to anyone who can provide information that leads to an arrest and conviction of the woman who drugged me, and most importantly, who exploited this poor child."

Marsha Robbins tilted her head and peered intently at her. "O.J. offered rewards too, Cara."

Cara chose to ignore her obvious attempt at provocation. "What has been done to me has been dastardly," Cara said, "but it's nothing compared to what has been done to that poor boy. I don't want anyone to lose sight of that. When I heard about how prevalent sex trafficking is during the Super Bowl, I spent this afternoon learning more about the human sex trade, and I'm horrified at what I've found. According to the U.S. State Department, approximately 2 million people are trafficked worldwide each year. Many of the victims are children. It's a global scandal. With the Super Bowl coming to the city, attention has been shed on the problem, but it's not only here during sporting events; children are being used sexually every day on our streets. If any good comes out of this whole sordid affair, I hope that it brings attention to this problem and compels people to take action to save these children and prosecute their traffickers."

"Sounds like you've got another worthy cause on your hands."

"You know," Cara said with a smile and a tilt of her head. "I hadn't thought about that, but yes. Maybe I've been the unfortunate victim of a crime, but maybe it's God's way of shining a light on this despicable problem."

Marsha Robbins turned to stare into the camera. "There you have it. Our exclusive interview with Cara Hawthorne. Visit our *In the Spotlight* website where you can voice your opinion on this interview."

The lights went dark and Marsha rose. She shook Cara's hand again and thanked her. Cara felt a bit like she had been pillaged. The technician removed the microphone, while another stagehand escorted her to the dressing room. She would not give them the satisfaction of seeing her cry. She took a tissue and wiped off some of the heavy makeup, donned her coat, and grabbing her gray Gucci purse, she headed to the parking garage.

When she arrived at her car in the dimly lit corner of the garage, she was alarmed to see a man waiting there. Instinct told her to run, but when the man came walking toward her, she realized it was Jake.

Her shoulders relaxed with relief. "What are you doing here?"

"I like stalking beautiful women."

She smiled. "No, really. What are you doing here?"

"I took my evidence to the FBI while you were taping the interview."

Her heart quickened. "And?"

He stuffed his hands in the pockets of his black jeans. "They were a bit pissed that we solved the case."

"We? You solved the case, Jake. I had nothing to do with it."

His lips turned up into a crooked smile. "You are certainly not like the FBI. They were more than eager to point out how much work they've done on the case. Right now, they are readying arrest warrants for Wesley and Brianna as we speak."

"I guess that should make me happy," she said, "but somehow all I feel is sad."

"That's why I'm here," he said, taking her by the arm and guiding her away from her car. "It's time we channel that sadness into a celebration."

Chapter 31

"Have you eaten?" Jake asked as he started his car.

"Not since the pastry in your office this morning, which I guess doesn't count since I vomited that. I haven't had much of an appetite."

"You need to eat." He drove through town, heading toward the Strip District. "Ever been to Roland's?"

"Yes, of course." She looked sideways at him. "No. I'm a nerd. I was raised in a bubble. I never went out much or to bars when I was single because my grandmother always said nothing good 'went in or came out of one.' Her father was an alcoholic back in Ireland. And then I met Wesley."

"Sweetheart, then it's time to burst through that bubble."

When they arrived at the bar, it was that quiet time between lunch and dinner. The waitress seated them immediately at a table for two that overlooked the parade of humanity that coursed Penn Avenue— everyone from foodies looking for finds in the markets to tourists scooping up Super Bowl paraphernalia.

"I've been so caught up in all of my drama," Cara said, "I haven't thought much about the game except for all of the sex trafficking that may be going on." She shook her head. "Seems like everyone is pretty excited, though."

"Yes, you can feel the excitement building. Things are going to get crazy around here," said Jake, looking around the dimly lit bar. The television was on, and he hoped there soon would be breaking news on it reporting that Wesley and Brianna had been arrested. Although he wasn't sure how Cara would react to see her husband on television.

When the waitress asked what they would like to drink, Jake said, "I'm having a Yuengling." He turned to Cara. "I think you've earned a drink too."

"Since it's only a bit after three, I'd normally turn you down, but after all I've been through, I need something," Cara said, searching the laminated drink menu. "Ah, a hot fudge martini. That's what I'll have."

Jake laughed. "You are such a badass,"

Cara chuckled. "Chocolate fixes everything."

Jake knew from his days in the IDF that after a battle, soldiers needed to unwind. They both ordered fish sandwiches. Then Jake raised his beer. "To Cara, for standing up for yourself and Tam."

Cara raised her martini glass. "No, to you. You did all the digging and work." She looked about to cry. "Poor Tam. I keep thinking about him, wondering what will become of him."

The waitress brought their meals, and Jake took it upon himself to order Cara another martini. While they ate, they talked about the weather forecast for the Super Bowl, if she liked sports, how much the city would profit from hosting the game—everything but what was really on their hearts and minds. When the waitress cleared their dishes, Jake ordered Cara another martini.

Then as Cara became a bit drunk, she began to open up, reminding Jake of a rare flower uncurling its petals.

"You know, Jake," she said, then sipping her drink. There was a looseness about her speech and mannerisms now that he found utterly charming. "Everybody thinks you've got it made when you have money, but they are wrong. It just brings a whole new set of problems."

"That's why I walked away from it," Jake said.

Cara looked at him surprised. "You were wealthy?"

"I told you I came from the same world as you."

Cara brushed her hair back. "So you're rich?"

"Well, not as loaded as you, but yeah, my family wasn't hurting."

"And here I thought you hated me because of my money."

"I didn't hate you."

She looked at him skeptically. "When we first met, you did."

"Ok. I admit when I watched you in that press conference with Father Nicco, I thought you were another spoiled brat who had gotten herself into a jam and was looking for a way to wriggle out of it. But I was wrong."

"So what convinced you that I was legit?"

"How you seemed more concerned about the boy in the photos than your reputation."

Cara slapped the table. "I knew it. That's your problem. You're an idealist."

"My problem?"

"Yes, I've been trying to figure you out. What's behind the terse, no-nonsense, take-no-prisoners hard guy persona? And that's it. Beneath all of that you're an idealist."

Jake ordered them another drink. "So you've figured me out then." He could feel himself smiling against his will. She brought a lot out of him that was against his will. "Tell me more. Enlighten me."

Her blue eyes sparkled like her sapphire earrings. "So you probably grew up wealthy, got bored romancing all the Hadassah girls, dropped out of school, and wanted to do something meaningful with your life, make a difference."

"Doesn't everybody want to make a difference? That's why you do what you do, isn't it?"

"I want to spare people pain. I guess that's a bit idealistic." She stared at him. "So I pegged you then?"

"Not really."

"Then why don't you tell me," Cara said.

"Long story short. I grew up Jewish, with two successful parents who were both physicians and too busy to spend time with me. I was pretty much raised by my *zaide*—that's grandfather for you Gentiles—who was a Holocaust survivor and devoutly observant. I was steeped in Judaism and couldn't quite square my parents, who were really nothing more than cultural Jews, with what my grandfather had taught me. Oh, sure they didn't eat pork, but they couldn't recite the commandments if Moses threatened to break tablet of the law over their heads. When my grandfather died and they began to push me into following in their footsteps to become a doctor, I decided I'd had enough and took off for Israel, eventually joining the IDF."

"Wow. That's impressive."

"I don't know about that. It was a way of getting out from under their thumb and really pissing them off at the same time." He rolled his eyes. "Can you believe they wanted me to be a doctor? Another Jewish doctor." He shook his head. "What a cliché."

"With your charming bedside manner, I'm sure you would have done swell," she said, which made him laugh. He was lost in thought wondering if now that her marriage was over if he would ever get the chance to show Cara how charming he could be at her bedside and in it, when she said, "Funny, isn't it? My grandmother raised me. Both of us raised by grandparents."

"I read something to that effect about you. What was your grandmother like?"

"She was Irish Catholic and a tough cookie, but I guess she had to be. She came here with "nothing but dreams in me pocketbook," Cara said, affecting a brogue.

Jake laughed. "You sound like the Lucky Charms leprechaun."

She reached out and slapped his arm—his prosthetic arm

Aghast, she covered her mouth. "Oh my God, I'm sorry."

"Why? I can't feel a thing there." But he could feel other things like the stirring not just in his loins but in his heart for her. He needed to change the subject. "Are you a tough cookie like her?"

"Not by half, but she's really the reason I decided to fight back against the blackmailers. I've always been rather shy, and I don't know how many times she must have told me over the years, that I needed to stand up for myself because nobody else in this life will." Cara's face suddenly looked sad. "She was right. I thought my husband was in my corner, but now I know that wasn't true."

Jake touched her arm and noticed she was tearing up. "I stood up with you," he said softly.

"But you were being paid." Cara wiped her eyes. "Damn the money again. Wesley only loved me for my money, and you only helped me because of it." She was going from relaxed to maudlin. Cara didn't need to be seen in public drunk, or crying, or, God forbid, both.

"Let's get out of here." Jake signaled the waitress, threw down a stack of bills, and helped Cara on with her black wool coat.

He saw her recoil when they emerged into the cold evening air. She was a bit unsteady on her feet in her gray stiletto heels, so he took her arm and guided her down the sidewalk. "I'll drive you home."

"Oh, you don't have to."

"Cara, the last thing you need is a DUI. Take it from me. You're drunk."

"But what about my car. It's still in the garage?"

"We can get it later."

They walked down a side street, Cara wiping her eyes with the back of her gloves. "I'll make sure to add it to your bill."

He halted and whipped her to himself. "Stop that. There is no bill, Cara. There's not going to be any bill. I didn't do this for the money. I did this for you."

"No, you didn't. You took me on as a favor to Father Nicco. You admitted it before."

"But things changed along the way."

She looked defiant, not believing him. The first casualty of betrayal was innocence. "So you did it for me because you're such an idealist?"

He backed her up against the wall and kissed her like he was storming a rampart, like she was some landmark to be captured. And when his lips left hers, he held her away and looked into her eyes. "No, Cara. I did it because I'm a mercenary. I'm in it for myself and I want you."

Chapter 32

Cara reveled in his kiss. It was good to be desired with such passion, and it only made her realize how much passion had been lacking when she was with Wesley. *Wesley?* Even inebriated, she knew that the last thing she needed now was to get involved with another man. She was losing control of everything. She'd just been served the divorce papers and here she was kissing Jake. Cara pulled away and looked at him. His gaze was dark and imposing, but it wasn't his look that intimidated her. It was the knowledge that she was powerless to contain the desire she felt for him.

"Jake, I can't. I can't do this. We're in the middle of the street. What if someone sees me? I'm not even divorced, and I feel so . . . so damaged by all that has happened that I don't even know if I'm capable of making rational judgments anymore."

"That's OK," he said. "I'm a patient man. I'm trained to wait and watch and when the time is right, to strike."

Cara turned her head before he kissed her again. "But there may never be a time to strike," she said softly.

He kissed her neck, and then whispered in her ear, his breath hot on her skin.

"Don't worry. I create them."

*****

Jake was silent on the way home, and Cara felt so disoriented, she wasn't sure if it was from the martinis or his kiss. One thing she knew was that the life she thought she had was irrevocably changed. She could not go back; she could only go on. But how? She looked at Jake, his one natural hand and his one prosthetic one gripping the steering wheel.

"You never told me how it happened."

He looked over at her. "How what happened?"

"How you lost your arm."

"A really pretty client twisted it off when I refused to kiss her."

Cara smiled. "Seriously."

"We were on patrol and were ambushed. A grenade went off. I took a hit in that arm and in my leg," he said touching his right thigh. "Then I was captured."

Cara felt sick to her stomach thinking of Jake in that situation. "How long were you held?"

He looked straight ahead, emotionless, but Cara could see a slight twitching in his jaw. "Three days."

"Did they mistreat you?"

"No."

Cara sighed with relief.

"No, I wasn't mistreated. I was tortured."

Cara looked at him, any self-pity she felt for herself and her plight evaporating.

"They poured acid on my wounds and went through a few mock beheadings. They really loved me because I was an American and a Jew. I was the daily double."

Cara heard a sob escape her lips and felt warm tears running down her cheeks.

"I was rescued before they could actually go through with the beheading."

"I'm sorry," was all Cara could muster. The distress of thinking of Jake alone in another land in pain, terrified, and near death rendered her speechless.

"Don't be."

The sun was nearly set, leaving a glow of red on the horizon. After some miles passed, she found the courage to speak again. "Was it hard adjusting to the—the loss?"

"You can say it, Cara. The loss of my arm. I know I'm missing an arm. It was hard physically, dealing with the pain and learning to do things with a prosthetic. But the hardest part was dealing with it emotionally, psychologically. I mean who wants a one-armed man?" He smiled devilishly and looked over at her. "Besides *The Fugitive?*"

Cara laughed. "Oh, you are just awful." She wanted to tell him that anyone would want him, but it seemed inappropriate and besides he had pulled in front of her house. She looked at the huge Victorian. It would be so lonely now. Even though she was enraged at Wesley, she had liked being married and planning a future with someone.

"Come on," Jake said. "I'll help you in."

"I've gone through nothing like you," she looked at him. "But I feel like I've lost a piece of myself."

He took her hand. "You'll get used to it. And you'll find that every setback has its benefits. I save money on sunscreen now. I don't have to worry about putting it on that arm." She laughed. She hadn't noticed before how funny he could be. It was as if in kissing her, he'd let down all his defenses.

As Jake walked Cara up her stairs, she felt an even greater sense of loss. Now that she'd found out who was blackmailing her, there would be no need for them to see each other again. It was best that way, she thought, as they alighted to the landing. He was too much of a temptation for her, and she really needed time to straighten her life out.

"Thank you, Jake," she said, extending her hand. "For all of your help."

"You act like I'm going somewhere."

"You've solved the case. There's no reason for you and I . . . "

He stepped closer until he was mere inches from kissing her again, when suddenly the door opened, and Cara and Jake saw Sophia standing in the doorway with a small boy cowering behind her.

"Tam!" Cara exclaimed. "Jake, it's him. We've found Tam!"

"More like he found you," Sophia said.

Chapter 33

The boy backed away as Cara and Jake rushed inside. Cara bent and took his hand to speak to him, but he recoiled, crying something hysterically that she didn't understand.

Jake crouched and touched Cara's back. "You have to remember; he only knows you as the woman he was forced to pose with. He's probably still afraid of you."

"But he trusted me enough to come here." She turned back to the child. "I won't hurt you," she said, desperately trying to convey by her facial expression and body language that she meant no harm.

"When and how did he get here?" Jake asked Sophia.

"Only minutes before you two did. I was feeling a lot better, and I decided to cook dinner. I was longing for a steak, and I even took my rental car out to the store and bought some. I was about to light the grill outside when I heard the doorbell ring. He was standing on the porch shivering, and I thought he was selling candy or something for a school fundraiser. When I opened the door, he handed me this, and kept saying: 'Alex say trouble. Come here.'" Sophia handed Cara a business card.

"It's my card." She looked at Jake. "Remember, I gave Alex and him one that night on the street and told them to contact me anytime." She felt panic stirring in her.

"Is Alex in trouble?" Jake asked the boy, obviously arriving at the same conclusion that Cara had.

"Alex say trouble. Come here."

Cara sighed and rose. "I wish I knew Thai."

"I do speak a little from when I lived in Thailand as a child," said Sophia. "I understand it more than I can speak it. He keeps talking about someone called The General and Mama."

"General," said the boy. "Mama" and then he rattled off what sounded like gibberish to Cara.

Sophia strained to make out what he was telling her. "Something about this general character being very angry with him and Alex getting hit." Sophia listened some more. "Alex told him to run and go to the house on the card."

"However did he find it?" Cara asked.

Sophia said some words to the boy and by the light in his eyes, Cara could tell that he understood the question. "He said that Alex showed him how to get here before, and he also told him to hide money in the tongue of his tennis shoe in case he ever needed it." The small child showed the small slit on the underside of his shoe where he'd hidden the money. Cara could make out the word "taxi" in the string of Thai words.

"Alex must have known something bad was going to happen and showed him how to get here by taxi," Cara said, looking at the boy. "Where is Alex? Is Alex OK?"

Sophia translated and the boy became very upset. "I don't think he knows. He said they—I guess he means whoever this general is—was very angry. He said he was going to take care of Tam too." The boy was almost hysterical now.

"Ask him if the general hurt him?"

"Alex," said the boy, who boy became very animated and made a jerking motion toward Jake's crotch.

Sophia smiled ruefully. "I think he said that the general hurt Alex who was protecting him, and Tam escaped by yanking The General's 'chain,' so to speak."

Cara looked puzzled.

Sophia rolled her eyes. "Do I have to explain everything, Cara? Tam went for The General's crotch."

"I don't care what he did," said Cara, "I'm just glad he got away. But

I'm worried about Alex. What do you think we should do, Jake? Do we call the police?"

Jake thought for a moment. "We could, but if we do, they'll want to know how you know all of this. If you tell them about Tam, they'll put him into some kind of protective custody."

Sophia looked at Cara. "You can't do that. He came to you for help. You can see he's scared out of his mind. We have to watch over him."

Cara didn't know what to do.

"What do you think, Jake? What should I do?"

"When I'm uncertain, I usually advise doing nothing. Why don't you have him stay here for a while? Obviously, he's a throw-away kid so no one except Mama and whoever this General is will be looking for him."

"OK," Cara said, her head still reeling from the martinis. "Sophia, do you think you can take care of him? Make him something to eat? Give him a bath? Get him something to wear? I think Jake and I should go and look for Alex."

"You're going to trust me with that?" Sophia asked.

"Why, aren't you capable?" asked Jake.

Sophia smiled at him. "I'm very capable; it's just that I'm the family screw-up."

"Well, so am I," said Jake, "but I'm sure even a royal screw-up like you can take care of him."

"Thanks for the vote of confidence," Sophia said. She turned and said something to Tam in Thai and then led him into the kitchen.

"You should go put on warmer clothes," Jake said.

Cara was still wearing the suit she'd worn to the interview. She went upstairs and changed into fleece pants and top and boots. When she came back downstairs into the kitchen, Sophia was scrambling eggs for the boy. Jake stood and held out an aluminum insulated container. "Sophia made us some coffee."

Cara was surprised. "Thank you and thanks for taking care of Tam."

"Welcome. I know how to deal with lost souls," Sophia said.

*****

For the next three hours, Jake and Cara drove throughout downtown Pittsburgh and some of the areas Jake knew from his investigation where Alex often solicited. They asked dozens of people if they had seen Alex, but no one had. Cold, tired, and discouraged, Jake drove Cara home.

"Thanks, Jake. For helping me look for Alex," she said as they pulled in front of her house.

"Hey, I told you that you weren't getting rid of me so fast."

"I hope Alex is OK."

"He's street smart. He's probably fine." Jake touched her shoulder. "You look exhausted. Get some sleep, and I'll call you in the morning. Then we can see if we can find him."

He reached over and kissed her cheek and handed her the Thermos. "Go on in. Make sure Sophia hasn't taken Tam out clubbing."

Cara chuckled and walked up the stairs and let herself into the house. She waved to Jake who had watched her get in safely. When she closed the door, she noticed that the lights were dimmed and the house was quiet. She tiptoed into the kitchen and put the Thermos into the sink. Lights were flickering in the adjacent Family Room. She looked in. The television was still on, but curled up on the sectional was Sophia in a pair of flannel pajamas, her blonde hair hanging loosely about her face, looking like the girl next door who was babysitting and not the image of the party girl sexpot that the media had created. Lying next to her and holding her hand was Tam. He looked innocent too and was wearing a pair of Sophia's leggings and an old gray sweatshirt of Wesley's the he'd gotten on a ski trip to Colorado.

As Cara shut off the television, Sophia stirred and stretched. "Any luck finding Alex?"

Cara shook her head. "No." Cara's gaze fell on Tam. "How was he?" she whispered.

"Ate like a horse, poor kid. After the eggs, I made him two grilled cheese sandwiches too, and he gobbled them up."

"I guess we should put him in the guest room."

"I promised him I wouldn't leave him, so we can just sleep here for tonight until he gets used to us."

"OK. It's probably best not to disturb him anyway. He's sleeping so peacefully."

"What do you think is going to happen to him, Cara?"

"I don't know."

Sophia brushed his hair back. "Well, I want to keep him."

"I do too. But he's not like a stray cat. He's a child. Maybe daddy can help. He has so many connections."

"I'd wait a bit before telling him about Tam," said Sophia.

"Why?"

"He doesn't even know I'm staying here yet. Now, with Wesley filing for divorce. Let's not spring Tam on him until we tell him about all of that. We don't want to overwhelm him."

Yes, Cara thought, she had not spoken to her father about the divorce yet, and neither he nor Sophia knew that Wesley was behind the blackmail photos. It was probably wise to keep Tam with them if only because he could be a witness when charges were brought against Wesley.

"Yes, we don't want to give him a heart attack or compromise his chances for the ambassadorship. We'll keep Tam here with us for as long as possible."

"Good." Sophia stretched and covered Tam. "It's nice to take care of someone besides me. I haven't done too great of a job taking care of myself, but I'd really like to do better with him. He's never had a chance."

It was times like these when the real Sophia shined through that Cara wanted to hug her sister and forget all of the animosity that had built up between them.

Chapter 34

Exhausted, Cara slept deeply but with disjointed dreams of searching for lost shoes, jewelry, and her driver license. She woke with a start when Sophia touched her arm. "Cara, wake up. The FBI is here."

"FBI?" She rose to her elbows, her heartbeat going from zero to panic in two seconds. "What time is it?" Her eyes flew to the clock. It was nearly half past seven. Too early. "What do they want? Where's Tam?"

"They wouldn't tell me. They want to talk to you. *Immediately.* They stressed immediately. When I saw people at the door, I moved Tam upstairs and told him to be quiet. I put them in the den. I hope that was OK."

Cara's mouth was dry, and she had a dull headache. This was not the time for a hangover. "Do I have time to dress?"

"No, just throw on a robe and get downstairs," Sophia said, pulling her by the upper arm. "I hate entertaining them. Police make me nervous."

Cara shrugged off Sophia's grip on her arm and rose. "OK. Tell them I'll be down in a minute."

Sophia disappeared. Cara tucked her feet into slippers and wrapped her terry cloth robe around her, cinching it tightly around her waist. She went to the bathroom, brushed her teeth, and ran a comb through her hair. If they were expecting a glamorous heiress, the agents would be severely disappointed, she thought, as she looked in the mirror. Her face looked as drained as she felt.

Cara wasn't sure why, but she was nervous as she came into the den. She hadn't done anything wrong. Surely, there was nothing illegal about giving shelter to a child who had come to her home in the cold. "I'm sorry; I'm not dressed," she said to Agents Crosley and Pappas, who were standing in the doorway. "I guess you've met my sister, Sophia?"

"Yes, we met," Agent Crosley said.

"Please have a seat," Cara said. "How can I help you?"

Agent Pappas took a seat and leaned forward, his elbows resting on his knees like he was calling her into a huddle. "We'd like to ask you a few questions."

"About what?"

"Is this yours?" Agent Crosley held out a slip of paper. It was Cara's business card.

"Yes, it's my card. Can I get you coffee or something?"

"No," said Agent Crosley. "Can you explain what it might be doing on the body of someone we believe to be a male prostitute who was found slain last night?"

"Slain?" Cara felt her limbs begin to tremble. She slowly lowered herself onto the sofa. "What are you talking about?"

"A positive ID hasn't been made yet, but your card was found on his body."

Cara inhaled deeply in an attempt to hold back her tears as she asked, "Was he about sixteen and Asian? Did he have a tattoo of stars on his knuckles?"

Agent Pappas sat upright, looking highly interested. "We can't confirm that, but why do you ask? Do you know many male prostitutes?"

At that moment, the doorbell rang and whoever was there would not take his finger off the button as it kept on ringing, antagonizing Cara's aching head. "Sophia, will you get that?" Cara asked. Her sister left to get the door, and it seemed that instantly Jake came striding into the den carrying his briefcase like he was leading a charge. "Jake what are you doing here?"

"I was on my way to bring your car back when Sophia called me to tell me that the FBI was at your door. I came right over."

Sophia stood in the doorway. Jake looked at the agents. "What's this about?"

"This doesn't concern you," said Agent Crosley,

"They're here because they found my card on the body of a male prostitute. Oh, Jake, do you think it's Alex?"

"Don't say anything, Cara, without having a lawyer present," he said, setting his briefcase on her desk.

"Hold on, Rambo," said Agent Pappas as he rose to his feet. "She doesn't need a lawyer. We just want to ask her a few questions."

Agent Pappas turned back to Cara. "Now why would a young male prostitute have your business card?"

"If you'd have been doing your job and investigating the blackmail case, he might not be dead," Jake said, his jaw set with restrained rage.

"Yeah, why don't you concentrate on catching criminals instead of harassing innocent people," said Sophia.

"She doesn't need to be here," Agent Crosley said, nodding toward Sophia.

"She can stay," Cara said. "She may as well hear this. It will avoid having to explain it all again later."

"What is she talking about, Gold?" Pappas asked, staring down Jake.

"With all that was going on with securing the city for the Super Bowl, Cara was afraid that her investigation would be put on the back burner by the FBI. She hired me to investigate on her behalf. I followed some leads and obtained some surveillance photos of the perp and the kid, and a few days ago, we went uptown and started asking around, seeing if anyone could ID the kid. We got a nibble. A young Asian male named Alex. He said he knew the kid, and produced him, but both of them were terrified of someone they called 'The General' when Cara offered to help them. She even offered to take them in. When she couldn't persuade them to leave, she gave them her card and told them that if either of them ever changed their minds or needed help, to please contact her."

"Oh, so you were on a rescue mission?" Agent Pappas said sarcastically. "That still doesn't explain why this kid was hacked to death like he was a piece of meat. Perhaps someone was trying to shut him up?"

"Hacked to death?" Cara began to cry. Sophia came and sat next to her on the sofa, taking Cara's hand.

"When was he killed?" Jake asked.

Agent Crosley looked at her file. "Estimated time of death is between 2 and 7 p.m. yesterday."

"Cara and I were at a late lunch during that time. You can verify it with the restaurant, and I've got receipts to prove it."

"So what were you two doing together?" asked Agent Pappas.

"None of your business," Jake shot back, "but if you must know, we were solving her blackmail case."

Jake went to his briefcase and produced a folder. "Here is a still photo of the woman with Cara on the hotel's surveillance camera. Here she is in the parking lot with the boy—the same boy in the extortion photos. And here, Inspector Clouseau," Jake said, waving another photo in front of Agent Pappas' face, "is a photo of Cara's husband making out with the woman in his car and another of him secreting the boy into the hotel."

Sophia looked at Cara. "Oh my God!"

"I . . . we didn't know," Agent Crosley said suddenly looking sick.

"We've been busy sweeping the area for bombs and were just pulled in off that when they found this body," said Agent Pappas, looking a bit sheepish.

"Obviously, that's them," said Crosley. "No offense, Ms. Hawthorne, but for an attorney, your husband certainly isn't very bright. He was very sloppy. He left clues everywhere." Cara wanted to reply, Clues you never pursued, but she held her tongue.

"That's because he assumed that I'd cave to the extortion demands," explained Cara. "He never counted on me fighting back. I think he figured that I would pay the $250,000 and then sue me for divorce, citing that I had given into the blackmail scheme because I was guilty. Then he would use that to get as much from me in a divorce settlement as possible. "

"When did you all learn this?" Crosley asked.

"The day before yesterday," said Jake. "I took what I found to your superior officer early yesterday afternoon. You people need to get your signals straightened out."

"That still doesn't solve this boy's murder," said Agent Pappas.

"Where was he found?" asked Jake.

Crosley read from the file. "In a dumpster in uptown. The victim had numerous puncture wounds and lacerations. Now, let me show you a photo. We believe this is the murder weapon. It was found near the scene. Do you recognize this?"

When Crosley showed the photo to Cara and Sophia, they both gasped. It was an eight-by-ten glossy of Wesley's antique cheese knife.

Chapter 35

They tried to conceal it, but Cara could tell that the agents were ecstatic that both she and Sophia had identified the cheese knife as belonging to Wesley. They were probably relieved because solving the murder so quickly would absolve them from some of the responsibility for lagging on the blackmail case. After Crosley and Pappas confirmed that the cheese knife definitely belonged to Wesley, the agents left. They now had Wesley as an extortionist and murderer.

And I have him as an adulterer. Cara closed the door behind them and covered her face with her hands. "Oh, will this nightmare ever end? Now, we're not only dealing with blackmail, human trafficking, and child sexual abuse but murder as well. Poor Alex."

"Do you think they'll charge Wesley with murder?" Sophia asked.

"Yes," said Jake. "He has the motive, and they've found the murder weapon. I'm sure they will check for his fingerprints. It's all

JANICE LANE PALKO

circumstantial so far unless they have an eye witness, but probably enough to convict him."

"Tam," cried Cara, looking up at them. "Do you think he witnessed Alex's death? Do you think Wesley is The General? How could he be? Surely, I would have known if my own husband were running a child sex trafficking ring."

"Not to be critical, Cara," Sophia said, "but you would also think you'd know if he were cheating on you. Sometimes you can be a little slow on the uptake."

"He always said he hoped to be appointed Attorney General someday," Cara said in disbelief. "Maybe that's where 'The General' persona comes from."

"Where is Tam now?" asked Jake.

"He's sleeping in the guest room," Sophia said. "I hid him there when the FBI showed up. I didn't want them to take him from us."

"That might be best for now," Jake said. "He may be in danger. If he did witness Alex's murder, then it's best that no one knows he's here. It will be safer that way. Even if it turns out that Wesley has murdered Alex, I'm sure "mama" and the others involved in this shit will still be anxious to get one of their sex slaves back."

"Or shut him up," added Sophia.

Cara straightened. "I've been thinking all night about Tam and the

288

kids we saw on the street. I can't forget about them. I want to help them. I want to make it as hard as possible for people to exploit children and for the ones who have been, I want to rescue them from that life and give them a new one."

"What are you going to do? Start another foundation?" Sophia asked.

"Yes, unless someone has a better idea. I know Comfort Connection has been rocked with the blackmail scandal, but now that my name will soon be cleared, I hope things will start to turn around. I think I could manage both."

"I always like to strike at the root of a problem," said Jake. "If you don't mind working with me some more, I'd love to nail some of these bastards. Investigate who's behind all of this."

Cara smiled. "I think I could put up with you."

Sophia cleared her throat. "I know everyone thinks I'm some kind of screw-up, but, Cara, I've really enjoyed taking care of Tam. I don't know how I'd be able to help, but I'd like to work with you. Help kids like Tam."

"Really?" Cara took her sisters hand. "For so long it seemed as if we were working against each other. I'd love to work with you too."

"I was thinking maybe I could design those dolls I was showing you and then sell them to raise funds."

"That would be a great idea. As soon as we get some funding, I can front you the money."

"That's fine, but I think I have some favors to call in that should be able to fund my doll enterprise."

"You sure?" Cara said.

"I'm certain," Sophia said.

"You know this is going to hit the fan as soon as they find Wesley. Are you prepared to face that?" Jake said, eyeing Cara.

"I guess I should make some phone calls. I should alert father and the office. And, of course, Father Nicco. I'm going to need his advice on how to proceed with helping these abused children. He'll be invaluable; he has so many contacts."

"You might want to hold another press conference," said Jake. "Be out in front of this before everyone forms their own opinions from the media speculation that's bound to go crazy when a story as sensational as this breaks."

"What about *In the Spotlight*?" asked Sophia. "I think it would be smart to let them know what's going on before they air your interview."

While Sophia cooked breakfast for everyone, Cara called Father Nicco. He sounded deeply distressed when he learned that Wesley was now also a suspect in a murder. He offered to arrange for a press conference at five later that afternoon, that way the media could broadcast it live during their early newscast. Cara agreed but suggested that they hold it at Comfort Connection this time.

She then called the office and filled Lia in on what was going on and instructed her to arrange for a press conference. After Lia's shock had worn off, Cara also had Lia contact the producer of *In the Spotlight,* and the show was definitely interested in having Cara conduct a second, exclusive interview.

Her last call was her most difficult to make. It was to her father. She'd been putting him off. It was bad enough to have disgraced the family by a sensational divorce but to now have to tell him that Wesley was also wanted for murder was just too much.

When Sheila put her call through, Cara immediately sensed the buoyancy in her father's voice when he said, "Good morning, Cara dear. You're up bright and early. I take it you've heard the rumors?"

"I'm sorry, father. No, I don't know what you're talking about."

"It hasn't been announced yet, but I can tell you off the record, that I'm officially being nominated by the president to be the next ambassador to the U.N. I've been so monopolized with this vetting process I was never able to return your call. I don't know how the media got wind of it."

Finally, some good news, thought Cara. "That's wonderful. Congratulations! I can't think of anyone more qualified for the position. When will the news be made public?"

"In a few days. Then, of course, I'll need to be confirmed."

"But you should sail through that."

"I should hope."

Cara felt bad that her news was going to put the damper on her father's, but she needed to tell him, especially now that his son-in-law was wanted for extortion and murder. She hoped that would not have any bearing on his appointment."

"So how have you been?" he asked.

"That's why I'm calling. It seems the unpleasantness just keeps on multiplying. I'm not sure if you're aware, but Wesley is suing me for divorce."

"Seriously, Cara? I heard something to that effect in passing while I was in Washington, but I assumed it was some nonsense from the tabloids."

"Unfortunately, it is true."

"Cara, darling, I'm so sorry. Why is he doing this?"

"At first, I thought it was simply because he didn't believe that I was innocent, but other things have come to light that reveal that there is much more to it."

"Such as?"

"Jake Gold, the private investigator, and I have been trying to track down who was behind the photos, and we started working backward by identifying the child in the photos."

"Were you able to find him?" Her father sounded so hopeful.

"Actually, he found us in a manner of speaking. Unfortunately, it took the death of a young man to reveal that Wesley is not who he led us all to believe," she felt her lower lip beginning to tremble. She bit it to keep from falling apart.

"What do you mean?"

"Last night the boy in the photos showed up on my doorstep. He was hysterical."

"Out of the clear blue, he showed up at your house?"

"Yes, and no. Jake and I were able to trace the woman who drugged me, and it's someone named Brianna Hoffman. Jake discovered that she works with Wesley. Apparently, they have been having an affair."

"That bastard. Oh, Cara, I don't know what to say. I'm speechless."

She wiped a tear that had skipped down her cheek. "It seems that they cooked up this scheme using the child prostitute as a way to extort money from me, thinking that I would be too ashamed to fight the allegations. Then they would use my giving into the blackmailer's demands as a trap, making me appear guilty and taking me to the cleaners."

"How vile."

"I'm afraid it gets worse." Cara sighed, knowing that this tale of woe would be something that would be attached to her reputation for the rest of her life. There would never be any escaping it. "When I got home last night, the little boy who was in the photos with me was waiting on my doorstep. Terrified. He doesn't speak English so it was difficult to understand what he was trying to tell me."

"He came to your home?"

"Yes, but when the FBI arrived this morning, things became clearer."

"FBI? You called in the FBI? Why didn't you tell me? Why hasn't anyone alerted me to this? The president is going to be apoplectic when word of this gets out. He specifically stressed that he wanted no scandals associated with me."

"What has happened to me surely does not impugn your reputation. I'm sure the president will be able to see that."

"I hope so," said her father. "What did the FBI want?"

"A teen prostitute named Alex, who identified the boy in the photos for us, was found murdered yesterday uptown. Because I had given him my business card, telling him that if either he or the boy ever needed help, to please contact me, the card was found on his body. The FBI came looking for me, to question me about his murder."

"You a murderer? That's preposterous."

"We told them what we knew, what we'd found out about Wesley, and that I had an alibi for the time of the murder."

"It was probably his pimp who killed this Alex. I've been learning a lot about these sex traffickers from the news reports and how they love events like the Super Bowl. These people who exploit children are soulless. And can be very violent. Please be careful."

"I can assure you, we will," Cara said, closing her eyes to shut out the image of Alex being mutilated in her mind.

"Where is the child now?"

"He's here. We think he witnessed Alex's murder."

"Good heavens! Did you tell the FBI that? They'll want to question the boy."

"No, Tam—that's the boy's name—was so distraught, and I promised him he'd be safe with me until we can figure out what's best for him."

"Especially since the murderer is still out there. The boy could be in danger."

"I don't think so," Cara said solemnly. "They're going to charge Wesley with Alex's murder."

She heard him gasp. "Wesley? How do they make the leap from extortion to murder?"

"Because they found the murder weapon. And it belonged to Wesley.

They believe he wanted to silence Alex so that he couldn't expose the extortion plot."

"Oh, my goodness, Cara. I don't know what to say. I'm finding it difficult to believe that Wesley could ever murder someone."

"I had a hard time believing he could be guilty of adultery and extortion too," she said, hearing the bitterness sneaking into her voice.

"How do they know the murder weapon is Wesley's?"

"Alex was stabbed to death with an antique cheese knife. Wesley's antique cheese knife. I recognized it. There's no mistaking it. I'm going to hold another press conference this afternoon at five to get ahead of the scandal before it breaks and the media puts their spin on it. Father Nicco is going to accompany me."

"If you don't mind, I'd like to come as well, to offer my support. I am beyond heartbroken for you, the young man who died, this little fellow—what's his name?—Tram."

"Tam," she corrected her father

"And for Wesley," he said. "How did we not see him go so wrong?"

"I keep asking myself that."

Laurence Hawthorne sighed heavily. "I guess with some people, you just never really know them."

Chapter 36

When Cara came into the kitchen, Jake was eating pancakes. The radio was on and Sophia was humming along as she hovered near the stove whipping up another batch. "Have a seat," she said when she spied Cara. "Yours will be ready in a minute. How did your calls go?"

"As well as can be expected. Father Nicco suggested I hold another press conference. I've scheduled it for five at my office, and then I'm going to tape a follow-up segment for *In the Spotlight* at seven. And I don't believe it, but father asked to come to the press conference as a show of support."

"I bet he did," Sophia said. "Did he tell you that he's going to be nominated to become Ambassador to the UN? It hasn't been confirmed, but they just reported it on the radio. Nothing like wanting to hog the limelight."

"No, he seemed very concerned. He could be invaluable with his

297

diplomatic connections once he becomes the ambassador. He said to be careful. Some of these pimps can be very violent."

"You didn't tell him I was staying here, did you?"

"No, but don't you think you should?"

Sophia sat at the island, placing another stack of pancakes in front of Cara. "I'll tell him soon enough."

"I'm not worried about pimps," said Jake.

"Neither am I," said Sophia.

They all looked at her. "I'm not trying to sound like Mr. Commando here," Sophia said with a nod to Jake. "But no one knows I'm here. No one knows I know anything about what's going on."

"All the same," Cara said. "I think we all need to be on our toes as we will, so to speak, be starting to step on theirs."

As Cara and Jake brainstormed the best course of action to take next, Sophia fixed some more pancakes and decorated them with a smiley face of syrup for Tam. "I'm going to see if my buddy is awake yet."

Cara looked at Jake and lowered her voice as Sophia left carrying the plate of pancakes. "I can't believe she's serving him breakfast in bed—she's usually on the other end of that arrangement."

Jake gave her a penetrating look. "Things change, people change, Cara." Before she could ponder what he meant, Sophia came back into the kitchen, looking very worried.

"I think Tam's sick," she said. "He seems warm to me, and he wasn't hungry. When he went into the bathroom to pee, I heard him crying in pain. I think he needs to see a doctor."

"God only knows what kinds of diseases the kid has come in contact with while being shopped around to every pervert in town," said Jake.

"What do we do?" Cara asked. "We can't just show up with a strange kid at a pediatrician's office or go to the emergency room with him, not when he could be in danger."

"But he's really sick, Cara," Sophia said. "We have to do something."

"Let me call Father Nicco," Cara said. "There's a pediatrician we refer children from Comfort Connection to who's on the Board of Directors of Catholic Charities, but I'm afraid if I call her, what with all the suspicion cast on me, she'll hang up on me or turn me in for having a child that's not my own. Perhaps if Father Nicco contacted her, explained the situation, and vouched for us, she'd see Tam on the sly." Cara went to the den to make the call while Sophia began to look up Tam's symptoms on the Internet on the laptop Cara kept in the kitchen.

"OK," Cara said, coming back in. "It took some arm twisting, but we can take him to Children's Hospital. Father Nicco convinced the doctor. Sophia and I can drive him there."

Sophia looked up from the computer screen. "I'm still a bit banged up. I can't go. No one knows I'm here."

"That's right," Cara said, her shoulders slumping.

"I'll go with you," Jake said.

"You sure?" Cara asked.

"Hey, I'm in this as much as you are, and if they sic the cops on us, I want to be there."

"While you're gone, I'm going to pile on the makeup to cover the bruises and do some errands, and then go to the store to buy Tam some clothes," Sophia said.

"Are you sure you feel OK? How is your head?" asked Cara.

"As crazy as ever," said Sophia. "I'm fine, and I found an app for your iPhone that translates into Thai. It may help in a pinch. Give me your phone, and I'll download it for you."

Cara quickly ran ahead to get dressed while Sophia and Jake wrapped the lethargic Tam in a quilt. Sophia kissed his warm forehead before Cara and Jake carried him through the breezeway to the garage. Tam was crying when they pulled out, and Cara noticed her sister wiping away tears as she stood in front of the living room window and watched them pull away.

*****

At Children's Hospital, Cara pulled the car in front of the entrance to the Emergency Room and stepped out of the car, looking for the hospital chaplain, a young priest named Father Kieran Mulroney, who Father Nicco said would be awaiting their arrival. Inside the vestibule, she saw a fresh-faced young man bouncing on his toes wearing a black parka. *Could that be him?* As she tried to discover if he were wearing a clerical collar, the young man hustled toward her.

"Cara, I'm Father Kieran," he called.

Cara dipped her head into the car. "It's him, Jake."

Jake opened the door of Cara's car and unbuckled Tam.

"I'm Cara," she said, as the young priest held out his hand and she shook it. "Thank you for helping us." Jake emerged from the car and reached in and picked up the lethargic child. "This is Jake and Tam," she said. Jake nodded at the priest.

"Go inside with him while I park the car," said Cara, who left Jake, Tam, and Father Mulroney at the curb and quickly pulled her Escalade into a short-term Emergency Department parking space. She dashed back to them in the cold, her coat and scarf flapping in the breeze and met them in the vestibule.

"I was just telling Jake that the bishop called and explained the situation. He asked me to text the doctor when you arrived." His attention was on his phone's screen as he tapped in characters. The message sent, Father Mulroney, looked up and put a hand on Jake's shoulder. Now inside the lobby of the Emergency Room, the priest peaked inside the blanket at Tam and gently touched the boy's cheek. "Would you like me to bless him?"

Jake shrugged, deferring to Cara.

"Oh, yes. Please," she said. "That would be so kind of you."

Father Mulroney touched Cara's elbow. "Let's get him registered first."

With Jake carrying the boy, Father Mulroney led them to the woman at the registration desk. "This is the boy I was telling you about."

"Oh yes, we were notified that the doctor is on her way and to send you to Room 3."

The large doors separating the waiting area from the exam rooms opened and Father Mulroney showed them inside, ushering them into Exam Room 3.

"Tam," Jake said, "I'm going to lay you on the table, but we'll be here with you." The boy was so sluggish it was impossible to detect whether he understood what was going on or not.

Cara was amazed at the care with which Jake was taking with the child. How could a soldier, trained to kill and destroy, be so gentle?

The boy moaned as he was placed on the exam table. Cara sat near Tam holding his hand while Father Mulroney raised his hands over the boy and said:

"Lord, our God, your Son Jesus Christ welcomed little children and blessed them. Stretch out your right hand over Tam, who is sick. Grant that, he be made well again, that he be returned to his family and to the community of your holy Church and give you thanks and praise. We ask this through Christ our Lord."

"Amen," said Cara as the priest made the sign of the cross over Tam. As he was concluding, a small, slight woman with short salt and pepper hair wearing a white lab coat walked in accompanied by a young Asian man in scrubs that were printed with little monkeys.

The woman thrust out her hand. "Cara, Dr. Roth. Nice to see you again. This is Dr. Wu, he's a resident here. I asked him to join me since Dr. Wu hails from Thailand and can translate."

"Thank you both," said Cara. "This is my friend Jake Gold."

"Jake?" said Dr. Roth, her face looking as white as her lab coat as she swiveled to look behind her. "What are you doing here?"

"You two know each other?" asked Cara.

Jake scowled. "Yes," he said tersely, signaling to Cara that he did not wish to elaborate.

"How have you been?" asked Dr. Roth, obviously moved and distracted by Jake's presence.

If Jake was moved by her presence, he did not let it show. "I assume Bishop Fiorito told you about Tam's background and that his life may be in danger," said Jake.

Dr. Roth seemed to shake off whatever had come over her. "Yes, that's why we've already registered him in the system under the name Roger Crosby."

Dr. Wu smiled. "For Mr. Rogers and Sydney Crosby, my two favorite Pittsburghers."

"It will be so nice to finally be able to communicate with him," said Cara. "I can't thank you both enough. And any expenses? Please send them to me."

Dr. Roth gathered as much information about Tam as she could from Cara and Jake while Dr. Wu began to speak to Tam. The boy seemed to perk up a bit when he heard someone speaking his native tongue.

While Dr. Wu apprised Tam about each step of the examination, Dr. Roth checked the boy all over.

Dr. Wu looked at Cara. "Tam tells me that he comes from a poor family and that his mother died recently. His father could no longer care for him and his older sister so he sold them to someone."

"Sold?" Cara was horrified.

"It's not uncommon," Dr. Wu said. "People are so poor and desperate, they feel they have no choice."

"How did he wind up in America?" Cara asked.

"He says he was shipped here in a box with other children. Then all that he remembers is a big city and someone putting him into a van and a long drive here."

"Good Lord! He came here in a box!" said Cara, outraged to think of a child being shipped like a pair of shoes or a book.

"Does he know how long he's been in Pittsburgh?" asked Jake.

Dr. Wu translated and then turned to him. "He's not sure, but he said it was cold. It's so hard for him because he is so out of his element. To come from a rural village, uneducated, and be thrust into a foreign culture without being able to understand the language is all rather confusing."

"Can he tell you where he was staying and the name of the people who brought him here?" asked Jake.

Dr. Wu said something to Tam, who gestured animatedly. "He said near the big glass house with the statute of the men with clubs."

Cara and Jake looked at each other puzzled.

"He said he lived with a woman named Mama and some others. Alex. Mostly girls."

Dr. Roth furrowed her brow. "Since he's been through so much, I'd like to run some tests on him. Unfortunately, he may have been exposed to the HIV virus or any other number of sexually transmitted diseases."

Cara wanted to cry to think of an innocent child possibly having such dreadful diseases.

"Many of these children have never had any medical care whatsoever," said Dr. Roth, "and sadly I've learned from a symposium that I recently attended on child sexual trafficking abuse held in conjunction with the Super Bowl, few of these children live very long."

"Do you have any idea what may be wrong with him?" asked Cara, who was growing more worried by the minute.

"This is a bit unpleasant to have to bring up," said Dr. Wu, "but he told me that some of his clients liked to perform sex acts on him, specifically oral sex."

"I'm hoping it's a simple a urinary tract infection," said Dr. Roth, her tone sounding measured and reassuring. "But I won't know until I run a urine sample."

Cara wiped tears from her eyes, and Jake took her hand.

"I'm going to have Dr. Wu explain what he needs to do and accompany him to the bathroom for the specimen."

As Dr. Wu explained to Tam that he needed to pee in the cup, Tam became frightened and spoke rapidly. Dr. Wu listened and then looked at Jake. "He's afraid. He wants you to come to the bathroom with him."

Jake looked surprised. Cara turned to him. "Do you mind, Jake?"

Jakes smiled. "I guess I should be flattered."

As Jake stood, Cara spoke up. "Dr. Wu, can you please tell Tam that he is safe with us, and we won't let anyone hurt him again."

Dr. Wu translated and although Tam looked pale and sick, he smiled weakly and nodded. Then Tam held out his hand and for the first time and said the word, "Jake."

"Come on, buddy," Jake said, as he picked Tam up and headed to the bathroom with the sick boy.

"He is really attached to Jake," said Dr. Roth.

"So how do you know Jake?" Cara asked.

Dr. Roth looked at Cara. "I'm his mother."

Chapter 37

When Jake returned with Tam to the exam room, he was relieved to find that his mother was gone. However, the look on Cara's face told him that she knew that Dr. Roth was his mother.

"How did he do?" Cara asked as he laid Tam on the exam table once again.

"It took a little bit of coaxing, but he eventually went. But you can tell it's hurting him."

Cara stroked the boy's head. Then she looked at Jake. "And how are you?"

"Fine." He didn't want to get into his family dynamics with her.

"Fine? Dr. Roth is your mother?"

"She uses her maiden name professionally."

"I don't care if she calls herself Dr. Quinn Medicine Woman, Jake.

She's your mother, and you treated her like she's a stranger. I know you said you were a rebellious kid, but that was years ago. What's with that?"

"Nothing. You wouldn't understand."

Cara crossed her arms. "No, this is what I don't understand. I would give anything to see my mother again and here you are barely acknowledging yours."

"Look, I'm not a dutiful child like you are."

His mother stepped into the room at that moment, holding a chart. He felt his blood surging through his body and the familiar adrenaline rush he always got before going into battle, but this time, he was facing his mother.

"He's right about that," said Dr. Roth, quietly. "I've guessed you've come to some clarity on your role over all of these years."

Jake held up his prosthetic hand. "Don't start with me—"

"Or what?" asked his mother. "You'll leave? And kill me next?"

Jake looked at Cara. "There it is. You talk about Catholic guilt. That's nothing compared to Jewish guilt. The Jews have had thousands of years perfecting it. You can't top us."

"When his father heard that he had been taken captive," his mother was looking at Cara while she spoke, "he suffered a fatal cerebral hemorrhage."

"And so you blame that on me? Could it be that he worked himself to death? Could it have been the fact that you two never were home? You were always working, striving, to get your name in the latest medical journal or on the society page?"

"It may have appeared that way to you, but we were doing it all for you." She appealed to Cara. "My husband and I were children of Holocaust survivors, if anything, that taught us that we must be prepared for any eventuality, the day when someone would try to take everything away again."

"She doesn't want to hear your justifications," shouted Jake. At that, Tam started to whimper and cry.

"Jake, you're scaring him," Cara said.

Jake stared at his mother. She looked older and smaller, and he knew it was cruel, but the rage building in him could not be contained. "See, that's what people who care about others do. They protect them. You were never there for me. It was only *zaide* who cared about me." He narrowed his eyes, going in for the kill like he had been trained to do. "You know mother, how they always say that when soldiers are wounded, they cry out for their mothers? Well, I can assure you. I didn't. When they were pouring acid into my wounds, I didn't cry for you. I cried for *zaide*." Then Jake stormed out of the room.

*****

While Dr. Wu explained to Tam that he would be conducting several more tests and would need to come with him for a bit, Cara went to find Jake. She found him in the vending machine alcove near the Emergency Room and was about to call his name when she stopped short. He was transfixed by what was on the waiting room television mounted in the corner.

"We interrupt this broadcast to bring you some breaking news," said the pretty anchor. "Prominent Pittsburgh attorney Wesley Wells, husband of well-known socialite and philanthropist, Cara Cavanaugh Hawthorne, has been charged with the murder of a teen male prostitute, who was found stabbed to death in an alley in the Uptown section of Pittsburgh last evening. In addition, he is also implicated in the extortion plot of his wife. Details are sketchy, but a source has told us that Wells and a co-worker by the name of Brianna Hoffman, with whom he was having an affair, allegedly drugged his wife and procured a child prostitute to frame her with child sexual abuse. Just days ago, we also learned that Wells filed for divorce."

Cara whimpered, then watched dumbfounded as a video of Wesley, handcuffed, being escorted into a police car appeared on the screen.

Jake looked over and saw her there. He took her hand, and if it weren't for his warm flesh surrounding her fingers and grounding her to reality, she may not have believed what she was seeing. It was one thing to know something and still another to see it with your own eyes. It was one thing to know that Wesley was a criminal, but to see him in a perp walk staggered her.

He squeezed her hand as she began to tremble. "You going to be OK?" he asked.

She nodded and then found her voice over the lump in her throat. "How about you? Are you going to be OK?"

He bumped her shoulder. "We have to be. We have a sick little kid to protect."

Chapter 38

They headed back to Tam's room and waited for him and Dr. Wu to return. "God, we really need a translator," Jake said, taking a seat in the metal-framed chair. "I wish we could understand him."

"Maybe it's a blessing that we don't," Cara said, staring at a medical illustration of a child's inner ear hanging on the wall. "I don't know what I would say to Tam, how I would explain what's happened to him. And honestly, when I hear the doctors talking about him having HIV or an STD, I don't know if *I can bear* to have him tell me what he's been through."

"If we want to help him, we're going to have to face it," Jake said.

"I suppose I'm going to have to face everything—that my marriage was a farce, that my husband is a cheater, a liar, and a murderer. When I think about him taking Tam to my hotel room and . . ." She shuddered. "Doing what he did to him and me, I get sick to my stomach. What kind of a person does such a thing? How could I have been so trusting and stupid?"

Jake came and put his arm around her. "Don't beat yourself up. Your willingness to trust people and believe the best about them is what I like most about you."

"Seriously?"

The knock on the door interrupted their conversation. It was Dr. Roth. "Hello again," she said with a weak smile for Cara and a brief glance at Jake. "Preliminary labs show that he has a raging urinary tract infection. I'd like to admit him to start him on antibiotics and some fluids. In addition to being a bit dehydrated, he is somewhat malnourished. We can do all the necessary testing and monitor his condition."

"But do you think he'll be OK?" Cara asked.

"Unless further testing reveals something, I'd say that in a day or so he should be better . . . physically. But, Cara, children who have been through what Tam has been through need help emotionally and psychologically." She stared pointedly at Jake. "Sometimes those are the most difficult wounds to heal. When his situation gets straightened out, I can recommend some professionals who have great expertise with children who have been abused and traumatized."

"Thank you," Cara said. "Can we stay with him? I really don't want to leave him. I don't want to make him feel like he's been abandoned again."

"You can both stay. Whatever you feel comfortable with. Dr. Wu will be back in to talk to Tam while they start his IV and get a room ready for him."

Cara extended her hand. "Thank you, Dr. Roth. We certainly appreciate your going out on a limb for us, for Tam." Cara looked at Jake. "Don't we Jake?"

He stuck his hands in his pocket. "Yeah, sure."

His mother stared at him, pain in her eyes. "It was good to see you, Jake." He made no response.

"I'll be in touch, Cara," Dr. Roth said, gently touching her arm before leaving.

Cara turned to Jake, not quite sure what to make of him and the way he behaved around his mother. "I'll stay with him," Cara said. "Why don't you go home and get some rest. I'll call Sophia to see if she can bring some toiletries for me, and to see if she bought any clothes for Tam. He really needs something to wear, especially a coat, for when he's released."

"If you're staying, I'm staying too."

"Jake, there's really no reason—"

"Look, I'm staying. You haven't eaten, I haven't eaten. I can bring us back food, and we can take turns caring for him."

"I really don't think it's necessary."

"Cara, I don't want to hurt your feelings, but if you haven't noticed, he's still a bit wary of you. After all, the first time he met you, you were drugged and naked. You don't remember what went on, but he does. Until he understands that you and he were both victims that night, I think it's best that we both be here for him. And besides, I want to keep an eye on him. If word gets out that the boy who is at the center of this extortion case is here, he could be in danger."

Cara sighed. "You're right." Tears started to well in her eyes.

Jake took her hand. "What is it, Cara?"

She turned, but he would not let go of her hand.

"It hurts to think that Tam believes that I had anything to do with that night. I feel ashamed even though I know I didn't do anything."

Jake pulled her closer, and she found herself wanting him to take her into his arms. "Give it time, Cara. Things will get better. Now, remember you've got a press conference at five o'clock."

She broke away. "I guess you are right. I'll go home, get ready, and if Sophia's back, I'll send her over with food and the things she bought for Tam."

As she was about to leave, Dr. Wu returned with a smiling Tam, riding in a wheelchair. Dr. Wu popped a wheelie, making Tam squeal with delight. It was the first time that Cara had ever seen the boy smile, and it was like the first time the sun comes out after a long winter.

Cara patted Tam's cheek. "Jake is staying. I'll be back." She didn't know if he understood her words, but she hoped her concern was coming through to him via her expression.

*****

When Cara arrived home, Sophia was not there. She wished that Sophia had replaced her cell phone because her message went to her voicemail on the phone she'd left in Las Vegas. Sophia had said that her concussion was improving, and Cara hoped that she wasn't pushing herself. Cara reassured herself by remembering that the doctor had said it was a mild concussion and concluded that her sister's disappearance was probably just Sophia being Sophia. Cara shook her head. She'd hoped that Sophia was beginning to show some signs of maturity and responsibility, but just when you think you can count on her, she goes AWOL. Jake may think that being trusting and hopeful were desirable, but Cara had her doubts. She was weary from being disappointed, but she couldn't dwell on Sophia now. She had to prepare for the press conference. She spent several hours researching some information on the Internet and drafting her remarks until it was time to get ready.

After showering, Cara stood in her walk-in closet in her terry cloth robe wondering what to wear, what in her wardrobe would make her appear sincere, sad, and yet resolved to seek justice for Tam and all the other children like him?

She selected a somber black tweed suit then pulled out a brown shirtwaist dress. Finally, she hung them back up. "I'm wearing what I like," she declared to herself. "I'm so sick of caring about what other people think and feel about me." She pulled out an electric blue sweater dress and floral printed scarf. After drying and styling her hair into a sleek ponytail, she did her makeup and pulled out her grandmother's blue topaz earrings. She looked at her hand, at the glittering engagement ring and wedding band. She removed them from her finger and stashed them in her jewelry box. Cara pulled on her black leather boots, grabbed her phone and purse, and headed out the door.

When she arrived at Comfort Connection, Tess told Cara how beautiful she looked. Lia met Cara coming back from ushering the press into the small conference room. "The place is already jammed with reporters and their camera crews, Cara. Your father and the bishop are in your office waiting for you," Lia said

When she opened her office door, both men walked toward her. Father Nicco held out his hand. He smelled of sugar and vanilla. No doubt, he'd been baking pizzelles again. "Cara *mia*, how lovely you look."

"Yes, as usual." her father said as he came and kissed her cheek.

"I was just telling the good bishop here that I've been hearing many favorable comments on how he's running the diocese both from people here in the states and in Europe, and the rumor is that he's on the shortlist for being named a cardinal.

"That's wonderful," Cara said. She couldn't think of anyone more worthy of rising to the hierarchy of the church, but selfishly, she hoped he wouldn't have to leave Pittsburgh.

Father Nicco shrugged. "Whatever they call me, my mission stays the same, to bring the Good News of God's love to the lost. Whether that's while wearing a mitre or red biretta makes no difference. Now, enough about me." He waved to a container on her desk. "I brought you some pizzelles. Some more lemon, but this time I added the poppy seeds—making them black and gold—Steelers colors in honor of the Super Bowl."

"Thank you," she said.

"How are you holding up, my dear?" he asked, the concern making his deep blue eyes appear pensive.

"OK. I'm taking it one step at a time."

"And focusing on helping these children is the best way to channel your anger," her father said.

"Yes, that's what I want to focus on." She turned to Father Nicco. "Will you introduce me like you did at the last press conference, and, of course, you can introduce my father as well?" She looked at her father. "I don't know if you want to speak at all?

"Maybe something brief. I just want to be there to show my support."

"Thank you. I can't tell you how much it means to have the both of you in my corner."

Lia poked her head in the office. "It's time, Cara."

Cara stood and straightened her dress and scarf. "Let's get on with it then. No sense hesitating," she said, "or as Grandma Cavanaugh used to say: 'You'll never plough a field by turning it over in your mind.'"

Chapter 39

Cara sat at the table between the bishop and her father. She looked up at the throng of reporters and hoped that this would be the last press conference she'd ever have to schedule regarding the incriminating photos. She didn't know what was in store the for the rest of her life now that her marriage was over, but she was determined to make the best of it, if not for her sake but for Tam's and the other children like him.

Father Nicco tapped a microphone, silencing the buzz of conversation among the reporters, then spoke into the bank of microphones. "Thank you all for coming today. As you may remember, eight days ago, I appeared with Cara Hawthorne at another press conference where we exposed the dastardly extortion plot that had been perpetrated upon her. Today, as you most undoubtedly know, Cara's husband, Wesley Wells, has been charged in that case and sadly, with the murder of a young man. While we are not here to weigh in on those matters, we do ask that you remember

Wesley and the young victim in your prayers. Cara's father, Laurence Hawthorne," Father Nicco made a hand gesture toward her father, "and I are here to show our support for Cara as she endures these trying times and to offer our assistance to her as she begins a new journey."

He clasped Cara's hand and nodded. "My dear."

Cara looked at Father Nicco and then at her own father. She was breathing heavily from nerves, and she hoped the microphones weren't picking it up. "Thank you both for being here." She paused to calm herself and then looked at the reporters and said, "And thank you all for coming as well."

"As you know, my life since being honored with the Mother Teresa award has been turned upside down. My reputation has been tarnished, my marriage ruined, and my nonprofit organization, Comfort Connection, has suffered, but none of that compares to what the children who are victims of child sexual abuse and human trafficking suffer. While trying to clear my name and prove my innocence, I have discovered another side of Pittsburgh—almost a parallel universe—where children are ripped from their homeland and brought to our streets to be treated worse than animals. Where they are used sexually until they are used up and then are discarded like yesterday's trash. Pittsburgh is not the only place where this is happening. It's happening all over this country and the world, but for a city that touts itself as being one of the most livable in the nation, I'm here not only to bring awareness to this problem, but also to eradicate it."

Cara stared pointedly at the cameras, knowing that this conference would be picked up by the national news as well as the local. "Awareness is nice," she said, "but I'm a woman of action, and we need to work to eliminate this scourge upon on our city and society. While preparing my remarks today, I learned something that I believe to be very fitting and a Divine coincidence. On Sunday, February 8, it is not only the Super Bowl, but it is also the feast of St. Josephine Bakhita. I have had sixteen years of Catholic education, and yet I've never heard of this remarkable woman. Let me tell you a little of what I've learned about this saint. She was born in 1869 in Darfur, Sudan. When she was between the ages of seven and nine, she was kidnapped from her home by Arab slave traders and made to walk 600 miles barefoot to El Obeid where she was forced to convert to Islam. During the next twelve years of her young life, she was sold nearly a half dozen times. She was beaten, abused, tattooed, and scarified, enduring more than 100 patterned cuts into her breasts, belly, and arms. She was so traumatized, she forgot her given name, but the slavers called her Bakhita, which, ironically, is Arabic for fortunate.

"Eventually, Bakhita was sold in Khartoum to an Italian diplomat, who was a very kind man named Callisto Legnani. When he was forced to return to Italy, Bakhita begged for him to take her along, and he agreed. When they arrived in Italy, Legnani gave Bakhita to the wife of a friend, for whom she became the nanny to the woman's daughter, Mimmina. While Mimmina's mother traveled abroad, Bakhita and the child were left in the care of the Canossian Sisters in Venice. When the woman returned to claim them, Bakhita refused to leave the convent. The Italian court eventually ruled that she could remain with the sisters. On January 9, 1890, Bakhita was baptized Josephine Margaret and Fortunata, which is Latin for lucky. She entered the convent and in 1896, she took her final vows as a Canossian sister. She served the poor for forty-two years and was known as *Sor Moretta*, the little brown sister. She died February 8, 1947, and on October 1, 2000, she was canonized a saint by Pope John Paul II as St. Josephine Bakhita."

She looked up at the media. "While that story is remarkable, I tell you about St. Josephine Bakhita because of what she said when asked what she would do if she were to meet her captors, Bakhita replied, 'If I were to meet those who kidnapped me, and even those who tortured me, I would kneel and kiss their hands. For, if these things had not happened, I would not have been a Christian and a religious today.'"

"It is in the spirit of St. Josephine Bakhita that I'm announcing the formation of a new nonprofit called Bakhita's Hope. In addition to continuing Comfort Connection's work of helping grieving children, I am also determined to help children who are victims of human trafficking and sexual abuse so that they may find the courage to enjoy productive, joyful lives," Cara nodded to Lia, who was standing near the door to the conference room.

"My assistant, Lia Minor, is passing out information sheets on this crime, and let me assure you the statistics are horrendous. The U.S. State Department in 2004 estimated that 600,000 to 800,000 people are bought and sold across international borders, half of them children, most of them female. UNICEF estimates that there are 1.2 million child victims.

"Through this foundation, I aim to battle human trafficking and reclaim its victims. These children are our little brothers and sisters in Christ and are worthy of the same dignity and love the rest of us enjoy.

"Bakhita's Hope is in its infancy, so I am asking for your trust once again, and I'm also asking for your support. Thank you. I will be happy to answer any questions that you may have about Bakhita's Hope, but you must understand that I cannot comment on any ongoing legal matters concerning my husband."

Cara answered a few questions and gave the media the number of the FBI hotline where the public should call to report suspicions of child sexual trafficking. As they were wrapping up, a reporter shouted: "Mr. Hawthorne, do you think your son-in-law's arrest will hinder your confirmation as ambassador to the United Nations?"

Laurence Hawthorne seemed annoyed, but smiled graciously and smoothed his gray hair. "You flatter me. You must know more than I about my being mentioned for the ambassadorship. But no matter where my career takes me, the main thing is that I support my daughter's latest endeavor, and I pledge to help her combat this despicable trade."

Cara, the bishop, and her father rose and quickly retreated to her office before the press could accost them.

"That was quite impressive, Cara *mia*," Father Nicco said as Cara shut her office door behind them. "You surprised me with your new endeavor, Bakhita's Hope. I can't think of a more appropriate cause for you to apply your talents. You know you have my support and of any of the diocese's resources."

"I think they were a bit disappointed that I wasn't there to give them more salacious information on Wesley," Cara said. "You know that's what they really wanted."

"I think they were in shock to find out that child sex trafficking is taking place in Pittsburgh," said Father Nicco. "Everyone thinks it's a big city problem or something that only happens when the Super Bowl comes to town. But I've been making inquiries to other dioceses around the country, and it's a scourge everywhere."

Cara looked at her phone. She was hoping that Sophia would have called her by now. It wasn't unusual for Sophia to be impulsive and take off, but she had seemed so concerned about Tam, Cara didn't think she would abandon him. Her father still didn't know that Sophia had been staying with her, but she was becoming concerned about her sister. Lord, forgive me for lying, she thought before turning to her father. "Father, have you heard from Sophia lately?"

Cara asked. "When all of this mess erupted, she contacted me, and she's been in touch regularly, but I haven't heard from her in quite a while. Has she told you where she is?"

Laurence turned to Father Nicco. "Oh, Sophia, she's always been such a handful. I ask you to remember her in your prayers." He turned to Cara. "No, I haven't heard from her in a few days. She called for some advice on her annulment." He turned to Father Nicco. "I presume you heard about her Las Vegas wedding."

Father Nicco nodded.

"I fear I failed the child. She has truly suffered from not having a mother. She's such a talented and good soul, but she is so impulsive." He touched Cara's arm. "Don't worry. I'm sure she'll be fine. When I hear from her, I'll let you know."

"Thank you both for coming," Cara said. "It really means a lot to me. I'd love to take you both to dinner, but I want to get back to the hospital to see how Tam is doing."

She filled them in on the child's condition. Then Father Nicco said, "I hope they release him soon. I don't know how long I can stall the administration at Children's from notifying the authorities that he is in your care."

Cara put her hand on her hip, gazing at Father Nicco as if he were a naughty child. "Did you know that Dr. Roth is Jake's mother?"

"I seem to remember that from somewhere."

She kissed his cheek. "You knew all along and you purposely brought them together, didn't you?"

Father Nicco's eyes twinkled. "I do my best, and let God do the rest."

"I think we're going to need a miracle then," Cara said. "I don't know what went on between them, but they were at each other's throats the minute they saw each other."

"I hope the boy soon recovers," said Laurence Hawthorne "and can leave the hospital. That's no place for a child."

"It's especially difficult because of the language barrier," Cara said. "He speaks no English."

"If you would like to follow me to the office, I have a software program for learning Thai," said Father Nicco. "We had a seminarian from Thailand working in the office last summer, and we purchased it to help us better communicate. I didn't have much success with it, but it may help you. Even if you pick up some rudimentary phrases."

"Great," Cara said. "Your offices are on the way so I can pop in and get the CDs. I'll be relieved when he's released too. We won't be running the chance of someone there discovering his real identity. Jake brought up a good point: If whoever is responsible for smuggling the boy into the U.S. knows that Tam witnessed Alex's murder, Tam's life may be in danger."

"If it helps, Cara," her father said, "I may be able to put you in touch with some translators, especially now that I most likely will be appointed the ambassador."

"So it is true," Father Nicco said, turning to Laurence Hawthorne.

"Yes, but I'm not at liberty to speak about it until the president makes the official announcement."

Father Nicco offered him his hand. *"Buona fortuna!"*

Cara's father smiled and shook the bishop's hand.

"Thank you both again," Cara said. "This is the first day since those awful pictures arrived that I've been able to see that maybe something good will come out of this catastrophe."

Chapter 40

Cara picked up the Thai language CDs at Father Nicco's office in Oakland and headed back to the hospital, periodically calling Sophia. No answer. *Where are you, Sophia? Why can't I ever count on you?*

Worried, Cara called Jake and asked if Sophia had gotten in touch with him. He said no, but that they had Tam settled in a room, and that they had not been able to watch her press conference. She told him that it had gone well, and then she told him about Bakhita's Hope.

"You've really got this mapped out, Cara. When did you come up with this idea?"

"When I was lying in bed and couldn't sleep."

"You are a great strategist," he said. "You should have gone into the military."

In some ways she felt she had. She knew combating human sex

trafficking would be a battle, and she hoped that she was up to the task. As she drove, she whispered a prayer, "Dear God, help me to make something good come out of this mess I've found myself in. Help me to help those poor kids trapped in this, especially Tam. Lord, protect Sophia and please straighten her out. And Lord, finally there's Jake. I don't even know what to say about him. I'm just giving him to you because I don't know what to do with him." She laughed and shook her head. "Nothing like dumping on you, huh?"

As she drove, she noticed that ever so slightly the sun was setting later in the evening, and an odd sense of calm and balance descended upon her. It was the first time in weeks that she felt as if she were exactly where she was supposed to be and doing what was supposed to be doing. Then her thoughts drifted back to Wesley and rage smoldered in her heart, but as she thought about him and what he faced, she was filled with sadness. She knew as a Christian that she should pray for him, but she still felt a barrier in heart that could not allow her to pray for her husband. *I'd curse the ground he walks on,* Cara heard her grandmother's voice snapping harshly in her mind. Then her thoughts turned to St. Bakhita and how she had forgiven her captors and torturers. *How do I span the gap between bitterness and forgiveness? I can't. Maybe that's why she was named Bakhita. She was lucky enough to be given the virtue to forgive trespassers—something I don't ever foresee me doing with Wesley.*

When she had spoken to Jake before, he told her that he hadn't eaten yet. She stopped on the way and picked up sandwiches in the cafeteria. As she rode up the elevator, with the sandwiches and towing her overnight bag behind her, she thought about Wesley sitting in a jail cell. *Lord, if you want me to forgive him, you're going to have to work a miracle on me.*

When she arrived in Tam's room, she noticed that he was already looking better.

"Rehydrating him has helped so they tell me," said Jake.

As they ate their tuna sandwiches and bags of potato chips, Cara filled him in on some of the ideas she had for Bakhita's Hope, and then she turned serious. "I still haven't heard from Sophia. Aside from being worried about that, I was counting on her to buy Tam clothes and the things he needs."

"Is it like her to just disappear?" he asked, and Cara could see the private investigator's mind working behind his dark eyes.

"Unfortunately, yes. She's very impulsive. Once, she said she was going out for a pedicure and the next thing we heard of her is a report two days later on *Inside Edition* showing her cavorting at the Cannes Film Festival."

"Then I'm sure she's OK. She's a survivor, and don't worry about Tam. He has everything he needs for now," Jake said, crumpling his sandwich wrapper.

"Why don't you go home and get some rest? You've solved the case," said Cara.

"Are you certain?"

"I'm certain. There's no need for the both of us to be here."

"OK. I'll drive by your place, and if Sophia's home, she can drive me back to my car. If not, I'll take your car to my place and pick up the stuff Tam needs on my way here in the morning."

"Great. I'll stay here and occupy myself with learning Thai." Cara pursed her lips. "Darn, I left the CDs in my car." She explained to Jake that Father Nicco had given them software for learning Thai. "I brought my laptop from work with me, and I was going to load them onto it and try to learn some phrases while I sit here."

"Tam's sleeping," said Jake. "I'll walk you down to the car while you get them."

Cara looked warily at Tam. "You sure? What if he wakes up?"

"He'll be fine. We'll only be gone a few minutes."

While they descended to the garage in the chilly elevator, Cara found a pad of paper in her purse and began to scribble a quick list of things she needed Jake to buy for Tam in case Sophia had not yet purchased them."

"Oh, I almost forgot," said Cara as they rounded a concrete pillar in the dimly lit garage, the sound of her heels echoing off the walls. "Can I have my note back? I need to add my phone charger. If Sophia's home, she'll know where it is."

As Jake thrust his hand into his jean's pocket, they heard the squeal of tires. Their heads turned in unison toward the sound and saw a car come tearing around the bend. Its headlights painted them like a laser from a high-tech rifle. His military training kicking in, Jake shoved Cara down between two parked cars, and then to avoid being hit, he rolled over the trunk of a Buick Regal before landing between the next slot of space between another set of parked cars. The speeding car missed Jake by inches and then peeled out of sight.

"Are you OK?" Jake asked as he looked beneath the Buick to Cara who was lying on the other side of the car.

Cara sat up and examined her leg. "I tore my tights and skinned my knee. Goodness, what a reckless driver." She began to rise.

"Stay down," Jake said. "That wasn't a reckless driver. He aimed right for us, and he could have killed us if he wanted. I think someone is annoyed with us."

The next thing she knew Jake was standing above her, his gun drawn. "Looks like they're gone." He holstered the gun, and then held out a hand and pulled Cara up.

"You think it was deliberate then?" she asked, her trembling hands brushing off her coat. "But who even knows we're here?"

"Somebody. They could have tailed you from the press conference and been waiting for you to leave. I think we've hit a nerve. For too long, the people who brought Alex and Tam to Pittsburgh have been allowed to operate in the dark, but we've lifted up the rock and shined a light on them. Now all the vermin are crawling out. We're going to have to be very careful."

Cara's eyes widened and then froze in alarm. "Tam! Do you think he's OK?"

"Let's get back there." Jake pulled out his cell phone and began to call the nurses' station to tell them not to let anyone in the boy's room. "I'm not willing to take any chances." He grabbed Cara's elbow. "And I'm not leaving your side. If they want you or Tam, they're going to have to go through me first."

*****

When they returned to the room, they were relieved to find Tam sleeping as they had left him. The stress of the day came tumbling down upon Cara like an avalanche, and she found herself yawning. "This chair is a recliner," Jake said. "Why don't you take it, Cara, and I'll sleep on the floor."

"I can't let you do that. Why don't you crawl in with Tam? He's so small, you could share the bed."

Jake looked over the situation. "Nope, don't think so. Even though he seems to trust me, God only knows what he's been through. I don't think waking up in bed with a man would be helpful."

Cara removed her boots and went into to the bathroom and wet a washcloth. She came beside Tam's bed and bent to gently rub the blood and dirt from her skinned knee. "I certainly can't crawl in beside him after the pictures and all of that," she whispered.

"I'll sleep on the floor," said Jake softly.

"The floor? Oh, Jake."

He looked at Cara. "I was a soldier. I can sleep anywhere. I've even slept in a makeshift prison. This is nothing."

"I found an extra blanket in the closet," she said. "Why don't I call the nurse? Maybe they have one for you."

Jake took her by the arm and marched her over to the recliner. "Sit," he commanded.

Cara reluctantly did as told. When she was seated, he reclined the chair, then taking the blanket, he draped it over her, tucking her in. He then looked down at her and pushed the hair back from her face. "Goodnight, Cara," he said before gently kissing her lips.

"Night," she said, overcome with feelings of desire for him. She watched him in the dim hospital room lighting as Jake took off his jacket, bunched it up into a ball, and curled up at the foot of Tam's bed. It wasn't long before Jake's rhythmic breathing as he slept joined Tam's like another track laid down on a tape. When she was sure that Jake was deeply asleep, Cara quietly got out of the chair, took the blanket, and covered Jake with it. She returned to the recliner and covered herself with her coat.

*****

Whimpering and thrashing woke Cara. She hopped out of bed and came to Tam's side only to find, that he was sleeping peacefully and that it was Jake on the floor who was having a nightmare. She quickly knelt beside him and touched his shoulder. "Jake. Jake," she whispered, alarmed at how violently he was shaking. Finally, his eyes flew open, and he didn't seem to recognize her. "Jake, it's Cara. You were having a nightmare. Are you all right?"

He felt for his gun and then sat up, looking at her with terror contorting his face. She put her arm around him. "It's me, Cara. You're at the hospital with Tam and me."

He continued to look about the room. Then it became clear to Cara that he recognized where he was when he pulled his knees up and hung his head between them.

Cara stroked his thick curls, and laying her head on his shoulder, she whispered, "Are you going to be OK?"

He turned and looked at her, the watchfulness receding from his black eyes. "Sorry. Every time I think I'm going to be fine, something from my past reaches out and tries to pull me back into the pit."

She stroked his stubbled cheek. "If it comes back and tries again, it's going to have to take me with you because I'm not letting it get you."

Chapter 41

Cara winced as she turned, feeling the cold, hard tile floor beneath her palm. Her eyes flew open, and she was startled to find Dr. Roth standing over her, as she lay there cuddling Jake. Then Cara remembered where she was—the hospital, but she hadn't remembered falling sleeping on the floor next to Dr. Roth's son. She quickly sat up and nudged Jake. Like a hair trigger, he sprung, sitting up, scanning the room.

"Surely, this is not what I think this looks like," said Dr. Roth very calmly.

"I can assure you it's not," said Cara, rising and straightening her clothing. Her knee was stiff and bruised where she had scuffed it last evening during the attempted hit and run.

"Why?" Jake asked, slowly rising, and never taking his eyes off his mother, "Would it embarrass you?"

"Yes, Jake, it would," she said, looking on the verge of tears.

"You're here about, Tam?" asked Cara, trying to diffuse the tension.

Dr. Roth looked grateful that Cara had changed the subject. She glanced at the boy's chart. "Yes, I am. He's responding well to the antibiotics. I'm waiting on the results of one more test, and if it's normal, there's no reason why you can't take him home later today."

"That's great news," Cara said, looking at Jake. "Isn't it?"

"Yes," he said, smoothing his disheveled hair.

Dr. Roth raised her hand. "I'll be in touch." Then she left the room.

Jake clicked on the TV. "I wonder what the weather will be this weekend? If it snows, that will really screw up the Super Bowl."

Cara looked at Jake. "You certainly give no quarter?"

"What do you mean?"

"She's your mother, Jake. She can't be that bad."

"Cara, stay out of it."

"What could she have done so wrong to make you treat her that way?"

Before he could respond, Tam began to thrash and wail. Cara and Jake ran to his bedside. "What is it?" Cara asked.

"What's wrong?" said Jake, touching his shoulder as Tam buried his face in the pillows.

Jake looked up at the television and there on the screen was an image of Wesley.

Jake pointed at the television. "It's Wesley, Cara. He's afraid of him."

Cara hugged the child and kept repeating, "No, you're OK. You're OK."

"Damn, this language barrier is maddening," snapped Jake, who quickly grabbed the remote and turned on *Sesame Street.*

When Big Bird came on the screen, Tam settled.

"Wesley certainly gets a reaction out of Tam," said Jake. "Perhaps Wesley is 'The General.'"

"No. Not Wesley. He can't be 'The General.' I would know." Then Cara fell silent. But then I never thought he'd cheat on me or procure a child and drug me and pose me naked, thought Cara.

"Since Tam will probably be released soon, there's no sense in us leaving," said Jake.

Cara pulled out her cell phone. "Still no word from Sophia, and now I'm getting a low battery message. This is the last time I trust her with anything," Cara said.

"Here," Jake said, pulling out a battery booster. "You can use this."

Tam seemed to lose interest in *Sesame Street,* and Cara found some cartoons on Nickelodeon for him. The international language of slapstick humor made the child laugh, something she'd not seen him do before. Cara's phone rang, and she picked it up to answer it, hoping that it was Sophia, but the screen said, Lia. "Hello, Lia," Cara said. With that, Jake left the room.

"I couldn't wait to get in touch with you. I think we're going to be OK, Cara," Lia said. "After you left, we got a lot of phone calls inquiring about how they can help with Bakhita's Hope. We also compiled a list of our supporters, and next week, we'll start contacting them to make sure they are aware that you've been exonerated and that you are expanding your scope, launching Bakhita's Hope."

"That's fantastic. I'm hoping to be able to come in on Monday. I have a few things here that need my attention, but by then things will have settled down, at least, I hope so," Cara said, observing Tam's animated face as he watched cartoons. "Call me on my cell if anything comes up."

As Cara ended the call, Jake walked back into the room carrying two paper bags. "I went to the gift shop and bought us toothbrushes and toothpaste. The nurse gave us some more towels so we can wash up." He set that bag on the window sill. "I also got some breakfast. I hope you like bagels and cream cheese."

"Thank you, Jake. You are a life saver." Cara went into the bathroom and brushed her teeth and washed her face then came out and spread some cream cheese on a bagel. While Jake was freshening up, Cara's cell phone rang again.

"Cara, I'm so excited," Lia said when she picked up the phone. "I checked the voice mail just now and Sanford Coskins' office left a message. He would like you to call him."

"Oh my goodness," Cara said, gulping down her bagel and searching through her purse to find a pen and paper to jot down the number. "Thank you. I'll call him now."

After a bit of delay, Cara was put through to Sanford Coskins, who apologized profusely for doubting her innocence.

She accepted his apology. "I don't blame you for being wary," she said. "Appearances can be deceiving, and you can't be too cautious. I presumed my husband to be faithful and an upright man, but obviously, I, who lived in the same house with him, didn't know him."

"Cara," Coskins said, "I watched your press conference yesterday, and I like your pluck. Someone else would have gone into hiding to lick their wounds, but you're aiming to get beyond this horrible episode and help others. I admire that." He then told her of how they'd found victims of forced labor, children as young as thirteen being worked like mules, at a nearby ranch. "That is a disgrace. This cannot stand in a free country. You can count on me for support."

Cara thanked him and told him she would be in touch.

She hung up the phone and did a little dance. "Woo, hoo!" she cried.

Tam looked puzzled.

"What are you so happy about?" asked Jake, who had been busy tapping away on his cell phone.

"Sanford Coskins is going to back us."

"Sanford Coskins? Holy hell, Cara. *The Sanford Coskins?*"

"None other."

Jake high-fived her, and she giggled.

"What's so funny?" he asked.

"I've never done that before."

"Done what? High-five someone?"

"Yes."

"Seriously?" he asked, raising a dark brow in disbelief.

"Who would have high-fived me? My grandmother? My father? Not exactly Wesley's style either."

"Geez, what else haven't you done?" he asked, his eyes locking on hers.

She felt something ignite in her, like dry kindling sparking into flame. "This." She reached up and stroked Jake's cheek and was about to kiss him when Tam laughed loudly at the cartoon. Cara caught herself and pulled away.

"No, Cara," he said, sliding his hand behind her neck and pulling her close. "Follow your instincts."

She turned her head. "I'm sorry. My instincts are telling me this is not appropriate."

"That's not your instincts, that's your mind." He touched her chin, forcing her to look at him. "Go with your gut."

"But my gut has been proven to be untrustworthy," she softly, losing herself in the deep darkness of his black eyes.

"Mine hasn't. And my instincts are always right," he said as he swept her into his arm and kissed her.

Chapter 42

Tam was discharged later that day. Super Bowl hype had the city in a choke hold. Traffic was snarled everywhere. Even though it was bitingly cold, tourists and media from all over the country, and in some cases the world, clogged the streets, hotels, restaurants, and stores. With all that was going on in the city, few people noticed Tam leaving the hospital with Cara and Jake. Dr. Roth sent him home with antibiotics and the recommendation that Cara seek psychiatric counseling for the child as soon as possible, which should prove to be a daunting task, Cara thought, unless she found one that spoke Thai.

When Cara and Jake brought Tam into her house, there was still no sign of Sophia. Cara couldn't decide if she were more worried or angry with her sister. To put Cara's mind at ease, Jake made calls to the area hospitals and checked in with his contacts at the police department to see if they had any Jane Does matching Sophia's description. He was happy to report that there were none.

"I'm really tired," Cara said, "and I know you must be too. Sleeping on the floor wasn't exactly restful. Why don't you go home and get a good night's sleep."

"Are you sure you can manage with Tam alone?" Jake asked.

"I'll be fine. I'm going to catch up on things here and make him rest," she said, walking Jake to the door. He stood holding the knob and moved to kiss her, but Cara backed away. Miffed, Jake stepped outside without saying a word and pulled the door shut behind him with such force, the leaded glass panels on either side of it rattled and the chandelier in the foyer above her swayed and tinkled as the crystal prisms jangled against each other. She leaned against the frame, eyeing the swaying chandelier. Cara knew she had to show only the slightest bit of interest and Jake would have gladly stayed the night. It was tempting, and she found herself rationalizing why she should give in to her desire—that she had been wronged, that no one should have to endure what she'd had to without some sort of recompense. Then Cara caught herself. *I can't take up with Jake. I'm finally starting to reclaim my reputation; I can't allow myself to be vulnerable to him, especially since I'm still married. I can't encourage him.* But her resolve seemed as easily shaken as the prisms swaying overhead.

*****

The next day, Jake called at half past eight and woke Cara. "I'm sorry to call so early on a Saturday, but there's big news."

"What?" Cara said, pushing her hair out of her eyes.

"The anti-human trafficking task force made a major bust last night. The news is reporting that they picked up thirteen traffickers and one person they are describing as high-level."

Cara sat up in bed. "Do you think they've got The General?"

"I've been calling all my contacts, but no one knows for sure yet. Has Sophia surfaced?"

"No, and I really wish she would call to put my mind at ease and to let me know if she's coming back. I need her here so I can get some things for Tam."

"Why don't I come over this afternoon and sit with Tam while you run your errands?"

Evidently, he had gotten over his anger at her for rebuffing his kiss. "Only if you allow me to cook you dinner."

"Agreed," said Jake.

*****

Jake arrived around two, and he still hadn't gathered any more information on those who had been apprehended in the human trafficking sting. Cara went to Ross Park Mall and bought Tam several pairs of pajamas, underwear, socks, shirts, pants, and shoes. And even though he was not familiar with football, she couldn't resist buying him the commemorative Super Bowl jersey. She also dropped by Toys R Us and picked up some picture books. They were geared for toddlers, but she thought they might help him to learn English. Her last stop was the grocery store where she stocked up on food that she thought a child would like and items for that evening's dinner.

When she walked into the kitchen with her purchases, she found Tam still resting on the sectional sofa while Jake was sitting at the kitchen island engrossed in the round-the-clock Super Bowl coverage on the television in the kitchen. She had been unsure about what to fix them for dinner but decided to make baked chicken, macaroni and cheese, and roasted broccoli.

After dinner while Tam napped on the sectional beside them, she and Jake lit the fireplace and watched the Super Bowl pre-game special together. Though he protested, Cara insisted, once again, that Jake go home, that she and Tam would be fine. "The General is most likely in police custody," she said, "and besides, I have a security system that will keep us safe."

Once again, she moved to show him out. Cara turned the knob, but Jake held the door closed, staring her down as if issuing her a challenge. The smoldering black look in his eyes told her that unlike the previous evening, he wasn't leaving without a kiss. He put a strong, warm hand on her shoulder and leaned in and whispered, "Cara, with The General most likely apprehended, I know everything seems to have changed. But one thing hasn't." He stared at her fiercely. "How I feel about you."

Cara pulled away, but he grabbed her shoulders, the warmth of his natural hand burning through her clothing, and pinned her against the front door. As he closed in to kiss her, she turned her head. "Jake, this is all too complicated."

He paused then whispered in her ear. "I love complicated. I love unraveling puzzles." He kissed her neck, and she felt her resolve evaporating as her yearning for him grew. His warm lips followed the ridge of her collarbone with kisses, sending shivers down her spine, and just when she felt her resistance about to run like a loose stitch on a sweater, he opened the door and left. Her chest rose and fell in a deep sigh as she closed her eyes and hugged herself trying to order her senses, but it was futile. Jake Gold had dispersed her will, leaving it in shambles like a skein of yarn that had been scattered by a litter of kittens.

Chapter 43

On Super Bowl Sunday morning as Cara was about to make herself a cup of tea, the phone rang. She looked at the caller ID, expecting it to be from Sophia, but the display indicated that it was her father calling.

"Hello, Cara," His voice sounded solemn. She froze, hoping that something dreadful hadn't happened. "I was calling to let you know that I've heard from your sister."

Cara felt herself bracing for what he was about to say. "Is she OK?"

"Yes and no. She came here last night asking for money. Some silly nonsense about needing it to create some dolls—"

Cara didn't want to reveal that Sophia had been staying with her, but she also didn't want to lie. "She did mention something about that the last time I talked to her."

"But she was a bit incoherent."

"Was she OK? She didn't want to worry you, but she told me that she had suffered a concussion at the hands of her Vegas husband," said Cara.

"It wasn't from a concussion." And then he paused. "Cara, she was high."

"Oh, no!" Cara took a seat at the island. "Is she OK?" *I was a fool to believe that she would ever change.*

"She looked terrible, like she wasn't eating or hadn't slept in days. It was heartbreaking. I couldn't stand to see her that way. Such a beautiful child, and she's killing herself. At first, she denied that she was high, but she eventually admitted that she's doing heroin."

"Heroin?" Cara's head jerked as if she had taken a blow to it. "Dear God . . . I never dreamed. Alcohol or pot? Maybe. But heroin?"

"I know. I thank God she came to see me before something terrible happened."

"So what did you do? Where is she now?" Cara was trembling.

"I forced her into treatment."

"How did you ever get her to agree to that?"

"I told her that if she refused to go into rehab, I would call the police immediately and then take steps to have her declared incompetent so that she would not inherit her portion of your grandmother's wealth. That rattled her a bit. I know some people on the board at Life

Haven, and I contacted them and drove her out there and checked her in."

"That's a relief. At least, she's under medical supervision. How long will she be in there?"

"Three to six months. It depends. Life Haven has an excellent program."

"Is she permitted visitors?"

"Not for some time. Right now she's detoxing, and then when she's sober, I'm sure we will be encouraged to visit, maybe even sit in on her therapy sessions." Her father sighed heavily. "This was so difficult, Cara, but I felt I had no choice. She lashed out at me, accused me of being a terrible father, but I only did what I did because I love her."

For years, Cara had thought one of Sophia's biggest problems was how indulgent her father had been with her sister. She knew Sophia had grown up without the benefit of a mother as had Cara, yet her father hadn't given in to her every whim. I guess some parents have a favorite child, thought Cara, and she definitely knew she was not her father's. Perhaps she should be grateful for that rather than resentful, or she may have ended up as out of control as Sophia.

"I'm glad you insisted," Cara said. "At least, we will know where she is and that she's not harming herself."

"Also, Cara, I wanted to let you know that they are fast-tracking my nomination and confirmation as U.N. Ambassador. Ambassador Chamber's health is failing. They are going to announce my nomination this afternoon at three during the president's pre-Super Bowl interview."

"Congratulations, Mr. Ambassador!" Cara couldn't help but be proud of her father. Having the president select him for such an honor was not only good news for her father and family, but perhaps it would also spell good news for her charities. This appointment to the ambassadorship would go far in rehabilitating all of their reputations.

"Thank you. It's going to be quite crazy here. This evening, after the Super Bowl— where I'm entertaining dignitaries at the game in our corporate boxes—I'm flying up to New York City, and while I'm there, I'm going to search for an appropriate place to live near the U.N."

Her father then inquired about Tam and how she was holding up under all the stress. She didn't want to tell him about the attempted hit-and-run because she really had no proof that it was one, and he didn't need another thing to worry about anyway.

After she hung up the phone, Cara realized that it was probably the most cordial conversation she'd had with her father in a long time. Cara wondered if all of his reflection on his parenting skills had not only revealed to him that he was too permissive with Sophia but also that he'd been neglectful of Cara. Either way, she was glad that she could count on him. With his appointment as Ambassador to the

United Nations, she would have unprecedented access to a man of power who could do so much on a global scale to aid her fight against human sex trafficking.

Tam plodded into the kitchen, his improving health returning the sparkle to his dark brown eyes. He looked at her and then around the room before uttering what had become his favorite English word: "Jake?"

She made a hand gesture for sleep and the child ran out of the kitchen. She caught him before he went back upstairs. She shook her head. "Jake's not here. He's at his house sleeping." She made a motion as if she were driving a car. The boy's face fell. "He'll be back later," Cara said. She wasn't sure if Tam understood, but she decided to change the subject. "Are you hungry?" She mimed putting a spoon to her mouth. "Hungry?" He shook his head enthusiastically. Cara took his hand, and for the first time, he didn't flinch when they touched. His hand was so small in hers and he was so slight. How could anyone abuse this little one? How could Wesley? Her thoughts leaped to the nights she'd spent in her husband's arms, and she felt sick. Images of Wesley making love to her over the years flashed in her mind. She closed her eyes to shut out the memories. Now thinking of him in that way repulsed her more than the blackmail photos.

She sat Tam at the kitchen table and held up box after box of cereal until the boy nodded his approval for Cocoa Krispies. After administering his next dose of medicine, she finally settled in to have that cup of tea nearly an hour later. She was surprised at how much care a child required. Maybe she was a bit unfair to judge her father for sending her to live with her grandmother after her mother's death. *I'm sure it must have been overwhelming for him to be left with an infant and small girl.*

As Tam crunched his cereal and drained the bowl of milk, she sipped her tea, her thoughts drifting back to her mother. She knew from all her work at Comfort Connection that many children of parents who committed suicide often harbored deep anger toward that parent. Cara had never felt anger at her mother, but she was burdened by a nagging question: *Why? Why did she do it?* She didn't remember much of her mother or that fateful day. Any time she had questioned her father about her mother's death, he had made it clear that it was too painful for him to talk about. She also sensed that her father blamed her for her mother's suicide. She told herself that was ridiculous. How could a four-year-old child be responsible? Maybe that's why he favors Sophia; he blames me. But that was twenty years ago, she told herself. Time to leave it in the past. *I have a lot to leave in the past.* My mother and now Wesley. It seemed that life was nothing but trying to overcome what has already happened.

Cara had intended to spend the rest of the morning outlining how she wanted to proceed with Bakhita's Hope, but she was absorbed into the Internet while searching for information on heroin addiction. With each fact she learned about this addiction, her heart sank further. *Oh, Sophia. What ever possessed you to take the first hit? What have you done to yourself? God, please help her find you because there's no way she can beat this on her own.*

Thankfully, Tam was feeling better and was content to spend his time watching television or have Cara draw him pictures and pronounce the corresponding English name for the drawing. At five minutes before three, as she was about to switch the television channel from Nickelodeon to the news to see the president announce her father's appointment, her cell phone rang.

"Hey Cara, I hope I'm not disturbing you," said Lia, who sounded like she was calling from a fraternity party.

"No, I was just watching the TV. They are nominating my father to be the U. N. Ambassador," Cara said punching numbers into the remote.

"Wow, congratulations! We certainly have friends in high places. I can call back later."

"No, it will be all over the news, and I'm DVRing it now. What's up?"

"I forgot. There's something else I wanted to tell you."

"Where are you?" Cara asked, straining to hear her assistant over the racket.

"That's why I called. I'm at the Super Bowl. Francesco D'Amore came into town for the game yesterday and called me. He's singing the *National Anthem*. It seems he's a friend of the NFL commissioner, and he's invited me to be his date for the game."

Cara squealed. "You must be so excited!"

"I about fainted when I saw his number come up on my cell phone yesterday morning. I took him on a tour of the city, and we went to dinner on Mt. Washington last night. He also wanted to see our offices."

"I hope you didn't make hot Italian love on my desk."

Lia screamed. "You are terrible! But seriously, why I'm calling, other than to brag that I'm going to the game with the former Sexiest Man Alive, is that I when I took Francesco to show him our offices, I picked up some work to take home. I suppose you've heard that they are predicting that a ton of snow is headed our way, starting after midnight. While I was there, I also got the mail, and we received an unusual letter. It was marked 'Personal,' but half the mail that comes in is marked that way, and I opened it. Anyway, if I shouldn't have opened it, I'm sorry."

"What did it say?"

"It's kind of cryptic. The handwriting was shaky like an elderly person had written it. All the words in the first sentence were in caps and it said: TIME DOES NOT HEAL ALL WOUNDS! And that was underlined three times. Then it said, 'I saw your press conference. Pretending to be concerned about children. What a farce!

You should be ashamed. What you have done will never be forgotten."

"I don't understand," said Cara. "Who's it from? Did they sign it?"

"It was signed," said Lia. "It's from someone named Sally Metzger. Do you know her?"

"I've never heard of her. Does it have a return address?"

"No, but it was mailed from around here. The cancelation was a bit smeared, but it's a 152 zip code. I can't make out the last two numbers."

"I have no clue," said Cara, shouted.

"If the handwriting seems to be from an elderly person, could it be a grandparent of one of the children in Comfort Connection?"

"I guess it's a possibility," Cara said, "but 1 don't have any recollection of any of the children in the program having any problems." Cara sighed. "Could she be a donor who feels that we've misused her donation?"

"I can check the donor database when I get into work tomorrow, if you'd like. If the roads are passable."

Cara thought back to the car that had tried to run them over in the hospital garage. Was this letter and that car connected? "Would you please? And hang on to the letter, and please let me know if you get anything else out of the ordinary."

"You don't think it's anything to be concerned about, do you?"

"No, she's probably just an old crank who's sure I molested children even though my innocence has been clearly established. Keep me posted. Oh, and, Lia?" Cara said before hanging up the phone, "Don't run off to Venice with Francesco after the game. I need you."

Lia chuckled. "I wish. Look for me on the sidelines. I get to go on the field and stand off to the side while he sings."

"Have an awesome time," Cara said so excited for her assistant.

"Will do," Lia said before hanging up.

Cara stared at her phone's screen for a while lost in thought, wondering who Sally Metzger was and what could possibly have provoked her to pen such a strange letter. She hoped that the woman was merely a crank. Although Cara knew by declaring war on the human sex trafficking industry, she was not making any friends.

As Cara pressed the buttons to watch the recording of her father's press conference, her phone rang again. The word "Jake" flashed on the screen. "So much for watching this." Tam looked at her blankly as she clicked the remote back to Nickelodeon for him.

"Hey, congratulations about your father," Jake said. "I watched the president make the announcement during his Super Bowl interview."

"Thanks. I missed the interview. Lia called right when it started, and Tam was busy watching cartoons. But I recorded it. I'll have to watch it later. Now, how are you? Did you get some rest?"

"Some, but I find it hard to stop thinking about you . . . Tam. You know, the situation." he quickly added. "I hope you haven't started dinner. I was going to pick something up and then stop by to watch the Super Bowl with Tam. And you."

"He'd love that," Cara said. "I think he misses you." And she heard a voice in her mind saying, *And so do I.*

Chapter 44

Tam had been resting on the family room sectional watching Nickelodeon, but when he saw Jake walk into the kitchen around five o'clock, his eyes lit up, especially when he saw that Jake was carrying bags from McDonald's.

"Nice Super Bowl jersey," Jake said, touching the boy's shirt.

"Super Bowl," said Tam, with a broad smile.

"You certainly perked him up," Cara said, who'd quickly showered and dressed in black leggings and white cable-knit tunic sweater.

"It's not me. I speak the international language of McNuggets." Tam was chattering away, dancing, and reaching for the bag. Too bad neither of them could understand what he was saying, but they both understood when he dived into the meal that he loved his dinner.

"Sorry it took so long. I stopped at Kmart too. I also got him some LEGOs and a DVD, *Kung Fu Panda*."

"Thank you so much," Cara said. "At least, I can count on you."

"Traffic is a mess," Jake said, shrugging off his coat. "I'd like to kill the idiot who called in that bomb threat!"

"What? There's been a bomb threat?" exclaimed Cara, taking his coat. "We've been watching Nickelodeon all day. I still haven't been able to see my father's announcement yet."

"Yeah. Late this morning, some lunatic phoned in that there was a bomb on one of the boats transporting spectators to Heinz Field. They mobilized the River Rescue unit and cleared everything, but then an hour ago another one came in, saying that they were going to blow up the Fort Pitt Tunnel. The tunnel is shut down now, and traffic is at a standstill everywhere. People are trying to get to the game. I would have gotten us something other than McDonalds, but with the traffic, I was afraid I'd miss the kickoff."

"I hope my father, Father Nicco, and Lia are safe. They're all going to the game."

"Last report on the radio said the tunnels were being checked right now and were expected to be cleared in thirty minutes."

Cara handed Jake a plate. "What is wrong with people?"

Jake commandeered the remote from Tam so that he could tune into the pre-game show. Kick-off was scheduled for six. Tam crossed his arms and frowned with disapproval so Cara let him camp out in the den, where she turned Nickelodeon on for him on the small television in there.

As Cara and Jake dined on Big Macs and fries, she told him about her conversation with her father and sadly about Sophia.

"She's on heroin?" Jake asked, raising an eyebrow. "I notice things, and I didn't get the sense that she's a junkie. Did you suspect that? Did you notice any needle marks?"

"I Googled heroin addiction this afternoon, and I learned you don't always have to inject it."

"I know that," said Jake, "but usually there are other signs like being whacked-out or her having laxatives. Junkies get constipated because the drugs slow down their systems. What about other drug paraphernalia?"

"None."

"Was she acting strangely?"

Cara shrugged. "Strangely? We're talking about Sophia. And she had a concussion."

Jake shook his head. "I'll give your dad credit for getting her to go to rehab."

"Yes," Cara said, then she hesitated.

"What is it?"

"It's not nice to think this, but I can't help wondering if he wanted

Sophia out of the picture so as not to mess up his confirmation to the ambassadorship."

"Would he do something like that?"

Cara shook her head. "No, that's a crazy thought. He indulges her. She is literally his fair-haired girl." She stared at Jake. "But there is something else that's a bit of a mystery." Then she told Jake about the letter Lia had received at the office. "It's probably nothing to worry about. Just a cranky old lady."

"I don't like the sound of that. Not with nearly being run over." Jake pondered for a moment. "What has me puzzled is that phrase: 'Time does not heal all wounds.'" It sounds like someone harboring a grudge. Can you recall anyone ever threatening your family? A disgruntled employee maybe?"

Cara thought back over her life. "My grandmother had a housekeeper, but she was devoted to my family and passed away a few years ago. There were gardeners and other workers, I guess, over the years, but nothing that I can remember. If anything, they loved my grandmother. She treated them very well because she started out as a housekeeper herself." Cara shook her head. "No, I'm completely mystified by it."

"Either way. I'd like to see that letter."

Before settling in for the game, Cara checked on Tam. He was on the floor lying on his tummy watching *Teenage Mutant Ninja Turtles*. At six,

Cara and Jake took their seats on the sectional in front of Cara's huge television. She pointed to the screen excitedly when the camera took a wide-angle shot of Francesco D'Amore singing the *National Anthem*, catching Lia gazing at him adoringly from the sidelines. Moments later, the camera focused on her father in the Allegheny Food & Beverage luxury box, the announcers noting that this "son of Pittsburgh has made the city proud with his nomination to the ambassadorship to the United Nations today. This is probably the most prestigious appointment for a Pittsburgh native since President Bush appointed Paul O'Neill Treasury Secretary."

The game proved to be a bore because, by the end of the first quarter, the Redskins were already up three touchdowns on the Jaguars. To generate some excitement, Jake proposed that every time they broadcasted a clichéd shot of molten steel or a Primanti's sandwich as a background piece on Pittsburgh, that they do a shot.

Cara looked at him skeptically. "Are you serious?"

"Sure. Haven't you ever played a drinking game?"

"If I've never high-fived, do you think I've ever played a drinking game?"

Jake rose. "Where do you keep your liquor?"

Cara pointed to the walnut cabinet adjacent to the family room fireplace.

Jake opened the double doors and stared at the various bottles of liquor. "Name your poison, Cara."

She thought for a moment. "I'm not much of a drinker, but I do like Godiva. That's why I had the chocolate martini at Roland's."

Jake screwed up his face. "Godiva? That's for wimps." He crouched and moved some bottles aside. "Ah, ha," he said. "Jameson's. You're Irish—whiskey it is."

"I don't know about this," Cara said when Jake rejoined her on the sectional, plunking the bottle of whiskey and two shot glasses on the coffee table in front of them.

"OK, let's make this interesting," he said. "We both drink when they show molten steel or a Primanti sandwich, but you drink when they show the incline, and I drink when they show Point State Park."

Cara sighed. This seemed reckless, but at the same time exciting and fun. "OK. I guess."

By half time, they'd both had three shots apiece, and when the broadcast came back for the halftime show, they focused in on the incline before cutting away to Duran Duran. Cara took her fourth shot, shuddered, and exclaimed, "Duran Duran? I love them! When I took dance lessons, we did a routine to *Hungry Like the Wolf.* All the little girls in my tap class dressed like wolves, but I got to dance the part of Little Red Riding Hood. My grandmother hated that routine." Cara threw up her hands. "Why didn't I know they were performing?"

"Maybe because you've been busy fighting crime with me," said Jake. "It's their fortieth anniversary. That's why they selected them for this year's half-time show."

The lights dimmed in Heinz Field and Duran Duran took the stage to a blast of fireworks and thunderous applause, and Cara suddenly found herself singing and dancing to *Rio*, which sent Jake into fits of laughter. He ceased laughing when Cara grabbed his hand and made him dance with her. He resisted, but she persisted until he was forced to join her. The song over, Duran Duran next segued into the more mellow *Ordinary World*, and Cara felt Jake wrap his arms around her and pull her close. Her head was spinning as they swayed. She could feel Jake's warm breath on her neck, it smelled like whiskey. Then he began to whisper the lyrics in her ear.

Tears came to her eyes as she thought about all that she'd been through, how her extraordinary life had come crashing down around her. But as Jake held her and crooned softly in her ear about not crying for yesterday, Cara decided that she just might like the ordinary world.

Chapter 45

Jake poured himself a cup of coffee and stared out his living room window. Heavy snow was falling, making the world look like it had been covered with gauze, the kind that had bandaged his stump after the amputation. He'd thought his life was over when he lost his arm, and for a time, he had to admit, that he'd acted more dead than alive. But now he felt different and that was because or Cara. She made him want to live again. He pulled out his cell phone. It was ten forty-eight, on the day after the Super Bowl. He hadn't seen one car go by or a soul out on the street and it seemed that the entire city had a hangover—Lord, knew he did.

He wanted to call Cara. But he wondered if it was too early, and he also wondered how she was feeling. By the time the fourth quarter had arrived, they'd suspended their drinking game because he feared she'd end up in the hospital if they continued. The game had proven to be a gross mismatch so to enliven the broadcast, it seemed the anchors had resorted to touting the attributes of the city, and the cameras kept panning to the incline and Point State Park, obliging them to drink.

Jake helped Cara, who had fallen asleep on the couch, to bed. Still in her clothes, he removed her shoes and covered her with her comforter. Then he settled Tam into bed too. He then went downstairs, tidied up, and slept for a few hours in the family room until he was sober and then let himself out around four thirty to drive home. The frigid night air was bracing and snow began to fall as he pulled in front of his apartment. He entered and stripped off his clothes, crawling under the cold covers in his boxers.

Around noon, he called Cara, who answered the phone with a groan.

"You're sounding chipper," he said.

"The next time you suggest a drinking game, I'm confiscating your prosthetic arm so you can't pour drinks," she said.

May as well take my arm, thought Jake. You've already captured my heart. *God, get a grip, Jake. You sound like a lovesick teenage girl. You're going to frighten her away.*

He took another hit of coffee. "Feeling that bad?"

"Yes, and to boot, Tam is particularly wound up today. He wants me to play LEGOs with him, but I swear I can hear the bricks snapping together, and they sound like bowling pins crashing with this headache."

"*Zaide* always recommended matzo ball soup for hangovers, but Jews always think soup cures everything."

Cara laughed weakly. "Thanks for taking care of me and Tam last night."

"No problem."

"What are you doing today?"

"Not much. Recovering. Watching the snow fall." He didn't want to tell her that if he felt well enough after dinner, he planned to spend the evening trolling the streets of downtown Pittsburgh asking questions of the street people and prostitutes to see if any of them could help him find Mama or confirm if The General had been arrested. If he told Cara, she would probably want to go along again, but now she had Tam and she was needed. "Go lie down," he said. "I'll call you later."

After he hung up with Cara, he watched the Super Bowl wrap-up on ESPN and ate a late lunch of eggs and toast. When he left the apartment as dusk fell after taking a long, hot shower, he felt nearly human again. He headed uptown to the area where they had met Alex. He could still see the teen in his mind, his broad grin and the energy animating his gestures. What a tragedy to be so brutally murdered. Wesley was one sick freak. What did Cara ever see in him?

The heavy snow had tapered to flurries, and everyone he tried to engage who appeared to be working the streets seemed wary. But who could blame them? One of their own had been viciously murdered, and even though Wesley had been arrested for the crime, it seemed that those on the streets were still spooked by strangers. They were also wary because so many prostitutes and pimps had been rounded up as a result of the increased Super Bowl security.

Many assumed that he was a cop, but he assured them that he was not, that he was a friend of Alex and Tam's and that he did not want to arrest anyone. He only wanted information. Before long the enticement of an easy $20 bill loosened the lips of a street walker whose hair looked greasy and who was shivering badly, from the cold or from a dire need of a fix, he couldn't tell. Jake promised her a cup of coffee and another $20 if she gave him any useful information. Before long, he and the prostitute were seated in the McDonald's on Liberty Avenue. After adding nine packets of sugar to her coffee, she told Jake that her name was Princess and that at first the homegrown streetwalkers had been hostile when these foreign workers began to invade their turf, but Princess shook her head, "Alex and the others had it much worse." Princess had straight, perfect teeth and spoke intelligently. Jake thought she'd probably been raised in the suburbs with orthodontia, and a good education but had gotten herself messed up in drugs. She told Jake that Alex had told her that he thought he'd been recruited to work on a cruise ship when The General's people had come to his town. Alex never suspected that he'd walked into a human sex trafficking syndicate.

"So he told you about The General? Did he say anything more about him?"

"Only that he was a merciless bastard."

"Do you know where he lives or what he looks like? Anything?"

"The General is like the Wizard of Oz. No one gets to see behind the curtain. Even the pimps are afraid of him. I've never seen him. Mama is the one who runs the show on a day-to-day basis."

"Mama. What do you know about her?" Princess was eyeing the Big Mac on the young man's tray a few booths over. "Are you hungry? Would food help you to remember?"

"Yeah, couldn't hurt."

Jake bought Princess a Big Mac meal and had it Super-Sized.

"You know how to treat a girl," Princess said, quickly unwrapping the hamburger.

"Now, what can you tell me about Mama?"

"Not much. I saw her once about a year ago, but a lot of the business is moving online. I'm old school. I like to see my customers. There's a lot of freaks out there who like to get it on with little boys. You can't really peddle kids on the street. It attracts too much attention. Alex told me that Mama kept the young ones with her in a house in Uptown."

"Where in Uptown?"

"Below Mercy Hospital. There's a lot of old row houses. People are always coming and going there, moving in and out. No one pays much attention to their neighbors."

For the price of a warm apple pie, Jake learned that one of Mama's girls, one named Jittra, who had been beaten and disfigured by a john, leaving the child with a disfigured face had been taken off the streets and drafted to help corral the younger sex slaves. "She was too ugly to make any big time money anymore."

"Is there any way you get her to talk to me?"

Princess thought for a moment. "No, but she goes to the new Shop A Lot nearly every afternoon at four. Mama sends her to get stuff for dinner and such. I see her there when I get my cigarettes."

"Shop A Lot? The grocery store that just opened around Thanksgiving?"

Princess nodded.

"Thank you," Jake said. "You've given me a lot to work with."

"You already had a lot to begin with," Princess said with a leer. "You were so nice; I'd give you a discount."

Jake patted the tabletop. "Maybe next time."

On the way home, Jake called Cara and told her all that he had found out and that tomorrow, he'd be staking out the Shop A Lot with the mission of catching the girl who could possibly lead them to Mama.

*****

The next afternoon Jake headed toward the Uptown section of the city. As he was stopped at the light in front of the CONSOL Energy Center, he glanced over toward the larger-than-life Mario Lemieux statue outside the entrance gate to the center. And then it dawned on him. *Near the men with the clubs!* That was how Tam had described where he had lived with Mama. The statue was a recreation of Lemieux's famous goal against the New York Islanders when he broke through two defensemen to score. Of course, hockey sticks would seem like clubs to a small boy who'd probably never seen an NHL game. Jake's pulse quickened as he headed to the small parking lot of the Shop A Lot. His instincts told him he was in the right place. Now all he need was to be patient and for this girl, Jittra, to show up.

The trouble with being a private investigator was the weather. It was either too hot or too cold to be spending so much time sitting in a car. He was thinking how he was going to make sure that his next car had heated seats, when in his rearview mirror, he noticed a small Asian girl, poorly clad in leggings, puffy parka, and pink Crocs heading down the sidewalk toward the Shop A Lot entrance. The wind was whipping her long black hair across her face making it impossible for him to see if it was disfigured. Quickly, he got out of the car and hurried into the store and pretended to linger over the lottery machine near the entrance until the girl walked in. She brushed her hair from her face, and that was when Jake saw it. The scar. It ranged over her porcelain skin from her eye that drooped slightly to the bridge of her nose to across her upper lip. It would have to have been one sadistic bastard to inflict such a wound on a child. As if she could sense that he was looking at her, she hunkered into her coat and grabbed a cart.

He followed from a distance, watching as she filled it with soy milk, peanut butter, and eggs. As she headed toward the cereal, he went down that aisle. While she was mulling over the boxes of Fruit Loops and Cheerios, Jake casually stood next to her and spoke softly. "I'm looking for some cereal for a boy who is staying with me. Perhaps you can help me pick one."

The girl cast her eyes down.

"The boy's name is Tam."

By the way, her slight frame stiffened, he knew that she knew Tam.

"Yes, I'm a friend who's trying to help him."

She looked up at him with sad, black eyes. "Did you try to help Alex too?"

Jake was taken aback. *At least, she hadn't lost her fighting spirit.*

She picked up a box of Rice Krispies. Jake gently touched her arm. "Tam told me that The General killed Alex. I don't think the man they arrested killed Alex, and I want to find The General so that he can't hurt Tam. So that he can't hurt you or any of the others either."

Obviously terrified, she scurried down the aisle. Jake followed, but he didn't want to look as if he were harassing her.

When she stopped at the bread section, Jake stood near her again. "I know you are afraid, but I also know that you can help me and help all the others."

She looked at him and pointed to her face. "All men say I not hurt you. They lie."

"But I'm different. I'm working with Cara Hawthorne to—"

"Cara—pretty lady on TV?"

"Yes, she wants to help."

"Mama say, 'Hate that bitch.'"

"Cara and I are working to find The General. Do you know who he is?"

"No, never see General. He like ghost. Only call Mama when new product coming or if there trouble."

"Product?"

"Boys. Girls. New workers."

"How often do new workers come?"

"Don't know. Some are coming on Friday. Hear Mama talking. Making room for new. Need more since Alex dead and others arrested during Super Bowl."

"How are they getting here?"

"Way we all come. Box on boat."

"What do you mean?"

"Come on ship. Like banana or television. Kids like products too. No one cares."

"I care."

She stared at her Crocs.

"What is your name?" Jake asked.

"Mama call me June, but real name is Jittra."

"Jittra, where did the boat come into?"

"I go. Mama kill June if she find out I talk to you." She left Jake and entered the Express Line and checked out, handing over crinkled dollar bills as Jake watched her from the entrance. He stepped outside waiting for her.

When she stopped to put on her mittens, Jake approached her again. "Please, Jittra, I can help you. Wouldn't you like to be able to go home?"

"Can't go home," she said, transferring her bag to her other hand to put on the other mitten. "Orphan. General's men take me off the street. Tell me they feed me, give me place to live." A tear rolled over her scarred cheek. "They not tell me what I have to do to eat and have a bed."

She began to walk in the direction from which she had come.

"I can help you," Jake said walking beside her. "Cara will find you a place to live, a place where you can be safe. Where does the box on the boat arrive?"

She looked at the billboard and pointed. It was Liberty Mutual insurance billboard. "City with lady with lamp. I go now."

The Statue of Liberty. How bitterly ironic that her first view of Lady Liberty came while trapped as a sex slave. "Do you know where and when?"

"No," she said quickening her pace.

"Can you find out?" He said, increasing his stride to keep up with her. He grabbed her elbow, stopping her, and she looked terrified. Jake pointed to her scar. "If you find out, I promise to have a doctor fix that. To make you beautiful again." He could tell by the light that came into her eyes that more than anything she wanted to be safe and rid of that scar.

He pulled up his sleeve and showed her his prosthetic arm. "They can't fix this, but I wasn't beautiful to begin with." Even if he had to sell his prosthetic arm to pay for her surgery, Jake vowed that he would do it.

"Do you come to the store every day at this time?"

She nodded.

"Find out what you can, and I'll be here tomorrow, same time."

She didn't make any promises. And as Jake watched her walk into the cold, creeping twilight carrying the groceries, he thought that Atlas had it easier with his load compared to Jittra, who appeared to be burdened with the weight of a thousand lifetimes on her young shoulders.

Chapter 46

Cara awoke on Monday, the day after the Super Bowl, at six thirty-eight with a burning thirst. When she pushed back the covers, she was reminded that she was still in the clothes she'd been wearing the night before. Her grandmother would have been horrified, but as she plodded to the bathroom for a drink of water, she was so hungover, she didn't care what anyone thought. After drinking some water and being repulsed at how dreadful she looked in the mirror, she then checked on Tam, who was sleeping peacefully in the spare bedroom. She tucked the covers under his chin and hoped he'd sleep late.

On her way back to bed, she glanced outside and saw that nearly half a foot of snow had fallen during the night, and none of the roads looked as if they had been touched. If the schools declared a snow day, Comfort Connection followed suit. She went back to her room and clicked on the television. School closings were scrolling across the bottom of the screen. She turned off the television and phoned Lia. The call went to her voice mail. "If you're not in Venice with

Francesco, please contact the staff and tell them not to come in today. The roads look terrible. Call me later." *Much later*, Cara thought. She then sent a mass email message to the local media asking them to post that Comfort Connection was closed. That taken care of, she curled up under the comforter and hoped that when she awoke, she'd feel better.

She woke again near 11 o'clock when she found Tam standing over her, making the hand gesture of eating. There was no improvement in her hangover. As she lay in bed trying to raise the strength to get up, she wondered how Sophia was doing in detox. If a hangover was this painful, Cara couldn't imagine trying to kick an addiction. Finally, she dragged herself out of bed and went downstairs, where she toasted two frozen waffles for Tam. She then trudged to the shower and hoped the warm water would wash away the hangover. After drying her hair and dressing in yoga pants and fleece pullover, she headed back downstairs and made a piece of toast and cup of tea. She then swallowed two Tylenols, and she found something for Tam to watch on television while she lounged on the sofa.

Near noon, Jake had called to check on her and Tam. He thought it funny how awful she felt, but she couldn't be annoyed with him. Apart from Father Nicco, Jake, once he had gotten over his innate dislike for her, had proven to be her greatest advocate. He'd exposed Wesley's guilt, had helped her with Tam—why, he'd also saved her from harm when he'd shoved her out of the way of the car in the garage.

Jake. After she hung up the phone, she couldn't get him off her mind, and her thoughts drifted back to last night, him holding her and dancing. He was so different from Wesley. Jake was dark, laconic, and physical while Wesley, with his light hair, was fair, and as a lawyer, gifted with words both written and spoken as well as being cerebral. No doubt Jake was incredibly handsome, and when he wanted to be, charming, but he was deeply wounded both physically and psychologically. Cara had to admit that she was attracted to him anyway, and she also had to admit that no matter how she felt about him, she was still married. There is an annulment, she thought, but even if one were granted for her marriage, was Jake another mistake in the making? Cara wasn't sure they were compatible. "Lord, listen to me," Cara said, "speculating about being married again when I'm not even sure of Jake's feelings or desires. I may just be another hill to capture."

On Monday evening, Jake called again to tell her that he was making some headway with the investigation of Mama and The General, and said that as soon as he checked out a few more things, he'd give her a call. She said certainly, and then told him that Tam had learned his first English sentence: "When Jake coming?"

*****

Tuesday dawned sunny and without Cara feeling like she'd been sacked in the Super Bowl numerous times. Lia called her at eight and after Cara told her that she'd spotted her on the sidelines at the Super Bowl, Cara asked all about Lia and Francesco's weekend. "It was incredible," said Lia dreamily. "He flew out right after the game to beat the snow storm, but he said he may be coming in the spring. I hope so. I was so glad when you called off work yesterday. I needed an extra day to recover."

Cara told Lia that she wouldn't be in the office for the rest of the week. She hadn't told her yet that Tam was living at her house, but soon she would have to. She couldn't hide the boy forever, and she had to go into the office eventually. "Call me if anything comes up," Cara said before hanging up.

While Tam watched *Kung Fu Panda*, for, it seemed to her, the millionth time, she brainstormed a logo for Bakhita's Hope. She downloaded a biography on St. Josephine Bakhita onto her Kindle and intended to scan the book for some inspiration, but she soon found herself curled up on the sectional in the family room absorbed in reading more about the life of this remarkable woman. It was fitting that she named her new nonprofit Bakhita's Hope because merely reading about her encouraged Cara. If she could endure being kidnapped, abused, sold into slavery, and physically tortured, then Cara felt the smallest spark of hope that she could rise above all that had happened to her as well. And so could Tam. And for that matter, so could Jake.

*****

On Wednesday morning, Jake called and said that he'd be over around one to tell her what he'd learned. Cara spent the day on the telephone. First, she called her father, who was in New York. He said that he'd had reports on Sophia and that she was doing as well as could be expected. He had been busy conducting interviews with the media and preparing for his confirmation hearings.

She then called Father Nicco, and she found his call upsetting.

"Did you enjoy the game?" Cara asked him.

"Oh my, yes. American football is still inferior to football, or soccer as you call it, but I thoroughly enjoyed giving the invocation in the locker room for the players and the spectacle of it all."

Cara filled him in on what she'd been doing, leaving out the part about the drinking game and her hangover.

"I visited Wesley yesterday at the jail," Father Nicco said, casually dropping that piece of news into the conversation.

"Oh," Cara said, a bit caught off guard. "How is he?"

"Bad, Cara. He's despondent, and he asked me to tell you that he is sorry."

Cara felt tears stinging her eyes, and she wasn't sure if they were from pity or anger.

"I think he was seduced by his accomplice. I think she turned his head, played into his feelings of inferiority."

Cara didn't know what to say. Admitting the anger raging in your heart to a priest would only prompt an admonition from Father Nicco that she should forgive him, and right now, she didn't even want to think of that.

"He takes responsibility for the blackmail, but he is adamant that he had nothing to do with that young man's murder."

"For his sake," Cara said bitterly, "I hope that's true."

"Cara, *mia,* I know this is hard for you, and please don't think I'm advocating for Wesley because, in my heart of hearts, I'm furious with him as well, but in the better part of my nature, I have to honor his request."

"Request?"

"He would like you to visit him."

Cara heard herself sputtering, "Me . . . me? Go visit him in jail? No, I can't. After what he did to me, my life?"

As she rambled on about why she couldn't possibly visit Wesley, all she heard was Father Nicco softly repeating, "I was in prison, and you visited me. I was in prison, and you visited me. I was in prison, and you visited me." He was citing the gospel of Matthew, preying on her conscience. She stopped talking and just listened to him reciting the scripture like a mantra.

She began to sob.

"Cara, *mia,* dear heart. I'm not advising you to go for Wesley's sake, but for yours."

Tam came to her and looked up as she wept. He wrapped his arms around her waist and clung to her. *If Tam can reach out to you, how can you not reach out to Wesley?* asked a small voice in her conscience. She stroked Tam's silky black hair.

"I don't want bitterness and anger to devour you," said Father Nicco.

"I'll think about it," she said, wiping the tears with the back of her hand before she gently hung up the phone.

Chapter 47

Around one o'clock, Jake phoned Cara. "Hey, I've been thinking a lot about that letter you received. Do you think I might stop by your office and get it? I'd like to have a look at it," he said.

Cara glanced at the clock. "Lia should be there. I'll tell her that you will be dropping by for it."

No sooner had she hung up with Jake than the doorbell rang. Cara, ever on guard now, peered out the side panel. It was Lia, bundled up in a camel coat. Should she let her in? She had told no one other than her father and Father Nicco that Tam was staying with her. She knew she could trust Lia, but should she involve her in this mess, especially since a possible attempt had been made on her and Jake's lives? She couldn't leave her freezing outside so Cara opened the door. "What a surprise."

Lia entered and gave Cara a hug. "I've missed you. We've barely had a chance to see each other ever since all hell broke loose, and I wanted to check on you to see how you are holding up. And give you that letter," Lia said. Her cheeks were red. Cara quickly scanned the house as Lia embraced her. There was no sign of Tam; no doubt he was probably hiding in the family room because he was still so frightened of strangers. Cara decided that she would lead Lia into the living room and then get them a drink. While in the kitchen, she would tell Tam to stay put.

"It's so good to see you," Cara said as she shut the door.

Before Cara could even take a step toward the living room, Tam came wandering into the foyer in his pajamas saying, "Jake? McDonald's?"

Lia's eyes widened. "Well, who is this?"

"I wasn't sure if I should involve you in all of this, but this is Tam. The boy who appeared in the blackmail photos."

Lia looked puzzled then troubled. "So you did know him then?"

"No, it's not what you think. Come into the family room and I'll explain. The private investigator I've been working with, Jake, was going to stop at the office for that letter, but I'll text him that you brought it."

"Jake? McDonald's?" Tam said again, staring up at Cara.

She patted his shoulder. "Later. Jake's coming later." Cara pulled out her cell phone. The message sent and received, she poured glasses of iced tea for them while Tam inserted the disc for *Kung Fu Panda* again. After they had taken seats on the sectional, Cara filled Lia in on how she and Jake had tracked down Alex, who led them to Tam. She then told her how she instructed Alex and Tam to come to her if they ever needed help.

"The night Alex was murdered," Cara said, "Tam showed up here scared out of his mind." She told Lia how Tam had gotten sick and how they had nearly been run over in the hospital parking lot. "Someone is very angry with us for poking our noses into this human sex trafficking racket. That's why we haven't told anyone where Tam is. We believe he may have witnessed Alex's murder."

"What do you plan to do with him?"

"I don't know. When he's out of danger, we'll cross that bridge, but right now, I want to make sure that nothing can ever harm him again."

The doorbell chimed once again. "That's probably Jake," Cara said.

Cara answered the door. This time, Jake was holding a bag from Wendy's. "My God, if they don't throw us in jail for failing to report that we have Tam, they will surely do it for feeding him a diet of fast food."

"The kid loves hamburgers, and it wouldn't hurt for him to gain some weight."

"You are not kidding me, Jake Gold. You're just an old softie when it comes to Tam."

"Where is he?" said Jake, looking for the boy.

"He's in the family room watching *Kung Fu Panda* again."

"So he liked the movie?"

Cara laughed, shutting the door behind him. "He's watched it so many times, I think I could recite it by heart."

"Sorry."

"No, it's good. It keeps him occupied, and it's helping him to learn English."

"Then you'll be happy that I bought him *Kung Fu Panda 2*."

Cara groaned and then led Jake into the family room where Lia was sitting next to the boy on the sectional and helping him to write letters on a tablet.

"Lia," Cara said. "I'd like you to meet Jake Gold. He's the private investigator that I hired to find out who staged the photos, and who has now evolved into a junk food pusher."

Jake shrugged. "So the kid likes fast food. What can I say? I brought extra. Care to join us?"

"Why, thank you," Lia said.

"Great," said Jake, who headed to the kitchen with the food and Tam trailing along.

Lia looked at Cara and whispered. "He could investigate me anytime."

Cara rolled her eyes. "I thought Francesco was your dreamboat?"

"He is," Lia said. "But I'm thinking about you. He's good looking in a bad boy sort of way."

"Me?" Cara whispered. "I'm still married. How would it look if I was caught carrying on with him?"

"Oh, loosen up, Cara. Who cares what it looks like? You won't be married for much longer, and no one could blame you after what Wesley did to you. And besides, he's incredibly hot. Don't tell me you haven't noticed."

"Of course, I've noticed."

"Good," Lia said as they walked into the kitchen. "I'm glad to see that you are human."

As Cara watched Jake unwrap Tam's food and insert his straw into his drink for him, Cara never felt more human in her life, and more vulnerable to Jake's magnetism.

*****

As they lunched over Spicy Chicken sandwiches and chocolate Frostys, Jake told Cara and Lia what he had discovered from Jittra about the transporting of the sex slaves and how he hoped she would have more information for him when he staked out the Shop A Lot again later that day.

"Do you think she will show up?" Cara asked.

"I'm hoping so. I told her you and I would help her. I promised I'd find a doctor to fix her scar," Jake said. "I know I shouldn't have committed you. But even if you can't help her, I'm going to. No one should have to go through life disfigured like that."

Cara felt a vise-like clamping of her heart. Jake certainly knew what it was like to be disfigured. "You know I would want to help her. I've been doing research on human sex trafficking, and not only are we going to have to help provide these kids with the basics of life, but also many of them are going to need counseling after all they've been through," said Cara. "We've got our work cut out for us."

"If anyone can do it, you can, Cara," said Lia.

"Which reminds me," Cara said. "Lia was about to give me the letter we received at the office when you arrived."

"I checked through our donor database too," Lia said, "but I could find no one named Sally Metzger. Let me get it for you." Lia went to her Vera Bradley tote and retrieved a manila folder and brought it to the counter. She pulled out a personal-sized envelope and a sheet of white paper.

"You look at it, Jake," Cara said, "while I give Tam his medicine." She went to the cabinet, wrestled with the child-proof cap and finally was able to get into it to get the pill. She filled up a glass of water from the dispenser in the refrigerator door. After Tam swallowed his pill with a large gulp of water, Cara gently patted his shoulder. "Good, Tam."

"Watch *Panda*," he said with a look of mischief in his dark eyes.

Cara rolled her eyes. "Let's ask Jake."

They walked back into the kitchen. Cara touched Tam's shoulder. "Tam wants to know if he can watch *Kung Fu Panda* again?"

Jake made a stern face. "No."

Tam looked crushed.

"But you can watch *Kung Fu Panda 2*," said Jake as he whipped the disc out of the plastic bag.

Tam laughed and grasped the disc. Cara made him repeat the words "thank you" before she took him into the family room, fluffed his pillows, and tucked him snuggly under blankets on the sectional couch. She hit the remote and the DVD player cued *Kung Fu Panda* 2.

When she came back to the kitchen, Jake handed her the letter. "Since the writer signed the letter, I'm not too concerned. I seriously doubt that she intends any harm. From the tone, though, it seems more like she has some kind of beef, and I get the feeling that it happened a while ago."

Cara studied the letter. The handwriting looked shaky. "I could ask my father if he remembers anyone by that name. He's had so many employees over the years, maybe it's from one of them."

Jake was tapping his iPhone.

"I find it odd that the letter isn't addressed to anyone in particular," said Lia.

"What does the envelope say?" Cara turned it over and noticed that it was just addressed to Comfort Connection.

Jake looked up from his phone. "I Googled her, and all I got was an article on how she volunteers at the local Meals on Wheels program at her church even though she's in her late eighties."

"She hardly sounds like someone we have to worry about. She doesn't seem like she'd be the type to mail us Anthrax," Lia said.

"She says 'your press conference.' Father Nicco was also at the press conference as well as you and your father. Maybe it's someone else with a complaint against one of the diocesan priests," Jake said.

"Then why wouldn't she have written to the diocese or come forward when Father Nicco was always on television commenting on the cases against the diocese?" asked Lia.

"The big question," Cara said, "is what do we do about the letter? Do we ignore it? Should I try to phone her?"

"I'm the investigator here," Jake said. "Why don't you let me see what I can find out for you?"

"You've had two press conferences. I wonder why she didn't write it after you held your first one?" asked Lia.

"Have *you* ever thought about being a private investigator?" Jake said, looking at Lia.

Lia laughed. "When you've been on as many blind dates as I have, you know how to do research."

Cara began to tap on her phone's screen. "I'm going to call my father to see if that name rings a bell with him." She set the phone down when the call went to his voicemail.

"In the meantime," said Jake, "I'll do a little more digging on Sally Metzger, and if I can track her down, I think I'll pay Ms. Metzger a visit to see what's gotten her Depends in a twist."

Chapter 48

Jake left Cara's and arrived at the Shop A Lot around three-thirty. He spent his time waiting for Jittra by trying to find more information on Sally Metzger. When he called the Social Security office, he even charmed a clerk there into checking to see if a Sally Metzger was still collecting checks and was delighted to learn that she was.

When he hung up the phone, he looked out the window and noticed that it had started to sleet, making the sidewalks treacherous or as they say in Pittsburgh, "slippy." He got out of the car and waited under the overhang at the Shop A Lot, wondering if Jittra would be a no-show since the weather was so inclement. Then out of the gray and sleet, came her little figure. She was wearing an old Pittsburgh Penguins hat pulled over her straight hair, her face wrapped in a ratty green and white striped scarf. The navy puffy down coat gave the appearance of more bulk on her tiny frame as she carefully picked her way over the icy sidewalks. Jittra looked poor, but not so destitute as to attract attention from the authorities. His guess was that Mama and The General took great care not be conspicuous.

"Jittra," he said softly, "Here. I got you this."

He handed her a hot chocolate that he'd gotten at Starbucks on his way there. She looked at him warily. "It will warm you up."

She glanced over her shoulder.

"Come to my car with me. It's right there," he said, pointing to the lot. "I promise you will be safe."

"Like Alex was safe?"

"No. We offered him safety, but he refused. I promise. If I have to come into the house commando-style and rescue you, I will. I promise you'll be safe."

"How can you say that?"

"Here," he handed her a cell phone. "You call any time you need me."

"I can't take. If Mama finds . . ." she shuddered and looked over her shoulder.

"Please get in the car," he said. The girl followed him and sat in the front seat. "Give me your coat while you drink that. He held the hot chocolate while she pulled her red mittens off with her teeth and slithered out of the coat. The bones of her shoulders jutted out under her thin T-shirt.

The windows steamed over as she drank deeply from the warm chocolate while Jake took out a knife.

Jittra gasped and flinched.

He could understand her fear of knives. "You're fine. I'm just going to make a slit in the pocket and put the phone inside the lining of the coat. Does Mama ever search your clothing?"

"No, Mama always say Jittra good girl. Never steals Mama's change when I come home from the store. I not steal because I don't want to be like Mama. She steal children, their goodness, their life. Never be like Mama," she said with an air of defiance, which gladdened Jake's heart. Mama hadn't been able to steal Jittra's will to survive and her dignity.

Jake slit the pocket at the seam. Then he showed Jittra the phone, how to turn it on and how he had programmed two numbers into it, his and Cara's. He also instructed her how to dial 9-1-1 to call the police.

Jittra was shaking. "I don't know. What if Mama finds?"

"Then you tell her that a man at the store who likes you gave it you so he can contact you for fun."

"She not believe that. She say nobody want Jittra anymore. Too ugly."

He touched her bony shoulder. "You tell her the man at the store thinks you are beautiful. And you are."

Jake shut the phone off and slid it behind the lining of the pocket nestling it in the cheap fiberfill of the jacket. He squeezed it. "The battery should last for several days. See, you can barely feel it in there."

Jittra squeezed the coat.

"Now, I'm going to sew this up with very loose stitches, so if you need to get at it, you can just break the thread."

Jittra giggled. "You sew?"

"Yes, I sew. I learned in the military." He bit off the string and then handed her the jacket. "I saw Tam last night. He's doing fine. My friend is helping him, and we'll help you too as soon as we can help the others."

She touched her cheek.

"And yes, we are going to find a doctor to fix your scar."

She held the hot cup to her cheek.

"Have you learned anything about the next shipment?"

She found her mittens which were lying in her lap, and then pulled out a rumpled napkin from inside one of them. "I find this. Copy what mama write down when she on phone."

He looked at the soiled napkin and the characters written in crayon.

They were barely legible, and then it occurred to him that Jittra did not know our alphabet and had gone to great pains and risk to copy what she saw. He looked at her and wanted to hug this brave, small soul. She was as heroic as the soldiers he'd fought alongside.

"Mama say 'Monday night, Pier 17.'" She looked at him imploring him. "You stop them. You help boys and girls."

"I will."

She glanced nervously out the car window. "I go before Mama wonder where Jittra be so long."

As she reached for the door, Jake leaned over and touched her small hand. "Thank you, Jittra. You are very brave. It won't be much longer."

It was Wednesday. No, it wouldn't be much longer. Monday would soon be here, and he had better get to work if he intended to bring down an international human sex trafficking ring.

*****

Jake was so excited by what he'd learned that he dropped by Cara's house. He called on his way to see if she wanted him to bring dinner, and she explicitly forbade him to bring anything.

As he walked up the door, he could smell that something good was cooking.

When Cara let him in, she was dressed in black jeans and sapphire blue turtleneck and Tam appeared behind her smiling. His coloring was improving. "Yo, dude." the boy said, raising his hand for a high-five.

Jake laughed and slapped him five. "Where did he learn that?" he asked Cara as he watched the boy scamper toward the family room.

"He's been watching the *Fresh Prince* marathon ever since you left. Lia turned him on to it before she went home this afternoon," Cara said. "I don't know how much he understands, but obviously, he understands that."

Jake smiled and then lifted his head. "What smells so good?"

"Pad Thai. I found an easy recipe online. Lia stayed with Tam while I went to grocery store and picked up some more things for him. I got him *Kung Fu Panda 3* to break up the monotony."

Jake laughed. "You're as bad as I am."

When they entered the family room, Tam was giggling at Carlton on television as he danced to *It's Not Unusual*.

"Ah," said Jake, "the Carlton dance. It crosses international boundaries."

Tam was trying to imitate Carlton but was not quite getting it. Jake walked into the room. "It's like this, buddy." Jake broke into a feverish Carlton, which sent Tam collapsing onto the couch holding his stomach in a fit of laughter.

Shocked, Cara covered her mouth and then burst into laughter too.

"What's so funny?" asked Jake, whipping his arms into the air, his prosthetic one looking a bit stiff.

"I didn't know you could do that," Cara said.

Jake grabbed her hand. "Yo dude, come on. Everyone can Carlton."

Tam began to clap his hands.

"Not me," Cara said as Jake pulled her toward him.

"Come on," Jake said. "Surely, you must have danced at those debutante balls. Or maybe you are so prissy you don't know how to get down."

Cara broke free. "Who you calling prissy?" she asked, putting her hands on her hips.

"You, Miss Goody Two Shoes."

Cara set her jaw and glanced at Jake and then Tam. "Look out, wallflowers!" She then moonwalked across the floor.

Jake couldn't believe what he was seeing, and he and Tam stopped dancing and watched with their mouths agape as Cara effortlessly glided across the kitchen floor backward and then struck a pose, raising one arm triumphantly into the air.

Tam came running to her and threw his arms around her legs laughing; his outburst of joy had taken her off guard and knocked her off balance. Jake caught her in his arms before she and Tam toppled onto the floor.

"That was pretty amazing," Jake said as he held Cara and gazed into her eyes. "Where'd you learn how to do that?"

"I took dance lessons for years. Don't you know all society divas do?"

Then Jake suddenly kissed her, while Tam clutched them both around the legs.

And as his lips softly caressed Cara's, what was truly amazing to him was that for the first time in many years of suffering and discontent, he was happy.

Chapter 49

While they ate dinner, Jake told Cara about what he'd learned from Jittra, about the shipment of people coming into New York on Monday.

"So what do we do now?" Cara asked.

"I have calls into ICE and the FBI. When they call me back, I'll tell them what we've learned. This is an international crime and the big boys will have to be involved."

"Do you think it would help if I called my father? He might be able to use his clout."

"I don't suppose it would hurt."

"I also want to call him and ask him if he knows anything about Sally Metzger."

While Jake took Tam into the family room to play with his LEGOs, Cara went into the den and called her father.

"Hello, Cara dear," he said. "I was just thinking of you, wondering how things are going with your newest project?"

"I'm fine, but I need your help with two things. But before I get to that. Have you heard anything more on Sophia?"

"I spoke to her physician today before I left for New York, and she's doing as well as can be expected. I gather detox is a rather unpleasant affair, but they tell me that she's holding up well. Once she has sobered up, they can begin to delve more deeply into her underlying problems in therapy."

"I didn't realize she was in such bad shape," Cara said, as she scoured her brain, once again, for any indication that Sophia was using drugs.

"Sophia is adept at concealing things. We all know she tries to appear a *bon vivant*, but I'm afraid your mother's suicide deeply wounded her."

It wounded all of us. How different her life would have been had her mother believed that her life was worth living. *Would Sophia be such a mess? Would I feel the undercurrent of blame from my father? Would I feel as equally as loved as Sophia?*

"Now, how can I help you?" he asked.

"First, Jake and I have been investigating the sex trafficking in the city, and we've gotten a tip that a cargo ship from Asia will be arriving in New York on Monday. It's transporting victims of human trafficking."

He was silent. "How dreadful, but I thought they reported on the news that they arrested numerous traffickers during the Super Bowl."

"Apparently, not all of them. Jake is waiting to hear back from ICE and the FBI to tell them what we've learned. I thought you should know since you will soon be the ambassador. I don't know if there is anything you can do?"

"Certainly, I'll do whatever I can, but I'm going to have to know details. How did Jake learn this? Is this tipster credible?"

"Jake found a girl in the city who lives in the place where these poor children are kept hostage." Cara sighed. "These people need to be stopped. I haven't met this girl, but Jake said her face was slashed severely. I don't know if it was a client or her trafficker who did it."

"I'm sickened just thinking about it."

Cara heard the anger in his voice. "This has to be stopped," he said.

"It's great to have your support."

"You said there were two matters."

"Yes, this is a bit odd, but do know anyone named Sally Metzger?"

Silence.

"Father, do you know anyone named Sally Metzger?"

"Sorry, Cara. Someone walked into the office. Sally Metzger? No, I can't say that it rings a bell. Should I know her?"

"No. This Sally Metzger person sent a very strange letter to Comfort Connection, and I don't recognize her name." She filled her father in on the contents of the letter. "Since we were both at the press conference and the letter wasn't addressed specifically to anyone, I thought perhaps you may know who she is."

"She's probably suffering from dementia. You know how some of these elderly people are always sending letters to the editor complaining about something or other. She most likely saw you on TV and was annoyed because they were having lime Jell-O at the home instead of strawberry and decided to take it out on you. I wouldn't attach too much importance to it."

"She wouldn't have been a former household employee, one that was fired years ago?"

"I don't recall any incident, but you are welcome to go to my apartment and search through the old accounting books for Hawthorne Manor. Your grandmother kept meticulous records."

"When you come home, I'll take you up on that."

"I'm going to be here for a few more days. You don't have to wait until I return from New York. You've been cooped up in the house taking care of your little charge. You know the security code. Why don't you get a little fresh air and go while I'm away?"

"Thanks. If I can get Lia to babysit him tomorrow, I'll go check them out."

"Why don't you take Tam with you? The view will amaze him, and he's seen nothing but the underbelly of this city. Let him see how beautiful Pittsburgh truly is."

"But I hate to take him out. No one knows he's with me."

"No one will see you. You know how few people are in the building during the daytime and many of the other residents are wintering in Florida."

"When you go through the books, be sure to look at the guest logs— all the celebrities and dignitaries that visited Hawthorne Manor— Gloria Swanson, Humphrey Bogart, Winston Churchill—it's really quite incredible."

"That sounds like a wonderful idea. Thank you, Father. I'll go tomorrow."

"See you when I return from New York."

Cara hung up the phone and walked into the family room, where she found Jake on his cell phone while at the same time he was snapping LEGO bricks with his good hand onto what looked like might be a car. She whispered to him that she was going to give Tam a bath.

She led Tam upstairs and ran the water. Before she left the bathroom, she made gestures that she wanted him to remove his clothes and get in the tub and scrub himself. He nodded, indicating that he understood. Then he said, "Cara, Tam." and he tried to moonwalk.

"You want to learn how to moonwalk?" She moonwalked a few steps, and he shook his head laughing. It was so good to see the child happy. "Bath," she said making a motion of scrubbing her arm, "then moonwalk."

She left the bathroom ajar in case he needed her, and she parked herself at the top of the stairs while Tam splashed and chattered away in the bathroom. How strange life is, thought Cara. A month ago, it was just Wesley and me living a quiet, well-planned life and then the hand of fate had come along and torn that life up into little pieces and thrown them into the air. Wesley and his mistress were sitting in a jail cell, a partially disabled Jewish IDF veteran turned private investigator was downstairs in her den working to bring down an international crime ring while a small Thai boy was splashing in her bathtub.

Certainly, the last few weeks had been awful, but Cara could not say that she was unhappy. Tam had stolen her heart, and Jake had brought out a side of herself that she hadn't known was in her. She felt a bit prideful, but she thought she brought out something in Jake as well. He was far from the surly, brooding man that she had met in his office the day she had hired him. Cara bit her lip. *I haven't paid Jake yet.* When he got off the phone, she would have to rectify that.

Tam emerged from the bathroom wearing thermal printed pajamas, his hair a riot of black, wet spikes. She took him back into the bathroom, towel-dried his hair, and then combed it. First she combed it into a Mohawk, which made Tam smile. Then she arranged his hair into devil horns and he laughed even harder. Tam took the comb from her and combed his bangs into a point, whose vee terminated between his eyes.

"Show Jake," he said as he took off down the stairs.

Cara followed, and they found Jake sitting on the family room floor searching through the LEGOs for another yellow brick. Tam came and stood in front of him.

"Nice do, buddy," Jake said. "You look like Eddie Munster." Then he reached out and with a flick of his wrist, turned the vee into a large curl in the middle of the boy's forehead, making Tam laugh even harder.

"Enough with the hair styles, guys. It's time for his medicine," Cara said taking the child's hand and making a spooning motion.

Cara took him to the kitchen and gave him his medicine. Then Tam looked at her. "Cara, moonwalk."

"What did he say?" Jake called from the family room.

Cara rolled her eyes. "He wants me to teach him how to moonwalk."

For the next fifteen minutes, Cara helped the boy learn to glide backward across the floor in his socks while Jake watched from the family room with a look of bewildered mirth on his face.

Tam yawned loudly.

"No more," Cara said. "You've been sick. You need to rest." Cara pantomimed sleep.

Then Tam became visibly upset.

"What's wrong with him?" Jake asked, rising and coming into the kitchen.

"He's not been sleeping very well. He's been having nightmares."

"I can't imagine why," Jake said sarcastically.

"I've been letting him fall asleep on the couch then carrying him up to bed. I'd let him sleep with me, but after what he'd been through with me, I didn't think it was such a good idea."

"This language barrier is such a pain in the ass," Jake said. "If I could only speak Thai, I could teach him some of the things I learned to cope with PTSD."

Cara was a bit taken aback. She knew from the night in the hospital that Jake had had nightmares, but he had never confided before that he had suffered from PTSD.

"When I was small, and I was sent to live with my grandmother after my mother's death, she used to lie with me, holding my hand until I fell asleep. That's what I've been doing with him."

"Works for me," Jake said.

So Cara made up the couch as a bed for Tam; she turned on the gas fireplace, dimmed the lights, and sat next to Tam on the couch with Jake on the boy's other side. She picked up Tam's small hand while Jake took his other one. Cara knew this was to comfort Tam but sitting together, their hands linked like paper dolls, Cara never felt more contented in her life.

Chapter 50

Cara awoke the next morning and found herself lying under a fleece blanket on the couch opposite Tam, who was also covered with a fleece blanket. She popped her head up, looking for Jake, but he wasn't there. He must have gone home, she thought. So as not to wake Tam, she slowly pushed back the blanket and rose. Slipping her feet into her pink suede moccasins, she padded out to the kitchen.

Cara was surprised when she found Jake sitting at the island, sipping coffee, the tips of his black curls damp. He looked fresh-scrubbed, but he was still wearing the clothes he'd had on from the night before and his stubble was on the verge of crossing the line and becoming a beard.

"You're still here?"

He looked at her above his mug. "That sounds so welcoming."

"Sorry, it's just that I thought you had gone home. I didn't know you slept with me—I mean us."

"You kind of zonked out. You seemed so tired I didn't want to wake you when Tam woke up with a nightmare?"

"He had another?"

"Yes, it's to be expected after what he's been through." He took her hand. "He'll be OK. We'll get him some help as soon as he's safe."

"I guess," Cara said, pulling her hand away.

He tilted his head, gazing at her. "What is it, Cara? What's wrong?"

"Everything. I've got a boy living with me for who knows how long and God knows where he'll end up. And then there's you. I have you here drinking coffee in my kitchen like you live here when I'm still married. Where's this all heading, Jake?"

He set the mug down. "I don't know, Cara. Do we have to know the destination right now? Can't we just enjoy the ride?"

"No, I can't. I'm not that kind of person. I'm not Sophia; I need definition in my life, to know where things stand. I'm trying to restore my reputation and get my life back, and I've got men spending the night at my house while my husband is sitting in jail for blackmail and murder. I'm now in charge of two charitable organizations that are supposed to help people, yet look at my life. What does this look like to the outside world? Like some kind of sick reality show?"

He stood and took her by the shoulders. "You don't have 'men' spending the night. You have me. The one who's in this mess up to my eyeballs too. The one who loves you, and I don't care what anyone else thinks!"

Cara stepped back from him. "What did you say?"

"Which part?"

"The part about loving me."

"Yeah, I love you. The one-armed Jewish cynic has fallen madly in love with the queen of the debutante ball. I know that doesn't help your reputation much or fit in with your champagne wishes and caviar dreams, but deal with it."

"I don't know what to say."

"Say you love me too because I know that you do, and I know you want to kiss me."

Cara turned her head as if to deflect his words. "I'm still married and I—-"

He pulled her tightly to his chest and kissed her. Then he looked into her eyes. "As you were saying, 'And I—' What?"

"And I haven't even brushed my teeth yet."

"Welcome to the real world, Cara, where people kiss before brushing, love before being available, and learn to adapt to circumstances beyond their control and forget what people think."

"But I can't Jake." She lowered her eyes. "I can't be someone I'm not. I do care how things look and what others think of me. How can I not? You haven't been raised under a microscope with everyone watching your every move, criticizing everything you've ever worn, weighing in on everything you've ever done."

"Tell me that you don't love me, Cara."

He took her chin in his hand and made her stare at him. "Tell me you don't love me."

"I do love you, but I shouldn't. There are two kinds of love, Jake— the good and life-giving and the wrong and suffocating—and ours is wrong and will only lead to heartache for the both of us."

"Good and life-giving love—like the one you had with Wesley? I'm not buying that crap, Cara. So you've been raised in the spotlight, who gives a damn what people think?"

"But I care what I think. I think—no, I know it's wrong to get involved with someone while I'm married. What would my father think? Or Father Nicco? Or Comfort Connection's supporters?"

"Do you care what I think?"

"Certainly."

"Here's what I think. I think you really are a stuck up society snob. You're hiding behind virtue when you think you are too good to love a Jewish cripple."

"That's not true," Cara said, wiping away tears. "You know me. You know I'm not like that."

"Do I really know you? I don't think there is a you. You're just a glamorous façade. You're like a Hollywood set, the buildings look real, but inside there's nothing. You only do good things to feed the beast that is your image. There's nothing genuine in your heart."

"There is too something in there," Cara said, pointing to her heart, "because I can feel it breaking."

"I don't know what you want from me, Cara. I love you, but I'm not supposed to have you? What kind of madness is that? I've been tortured, but what you're doing to me is far worse."

"I don't mean to. For now, can't we just be as we have been friends and teammates in our fight against whoever is behind this human trafficking ring?"

"Teammates? Like Wonder Woman and Captain America?" He headed for the door. Cara followed him as he retrieved his coat and put it on.

"Where are you going, Jake?"

"I can't take this, Cara. I'm going to meet with the ICE and FBI agents to try to solve this mess. And being friends and crime fighters is the stuff of comic books. When you want a real man, you know where to call me."

Jake slammed the door behind him as Cara burst into tears. Suddenly, Tam came around the corner. He stared at Cara and then at the door. "Where Jake?" he asked.

She didn't want him to see her upset, so she quickly wiped away the tears with the back of her hand and pasted on a phony smile. "Gone. Jake's gone."

Chapter 51

Jake was still fuming from his argument with Cara when he arrived at FBI Headquarters on East Carson Street, and he was in an even worse mood when he left their office an hour later. He had arranged to meet with the agents and an official from ICE, who thanked Jake for what he'd told them. Jake, however, was enraged when the ICE agent told him that there would be no raid. Not at the pier in New York or at Mama's to rescue Jittra and all of the others. And even though he had turned over all the information he'd gleaned, including Jittra's poorly written note, to his dismay, they felt it would be more beneficial to observe these operations to learn as much as possible about them so that they could apprehend The General.

"So the 'high-level trafficker' that was arrested and reported on the news is not the ring leader?" asked Jake. They wouldn't confirm or deny that, and it pissed Jake off that while he had given them all his information, they would share none of theirs. "I want something in return," said Jake pounding his fist on the conference room table.

"I've solved two crimes for you. If Jittra is in the least bit of danger, you have to rescue her. Promise me, or I'll expose how lackadaisical you were in investigating Cara's blackmail case." Before he walked out on them, he extracted a promise that if Jittra called him for help, they would rescue her.

With nothing left to do on the human trafficking investigation, Jake was at loose ends. All he thought about was Cara. On the off chance that Father Nicco was available, he called the bishop's office. He was thankful that the good bishop was in town and arranged to meet with him for lunch at Lidia's at one in the Strip District.

When Jake arrived, he found Father Nicco waiting for him.

"So good to see you, Jake," said the bishop as he motioned for Jake to take a seat. "I've been in touch with Cara throughout this whole ordeal, but I haven't heard much from you. How are things going?"

"Great," Jake said, then lowered his head, running his hands through his hair. "Awful."

"Really? My, my. This calls for some wine." Father Nicco signaled the waitress who brought another glass for Jake and poured from the bottle of Cabernet that Father Nicco has previously ordered. "So tell me."

Jake leaned back from the table. "I don't know where to begin."

Father Nicco tapped Jake's real hand. "When I hear confessions and someone doesn't know where to begin, I usually tell them to start at the beginning. So let's begin with Cara. Were you able to work with her?"

"Work with her?" Jake shook his head. "Dammit, Father, I love her."

"She is quite a woman—kind, charitable."

"I'm not talking like that. I mean I love her—love her."

Father Nicco sipped from his glass. "Oh, I see. Does that fall under the "great" or "awful" category?"

"Both," said Jake.

And as they finished the bottle of Cabernet and dined on Caesar salad and veal parmesan, Jake told him about the progress he'd made on the human sex trafficking ring, to which Father Nicco shared with him the measures already being implemented throughout the diocese to help the victims.

"Now, back to Cara," Father Nicco said.

Jake rubbed the stubble on his cheek. "It feels kind of awkward telling a priest that you have feelings for a woman who is technically still married."

"Jake, you can't shock me. I'm a grown man. I know people fall in love all the time with people who are off limits. Think of me as your friend because I am. I only want the best for both of you."

Jake poured his heart out to Father Nicco, telling him how much he loved Cara, and how frustrated he felt by her insistence on maintaining proprieties. "I know you can't advocate for her to violate her marriages vows, but her husband tried to frame her with a crime for God's sake. Then he murdered someone. Surely, there can be exceptions made for that?"

"Oh, Jake," Father Nicco said, "I know you are a man of action, a warrior, but you must learn patience. If this love is ordained and blessed by God, nothing can stop it. But if it is not, nothing can redeem it."

"So what do I do in the meantime?"

"Pray. Wait. Keep yourself busy. In your haste, don't pressure Cara to be something she isn't, for no matter how frustrating you find her reaction to be, it is her essence and what you have fallen in love with. Remember, how you came to me so disillusioned by people who did not live by principles, how you wish you could find one person who did? My friend, God has answered your prayer. He has brought you Cara—a woman of principles. Be patient. Perhaps God will answer another prayer as well."

*****

Jake and Father Nicco parted outside the restaurant but not before the bishop extracted a promise from Jake—that he would call him any time, day or night if he wanted to talk. He shook Jake's hand and patted his back. "I was once in love with someone before I entered the seminary, but it wasn't to be. Still, my life turned out quite well—

thanks be to God."

"What happened to the woman?" asked Jake turning his face toward father, the February wind blowing his curls.

"She fell in love and married someone else."

Jake frowned. "Oh, man. I'm sorry. Do you ever see her?"

Father Nicco closed his eyes for a moment. "Sometimes in my dreams." He looked at Jake with a wistful smile. "But that is the beauty of love, Jake. If you nurture it, it never dies. Love and wisdom are the only two things we take out of this life and into the next."

"When you found out she was married and you couldn't have her, weren't you devastated?"

"For a while, but then I realized that just because I couldn't be with her, didn't mean I loved her any less. Besides, I loved God too, so I set myself to serving Him so that one day when I died, I would be welcomed into His kingdom of love where both He and all of us who love Him will live in eternity."

Jake admired Father Nicco, but as he headed to his car, he sincerely hoped that he wouldn't have to wait until eternity to have Cara.

*****

As Jake drove back to his office, he thought about what Father Nicco had advised about keeping busy. With Wesley sitting in jail charged with extortion and murder and the FBI and ICE in charge of the human sex trafficking case, there were only two remaining loose ends—rescuing Jittra and investigating Sally Metzger. He wanted to take matters into his own hands and spirit Jittra away when he would meet her later this afternoon, but he didn't want to jeopardize the FBI's plan to bring down the entire child sex trafficking syndicate.

Back at his office, he decided to occupy himself by trying to locate Sally Metzger. He started with the obvious, a search of the White Pages, but had no luck. As he dug some more on the Internet, Sally Metzger's name showed up in a photo accompanying an article written this past Christmas about octogenarians living at Ross Park Care Center and receiving Christmas gifts donated by school children. He wondered if she were still a resident at the care center. It wouldn't hurt to try to reach her. On a whim, he hopped into the car and began the half hour drive to the nursing home.

Jake hated nursing homes. *How could my mother have put* zaide *in a home after all that he had been through?* Jake still couldn't understand. *Zaide's* mind had been failing him, and his mother said sending him to a nursing home was for his safety. Jake knew that his grandfather's life was coming to an end and even offered to defer college to take care of him, but his parents had insisted that he leave for Columbia. Before departing, Jake visited *zaide* in the home, where his grandfather had called the nurses by the names of the guards in the Jasenovac concentration camp where he'd been sent as a child.

When they brought his grandfather his dinner on a tray, the old man looked terrified, grabbed the dinner roll, and stuffed it into the pocket of Jake's jacket. "Here, take this before the guards see it," *zaide* said, terror in his eyes. Then his grandfather tore into the meal with his hands, greedily stuffing the turkey and mashed potatoes into his mouth, much the way Jake imagined his grandfather had done in captivity many years ago when he was starving. It was bad enough that *zaide* had had to endure the Holocaust once in his life, but when Jake's parents had sent him to the nursing home, it outraged Jake that he was reliving it for the second time. Sadly, *zaide* lasted only a few weeks before dying. Heartbroken and filled with anger for his parents, Jake left college and headed to Israel.

Jake shook off the painful memory and walked into the facility, which was done in soft blues and roses. No matter how tastefully decorated, it still was a glorified institution to Jake. He thought he'd take a stab at finding Sally Metzger by checking in at the front desk, where the receptionist was on the phone.

"Hi," he said when she hung up. "Perhaps you can help me. I'm looking for my Great Aunt Sally Metzger. I live in Burlington, Vermont, but I happened to be in Pittsburgh on business, and I thought I'd stop in to see her. I'm afraid my family has lost touch with her since my mother—her sister—developed Alzheimer's."

"Sally Metzger? Oh, she's a dear and sharp as a tack. Isn't it strange how in the same family one can lose their physical health while another it's their mind that goes?"

Jake was delighted that the receptionist was buying his story. "I hope

I get Aunt Sally's mind and my mother's physical strength."

"You and me both. She's in Room 226. You go down that corridor to the elevators. She's going to be so happy to have a visitor. She's been so sad since her son's death."

"I'm sure," Jake said, shaking his head at the tragedy, but he wanted out of there before he blew his cover. "Thanks," he said as he headed toward the elevator, which was so slow in ascending he pushed the elevator button several times until he remembered Father Nicco's admonition to have patience.

He hated the way nursing homes smelled—a mixture of human waste masked by air freshener. On his way to Sally Metzger's room, he passed several elderly patients who were sitting slumped in wheelchairs near the nurse's station. Some looked at him while others stared straight ahead. He knew the will to live was strong. He'd learned that when he'd been tortured and from *zaide's* life, but it seemed for many of these elderly people, the only thing remaining of them was their will.

He found Room 226 and the name card outside the room said Sally Metzger. Her name had been written in pen. I guess when you are that close to death, nothing is engraved. He peeked inside the room. Sitting in a wheelchair next to a hospital bed was a small woman with sparse gray hair. She was wearing a colorfully printed nightgown and a white knitted sweater. The other bed was unoccupied.

"Excuse me, are you Sally Metzger?" Jake asked as he stepped into the room. He tried to look relaxed and not as if he was storming the place.

"Yes? Last time I checked. Who are you?"

"Jake Gold. Do you mind if I talk to you for a moment?"

"Are you a lawyer?"

"No, I'm here about a letter you sent to Comfort Connection."

"Your name sounds Jewish. Are you sure you're not a lawyer?"

He smiled. Evidently the PC police were not on duty here. "I am Jewish, but I'm not a lawyer. I'm a friend of Cara Hawthorne's, and we were concerned about your letter."

She shook her head. "For a time, I had thought that she'd turned out different, what with her helping little kids with her charity, but she turned out just like him. I guess the apple doesn't fall from the tree—or I should say rotten apple."

"I don't understand?"

"Her being a pervert. Just like her father."

"Her father? Laurence Hawthorne? He's a pervert?"

"Pervert, sick son of a bitch. I don't care what you call him. Anyone who bothers young boys is a bastard in my book."

"He bothered young boys? Why do you say that?"

"Because I worked in his home as the Hawthorne's housekeeper, and I caught him when he was home from college pleasuring himself while he had his hands down my son's pants."

This news was as jolting mentally as the grenade that had taken his arm had been physically. "What? Are you sure? You're talking about Laurence Hawthorne—the nominee to the Ambassadorship to the United Nations?"

"Yes, I saw his rat face on TV with his daughter, acting like butter wouldn't melt in his mouth while my poor Bobby is dead." Her wrinkled hands shook. "Oh, his parents thought they could cover everything up by paying us off, but Bobby was never the same after that. He got into trouble at school. I think that led him to drink, and no matter how many times he tried to sober up, he fell off the wagon." She wiped a tear away from her lined face. "He hanged himself a year ago, you know."

Jake shook his head. "Sorry, I didn't know that."

"Yes, and a few months later, I had a stroke. Now, here I sit in my old age with all these cretins when I should be in my own home with my son."

"Forgive me, Mrs. Metzger, but I have to be clear about this: You are accusing Laurence Hawthorne, the future Ambassador to the United Nations, a well-respected businessman, of being a pedophile. Do you have any way of proving this?"

"I have a bank statement from forty years ago showing a deposit of $300,000 from the Hawthorne's." She shook her head. "And a report from Bobby's pediatrician. How stupid I was. At the time, it sounded like a fortune. I was widowed and I needed that job. They told us if we just kept quiet, we'd be taken care of. But there was no amount of money that could fix what Laurence Hawthorne did to my son."

"Why have you kept silent for so long?"

"Because of Bobby. He never wanted anyone to know that he had been molested. I used to argue with him all the time—Who gives a shit what others think? I'd tell him. But I guess unless it's you, you can't know what it feels like to be that person."

She wheeled over to a dresser drawer and opened it. After rifling through some nightgowns, her shaky, gnarled fingers pulled out a slip of paper. She handed it to Jake. It was an old, faded deposit slip from Mellon Bank showing $300,000 was deposited on June 18, 1974. Then she pulled out a medical receipt from Boothby, Watkins & Rosenberg Pediatrics dated June 9 of that same year.

"What did you hope to accomplish with the letter?" Jake asked, handing her back the papers.

"Mr. Gold, I'm old. I have nothing left—but I'll die a happy woman if I can provoke in Laurence Hawthorne a small amount of the shame and fear he inflicted on my Bobby. 'Master Laurie,' was how I had to address him." She turned her nose up. "Like he was a British lord or something. He was always such a smart little shit. His parents weren't bad people. Truth be told, I think they were a bit afraid of him. He was a brat when he was small. I once saw him push a child down the stairs at his eighth birthday party. Oh, but as he grew older," She rolled her eyes in disgust. "Ordering everyone around. No wonder the staff called him *The General* behind his parents' back—that is until they caught the chef calling him that and fired him."

Jake's heart skipped a beat. "What did you say they called him?"

"The General."

Jake bolted out of the chair. "Thank you, Mrs. Metzger. I can assure you Cara Hawthorne knew nothing about this. Here is my card. We'll be in touch."

Instead of waiting for the pokey elevator, Jake took the stairs. As he breezed past the receptionist, he nodded. "Thanks."

"Enjoy your stay," called the receptionist.

He waved and as he sprinted out the door, he was calling Cara.

Chapter 52

On the third ring, Lia picked up the phone. "I thought I called Cara's home, Lia. I must have dialed her office number instead," Jake said as he opened his car door. "I'm sorry."

"No, you called the house. I'm watching Tam. He seems to be coming down with some kind of virus now. I had brought her over some work, and I offered to watch him while she went to her father's apartment to do some research."

"She went to her father's?"

"Yes, she just left. Apparently, she told him about that letter, and he said she could come and look through his family's records to see if she could find anything."

Jake's heart was beating against his breastbone. "Do you know if he's there with her?"

"No, she didn't say."

"I know this is going to sound strange, but do you have your iPhone handy?"

"Yes, why?"

"Can you pull up a photo of Cara's father? There should be plenty of them on the net what with his recent nomination."

"Let me get my phone," Lia said. Jake checked his watch. If Cara had just left, perhaps he could reach her in time before she entered her father's place.

"OK," Lia said, a bit out of breath. "A photo is loading now."

"Can you do me a favor and show the photo to Tam?"

"OK," Lia said, sounding very puzzled by the request.

He heard her walk into the family room and call, "Tam, sweetie. I need you to see something."

Tam's terrified scream and his word *General* told Jake all that he needed to know.

*****

Cara marveled at the low hanging clouds cloaking the city as she cruised down Grandview Avenue. The gloominess matched her mood. She was still upset about Jake. It was true she did love him, but she couldn't help being the way that she was. Why couldn't he understand that?

She pulled into the driveway of her father's apartment complex and drove into the parking garage. Although she loved Hawthorne Manor, she could see why her father had chosen to live in this penthouse on Mt. Washington; the view of the city drew the soul like a magnet. She parked in the visitor parking space and headed to the elevator. When she punched in the code, it took her to the eighth floor. The glass elevator looked over the city, which gleamed like platinum in the dull winter sunshine. It looked so sleepy today in the grips of winter, it was hard to believe that there were sexual predators in the city. If she had her way, she'd see to it that they were no longer there.

When the elevator doors parted, she stepped into the vestibule. Once again, she punched in the security code, entering her father's apartment. She walked into the foyer and turned on a light, the chandelier glowed and beams bounced off the marble floor. As she walked into the spacious, ultra-modern living room, she nearly jumped out of her boots. Her father was seated on the white leather sofa sipping scotch. There were no lights on, and his white hair and silhouetted figure blended into the background of the gray sky and cold, silver city behind him.

"Father, I'm surprised you're here," she said, covering her thumping heart with her hand.

"Yes, I thought you'd be." Laurence turned and faced her wearing a small smile.

"I thought you were still in New York."

"I returned suddenly because I had some business to attend to, some loose ends to tie up."

"I won't bother you."

"That is the plan."

Cara looked at him. He was talking rather strangely. Was he drunk?

"Father, is something wrong?"

Before he could answer, Cara heard a noise to her right. She turned and saw Sophia, emaciated and disheveled, shuffling into the room.

"Sophia!" Cara exclaimed, rushing to her sister's side. "You're here? What happened? Are you OK?"

Sophia's eyes bore into her father. "Ask our dear father."

Cara turned to look back at her father, and she was shocked to see him stand and withdraw a handgun from his breast pocket. "What are you doing?" she exclaimed.

He shook his head. "Cara. Cara. Cara. Always the do-gooder. Always putting your nose where it doesn't belong."

Cara began to tremble. She looked to Sophia. "I don't understand."

At that moment, Cara's phone began to ring inside her purse; she made a move to retrieve it, but her father pointed the gun at her. "Don't answer it, Cara dear."

She took Sophia's hand. It was cold and clammy. "Did he do this to you?" She turned toward her father. "What did you do to her?" she screamed at him, not caring that he had a gun.

He took a step closer to them. "Oh, Cara, what a devoted big sister you are. Why, if you weren't such a good girl, your mother would still be alive."

She felt tears come to her eyes at the mention of her mother's death. Did he still hold her responsible? Had his grief driven him mad? "What are you talking about?"

"Everything was fine until you had to report to mommy that daddy had his hands down baby Sophia's diaper. If you hadn't told your slut of a mother, I wouldn't have had to throw her off the balcony."

Cara gasped while Sophia began to cry.

He shook his head in mock sympathy. "Such a shame, but postpartum depression can be a bitch."

"You molested Sophia and killed our mother? How could you do such a thing?"

"Because he's a monster," Sophia said flatly. "I saw him steal the cheese knife from your kitchen, the knife that was used to murder Alex. When I went to confront him about it and demand my inheritance before turning him in, I learned that he's the mastermind behind the sex trafficking ring in the city." Tears flowed freely down Sophia's hollow cheeks. "I thought he took out his perversion on me only because I was a bad girl and you were the good girl, that he loved you more, but he's incapable of love."

"He said you were in rehab."

"I was never in rehab. He drugged me and has kept me here as his prisoner."

"Now, Cara, don't fret. Your and Sophia's troubles will soon be over. When she overdoses in front of you, it will be so much easier to explain your death as a suicide when you leap from the balcony. See, you've lost it all—your reputation, your husband, your livelihood, and now your mess of a sister has OD'd. Everyone will understand that it's all too much to bear. Suicide runs in families, you know. You take after your mother so much."

"You'll never get away with this," Cara said.

"You really are rather tiresome. Do you know how many times I've heard that? When you have money, good looks, and a spotless reputation, you can get away with anything." He put the gun to Cara's head. "Now, let's get on with our little Shakespearean tragedy. Open the sliding glass door to the balcony, Cara. While you, Sophia, sit on the chair."

Cara's mind was racing. At least, he'd taken away the element of surprise. She knew how he was going to kill them; it was just finding a way to stop him. With unsteady legs, she went to the sliding glass door and removed the security bar. Who did he think was going to break in this many stories up, Spiderman? But perhaps when you are harboring as many secrets as her father was, you take extra precautions. She slid open the door, a blast of cold air swept into the room.

"Throw the security bar on the balcony."

She cast the metal rod out on the balcony; it clanged as she averted her eyes from the height of the building. *Please God, help us.* "No one is ever going to believe this," Cara said.

"You are so naïve. I have contacts everywhere. Flash a little money around and you can eliminate foes and cover up anything. Or anyone." He motioned with the gun. "Now, Cara, come here."

Sophia was seated on a dining room chair looking catatonic. In that state, Cara knew she could not expect Sophia to help them out of this situation. Their father was behind the chair holding the gun on Cara.

"There are rubber gloves and a syringe. Put on the gloves."

The phone rang again in her purse. It was probably Jake, but he'd no reason to suspect that Cara was in danger. Who would ever believe that her father was so evil? She struggled to put the latex gloves on over her shaking hands. "Since your prints won't be on the needle, no one will ever suspect that you gave Sophia her overdose."

"You can't expect me to kill my own sister!"

"You are such a diva. Put them on," he said pointing with the gun.

Suddenly, Sophia snatched the hypodermic needle, and in one sweeping motion, reached behind her and jammed it into Laurence's eye. He recoiled in pain, dropping the gun, as Sophia tumbled from the chair. Cara dove for the gun at the same time that he did. He reached it first and trained it on her again. Pulling the needle from his eye, he rose and viciously kicked Sophia in the head as she struggled to stand. "I'll finish her off after I take care of you," he said, covering his injured eyes as he stepped over Sophia who lay in a heap on the floor.

"Walk," he commanded as he held the pistol on Cara, backing her through the sliding doorway onto the balcony. The wind howled and shocked Cara with how biting it was, but it helped to sharpen her senses. The apartment complex was built into the side of Mt. Washington, and she couldn't bear to think how far of a drop it was over the railing. She could hear cars below and off in the distance, the faint rattle of a freight train. How strange that life could be happening all around her while she was about to lose hers.

Her back against the railing now, Cara pondered whether it would be better to take the bullet or plunge to her death.

He pointed the gun at her temple. Tears began to flow as she trembled. "Father, please."

"Stop calling me father."

She gritted her teeth. "You are going to have to shoot me," she said defiantly. "I will not take my own life."

"Even in death, you have to be a paragon of virtue. "He aimed the pistol. "Have it your way."

There was no way out. Cara closed her eyes and waited for death. *Dear sweet Jesus, save me!* Then suddenly there was a loud pounding at the door. And Jake calling her name. "Police. Open the door."

Cara's eyes flew open. Startled, her father looked over his shoulder. She swiftly bent and grabbed the security bar, swinging it with all her might, striking him in the arm. The gun went off. Cara recoiled as a searing pain radiated in her shoulder and she fell to the floor. Jake and the police broke through the door.

Panicked, Laurence scrambled to the railing. Cara, in pain and bleeding profusely, rose to her knees, reached out, and grasped his leg. "Don't jump. We'll get you help."

For a moment, Laurence Hawthorne's eyes locked on Cara's as she pleaded with him to not to commit suicide. Then a blackness came over them. He grinned and then kicked Cara in her wounded shoulder. She fell backward, writhing in pain, and watched in horror as he quickly mounted the railing and cast himself off the balcony.

Chapter 53

Four days later Cara awoke in the ICU. When she opened her eyes, she saw Jake with the beginning of a wooly beard and rumpled clothing sleeping in the chair. His prosthetic arm was lying on the nightstand next to her bed.

"Jake," she said hoarsely. "How long have I been in the hospital?"

"You're awake!" he said and came to her side. "How are you feeling?"

"I'm in a bit of pain. What happened?" Then she remembered. "Where's Sophia? Is she OK?"

"You will be fine. They operated, but you won't lose your arm. Which pisses me off because I thought maybe we could get a buy-one-get-one-free on prosthetic limbs."

Cara smiled weakly and winced from the pain. "And Sophia?"

"She will be fine. Everything will be fine."

"He tried to kill me. My own father." Then she remembered and shook her head. "No, wait. He said he's not my father."

"I know."

"How did you know?"

"Because you're good and kind and he could have never given life to someone like you."

Cara smiled. Then dozed off.

The pain medication made her drowsy so she wasn't fully conscious until a day later when she was moved into a regular room. Jake was with her when she made the transition.

"Where is Tam?" she asked, her eyes sweeping the room and taking in all the flower arrangements that had been sent to her.

"He's at your house with Lia. He's fine."

"And Sophia?"

"Before I came to see you, I stopped by her room and checked on her. She's got a long road ahead of her, but she seems determined to get her life back on track. As soon as you get settled in here, they're going to allow her to come visit you."

Cara lay back on her pillow and exhaled deeply. "Thank goodness. I still can't believe what happened. Some of it doesn't make sense.

How did you know that I was in danger at my father's?"

"After we had our little disagreement, I decided to investigate the letter you received. I found Sally Metzger at the nursing home." He explained to Cara about how she had worked for the Hawthorne family when Cara's father was young, and how he had molested her son. "What tipped me off was when she said everyone on the staff called your father *The General* because he called all the shots." He then told her how he had Lia show Tam a photo of Laurence Hawthorne on her cell phone and the child's hysterical reaction. "I called the police as I sped to your father's—I mean Laurence's house. At first, they didn't believe me, but then I called my mother. She was once on staff at Boothby, Watkins & Rothenberg Pediatrics, and she persuaded their office manager to open Bobby Metzger's file, which corroborated that Sally Metzger had brought her son to the doctor because she suspected he was having psychological difficulties because he had been molested."

"You called your mother?" Cara said mystified.

"Yes, to save you. Now, don't get all excited. Our relationship is still shaky."

"So she helped to convince them?"

"Yes, and they were trying to get in touch with you about another matter as well, so I convinced them to come with me to the apartment instead of your house."

"Another matter?"

Jake's face became very serious. "I don't know if you're up to hearing all of this."

"Jake, what is it?"

"The police were looking for you to tell you," he paused and took her hand, "that Wesley hanged himself in jail."

She gasped, and her eyes welled with tears. Was it because she still had some small vestige of love for him, or because it was such a tragedy? If he'd only waited, he'd have been cleared of Alex's death. She felt a twinge of guilt for not visiting him in jail. She brushed away the tears. Cara wasn't sure what she now felt for Wesley, but she certainly hadn't wanted his life to end this way. It took her breath away how one evil act could mushroom into an epic tragedy. Wesley had been so gifted and blessed, and he'd thrown it all away.

"I'm sorry," Jake said, handing her a tissue.

"How did it happen?"

He tore his jumpsuit into strips and braided it to make a rope.

"At least, he will be exonerated in Alex's death. You know my father is responsible for that as well. Sophia saw him steal Wesley's cheese knife, the murder weapon."

"Yes, apparently when your father found out about the blackmail photos, he did some investigating on his own and discovered that

Wesley was behind the scheme and decided to kill two birds with one stone: kill Alex, who had blabbed about The General to us, and frame Wesley with Alex's murder. Sophia told the police how she confronted him about the knife and Alex's murder, and how he beat and drugged her, keeping her a prisoner in his penthouse. Sophia has proven to be a treasure trove of knowledge as she was present for much of your father's plotting. She was able to give ICE a ton of information."

"Because of her, they were able to infiltrate the human sex trafficking ring and pose as your father, and they were able to set up a sting that rescued 143 people on that freighter as well as arresting traffickers in the State Department, Thailand, New York, Buffalo, Philadelphia, and Pittsburgh." Jake smiled. "They were able to rescue Jittra too."

Cara smiled. "Where is she?"

"They took her to a really safe place. Your house."

"My house? How did you arrange that?"

"Actually, Father Nicco and my mother threw their weight around, vouching for your character. Lia is with Jittra and Tam now. It's only temporary; we're going to have to go to court to petition them to award us permanent custody."

"Us?"

"Yes, Cara, it may be too soon to talk about it, what with Wesley's death, but you know how I feel—"

A knock at the door interrupted Jake.

A nurse poked her head around the door frame. "You have a visitor," she said and then escorted Sophia into the room. When Cara saw her sister again, she could not speak she was so overwhelmed with emotion. Cara inched up in the bed, sobbing. Sophia, with a nasty purple bruise on the side of her face but looking much more alert, began to cry as she drew to Cara's bedside. Cara reached up with her undamaged arm and held Sophia, stroking her silky blonde hair. "Thank God you are safe." When their tears subsided, the nurse left and said to buzz her, and she'd come back to help Sophia to her room.

Jake moved a chair over for Sophia. "I'll leave you two alone," he said and then left the room.

"You refused to kill me," Sophia said quietly, gazing at Cara as if it was the first time she'd ever seen her.

"And you tried to save me," Cara said, taking Sophia's hand, marveling at the love she felt for her younger sister.

"How stupid I've been," Sophia said. "All these years I thought he did what he did to me because he loved you more, that you were the good daughter, and I was the bad and deserved his perverted attention as punishment."

"And the way he defended everything you did and criticized me," Cara said, "I always thought you were the most highly favored daughter."

Sophia set her jaw angrily. "If I was favored, I'd hate to have seen what he'd have done to me if I was the one he despised."

Cara's heart was breaking for her sister. "I never knew, Sophia, and I'm sure grandmother didn't either. I swear, had either of us known, we would have done something, brought you to live with in Pittsburgh. How long did it go on?"

Sophia looked out the window. "From as far back as I can remember and from what he revealed about our mother's death, he must have started molesting me as soon as I was born."

"Oh, Sophia, I'm so sorry."

It felt odd to admit it, but Cara wondered why her father had never molested her. Because Sophia looked more like him? Was he that narcissistic? Was it because she was not his daughter? And who was her father? There were so many questions still to be answered.

Sophia looked at Cara with tears pooling in her blue eyes. "You know what's the worst thing he ever did?"

Cara looked at Sophia quizzically.

"He pitted us against each other."

Cara had a lump in her throat. "He's gone, and we now know that he didn't favor either of us. He loved only himself. He destroyed so much, but he couldn't destroy one thing: How much I love you."

Chapter 54

On Cara's last night in the hospital, Father Nicco stopped by. Other than being there the first day when he'd been brought in to give her the Anointing of the Sick, he'd been busy working with the authorities to either repatriate or find loving foster homes for the children rescued from Laurence Hawthorne's sex trafficking syndicate after the ICE raid.

When he came in, he hugged Jake and handed him a box. "Some pizzelles for you to snack on. They're chocolate cherry for Valentine's Day." Then he turned and took Cara's face in his hands, kissing her cheeks. "Ah, Cara *mia*. It is so good to see you looking so well. How are you feeling?"

He and Jake sat in the chairs next to her bed. Cara told him that she was feeling sore but much better and was looking forward to going home. They discussed all that had happened, and she was particularly concerned about Sophia.

Father Nicco reached out and patted Cara's hand. "I've been visiting with Sophia too, and we've been praying for healing and the capacity for forgiveness. We can only pray and let God do the work."

His blue eyes focused on her. "Spiritually, my dear, how are you doing?"

"My father, rather the man I thought was my father—I'm so angry at him. And Wesley?" She shook her head. "I feel so conflicted. Half of me hates him for what he did and the other half pities him." She lowered her eyes. "And I feel guilty. I keep thinking that maybe if I had gone to see him after you told me that he wanted to see me, he wouldn't have killed himself."

He squeezed her hand. "You can't know that, Cara *mia*. Ultimately, what he did was his responsibility."

"I worry about his soul, whether I did something that drove him to such horrific lengths."

"I can leave," said Jake.

"No, stay," Father Nicco said. "Cara, the funeral we held for him was lovely. Rest assured, Wesley is in more merciful hands now than he would have ever been here on earth."

"I feel like my world has been turned upside down. Like everything I have ever believed has been a lie—my marriage, my family. No one is who or what I thought they were."

"How so?" asked Father Nicco.

"I thought my husband loved me, but he turned out to be more concerned with my money and was in love with another woman. I thought Sophia was a major screw-up and my rival, but she turned out to be more wounded than I am and my most loyal ally. I thought my father was my father, and now he's not." She squeezed Father Nicco's hand. "You're the only one who hasn't changed."

Jake cleared his throat. "I don't know if this is the right place or time, but there's something I need to share with the two of you."

"What is it?" Cara asked.

"Yes, Jake, what is it?" said Father Nicco.

Jake rose and closed the hospital room door.

Then he came and sat at the end of Cara's bed. He touched her foot and facing her and Father Nicco, he exhaled deeply. "After meeting with Sally Metzger and while you were recovering, I did some digging into your father's—I mean Laurence's past to see if he had abused any other people, and I found something that you may find shocking." He paused. "There was a housekeeper who came shortly after Sally was dismissed, a woman named Esther Wright. She lives in Florida now, but I was able to get in touch with her. And she remembered how your mother came to marry Laurence. It seems it was to keep him from being charged with pedophilia. His parents thought it best for him to marry, and then ship him overseas to work for the company internationally."

"So he married my mother?"

"He was forced to marry her, and from what I've learned, she was forced to marry him."

Cara frowned. "Why was she forced to marry him?"

"Apparently, the Cavanaughs and Hawthornes knew each other socially," Jake said.

"Yes, they belonged to the same country club," Cara said.

"Your mother agreed to marry Laurence because she needed a cover too." Jake picked up Cara's hand. "You see, Cara, she was already pregnant with you and needed a husband to avoid a scandal."

"Then it's true. Laurence isn't my father." She felt a bit relieved but still puzzled. "But who is my father then?"

Jake reached out and clasped Father Nicco's hand, noticing how the priest had suddenly gone pale.

"A young, handsome, poor Italian student who had gone back to Italy for the summer," Jake said.

Father Nicco's blue eyes were swimming with tears as he softly added. "And who came back for the fall term with the intention of proposing to the love of his life only to find that she was already married and living in Asia."

As tears rolled down his cheeks, Father Nicco looked at Cara. "I never knew, Cara *mia*. I swear to the Lord above had I known, I would have been there for your mother. When I went to your mother's house, your grandmother Cavanaugh told me that she 'hadn't scrubbed her fingers to nubs working as a maid and risen above her circumstances only to have her daughter take up with a poor 'Eye-talian.'" He doubled over onto her bed, burying his face in his hands, sobbing. "I thought your mother had fallen in love with Laurence. Please forgive me, Cara," he wailed. "I'm so sorry."

Cara reached for him and touched his shoulder with her good arm. "Sorry?" she sniffled. "There's no reason to be sorry. I love you. I only wish you were Sophia's father too."

He pulled back and looked at her adoringly. "Ah, Cara, *mia*, you are too kind, but all fathers fail their daughters in some way. She has a perfect, heavenly father who loves her and that is all that matters."

"That may be so, but I'm still thrilled that you are my true father."

He kept looking at Cara as if searching to find his contribution to her life. "When we first met, I remember telling you that I knew your mother, but I had no idea that you were mine. I can't believe that you are my daughter." He raised his hands and looked to the sky, ebullient. "'The Lord has done great things for us; we are filled with joy.'" He turned to Jake and hugged him. "Thank you, Jake. For all of your hard work."

Jake looked troubled. "I wasn't sure you'd feel that way—not because you wouldn't be happy to learn that Cara is your daughter, but because of your position in the church. I've heard the rumors that you are under consideration for being named a cardinal."

"Yes, oh my goodness," said Cara. "This could cause all kinds of problems for you. We don't have to tell. It can be our secret."

"Nonsense," Father Nicco said. "I want to tell the world— proclaim it from the rooftops. This is a *primo* example of how 'God makes all things work together for the good of those who love him.'" He stroked Cara's hand. "Are you up for another press conference?"

"Another one. Whatever for?" Cara asked.

"To introduce the world to my beautiful daughter . . . unless you prefer that I do not."

Cara beamed. "No, I'm proud to call you my father."

He patted her hand. "And vice versa, Cara *mia*, my *bella bambina*."

Chapter 55

After Father Nicco left, Cara was elated but exhausted. She lay back in the hospital bed, and closed her eyes, wearing a contented smile. Life was funny, she thought. You could go from utter devastation to sheer delight in minutes. Jake had walked Father Nicco to the elevator, and when he returned, he sat in the chair beside her bed.

"You know you really should go home and get some rest," she said. "You've been here continuously."

"I don't want to be anywhere else."

She sighed. "We really haven't had a chance to talk since our little spat in my kitchen."

"I know," Jake said, leaning on his elbows.

"I've been doing a lot of thinking," Cara said. "You know how I said that everyone turned out to be not as they seemed?"

"Yes,"

"The same goes for you."

"How's that?"

Cara smiled at him. "At first, I thought you were a cold-hearted cynic."

"And what did I turn out to be?"

She reached for his hand. "The most kind-hearted, brave, and loyal man I've ever known. And I love you."

"Oh, Cara. I was all of those awful things, but it was you who changed me. You know how I feel. I love you."

"Come here," she said. He came to the side of the bed. She reached up and kissed him.

"Why, Ms. Hawthorne," he said, "what will people think of you kissing me like that?"

She caressed his cheek. "Actually, Jake. I don't care what people think of me anymore. All I care about is loving you."

Epilogue

Jake looked rather overwhelmed, Cara thought. The first time she'd been here, she came away with a stiff neck from looking up so much. As she watched him, his mouth gaping in amazement as he gazed at the opulence overhead, she thought that he'll surely suffer from a stiff neck too. But who could blame him? The Vatican was overwhelmingly magnificent. She, Jake, his mother, Tam, and Jittra had spent the previous day touring the enormous Vatican museum. Now here they were seated near the front of St. Peter's Basilica where Father Nicco, her own father, would shortly be installed as a cardinal.

After all the walking they had done yesterday, it was a relief to sit. She held out her feet and appraised her ankles. They were a bit puffy, but when you're in your sixth month in sweltering Rome, that was not surprising.

Jake picked up her hand and fiddled with her wedding ring. "Your hands aren't swollen," he whispered, "but your ankles are bit. Are

467

you sure you're not overdoing it?"

"I'm fine," she whispered and squeezed his hand.

Sophia passed her a bottle of water. "Keep yourself hydrated."

No matter how many times she'd seen Sophia since she'd entered the Postulancy with the Missionaries of Charity, Cara could not get used to seeing her younger sister looking so modest and gloriously peaceful. Her blond hair had been bobbed, and she wore no makeup, only a simple, cotton dress, but Cara thought she looked the most beautiful she'd ever seen her.

Her gaze traveled to Father Nicco sitting on the altar, and she couldn't have been prouder. When they had revealed in their press conference their familial relationship, initially, the world was shocked. To their delight, the pope had spoken out on their behalf, citing God's infinite mercy and how some of the saints, specifically St. Augustine had fathered a child out of wedlock before his conversion. Gradually, as the weeks passed and the media attention subsided, they were embraced by the church and the public. Cara attributed it to her father's gift for making the world see that God is the God of second chances and of making beauty from ashes.

She flashed a broad smile to Lia across the aisle, who looked sublimely happy as any newlywed should after watching Francesco D'Amore, her husband, rise and sing *Ave Maria*.

Afterward, the happy group posed for pictures in St. Peter's Square, and Cara couldn't help but wonder what people thought of her family. *Here I am pregnant standing next to my father, the Italian Catholic Cardinal; my husband, the Jewish wounded warrior; his mother; my children, sixteen- year-old Jittra, who had recovered nicely from plastic surgery and was gaining more confidence with each day; and ten-year-old Tam, the child who'd grown to trust and love me. And my sister, Sophia, the scandalous socialite and soon-to-be one of Mother Teresa's Missionaries of Charity. God does work in mysterious ways!*

As the cameras clicked and they said *formaggio*, the Italian word for "cheese," Cara knew the photos would be published in tabloids and newspapers all over the world. She smiled broadly realizing that she was free from the prison she'd constructed for herself, the one whose bars were created by caring about what everyone thought of her. She no longer cared what people thought of her or her *avant-garde* family. She only cared what God thought of her, and she knew that no matter whatever befell them in this life, both she and Sophia, as well as all women who love him, are His most highly favored daughters. Eternally.

The End

DISCUSSION GUIDE FOR
MOST HIGHLY FAVORED DAUGHTER

1. If you have a sister, you may be interested to know that researchers say that the sister relationship will most likely be the longest relationship of your life, notching more years than those with your parents, spouse, or children. Does that bring you comfort or trepidation? And why?

2. In the beginning of the novel, Cara is very concerned with what people think of her, but by the conclusion, she no longer cares. Has there ever been a time when you were overly concerned with how others perceived you? How did that make you feel?

3. The main characters all live behind a façade. Have you ever known anyone whom you felt was living behind a façade? Why do you think they were doing so?

4. Eventually, every character in the book has something from the past that catches up with him or her. Do you believe you can ever escape your past?

5. Many of the main characters are transformed by the end of the novel. Do you believe that transformation is possible for people in real life?

6. Although it is not described in detail in the book how the public reacts to the revelation of who Cara's father is, how do you think it would react today if this were to happen in real life?

7. The epigraph at the beginning of the book states: "A sister is both your mirror—and your opposite." In what ways are Cara

and Sophia alike and opposite? Which do you think predominates?

8. Have you ever been unjustly accused of something? How did that make you feel? Did you fight back like Cara or did you cower?

9. Today, we read about girls being kidnapped by radical Islamists such as Boko Haram and being abused and used as slaves. Were you surprised to learn about St. Bakhita and how her story mirrors today's terrorism?

10. Cara quotes statistics about human sex trafficking at her press conference. Were you aware of the prevalence of this horrific crime?

11. Laurence Hawthorne's parents cover for his crimes, enabling him to perpetrate more. Do you know of an instance where an initial transgression that is overlooked resulted in even more wrongdoing?

12. The names "Cara" and "Sophia" were purposely chosen. Cara is derived from the Latin and means "beloved." Sophia means "wisdom." In the beginning of the novel, Cara lacked love, while Sophia lacked wisdom. By the end of the novel do you believe either of them acquired what they were lacking?

13. Why do you think that Laurence only abused Sophia and not Cara?

14. Have you ever been envious of another's life and then found out what their life has been really like and been glad that you were not that person?

15. Cara and Jake are very different. Why do you think they eventually clicked?

16. Cara and Jake both come from privileged backgrounds. Jake rejected his, but Cara did not. Do you think being wealthy would be a blessing, a burden, or both?

17. If you were casting a movie of *Most Highly Favored Daughter*, which actors would you cast for each character?

18. We learn that St. Bakhita forgave her torturers, and yet when Cara is prompted by Father Nicco to forgive Wesley, she finds that she cannot. However, at the end of the novel, she reaches out to Laurence after all that he's done to her, begging him not to commit suicide and to save himself. Do you think Cara would have eventually been able to forgive Wesley after this had Wesley still been alive?

19. At the end, Cara has a new family composed of Tam, Jittra, and Jake. Do you know of a family that has been created out of unusual circumstances?

20. Although deceased, Cara's grandmother figures largely in Cara's life. Do you have someone from your past who still influences you today?

21. At the conclusion, Cara says that "God is the God of second chances." Do you believe that God gives second chances?

22. Cara believes that Sophia is her father's favorite while Sophia believes that Cara is the favored daughter. Were you or any of your siblings a favored child? How did that make you feel?

ABOUT THE AUTHOR

Janice Lane Palko has been a writer for more than 20 years working as an editor, columnist, freelance writer, teacher, lecturer, and novelist.

She is currently a staff writer for the website PopularPittsburgh.com and has had numerous articles appear in publications such as *The Reader's Digest, Guideposts for Teens, Woman's World, The Christian Science Monitor, The Pittsburgh Post-Gazette,* and *St. Anthony Messenger.* Her work has also been featured in the books *A Cup of Comfort for Inspiration, A Cup of Comfort for Expectant Mothers,* and *Chicken Soup for the Single's Soul.*

In addition to *Most Highly Favored Daughter,* she has written the romantic comedy *St. Anne's Day;* the Christmas novel, *A Shepherd's Song;* and the romantic suspense, *Cape Cursed.* She is currently working on a spin-off of *St. Anne's Day* called *Our Lady of the Roses* and the second novel in her Sanctified Suspense line, *Mother of Sorrows.*

Visit her at:

Amazon:	www.amazon.com/Janice-Lane-Palko/e/B008PZ3DL0
Website:	www.janicelanepalko.com
Blog:	www.thewritinglane.blogspot.com
Facebook:	www.facebook.com/janicelanepalko.writer
Twitter:	twitter.com/JaniceLanePalko
Pinterest	www.pinterest.com/janicelanepalko

.

Made in the USA
Charleston, SC
28 November 2016